THE QUEEN AND HER COURT

"Why don't you sit back down on your throne," Lance suggested motioning toward the big rock, "and regale me with tales about your life in merry old England."

Rebecca giggled at his foolishness.

"Ladies do not sit on thrones. Queens sit on thrones. But queens never entertain. They summon their jesters who perform for *their* amusement."

Caught up in the levity of their conversation, Rebecca guilelessly played with an escaping lock of hair wrapping it loosely around her finger. She was unaware of the effect her youthful lightheartedness was having on the man standing so close to her.

Striving to gain some semblance of control, Lance asked solemnly, "And what if the queen is not amused?"

Green eyes sparkled with mischief as Rebecca replied knowingly, "Oh, one way or another the queen is always amused for there is nothing so funny as a headless jester!"

The consequence of her efforts to shock Logan's sensibilities with her farcical narrative differed greatly from what she had anticipated. For without warning she was snatched up by two powerful arms and enfolded in his warm embrace as he bent his head to taste the nectar from her honeyed lips . . .

KATHY WILLIS
Tropical Thunder

ZEBRA BOOKS
KENSINGTON PUBLISHING CORP.

Dedicated in Memory of Mom, Dad, and Katy.

ZEBRA BOOKS

are published by

Kensington Publishing Corp.
850 Third Avenue
New York, NY 10022

First printing: April, 1992

Printed in the United States of America
10 9 8 7 6 5 4 3 2

Chapter 1

Southampton, England.
Spring, 1824.

As wind filled the sails of the *HMS Victoria* heading the ship in a westerly direction, Captain Jeremiah Higgins stood on the upper deck. His legs were braced apart seaman fashion as his keen blue eyes examined the activity on the deck below. He observed that each sailor under his command was properly carrying out the duties assigned him.

After twenty years of sailing with a well-trained crew, one he had trained himself, his observations were somewhat cursory. He anticipated no unusual problems on this voyage which was why it took some minutes before his gaze fixed on the young woman in forest-green velvet. A lady of quality judging by the rich material of her gown whose tight fitting bodice tapered perfectly to encircle her tiny waist. The tips of matching green slippers peeked out from beneath full skirts which flowed down to barely touch the smooth boards of the deck. A lovely sight for any man to behold.

During his many years at sea, Jeremiah had become a remarkably astute judge of both quality and character. His occupation as a sea captain brought him into contact with people from all walks of life—impoverished immigrants who risked their meager savings on the prospects of a better life in the young country called the United States of America, to members of the royal house who crossed the ocean out of curiosity then returned to England shaking their heads over the lives and money that had been wasted on a war for what they could only view as worthless land, and all manner of men and women who fell somewhere between the two. Jeremiah was rather quick at judging quality, and although judging character took a little more time, the perceptive sea captain was usually right on the mark

He had no doubt about one thing. The woman standing on the lower deck was definitely quality. He was equally certain that the woman had to be Lady Rebecca Winslow since only one female had booked passage on this crossing. As Jeremiah studied the petite figure whose golden-blond hair seemed to radiate light without benefit of sunshine, a suspicious frown creased his weathered brow. Why would a bluestocking such as Lady Winslow venture halfway around the world to the wilds of North America unchaperoned and apparently heedless of the dangers she would be facing?

Jeremiah hugged his substantial stomach with one arm as he stroked his full gray beard. He continued to stare at the diminutive figure below. Deep within him he felt a stirring of unease. He lifted his eyes to the sky in an effort to see beyond the dense fog covering any trace of early morning sunlight then lowered his gaze to look again upon the lovely lady in green. It was still there—the unexplainable certainty that trouble lay ahead.

Rebecca Winslow, unaware of the captain's scrutiny, leaned forward and silently bid farewell to Southampton now only a distant silhouette in the heavy gray morning mist.

"I'll be back," she promised resolutely. Her softly spoken words drifted out to sea on a breeze just strong enough to fill the sails and gently point the ship toward the new western world.

Wisps of golden hair escaped the braided coronet crowning her head to frame a small, heart-shaped face. Luminous green eyes sprinkled with amber flecks scanned the gloomy skies overhead. *Too late to turn back now. I've made my decision and right or wrong I am on my way,* she reminded herself.

Despite the painful losses she had suffered during the past few years, Rebecca had managed to maintain an optimistic outlook on life. Her beloved older sister Mandy had died in childbirth when Rebecca was only fourteen leaving her children motherless. Her parents had been taken from her two years ago in a carriage accident that should never have happened. Now as a lady of means at the scant age of twenty, Rebecca realized how much more fortunate she was than most young women to whom fate had dealt a similar blow. Lord Winslow had made certain that Rebecca inherited not only his sizable estate but also the title which went with it, a title handed down through many generations of Winslows.

Though not without precedent, it was rather unusual to place such wealth in the hands of a female "barely out of the schoolroom," as one distant cousin had remarked with disdain. Rebecca remembered her father with gratitude. Because of his trust and foresight she would never be relegated to the role of governess or, God forbid, become dependent on the charity of some distant relative. She had much to be thankful for. Yet, as Rebecca folded her arms and leaned back against the damp railing of the ship, one slender green-slippered foot began tapping out her irritation. Amber sparks overshadowed emerald irises as her dainty, slightly tipped nose wrinkled with distaste. She knew exactly why she felt less than euphoric about her situation.

Damnation! The small foot tapped furiously. *Why, along with the good fortune bestowed on me, must I be cursed with the twins? If not for Edward and Elizabeth, my sister's children, I would right now be riding from the manor house with William Pennington at my side.*

Her expression turned dreamy as she thought of the carefree days of her youth when she and William had raced across the smooth green meadow together. A mischievous smile curved her full pink lips as she remembered the many times she had found it necessary to restrain her swift flying mare so that William's horse would finish first even though hers had the greater speed.

Predictably William would suggest that they rest the horses beside the clear blue waters of the lake which formed the boundary between the Winslow and Pennington estates. A few brief stolen kisses would follow but never the words of love Rebecca had waited a lifetime to hear, nor did William speak of their future together. A small frown appeared to mar her smooth brow.

As time passed and still no firm commitment was forthcoming, Rebecca managed to convince herself that their eventual marriage had simply been taken for granted by everyone—including the young man himself. But something else had happened in recent months that caused her no little concern. A subtle change had taken place within her which defied explanation. She had actually felt a sense of relief when William took his leave without coming any closer to declaring his intentions.

It was really quite extraordinary. As a child, younger even than the six-year-old twins, Rebecca had decided she would someday marry William Pennington. Having once made up her mind, she stubbornly refused to consider any other alternative. Why then did she lately feel so uncertain when she contemplated spending the rest of her life with the man?

It wasn't just the rumors she had heard about his drinking and gaming. If true she blamed his actions on the influence of the rowdy London crowd with whom he associated when visiting the city. And when his name was mentioned in connection with other women, she dismissed it as jealousy on the part of her female acquaintances who felt it their duty to keep her apprised of the latest gossip. Rebecca could excuse the spiteful and malicious stories that found their way to her ears. And though William's tendencies toward irresponsibility often provoked her, she had accepted his shortcomings years ago.

Yet if she were honest with herself, she would have to admit that the cause of her suddenly mixed emotions had to do with something her best friend Amy Dickerson had said. Amy had been married nearly six months when she confided to Rebecca her feelings for her handsome young husband.

"Just looking at him makes my stomach churn and my legs turn to jelly," she had said rapturously. "And when he touches me . . . Oh, Rebecca! There's no way to describe how he makes my heart flutter. I suppose it's something one has to experience for oneself."

Amy had always been an incurable romantic and Rebecca found her description of marital bliss just a trifle nauseating, yet she knew that William's kisses had never caused the tremulous, heart thumping giddiness that made Amy's rather plain face light up with a radiant glow. Rebecca, of course, could never be affected that way. Still she wondered what it might be like.

She was brought back to the present with a start as the ship glided from the calm bay into the open waters of the Atlantic and a sudden gust of wind whipped against her full skirts molding the heavy material to her small form. She chided herself for daydreaming while her elbows grew numb propped against the cold metal rail.

Enough! It wasn't her parents' fault that she had the responsibility of her niece and nephew, Elizabeth and Edward. They certainly hadn't planned to die! And it

10

wasn't Mandy's fault for being too delicate to withstand the rigors of childbirth. It was Andrew who had shirked his responsibilities as a father. Because of him she was now on this damned ship bound for a primitive land where in all likelihood the natives ate raw meat with their fingers and communicated by grunting.

Rebecca scowled remembering how her heart had gone out to her brother-in-law so plagued with remorse over the death of the woman he adored above all others. At the time Rebecca thought she understood how he felt. She watched him stare dejectedly out over the fertile green fields of the well-managed estate which was of no interest to him without Mandy by his side.

His love for Edward and Elizabeth was obvious in the way he gazed down at the tiny infants one could only tell apart by the blue or pink of their gowns. Only when he looked at his children did the sadness in his face lighten with a hint of a smile. And never had she seen any indication that he held the innocent babes responsible for the grief he suffered. Andrew affixed that guilt firmly to himself.

Rebecca was the one who understood his need to build a new life for himself far away from the painful memories he could not escape in England. She had never doubted that he would do as he said and send for the children once he had established himself. *But damnation! That was nearly five years ago!*

It was easy to sympathize when the children were under the protection of their well-to-do grandparents. Never had she imagined that they would become her responsibility or that they would detest William

11

Pennington so intensely. Neither would she have believed that children of Edward and Elizabeth's tender years could express their dislike with such dramatic flair. Rebecca quickly learned that the combined imagination and ingenuity of the twins knew no bounds.

Shaking her head in resignation, Rebecca turned to find a portly gentleman immaculately garbed in the uniform of ship's captain making his way across the deck in her direction.

Her radiant smile nearly took Jeremiah's breath away. Deep dimples added to her loveliness. And those eyes . . . they were the color of the waters close to the coral reefs in the Caribbean Sea. A man could drown in those eyes and look forward to the dying.

"Good day to you, Lady Winslow. Please allow me to introduce myself. I am Captain Jeremiah Higgins at your service." The captain executed a surprisingly courtly bow for all his bulk.

Rebecca responded with a half-curtsy, not due to any lack of respect but rather to wind conditions. Her skirts were now wrapping themselves around and between her legs.

"I am pleased to meet you, Captain," she responded politely. "And there is one service I would ask."

Jeremiah tried to hide his irritation. Lady Winslow had quickly seized upon his offer to render her assistance. His words had been spoken more out of courtesy than anticipation of need. With a sinking feeling he wondered if this trip would be complicated with unreasonable demands by the beautiful young woman.

"Of course, Lady Winslow," he acknowledged hoping his smile did not appear forced. "What can I do for you?"

Rebecca glanced around to see if anyone else might be within hearing, then leaned a little closer to the stout sea captain bringing with her the delicate scent of wild flowers.

"Actually, sir, I would deem it more appropriate and not in the least disrespectful," she assured him, her green eyes darkening with intensity, "if you would not address me as 'Lady' Winslow."

Rebecca misinterpreted Jeremiah's shocked expression, failing to recognize it as one of relief. He had expected her to ask for fresh hot water each day delivered to her room in a porcelain tub or something equally outlandish.

"You see, Captain Higgins," she hurried to explain, "although I do not know a great deal about this new territory of Florida where we are going, it is my understanding that the natives feel a certain reluctance when it comes to accepting people who bear titles of nobility. And regardless of the brevity of my stay, I would not wish to incur the wrath of the local populace by appearing to be above myself."

Jeremiah found himself utterly speechless as he looked into the innocent green eyes of the woman standing before him. In fact, it was to his credit that he was able to contain the laughter which rose from within his chest threatening to explode at any moment. Reluctance, indeed! Didn't she realize that a bitter war had been waged and won to ensure that no class structure would ever exist within the colonies of the

13

United States where all men regarded themselves as equals?

"You do understand. Don't you, Captain?"

Jeremiah was touched by the guilelessness he heard in her voice, a melodious voice that floated, soft and soothing on the wind, completing a picture like the final brush stroke of a master painter.

"I will certainly respect your wishes, Lady ... I mean, Miss Winslow," he nodded gravely.

Then anxious to learn more about his fascinating young passenger, Jeremiah continued, "I suppose you must feel some regret at leaving your homeland. Is this your first sea voyage?"

"No and yes, Captain. The 'no' meaning I am not missing England and the 'yes' meaning this is my first sea voyage." Rebecca's voice held a hint of teasing but was so sweet no one could take offense. And to her surprise she realized that what she said was true. She looked forward to the journey ahead as an adventurous undertaking with which she could regale her children in the future.

"Miss Winslow, I do hope you won't think me impertinent," he apologized. "I have no right to question your reasons for being aboard my ship. However, I do feel it my responsibility to ask if you are aware of the dangers we face on our crossing and of the dangers which may await us once we arrive at Fort Brooke?"

"I suppose you mean pirates and Indians," she replied lightly. But noting the captain's grave countenance she felt her first sense of foreboding.

Raising bronze-green eyes, their golden flecks

glowing with fire, she assuaged his curiosity by replying determinedly, "Let me assure you that this is not a pleasure trip, Captain Higgins. I have vowed to return what rightfully belongs to another regardless of the possible danger such an undertaking may entail!"

"Ho! Captain!"

They were interrupted by a shout from above. Jeremiah and Rebecca looked up. The sun was just breaking through the mist in the eastern sky, throwing into shadow the man in the crow's nest. The sailor was leaning over the barrier which kept him from falling as he watched for unknown dangers in the water including ships which might or might not be friendly toward the Crown.

The sailor was pointing toward something that seemed to be attached to the beam used in climbing to the watch post, the "something" being about half the distance between the deck and the perch.

Jeremiah's voice roared up at the man on watch. "What the bloody hell is that?"

At the same time Rebecca whispered disbelievingly, "Edward!"

Running to the ladder leading to the upper deck, Rebecca gathered her full skirts and climbed to the top. She could hear Captain Higgins breathing heavily behind her and muttering unintelligible words under his breath. She crossed the deck and stood at the base of the beam which had rungs nailed crosswise, a foot or so apart, forming a ladder to the watch station high above.

"Edward! Come down here at once!" Rebecca demanded. Standing with hands on her hips, her foot tapped out a furious staccato rhythm as she waited impatiently for her edict to be obeyed.

A small voice cried back, "I can't Becca. I'm too afraid."

"Of course you can, Edward. I'm sure you remember how you got up there. Just do what you did going up in reverse," she suggested firmly as she peered toward the heavens trying to think of a punishment befitting the crime. *Would the kindly Captain Higgins take exception to keelhauling,* she wondered absently.

"Becca, I can't let go. I'll fall into the sea and drown!"

Rebecca bit back a tempting retort knowing Captain Higgins was standing close behind her breathing laboriously.

"I beg your pardon, Miss Winslow, but would you kindly tell me what is going on?" The volume of his voice increased with each word so that his next question came out in a shout. "Who is that up there?"

Rebecca watched as the wind lifted Edward's red-gold curls. Her eyes widened as the reflection from the brightening sun created the illusion of a halo above the small head. *A halo of all things! It is nature jesting with man or woman as the case may be!*

For a moment she could only stare at the small figure clutching the beam overhead. "That, sir, is the thorn in my side, the albatross around my neck, my vulnerable point. In short, Captain, that is my nephew, Edward."

"Wentworth! Can you bring him down?" the captain shouted to the man in the watch.

"No!" It was Edward's voice that answered. The one word held not only fear but intractability as he glared at the seaman above and shook his head daring the fellow to come closer.

In all his years as a sea captain, Jeremiah had never faced a situation such as this. He turned to Rebecca hoping she could shed light on why the small person overhead was wreaking havoc on his ship. His crinkled blue eyes widened as he watched her tuck her skirts into the sash encircling her waist.

"Miss Winslow," he spluttered. "Surely you aren't considering—"

"Captain," she interrupted before he could say more, "that is my nephew. And for a few weeks longer he is my responsibility. Mark my words, sir," she said tapping on his chest to emphasize each of them, "I will bring him down!"

Before Jeremiah could say another word she began ascending the ladder. As she climbed higher, the wind fought to loosen her skirts from their binding. Rebecca paid no attention for she was trying to remember the details of a particularly gory novel her friend Amy had smuggled into the room they shared at Mrs. Haversham's Academy for Young Ladies. The spine tingling adventure had included one scene in which a disobedient young sailor had been forced to walk the plank over shark infested waters. *Just retribution,* Rebecca mused pausing to catch her breath.

At last she reached a spot just below the point where Edward's feet should have been. But with his arms and legs hugging the pole, it was his small rounded derriere that rested on the rung above her. Exhibiting what she considered remarkable control under the circumstances, she silently congratulated herself on her restraint.

"I am right behind you, Edward." Her voice held a note of calm she was far from feeling for being in high places tended to make her dizzy. "I'm going to put my arm around you. Lean back on me and we shall climb down the ladder together."

When Edward remained stubbornly clinging to the post, she tried again. "Come now, Edward. I won't let go of you. I promise."

"No, Becca! I'm too scared. Just stay here with me," he pleaded.

"I am sorry, Edward, but I do not plan to spend the rest of my life suspended from this beam," she stated emphatically for she had reached the limit of her patience. She would have at that moment grabbed him by the seat of his pants and hauled him down were she not afraid they would both lose their balance.

"Whatever possessed you to pull such a henwitted stunt?"

"Be-Beth dared me," came the sheepish reply.

"Oh well, I suppose that explains it." Her sarcasm was lost on the frightened child. "And where, may I ask, is Elizabeth now that you are in such dire straits?"

"Sh-she's holding the net."

"The net? Yes, of course. What net, Edward?" Her hands were numb from holding so tightly to the narrow rung. An unbidden vision popped into her head: Two small red-headed children stood on the sandy shores of a deserted island waving goodbye as she smiled back gleefully watching their images grow smaller as the ship sailed away.

Edward nodded his head indicating the deck below. "Sh-she said she would catch me if I fell," Edward explained, his quivering voice evidencing his doubt.

Rebecca dared to glance down and then wished she hadn't. The distance looking down seemed much farther than it had when she was down below looking up. But in that brief glance she had spotted Edward's six-year-old, twin sister, Elizabeth. Indeed, her bright red curls were like a beacon as the sun beamed down upon her.

Rebecca swallowed then looked down once more hardly able to believe what she was seeing. Elizabeth stood some distance from the base of the support beside a hammock made of net which had been strung between the rail of the ship and the inner cabin wall. The bottom of the hammock was perhaps two feet above the hard wooden deck. Rebecca knew then that the children had finally managed to push her over the brink of sanity for she had the most absurd desire to giggle as she thought about the preposterous situation in which she found herself.

"I don't think it will work, Edward," she offered, sobering immediately.

"Wh-what won't work?" he stammered turning his head to look at her.

"The net, of course. I don't think the net will work."

"Wh-why not? Beth said it would work."

"Be that as it may," she reasoned, affecting the tone of one most knowledgeable about such things. "Assuming you can reach the net from this angle, I would imagine that the force of your body will push the mesh down against the wooden deck and you will burst like an overripe melon."

All color drained from Edward's round little face

19

leaving the spattering of freckles to stand out like cream dusted with nutmeg. With a pitiful moan he released his grip on the pole, turned, and hurled himself toward his aunt, his arms encircling her neck so tightly she could scarcely breathe. Rebecca would never know how she managed to hang onto the rung without dropping the trembling child.

Awkwardly she made her descent with Edward clinging to her like a baby possum while the wind continued to tear at her skirts. Golden-blond hair, blown free from restrictive pins, whipped across her eyes forcing her to feel her way down. When she was once again on solid footing she pried Edward's arms from around her neck and stood him none too gently upon the deck.

"How could you do such an addlepated thing?" she railed unmoved by pathetic blue eyes brimming with tears.

The man standing watch in the crow's nest had climbed down the timber much more rapidly than Rebecca who was hampered by her frightened burden and the gusting wind. Even though he had come the greater distance, he was only a few steps behind her by the time she reached the deck.

Her tirade was interrupted when he asked, "Is the boy all right?" Concern showed in his pleasingly handsome face and Rebecca was startled by the cultured English voice of the young man dressed in rough sailor attire.

"Yes, thank you for your interest, Mr.—?"

"Wentworth. Justin Wentworth," he supplied.

"Thank you for your interest, Mr. Wentworth,"

20

Rebecca repeated. "But you mustn't worry for I can assure you Edward's recuperative powers are without equal."

Justin's ready smile was contagious and Rebecca felt herself dimpling in response, unaware of the charming picture she presented. But the young Englishman was quick to recognize the enchantment of her grace and beauty. And suddenly instead of dreading the long weeks ahead as the *Victoria* made her way slowly across the Atlantic, there seemed much for him to look forward to. *Yes, indeed!* he anticipated hopefully. *If the first day was any indication of things to come, this might just prove to be a very interesting voyage!*

Chapter 2

Fort Brooke, Florida Territory.
Spring, 1824.

"God damn it, Kearny! This time your men have gone too far!"

The exceptionally tall, deeply tanned man clad in buckskins slammed the door behind him with such force that the walls of the small office vibrated. He carried with him a current of barely harnessed energy. His handsome, rough chiseled face exuded raw masculinity while powerful muscles rippled down long arms and across wide shoulders beneath his fringed shirt as he clenched and unclenched huge fists. His stature and dress combined with the obvious fury in his slate gray eyes, punctuated by a muscle throbbing at his left temple, would have sent most men running for cover.

Unruffled by the sudden appearance of the awe inspiring giant, Navy Lieutenant Lawrence Kearny stood up from behind his desk squarely facing angry army scout, Lance Logan. Though Kearny was an inch or so over six feet tall, he still had to look up to meet the livid smoke-colored eyes boring down at him. But the lieutenant felt no threat, for despite Logan's truculent demeanor he was one of the few men with whom the young naval officer would entrust his life.

Kearny arched his eyebrows questioningly. "Might I suggest that you calm down and tell me what has happened?"

The man's suggestion only served to further irritate the already enraged army scout.

"Calm down, hell!" Lance Logan exploded. "And don't you patronize me, you son of a bitch!"

Dark brown brows rose higher still as Lance leaned forward, his muscles straining against the material of his soft leather shirt. The knuckles of his hands whitened as he gripped the edge of the desk.

"Your men were sent to Fort Brooke to rid the Gulf of pirates, not to rape innocent Indians! And you call the Calusa savages!"

He straightened, eyes blazing, chest heaving with emotions he found near impossible to control.

"Now you wait just a minute, Logan!" Kearny thundered back defensively. "First of all, to my knowledge no one has been raped! Secondly, I have never called the Calusa savages!"

"The reason there was no rape, Lieutenant," he forced the words through tightly clenched jaws, "is because I happened to be close enough to hear Lona's screams. Your men caught her near the creek. When I got there they had her on the ground, one man straddling her, ripping off her clothes while the others held her arms and legs!"

Kearny didn't like the scene Logan described, but he never doubted the truth of the army scout's words. His men had been too long without women and there was no way of knowing when they would be able to leave this mosquito infested inferno.

Most of the men assigned to his command were young, still wet behind the ears, but basically honest and hard working. They were just trying to relieve the boredom of fort living and the lonely life they were subjected to aboard ship as they roamed the Gulf searching for the elusive pirates.

There was, however, a small ruthless element among his sailors; those who could not claim youth or inexperience as an excuse for their actions. These few seemed to think the Indians were here simply to satisfy their baser needs, and they encouraged the younger men to adopt their own distorted philosophies.

"Logan, you have my promise. I will talk to the men," he assured the scout, taking his seat once again. "Sit down and have a drink," he said motioning toward an empty chair.

As he spoke he opened a drawer and withdrew a bottle of whiskey and two glasses. Having vented some of his anger and frustration over what was happening to the local tribe, Lance could feel reason gaining strength over his emotions once more. He sat down in the chair the Lieutenant offered and accepted the glass. As he took a long swallow of the amber liquor, he began to relax. He felt a certain rapport with Lawrence Kearny which he felt with few other white men. Kearny was a dedicated naval officer and Lance knew he would do his best to accomplish the assignment he had been given. But he wondered if it would be enough?

He stretched his long legs out in front of him as he massaged the back of his neck with one large hand, the other balancing the glass on his hard, flat belly. Kearny noted the signs of fatigue and strain evident beneath the dark tan of his friend's face and knew the cause to be worry rather than anything physical in nature.

"You have to understand, Logan, that my boys don't feel the same way you do about the Indians. I know how much Little Dove meant to you but you mustn't allow her death to turn you against your own people. Most white men look upon the Indians as primitive heathens, little more than animals." Lieutenant Kearny's tone was defensive and at the same time sympathetic.

Lance stared coldly at the officer across the desk then his lids dropped to completely conceal his thoughts. The deadly silence began to grate on Kearny's nerves.

"Damn it, Logan! Whether you admit it or not there is some justification for the way white men feel about the Indians!"

Lance raised his eyes to the man addressing him, "What justification?"

"You've seen the results of an Indian attack. Mutilated bodies, poison arrows that cause a man to writhe in agony before death comes," the Lieutenant replied heatedly.

Lance stood up, placing his half empty glass on the desk.

"Careful, Kearny," he smiled, but there was no humor in his smoldering gray eyes. "Your prejudices are showing."

The younger man came out of his chair slamming his

fist against the desktop. "Damn it! This is not a question of prejudice! I know we have to find a way to live peacefully with the Calusa as well as the Seminoles, the Timucua, and all of the other Indians who inhabit the territory." He ran his hand through his hair again in an unconscious gesture of frustration. "You're right of course. We were sent here to fight pirates, not Indians. Again I assure you I will talk to my men."

They sat back down declaring an unspoken truce for both knew nothing would be accomplished by continuing to hurl accusations at each other. Lance reached for his drink, sipping slowly, enjoying the slightly numbing effect of the fiery liquid. He twirled the glass with his fingers as he stared thoughtfully at nothing in particular.

"You know, Kearny, the Calusa are a dying nation." His casual tone did not fool Lawrence Kearny for he knew what caused the sadness, the bitterness, and the anger that drove Lance Logan. He also knew that Logan would do everything possible to safeguard the people he loved and had adopted as his family.

"We've made some progress," Lance continued tiredly. "Chief Nokomis feels safe in leaving his women and children near the fort while he and his braves fish and hunt, and we can protect them to some extent from their human enemies. But how in God's name can we protect them from themselves—from poverty and disease—when they are determined to live the same way they have lived for a thousand years?"

Lawrence Kearny had no answer to give but he felt he had to say something.

"If anyone can help these people, I believe it's you. But at the moment the Colonel's not very sympathetic to their plight. Not with that renegade Chikiki and his band on the loose. Their murderous plundering has the settlers between here and Fort King scared to death and with good cause. Something has to be done to stop them! If only we could discover who is supplying the bastards with rifles and ammunition!"

"I have my suspicions," Lance answered, his slate-gray eyes narrowing dangerously as he took another swallow from the glass.

"I know. You still think it's those two ragtail trappers, Martin and Brady," Kearny sighed impatiently. "But damn it man! You have no proof!"

"Proof!" Lance gave the lieutenant a humorless smile that was little more than a slight tilt to the corners of his mouth. "I don't need the kind of 'proof' the military seems to require. Just let either of those lowlife scum so much as look crookedly in my direction and I'll show you justice! Indian justice! Slow and painful!"

Kearny shook his head dismissing the other man's words as an idle threat stemming from exhaustion. He knew Lance Logan was as much a part of the military establishment as any man on the post and he was certain Lance Logan would never take the law into his own hands.

"That would be stupid and you know it. Those two aren't worth hanging for. Besides, you aren't an Indian even if you think like one most of the time."

Few people would have dared to talk to the rugged scout in such a way. Fewer still would have had all their teeth left when they were finished. But Lance didn't move a muscle. He remained as he had been, sprawled in the chair seeming not to have heard what the lieutenant had said.

"It doesn't make any sense," Kearny continued, rising to pace the small confines of the office. "If Martin and Brady are supplying guns and ammunition to Chikiki, and I'm not saying they wouldn't do just that if the profit were great enough, what the hell are the Indians paying them with? They have no money and I hardly think there's a ready market for shells and baubles."

He looked bewildered as he tried to think of a plausible answer to his own question.

"Not shells or baubles," Lance spoke with certainty. "Gold!"

Lawrence Kearny's mouth gaped open as he reached up to run his fingers through his hair.

"Gold?" he repeated incredulously. "Where the hell would Chikiki get gold?"

The lieutenant sat down heavily in the chair behind his desk wondering—somehow hoping—that Lance was joking. Such hope was dashed with Logan's next words.

"According to Nokomis, the Spaniards have been trying to subdue the Indians here in the Florida territory ever since they discovered the world wasn't flat. But their conquests never lasted. The Indians were always able to drive their enemies out or in most cases leave their bones to bleach in the sun. And the treasures the Spanish left behind over the centuries are worth a fortune."

"And you're telling me Nokomis has such treasures?" Skepticism was apparent in Kearny's voice. "If you're right then explain why he and his people live in abject poverty."

He waited wondering what possible explanation

Logan could give.

"Because what we call 'treasure' the Calusa call a sacred heritage to be handed down from generation to generation as it has been handed down for hundreds of years."

"And you think Chikiki is exchanging valuable artifacts for guns and ammunition?"

"I'm certain of it! Nokomis has admitted that a number of priceless objects have turned up missing from their temple. But he refuses to believe his son could be responsible for the thefts. Stealing a sacred object does dishonor to their ancestors and the punishment for such an act is death."

"What are you going to do about it?"

"For the moment, nothing. The more immediate problem is not the missing gold but what happened to a different kind of treasure—one left here at the fort for 'safe keeping'!"

"Lona," Kearny groaned remembering the despicable actions of his men against the beautiful young Indian maid.

"Yes, Lona," Lance acknowledged rising slowly from the chair, setting the glass on the edge of the desk. "I'm on my way to talk to Chief Nokomis to assure him that what happened today will not happen again." Determined gray eyes locked with amber brown. "Can you give me that assurance, Kearny?"

Tense moments passed before Kearny answered.

"No," he replied honestly. "You know I can't. But I will do my best to keep the men in line while we are at the fort."

Lance Logan braced his hands against the desk once again leaning forward. "Heed my word, Lieutenant!

We may think of ourselves as being more civilized than the Calusa but don't ever lose sight of the fact that we are now the intruders in a land that has belonged to their tribe for hundreds of years. They won't give it up without a fight and they won't allow their women to be abused by the men at this fort."

He studied the other man who sat silently looking at the empty glass before him.

"Damn it, Kearny! I'm not asking you," Logan thundered. "I'm telling you! Keep your men in line or be responsible for starting a war with the Indians. A war in which, I remind you, we will be greatly outnumbered!"

With that, Lance turned and stormed from the office, forcefully slamming the door behind him.

The *Victoria* had rounded The Keys, a series of small islands at the southernmost tip of the territory called Florida, several days before. Now, heading north through the calm, aquamarine waters of the Gulf of Mexico, she was within one hundred miles of her destination.

Rebecca leaned against the ship's rail talking companionably to Justin Wentworth who was admiring the way the gentle breeze lifted wisps of her shiny blond hair. She had no idea that she was at that moment the object of attention for an equally admiring but much more sinister pair of eyes studying her from the far distant shore.

Standing on a small parcel of land known as Gasparilla Island the infamous pirate, Jose Gaspar, held a spyglass steady as he focused on the British merchant ship far out at sea.

"Be damned!" he exclaimed turning toward his cousin, Leon. "Just look at her! Have you ever seen such a beauty?"

Leon studied the ship through a similar glass. "Aye," he agreed. "Ripe for the plucking! See how her belly rides low in the water?"

Gaspar lowered the instrument and gave his cousin a vicious jab in the arm.

"Idiot!" the pirate leader roared. "Have you got barnacles for brains? I'm talking about the woman. Not the vessel!"

Leon turned his spyglass once more toward the passing ship this time focusing on the two people standing on its deck. Even from such a distance he could see the woman's glorious golden hair from which rays of light seemed to radiate. Seldom had he beheld such rare beauty.

Gaspar resumed his scrutiny feasting his eyes greedily on the figure of the unsuspecting woman who seemed to be enjoying the mild tropical breeze stirring loosened tendrils of hair about her delicate featured face. Never had the notorious pirate been so entranced by the mere sight of a woman. He admired the way her lavender skirts billowed gracefully as she turned to smile up at the sailor by her side. Gaspar sneered in disgust as he watched the two laughing together. Without even knowing his identity he felt a twisting, wrenching hatred toward the man who commanded the attention of the lovely temptress.

"She would bring a king's ransom," Leon agreed interrupting the pirate's unsettled thoughts. "But there's nothing we can do. It's going to take several days to repair the damage done to the *Dona Rosalia* by that bastard French vessel we sank yesterday."

As he spoke Leon looked toward the mangrove-lined banks at the mouth of the river the Indians called the Caloosahatchee. Hidden by tall moss-shrouded cypress trees, the pirate ship lay at anchor, her flag emblazoned with the dreaded skull and crossbones barely fluttering in the breeze.

"Ah, what treasure such a woman would add to our coffers. But not until I became tired of pleasuring her," Gaspar laughed arrogantly, for though he was no longer young he refused to see the dissipated male-factor he had become. He chose to remember himself as the handsome Spanish naval officer he had once been, a man much sought after by the women at the Royal Court of Madrid.

Lustful thoughts of what it would be like to have the golden-haired creature writhing beneath him caused a tightening in the loins of the debauched pirate and unconsciously he reached down to rub the front of his dirty breeches.

Then lifting his hand to scratch his scraggly beard, now more gray than black, his expression became speculative. "Tell me, Leon. How does our little French 'visitor' like the hospitality of Captiva Island?" He glanced at the neighboring island bordered by a sturdy wooden fence where prisoners were held until they could be ransomed or sold into slavery.

Leon had known it was just a matter of time before his cousin remembered the young girl they had taken aboard the *Rosalia* during the battle of the previous day. He knew likewise the meaning behind the dangerous gleam of anticipation in the coal-black eyes, anticipation that boded no good for their newest captive. He wondered how a man long past his prime could continue to have such an insatiable appetite for carnal pleasures.

"I'm afraid she doesn't appreciate her good fortune in being the ship's only survivor," he answered with words meant to justify whatever actions Gaspar might choose to take. "Her threats of retaliation are making the others uneasy."

"Is that so?" The pirate captain's eyes took on a feral glow. "Well now," he reasoned. "We can't allow discontent among our 'guests,' can we?"

Turning toward a rowboat resting upon the glistening white beach, he called over his shoulder, "I'm going to the *Rosalia*. Have the girl sent to my cabin at once."

Knowing his command would be obeyed without question, he did not wait for a reply. He strode across the sand, paying no heed to the delicate shells crunching beneath his bare feet.

Jose Gaspar poured himself a drink and sat down at the scarred desk carelessly brushing maps and papers onto the filthy floor where piles of dirty clothing lay side by side with dried scraps of food, the remains of meals eaten over a period of several days. The airless cabin reeked of dirt, sweat, and human waste.

The pirate captain propped his sand and salt crusted feet upon the desk taking several long swallows of rum as he glanced at the bed where a grimy, tattered blanket had been thrown haphazardly across the soiled mattress

A knock sounded on the door and after giving leave to enter Gaspar felt a stab of disappointment as he looked at the young girl who had been roughly pushed through the opening and was now standing before him. She was little more than a child. While awaiting her arrival his mind had conjured up the vision of a small woman with golden hair. Unjustly he blamed his disappointment on the innocent captive facing him near the cabin door. He was determined to make her pay dearly for what he considered her duplicity.

"What is your name?" he demanded studying the girl's slim boyish figure.

"Nanette," she answered. "Nanette Dubois. My father is a very wealthy, very powerful man in New Orleans. He will pay anything you ask to get me back, but should I come to harm he will kill you!" she proclaimed with false bravado.

The buccaneer threw back his head and laughed uproariously for he could see the fear she was trying unsuccessfully to hide as she clasped her hands tightly in front of her to still their trembling.

For all her youthful innocence, it took only a moment for Nanette Dubois to realize neither promise of reward nor threats of reprisal would steer the man before her from whatever course he had set. Her resolve to face the bandit leader with courage disintegrated within a moment.

"Please," she begged, as tears pooled in wide frightened eyes. "Let me go!"

"You are hardly in a position to bargain with Gaspar." He smiled wickedly baring yellow-stained teeth as he raked her body, noting every detail from her nondescript brown hair to her water-stained pink slippers. He scoffed at the unpromising flatness of her chest beneath the bodice of her soiled satin dress.

Nanette squirmed nervously as minutes ticked by

and the pirate captain continued to stare at her, a frown on his bearded face. She felt like a piece of cattle on which he had decided not to bid. Finally he spoke and her mounting fear turned to pure terror.

"Take off your clothes," he commanded twirling the glass in his hand before taking another long swig of the fiery liquor.

She stood motionless hoping against hope that she had heard him incorrectly.

"I said take off your clothes," he repeated enunciating each word carefully while he bewitched her with his deep penetrating black eyes.

"No, please," she pleaded taking a step backward against the door. She put her arms out frantically groping for the handle as tears of anguish rolled unchecked down her colorless cheeks. She felt the cold metal beneath her fingertips, but Gaspar rose before she could turn. He circled the desk to move within a foot of where she stood. Air swished as the angry brigand drew back his arm and slapped her a stinging blow across the face.

"You will do as I say!" he ordered furiously, unswerved by the blood that trickled from the corner of her mouth making an uneven ribbon of red down her chin.

Weeping openly Nanette reached shaking fingers to the top button of her bodice. After several fumbling attempts at undoing the fastening during which time her gaze remained fixed on the hypnotic eyes of the satanic pirate, she finally gave up, burying her face in her hands.

With an impatient growl, Gaspar lunged at her. Grasping the fragile material, he ripped the gown down to the waist exposing barely developed breasts below which her ribs were clearly visible beneath a thin layer of pale white skin.

Gaspar reached behind him picking up a long bladed knife that lay on the desktop. It pleased him to hear the girl's sudden intake of breath as he grabbed the band of her dress and slowly slit the material until what was left lay in a circle at her feet. He then continued to slice away at the bindings of her petticoats and pantaloons.

Even fully clothed, Gaspar had found nothing desirable about Nanette Dubois. A naked and shivering Nanette made him feel repulsed as he looked at straight hips, thin legs, and a triangular mound covering what he was sure would be a very narrow opening.

Infuriated by the puny figure standing before him yet determined to satisfy his desire even if he found the means for sating his hunger offensive, he grabbed her arm in a merciless grip dragging her toward the dirty, rumpled bed. As he threw her ruthlessly on her back, Nanette began to scream. Her screams went on and on, echoing off the paneled walls of the small cabin to mingle with the demented laughter of her captor.

She fought as best she could; scratching at his face and pummeling him with her fists but she was no match against her enemy's greater strength. The struggle to conquer excited Gaspar as the girl's lean body never could. He held both her arms with one hand in an unbreakable grip, his legs quickly pinning hers beneath him as he sought to loosen his breeches and free his now bulging manhood.

Spreading her legs with his knees he raised himself and foregoing any of the usual preliminaries to lovemaking rammed his shaft deep into the very core of her womanhood, unaware of the moment when he ripped her maidenhead asunder. But Nanette knew and at last her screams ceased. With the pain, an engulfing black void came which freed her from her torment as she sank into oblivion.

Gaspar, neither knowing nor caring that Nanette had lost consciousness, continued to plow into her with no more feeling than that of a rutting animal seeking only to satisfy his selfish need. When at last he had spilled his seed within her, he rose quickly to his feet adjusting his pants and staring down with distaste at the seemingly lifeless figure sprawled across the bed.

"I never did much like bedding boys," he spat discontentedly.

He had known all along he would find no satisfaction in ravishing the weepy, shapeless virgin. What he needed was a real woman. A woman worthy of his expertise. A woman full of fire. A woman with golden-blond hair that put the sun to shame.

Kicking aside the litter in his path he walked to the small grime-streaked porthole and slowly wiped the dirt away with the heel of a clenched fist. Malevolent eyes searched the blue-green waters fixing on the horizon in the direction the British ship had taken. Thin lips stretched into the evil antithesis of a smile.

"By all that's holy, I will have you, my fair-haired beauty!" he vowed giving not a thought to the irreverence of his oath.

Chapter 3

Rebecca, unaware that she had been indirectly responsible for the brutal rape of a young girl aboard Gaspar's pirate ship, smiled; her cheeks dimpled prettily, for she knew her journey was nearing an end. After eight monotonous weeks at sea, she looked forward to standing on solid ground again.

Once the children were handed into their father's keeping, along with a few choice words which would leave Andrew Townsend no room for doubt as to her opinion of him, she hoped to spend no more than a few days at Fort Brooke before embarking on the return voyage to England.

The ship remained well offshore, away from the western coastline of the Florida territory making it impossible to form a clear picture of the land itself. But Rebecca found the flat terrain unrelieved by hill or valley tedious in the extreme.

As they cut through the water changing to a northeasterly course a dark shadow appeared overhead momentarily blocking out the unrelenting rays of the sun beating down on Rebecca as she gazed at the distant shore.

Elizabeth, who had been standing beside her staring wonderingly at the strange land that would soon be her home, shrieked and grabbed her aunt around the legs.

"Don't worry, Beth! It's just an old pelican," announced Edward, who had been dancing around the deck shouting "Land Ho! Land Ho!" just as the sailor on watch had done when he spotted the eastern coast of Florida days before. Putting up a small hand to shade his eyes, he studied the ungainly creature soaring overhead. Edward made the most of every opportunity that came his way to impart a bit of what he had learned by constantly pestering the ship's crew during the voyage.

As they watched, the pelican, despite its awkward appearance, swooped down diving beneath the surf then reappeared to float gracefully atop the water. The passing ship seemed not to disturb the giant bird in the least as it bobbed along apparently admiring the wiggling fish held in his long bill. After a moment the pelican swallowed the fish whole, its outline defined as it traveled down the bird's long, rubbery throat.

"Ugh!" Elizabeth shuddered hiding her face in Rebecca's skirts for Elizabeth adored all animals and did not like to see even a fish come to harm.

Rebecca felt rivulets of perspiration running down the valley between her breasts and removed her wide-brimmed hat to fan her hot face. Though she had long since changed from her warm heavy dresses to lightweight cotton gowns, she knew it would take time to adjust to the humid heat of the tropical sun.

"I imagine the heat is only one of many things we will

have to get used to," said Justin Wentworth coming to stand beside her.

"Fortunately, I will not be here long enough to have to concern myself with adjusting," Rebecca answered airily smiling at the handsome Englishman.

Rebecca enjoyed the company of the young man whose laughing eyes seemed to look with keen enjoyment on all life had to offer. Even attired in baggy white pants and the loose-fitting striped jersey worn by the sailors, self-assured and well-spoken Justin Wentworth did not belong here among the common men comprising the ship's crew. Rebecca recognized this when they met, and in her usual forthright manner she had asked what circumstance had reduced a gentleman like himself to serve as a lowly seaman.

Not the least offended by her erroneous assumption, he had replied with a merry twinkle in his eyes, "My father holds a title in England and I, alas, am a younger son with three brothers standing between me and an inheritance that would allow me to live a life of ease." The lighthearted way in which he spoke belied his words and Rebecca decided he was far from disappointed with the hand fate had dealt him.

"I have listened to tales of the American colonies and the opportunities just waiting for an intelligent, able-bodied man such as myself," he grinned at her confidently. "Captain Higgins was kind enough to let me play sailor to help pass the long days at sea."

It was obvious to Rebecca that here was a man who preferred action and adventure to the secure life she was sure he could have had in England. Such an attitude was beyond her comprehension and she greatly feared he would find only disappointment and hardship following the path he had chosen in venturing to the new world.

Rebecca was grateful for his company during the crossing. She admired his gentle patience with Edward and Elizabeth who followed him everywhere getting underfoot as he went about efficiently performing the varied duties assigned to him. But she was concerned by the smitten way he gazed at her when he thought she wasn't looking. She hadn't encouraged him to believe that their relationship could ever go beyond friendly banter.

Justin was at first baffled by the reserve Rebecca maintained. But while the beautiful green-eyed enchantress remained somewhat aloof, Edward and Elizabeth were outgoing and gregarious. Ever enjoying being the center of attention, the twins proved most enlightening as they sought to outdo one another in the telling of their escapades in England. And as the days passed, Justin gradually pieced together a most entertaining picture of the delightful Miss Winslow.

Finally the day came when the *Victoria* left the open waters of the Gulf and sailed into Hillsborough Bay. Justin, Rebecca, and the children were each anxious for different reasons to see an end to the journey. An already warm morning sun shone brightly down from a cloudless, powder blue sky sprinkling the gently swelling water with a myriad of sparkling diamonds.

"Why," Rebecca asked turning her delicately formed face up to Justin, "do they call this Hillsborough Bay? I should think having won their independence the 'natives' would want no reminders of their former rulers, especially the British Colonial Secretary of State, Lord Hillsborough."

"The few white men inhabiting Florida at the time of the revolution remained loyal to the Crown during the war though I doubt they gave much thought to battles taking place so far away. They had all they could handle trying to keep their scalps."

"Please, Mr. Wentworth!" Rebecca admonished looking quickly to where the children were hanging over the side of the ship, their heads protruding between the guard ropes.

"Sorry," he apologized but continued with undisguised excitement that reminded her of Edward wanting to share his knowledge about the land they were fast approaching.

"Florida didn't become a territory of the United States until three years ago in 1821. Guess they haven't had much time to think about changing names. But what puzzles me is why it took the colonials so long to recognize the untapped source of wealth so close at hand."

That Justin believed what he said, Rebecca had no doubt. But how, she wondered, could the unpromising habitat before her command such fierce loyalty from one who had yet to set his feet upon its soil?

The shoreline was now plainly visible as they made their way slowly toward Fort Brooke. Rebecca was again struck by the flatness of the land with nary a rise to offset its tiresome sameness. It brought to mind the flat effect of a poor landscape painting. In contrast the vegetation seemed to escalate to towering heights. Nearest the water pampas grass and sea oats stood guard against the elements, their roots protecting the beach from erosion. Just behind, clumps of palmetto bushes thrived alongside sharp-pointed bayonet plants whose stems swished in the breeze as if to dare closer scrutiny. Hickory and oak trees seemed at home among tall umbrella palms, some heavy with clusters of orange dates. While in the distance, forests of pine and bald cypress dominated the landscape. Remembering the tales she had heard about Indians and pirates Rebecca felt a touch of fear for any number of unseen dangers could be lurking nearby hidden within the thick foliage.

"Isn't it ugly?" Elizabeth pulled her head back and looked up apprehensively at Rebecca.

"It isn't ugly, Elizabeth. It's just different," she replied smiling so that the child would not sense her own misgivings.

When at last Fort Brooke came into view the first impressions of the four people standing on the ship's deck were as different as the seasons that make up a year.

"It's ugly, too," Elizabeth sighed as she looked suspiciously at the sturdy log stockade set some distance back from the water's edge, wondering what was behind its walls.

"Where are the pirates and Indians?" Edward asked, disappointed by the handful of ordinary-looking men standing on the beach awaiting their arrival.

Justin felt an instant kinship with the virgin tropical beauty of the land surrounding the fort. He was exhilarated beyond his wildest expectations. This was where he belonged! He had no doubt! Here he could chart his own destiny free from meaningless titles and the demands of a shallow society.

Rebecca looked around her at the strange, forbidding wilderness, then at the high, imprisoning walls

43

surrounding Fort Brooke. She shuddered apprehensively. *Oh, my God! What have I done?*

There were perhaps a dozen men waiting to greet the longboat carrying Rebecca, Justin, Jeremiah, and the children as they were rowed swiftly toward shore.

As the boat bumped against the sand, two sailors leaped into the shallow water and pulled it up onto the beach. Justin and Jeremiah assisted Rebecca and the twins, and for the first time in weeks they stood on solid ground.

Rebecca, who had adapted readily to the movement of the ship, now found it difficult to adjust to the land beneath her feet and she leaned dizzily against Justin as his hand reached out to steady her.

The men on shore greeted Jeremiah heartily, clapping him on the back, while all tried to talk at once.

Rebecca kept her amber-green eyes lowered, embarrassed by the curiously admiring stares directed her way. She did not see the angry, giant of a man elbow the others aside to stand facing Captain Higgins.

"What the hell is the meaning of this, Jeremiah?" the man roared jerking Rebecca to attention. She looked up—then still further up—tilting her head to an uncomfortable angle before she could look at the man's angry visage. He was at least a head taller than any other man in the group except Captain Higgins and he had shoulders as wide as the trunk of a mighty oak.

"Good to see you again, Lance," Captain Higgins responded jovially, deliberately ignoring the question he had been asked for he could guess what was on Lance Logan's mind.

"I asked you a question, Jeremiah." Lance glared at the older man not willing to be put off. "What in God's name possessed you to bring three children through pirate plagued waters into a territory on the brink of an Indian war?"

Rebecca, who had been shocked into silence by the stranger's rudeness, turned wondering who the third child could be.

"Three children?" Jeremiah chuckled. "Perhaps you should look again."

And with the Captain's cryptic reply came the realization that the obnoxious, arrogant, backwoodsman raving like a bedlamite thought she was a child. *Damn the insolent cur!* Drawing herself up as tall and as straight as her five foot two inch stature would allow, Rebecca lifted furious green eyes sparked with golden flames to meet the chilling gray stare of Lance Logan. Fire and ice!

As their eyes met and held, Rebecca once again felt the dizzying sensation which had swept over her as she stepped onto the beach minutes before. An indefinable force seemed to draw her toward the insufferable, overbearing oaf and she found to her astonishment that she did not want to lower her eyes from his. She was aware of a queasy feeling in the pit of her stomach as she fought to control emotions she did not understand.

Meanwhile, Lance was just beginning to see how very wrong his first brief impression of the trio had been. His intake of breath was audible as his eyes traveled slowly from the delicate beauty of the womanly face to the full luscious breasts straining against the thin material of her moss-colored cotton

45

gown, still crisp atop her numerous underskirts, the wilting heat of the noonday sun notwithstanding.

His anger began to ebb as he observed a waist so small he could easily span it with his hands. He allowed his imagination to take over envisioning soft rounded hips and perfectly proportioned legs beneath the layers of petticoats. His exploration ended as he noted small patten-shod feet peeking from below the hem of her gown, one foot tapping impatiently.

Lifting his gaze he encountered fiery-green eyes dancing with gold flames. Once Rebecca was sure she had the rogue's attention, she proceeded to let her eyes very deliberately rove slowly down his immense body studying him as he had studied her a few moments ago.

Rebecca was awed by the sheer size of the man. His dark brown hair was tied back with a piece of rawhide. The angles and planes of his deeply tanned face were too rugged to be called handsome, but there was an aura about him that made Rebecca feel a thrill of excitement just from being in his presence. His straight nose with slightly flaring nostrils reminded her of a picture she had once seen in a book depicting the ancient gods of Greece.

Muscles in his long arms and massive chest bulged beneath the fringed shirt. His upper body tapered to a narrow waist. Lean hips and long legs were covered by tight-fitting breeches and his feet were encased in boots made of animal skin which ended at mid-calf.

She brought her eyes back to his and caught a brief hint of amusement.

Elizabeth and Edward had been standing one on each side of Rebecca, their blue eyes wide as they took in the strange scene unfolding before them. Unnoticed by the two adults who seemed bent on outstaring one another, Elizabeth took a step forward.

Lance felt something prodding his hard-muscled stomach just above his navel. He tore his gaze from hypnotic green eyes and looked down into a round, freckled face frowning up at him. His jaw dropped as he saw the child's small finger pressing into his midsection.

Elizabeth, still pushing her tiny digit against him, stated with childish honesty, "I don't like you!"

Lance stepped back quickly, surprised by the child's words as much as by her action.

"Elizabeth!" Rebecca was mortified. Fearing the man's reaction, she swiftly pulled the little girl back against her skirts.

"Lance Logan, may I have the pleasure of introducing you to Miss Rebecca Winslow?" Jeremiah asked wedging his way between them.

"This is no place for women and children," Lance stated, modifying his original declaration while pointedly ignoring the introduction.

Rebecca felt her temper flare again as the unmannered lout continued to berate the good captain. Just as she was about to tell him what she thought of his brash behavior, a lilting feminine voice hailed them.

"Welcome to Fort Brooke!" Rebecca turned to see a handsome young couple walking arm in arm toward them. She spun back around searching the remorseless gray eyes of Lance Logan who had nearly managed to convince her that women were not welcome in this godforsaken wilderness.

"Mary! George! Good to see you again," Jeremiah greeted the pair, reaching to shake the hand of the tall,

47

blond man in military dress.

Rebecca wondered if all men born in this new country grew to such outlandish heights. Maybe it had to do with their diet. *Raw meat,* she wondered, slanting her sea-green eyes toward Lance Logan who stood silently apart from the little group.

"Miss Rebecca Winslow, this is Colonel George Brooke, Commander of the fort, and his lovely wife, Mary," he beamed, squeezing Mary around the waist in a familiar fatherly embrace.

Colonel Brooke bowed formally while Mary clasped Rebecca's hand in hers and said with warm enthusiasm, "Miss Winslow! What a wonderful surprise!"

If either of the two were curious as to Rebecca's reasons for being at Fort Brooke, George was apparently too polite to ask and Mary was too excited over the unexpected company of another woman to care.

Rebecca looked into Mary Brooke's pretty smiling face guessing her to be no more than a few years older than herself. The woman's ample, well-rounded figure brought to mind the phrase "pleasingly plump." She was astonished by the way in which the Colonel's wife allowed her long, curly brown hair to hang loose down her back. Rebecca, like most Englishwomen, wore her own golden locks secured atop her head or at the nape of her neck.

But the free, unconfining style seemed perfectly suited to the young American woman, and it was obvious that her husband adored everything about her. As George Brooke gazed lovingly at his wife, Rebecca thought how perfectly suited they seemed.

Her eyes, as if they had a will of their own, sought

and found Lance Logan who was staring at her, an expression of cynical amusement on his autocratic face. Lifting her nose, Rebecca sniffed haughtily trying to ignore the annoying man. Why should she care what he thought of her? She didn't, of course! Everything about him repelled her: his size, the strangeness of his dress, not to mention his boorish manners. And there was something threatening about his overpowering masculinity. Yet, in all honesty, she could not dismiss the magnetic pull she felt drawing her eyes to his against her will.

Rebecca could no more make sense of her contradictory emotions than she could suppress the shudder of apprehension that coursed through her slender body at that moment. Daring a glance at the rugged mountain of a man, she knew by the satisfied smirk on his face that he had noted her reaction and she wondered if he had read her thoughts as well.

Jeremiah introduced Justin Wentworth to the Brookes then motioned smilingly toward the twins. "And these two copper tops are Elizabeth and Edward, Miss Winslow's niece and nephew."

The Colonel acknowledged the children then drew Justin aside, ever eager to recruit strong young men to help settle the territory.

Mary lowered herself to one knee unmindful of the sand soiling her skirts. She held out her arms to Edward and Elizabeth.

"Oh, they are adorable," she said, a bubbly smile lighting her pretty face.

Rebecca rolled her eyes heavenward as Elizabeth came shyly forward and allowed Mary to embrace her. Edward frowned choosing to remain at Rebecca's side.

"It's going to be such fun having you here," Mary enthused. "George and I made sure when we built our home that there would be plenty of room for new arrivals."

"Mrs. Brooke . . ." Rebecca began.

"No, please, you must call me Mary, for I know we are going to be good friends."

The warmth in the woman's eyes made it difficult not to respond in kind. "Of course, if you will call me Rebecca," she heard herself saying.

The newcomers were startled by a raucous noise from above as a flock of white gulls with gray-tipped wings swooped down in search of the breadcrumbs Mary fed them each evening.

"Not yet, you greedy things!" Mary laughed as she flapped her apron to send the birds on their way. "Come, let's go to the house where it's cooler," she continued, smiling down at the twins. "If I'm not mistaken, Lona made her special spiced cookies this morning."

"Mrs. Brooke . . . I mean, Mary," Rebecca stammered, not wishing to hurt the kind woman's feelings but determined to make it clear that she would not be staying long at Fort Brooke. Indeed, from what little she had seen so far, her return voyage could not begin soon enough to suit her.

But the colonel's wife was paying her little mind continuing to coo over the twins in such a way as to make Rebecca wonder if all American women were slightly daft.

"Mary!" she repeated in a voice that sounded loud to her ears. "I came here looking for a man!"

As soon as the words were out, Rebecca felt her

cheeks flush. She didn't miss Lance Logan's raised eyebrows or the way one corner of his mouth quirked. *Evil minded jackass,* she thought.

Rebecca fought to regain her composure then looked into Mary's astonished face. "What I mean is that I am here to find my brother-in-law, Andrew Townsend. Andrew is Edward and Elizabeth's father and it's high time he acted like one." Golden sparks dominated luminous green eyes as she spoke.

Lance watched the little spitfire wondering why he didn't just turn around and walk away. She was trouble all wrapped up in a neat, self-centered little bundle. He could feel it.

"Andrew Townsend isn't here." His words were so unexpected Rebecca jumped turning toward him, alarm clearly written across her delicate molded features.

"He has to be here," she argued refusing to admit any other possibility. "He wrote to me and told me he had established himself at Fort Brooke. He seemed so happy, so sure he had found what he had been searching for. His letter plus certain other things," she eyed Edward, "convinced me that it was time the children were reunited with their father."

Lance wondered what the "certain other things" might be. "Sorry to disappoint you, Miss Winslow, but Andrew isn't here and may not return for months."

George and Justin had by now rejoined the others. George knew that Andrew Townsend had left last week to pick up dispatches at Fort King a hundred miles northeast of Fort Brooke. He would return soon, a couple of weeks at most. And he knew Lance knew it. He gave the army scout a quizzical look hearing him intentionally misinform the beautiful Miss Winslow.

"A moment, Lance. Let's not exaggerate," George interrupted, hoping to erase the frown marring Rebecca's lovely face. "It's true Andrew is away from the fort, but I can assure you he will return in no more than two weeks."

If he thought this would come as good news to Rebecca he found out quickly that he was wrong.

"Two weeks!" she cried. "But I can't stay here for two weeks!" she said looking around with something akin to horror. "I have to return to England, to Wil . . ." she stopped herself but not before Lance had heard enough to draw his own conclusions.

He gave Rebecca a hard look. He had been right. Hooded lids hid his disgust. She was nothing but a spoiled English miss thinking only of fancy gowns and balls. There was undoubtedly some dandy in high-heeled pumps waiting to welcome her home.

Oh, he understood, all right! Miss Winslow was here to thrust two innocent children on poor, unsuspecting Andrew then rush back to England and a life of selfish pleasure. Hadn't he been pursued by the same type in Charleston? Beautiful young women without a serious thought in their heads except finding rich husbands to support their frivolous demands. He hadn't been caught then and though he had to admit Rebecca Winslow was comely enough he wouldn't be caught now! *No, by God! He didn't need another woman! Not now! Not ever!*

Wondering at the need to reassure himself where the young Englishwoman was concerned, he glanced around and found himself staring down into the most extraordinary pair of eyes he had ever seen, eyes like rare jewels, topaz mixed with emerald.

"Oh, hell!" he swore under his breath.

Rebecca had almost forgotten Edward. He stood beside her so quietly. Now she felt the tug on her skirts and looked down into wide, excited, blue eyes.

"Look, Becca," he said in wonder. "It's an Indian! Becca," he whispered, "it's a real Indian!"

Rebecca could feel his excitement and apprehension as he nervously clutched the material of her full skirts. She followed his gaze to where a dark head peeked out at them then darted back behind the cover of a clump of palmetto bushes.

She jumped at the sound of Lance's deep command. "Come here, Davey."

The child walked forward unhesitantly to stand next to Lance. He appeared to be no more than a few years older than Elizabeth and Edward. His raven-black hair hung straight about his shoulders. Fringed bangs were held against his forehead with a bright colored band. Huge velvet brown eyes stared at the red-headed, freckle-faced twins. The boy's skin was dark and flawlessly smooth.

Lance placed his large hand on the child's thin shoulder. "This is my son, Davey," he announced.

Whatever Rebecca expected, it certainly wasn't this. She felt the blood drain from her face. "But he's an In—" her voice faltered.

"Indian, Miss Winslow?" Lance finished for her, smiling sardonically. "Your astuteness is truly amazing."

Rebecca flushed beneath his sarcasm.

53

"But you're only half right," he continued. "Davey's mother was of the Calusa tribe."

One of the many tales of the new territory with which Justin had entertained them during their ocean voyage had been about the local Indians so the name was not entirely unfamiliar to her.

Rebecca could not take her eyes from the young boy. She was fascinated by his dark perfectly formed features which were too foreign for her to label "handsome."

"I will show Elizabeth and Edward the fort?" The boy's statement was in fact a question and he looked at Rebecca waiting for her reply.

Davey must have been watching and listening from behind the bushes for some time, Rebecca thought, for he did not hesitate in calling the twins by name.

Elizabeth looked a little skeptical but Edward was wildly excited over the prospect of exploring. Rebecca nodded her approval refraining from admonishing them to be careful for Edward would say she was treating him like a baby.

To her surprise, the warning came from Davey's father. "See that none of you get into trouble, Davey. Remember this is all new to Elizabeth and Edward."

"Yes, sir," the boy answered politely.

What a complex man, Rebecca thought as she watched the children racing toward the gates of the fort, Elizabeth bringing up the rear. Just when she was certain Lance Logan was entirely without feeling she found him expressing concern for three small children.

The others had wandered further down the beach as George explained to Justin some of the problems involved in running the fort and what they had accomplished in the short time the fort had been established.

"Mr. Logan?" Rebecca tilted her head looking up at Lance. "What did you mean when you said your wife *was* of the Calusa tribe?"

The man beside her seemed genuinely puzzled. "My wife?" He stared down at Rebecca his expression one of bewilderment.

Annoyed by his seeming lack of comprehension and wondering if it was deliberate, Rebecca repeated, "You just said your wife *was* an Indian. I wondered what you meant, that's all." She shrugged as if it didn't matter to her one way or the other.

"Miss Winslow," Lance's tone clearly indicated impatience. "I am not married. I have never been married. And I have no intention of getting married . . . ever!"

Obviously, for Lance Logan the exchanging of nuptial vows held as much appeal as walking barefoot over hot coals. And Rebecca was glad because it meant some unsuspecting woman would be spared the inept courting of this barbarian.

Rebecca tried to imagine the man attempting to court a lady in the proper fashion and could not stifle the laugh such a picture brought to mind.

"I'm not known for my humor, Miss Winslow," Lance glared. "If I have said something funny I would hate to miss it!"

Rebecca sobered immediately. "I was not laughing at anything you said, Mr. Logan," she assured a frowning Lance.

Rebecca felt it would be better not to try to explain the source of her amusement and returned to the discussion at hand. "Forgive me if I pry. I was simply curious about Davey's mother."

"Davey's mother is dead." If he felt any loss it was veiled behind an emotionless voice and cold gray eyes.

"I'm sorry," was all Rebecca could think to say. And she wasn't sure why she was sorry. Because a young Indian maiden was dead? Because Davey was a motherless child? Or because Lance didn't seem to care?

He had spoken so curtly and with such finality Rebecca had not expected him to say more so she was surprised when he continued. "Little Dove, Davey's mother, was a gift from Nokomis, the Calusa cacique, the chief."

"A gift!" Rebecca's voice cracked as it rose several octaves. "Do you mean to tell me this . . . this chief gave you a young girl as a gift?"

She was momentarily shocked speechless while Lance stood staring, captivated by golden fire igniting huge, disbelieving green eyes.

Finally Rebecca found her voice. "I have never, ever heard of anything so . . . so heathen!"

Lance held his temper reminding himself that he was talking to a spoiled young Englishwoman who could not possibly understand what it took to survive in this raw new country and wondering why he had felt it necessary to explain his relationship with Little Dove in the first place.

"I could not refuse the chief's gift," Lance explained. "It would have been an insult. I saved Nokomis's life so he had to give me something of value in return, something that would be a great sacrifice on his part."

As she listened, many questions came to mind but

56

she knew this was not the time to ask them. Lance looked deep into Rebecca's eyes wanting her to understand.

"You've no way of knowing how great a sacrifice the chief made when he gave Little Dove to me."

Rebecca grimaced at the easy way Lance spoke of one person being given to another and Lance was not unaware of her censure.

"Miss Winslow. Little Dove was the eldest daughter of Nokomis and according to Calusa custom she was supposed to marry her brother, Chikiki. Nokomis went against ancient tradition by giving her into my care."

Rebecca found herself fascinated yet greatly disturbed by the story Lance was telling.

"Chikiki was furious. He broke away from the tribe. He and a renegade band that chose to follow him have been terrorizing settlers between here and Fort King ever since."

Lance paused disgusted with his discourse, certain that the woman staring up at him, her lovely mouth slightly agape, could neither understand nor sympathize with the plight of the Calusa. "Have I satisfied your curiosity, Miss Winslow?"

"I just have one more question, Mr. Logan," she replied genuinely trying to make sense out of what she had been told.

"And what might that be?" The corner of his mouth edged up in the beginning of a smile as Rebecca puzzled over how to frame her question.

"If you were caring for her, why is Little Dove dead?"

His expression changed so quickly Rebecca took a step backwards wishing she could recall the words she had just spoken. She thought for a moment that Lance was going to strike her as his strong hands clenched into fists at his sides. Instead he looked at her with such naked anguish she suddenly felt an inexplicable desire to hold him and comfort him as she sometimes did the twins when they ran tearfully to her with their scrapes or bruises. But she had no time to ponder her reaction before Lance turned without a word and walked away.

Chapter 4

As Logan disappeared into the nearby woods, Mary rejoined Rebecca.

"What's wrong with Lance?" she questioned watching his retreat with a worried frown.

"It must have been something I said," Rebecca replied musingly. "Actually, Mary, I believe everything I've said since I arrived has irritated that man, but for the life of me I don't know why."

She stared at the spot where he had disappeared.

Mary linked arms with Rebecca. "It's not your fault," she assured. "Lance has a great deal on his mind. He's sensitive to the needs of the Indians and he's worried about them. He cares so deeply."

"Sensitive? Caring?" Rebecca scoffed in an undertone. These were not words she would use to describe Lance Logan. Words such as "insufferable" and "boorish" came more readily to mind.

As the two women approached the gates of the fort, Rebecca saw a herd of cattle grazing in the meadowland nearby, but her attention focused on the strange village erected just outside the wall. Sturdy, dark-skinned women moved about stirring the contents of huge black pots hung over open cook fires. They wore loose-fitting dresses that fell just below their knees and strings of brightly colored beads were around their necks. Half-naked children played together never straying too far from where their mothers worked. "They're part of the Calusa tribe," Mary informed her. "While Chief Nokomis and his braves are hunting, they leave their women and children near the fort for safety." Mary paused to look at the cluster of huts.

"It was not always this way for the Indians, feeling it safe to leave the women and children. At first the Calusa were hostile. They tried their best to drive us away. When they saw their attacks were useless against the solders' weapons, they were afraid. But gradually they came to realize we were not here to do them harm. They learned to trust as much as an Indian can ever trust a white man."

Rebecca looked at Mary in surprise. "But I thought it was the other way around? White men didn't trust the Indians?"

"I suppose it depends on your perspective," Mary laughed.

As they paused before the open gates, Rebecca looked back trying to glean some understanding as to why men, and apparently women as well, were willing to risk their lives to make a home in this crude, tangled mass of tropical vegetation. In the distance standing beside a creek which ran west of the fort stood Lance Logan holding the hand of a beautiful young Indian girl. Though they were too far away for Rebecca to hear what they were saying it was obvious that they knew each other well.

As Rebecca turned to follow Mary, she felt a sinking sensation in the pit of her stomach. *Damnation! Why was it that just looking at the man made her feel peculiar? And who,* she wondered, *was the young woman he seemed so fond of?* She stole a quick glance over her shoulder but they were no longer in sight.

Fort Brooke was much larger than it appeared from outside the sturdy log walls. Rebecca glanced up at the walkway encircling the inner walls of the stockade where soldiers stood watch. She paused for a moment feeling the full weight of what she had done in bringing Edward and Elizabeth to this hostile land where guards were necessary for protection.

She was greeted by the noxious odor of a dozen or more hogs restrained within a pen made of cypress poles. Squawking chickens ran here and there pecking at the ground and each other, raising dust with their flapping wings. To her left was a long rambling building which Mary pointed out as the barracks where the soldiers were housed. The cook house stood next to the barracks with gray smoke rising from the chimney shooting sparks into the clear blue sky. She wondered how anyone could stand the heat inside as she stood there perspiring in spite of the gentle breeze swaying her skirts. As Rebecca scanned the interior of the fort, Mary indicated the supply house, the guardhouse, a large stable with a blacksmith shop at one end, and several one-room wooden structures used for offices and meeting rooms.

Rebecca's eyes came to rest on the house George

Brooke had built for his wife. It was two-storied, constructed of the same cypress wood as the rest of the fort, yet it was unlike the other buildings. Rebecca could almost feel the warmth and love that had gone into its creation.

A huge oak tree shaded the front of the structure. Like most of the area's vegetation, its branches were hung with stringy, hairlike moss. Squirrels chased each other, rustling leaves as they jumped from one limb to another. Rebecca noticed that like everything she had seen so far even the squirrels were different. Their tails were not as full and bushy as those that played in the trees at home. They certainly had no need of thick tails in which to wrap themselves in this climate, she thought, wiping perspiration from her brow then frowning at the brown smudges on her dainty handkerchief.

"It is said that the Spanish explorer, Hernando de Soto, signed a peace treaty with the Indians beneath that very tree nearly three hundred years ago." Mary's voice was low and held a note of reverence. "It's called the 'Charter Oak.'"

"Three hundred years?" Rebecca marveled. "That's a long time. It's funny," she continued after pausing to study the enormous shade tree, "I've only heard Florida described as 'the new territory.' It's hard to think of this land as having a past."

Mary laughed. "Don't let Chief Nokomis hear you say such a thing. The way he tells it, the Indians have been here since the beginning of time. And I'm sure he would be much happier without the intrusion of the white man."

Rebecca thought it would have made better sense to

leave Florida to the savages, but she knew her opinion would not be appreciated by anyone except perhaps the subjugated Indian chief.

"To tell the truth, Mary, I had never heard of Florida until Andrew decided to come here," she replied. "Even then it was only a name, someplace faraway. And now that I'm here, I feel so foreign." Her emerald eyes brimmed with tears. "I was wrong to bring the children here," she confessed crumpling her handkerchief into a ball as she spoke.

Mary's tender heart went out to the unhappy young woman so far from home. Putting an arm around Rebecca's waist, she smiled sympathetically. "I don't believe your coming was a mistake, Rebecca. Maybe it's because I am so happy to have your company, but I have the strangest premonition that here is exactly where you belong."

Rebecca could only stare at Mary, convinced now that American women were daft indeed!

"Come, Lona. Walk with me, please."

Lona recognized Lance's need having witnessed his angry leave-taking of the beautiful English lady. They strolled along the bank of the creek hand in hand.

"She's very pretty," Lona offered, breaching the silence once they were away from the fort.

"What?"

"I said she is very pretty. The English woman," Lona repeated knowing Lance had heard what she said and knew exactly to whom she was referring.

"Is she? I didn't really notice," Lance lied, fully aware of Rebecca Winslow's beauty but unwilling to admit to any attraction. He had already formed his opinion of the lady and had made up his mind to stay as far away from her as possible.

"Lance," she laughed, her dark eyes sparkling. "Don't try to fool me, brother," she said teasingly.

He turned letting go of her hands and then placed his firmly on her shoulders, shaking her gently.

"Lona, I have never tried to fool you." Lance turned somber gray eyes on her and Lona knew he was thinking solely of her now, forgetting for the moment their beautiful English visitor.

Anyone else would have been frightened by the strength with which he held her, bruising her shoulders beneath his grasp.

"I've held nothing back, Lona, in explaining the dangers that lie outside the gates of the fort. Why did you ride so far into the woods knowing what could happen to you?"

The Indian girl shuddered at the memory of the sailors' hands on her but she stared at the ground refusing to answer.

Lance raised his voice in frustration and shook her again. "You're just like Little Dove!" he shouted. "You won't listen!"

Lona stepped back and Lance released his hold on her.

"I'll never forget Little Dove," Lona said feelingly. "She was my sister and I loved her even though we were born of different mothers. She was more beautiful than I and of pure Calusa blood. Sometimes I feel tainted because my mother was Spanish. But, Lance," she sighed wistfully, "in one way Little Dove and I were very much alike. She could not be bound and neither can I."

Lance knew this was true. Like the bird for which she was named, Little Dove had to have her freedom, freedom to ride like the wind across open fields or unrestrained through the woods on the back of her temperamental black mare. The mare had been given to Little Dove by her father soon after she had come to live with Lance, perhaps the Chief's way of making amends to his daughter for what he felt he had to do but still regretted.

Lance had never admitted, even to himself, that he loved Little Dove. Yet during their short time together, the wall that had encased his heart since the deaths of his parents and his sister when a fever epidemic ravaged Charleston had begun to crumble. They had laughed together; they had made love; and his woman had given him Davey.

With Little Dove and Davey beside him he had finally been able to reconcile the guilt that had plagued him since learning his family was gone. He realized he could have done nothing to save them even if he had been in Charleston when it happened. Instead, he had been in Washington talking to people interested in gaining new territory to the south, urging men like Lance to become a part of their plans.

When the devastating telegram arrived and he realized he had nothing to return to in Charleston, he reluctantly agreed to do what he could for the United States Government.

"Hello! Are you there?" Lona had known the moment Lance retreated inside himself and she waited silently. She had seen it happen many times before and she respected his privacy, but she also knew when he had brooded long enough.

"Sorry, Lona," he apologized. "I've done it again, haven't I?"

"Yes, but this time I'm grateful. I was spared from most of the lecture you had planned. Now about this pretty English lady—"

Lance cut off her words by hugging her tightly against his big, hard-muscled body. She leaned her head back and looked up into the face of the man who held her.

"If you don't want to talk about the lady, then tell me about the gentleman."

"What gentleman?" Lance asked puzzled.

"The nice looking Englishman that arrived on the *Victoria.*"

"His name is Justin Wentworth and he plans to settle here. Why?"

"Just curious," Lona asked innocently.

"If I had any sense I'd ask George to send you back to Nokomis," he said sternly.

Lona shrugged away his idle threat. "I must get back to the fort. Mary will be worried," she giggled.

Before he could say more, she spun on her heels and ran back along the bank of the creek.

Lance leaned against the trunk of a willow tree, its green-leafed branches stretching over the calm surface of the water. He looked down at his reflection, staring but not really seeing the image that looked back at him.

Justin Wentworth. All he knew about the young Englishman was that he had attracted Lona's attention. But he was damned sure going to learn a lot more.

For he had read the look in the young girl's dark eyes.

He straightened and reached out his arms rippling the muscles in his wide shoulders until the seams of his buckskin shirt threatened to split. *Yes indeed,* he thought to himself. He would find out all there was to know about Justin Wentworth.

Why hadn't he paid more attention to the man when they had been introduced? Thoughts of sea-green eyes came to mind.

"Damn!" he cursed loudly as he turned and walked back toward Fort Brooke.

Mary Brooke's home reflected her warm personality. The delicious smell of baked goods permeated the air as the two women entered the large living room. At one end Rebecca noted the empty fireplace in front of which an overstuffed couch and matching chairs covered in a pretty floral print were grouped to encourage conversation.

"Does it get cold enough to need a fire?" Rebecca asked disbelievingly.

"You'd be surprised," Mary replied. "In January and February the temperature can be quite chilling though the cold spells seldom last more than a few days. The Indians even tell of occasional snow flurries but last winter was relatively mild."

On the opposite side of the room stood a long maple dining table surrounded by a dozen needlepoint-cushioned chairs. Beneath the table a thick rug patterned in rich hues of green, brown and gold covered the highly polished wooden floor.

Rebecca stared dumbfounded at the elegant little

spinet piano against one wall. She felt as if she had entered another world.

"How did you do it?" she asked unable to hide her astonishment.

Mary walked over to the piano and lovingly lifted an oval framed portrait of a handsome young couple.

"My parents," she said handing the frame to Rebecca. "My mother died when I was a child. My father knew that she would want me to have these things so he arranged to have them brought here by ship from Baltimore as a wedding present."

Rebecca studied the young woman in the portrait who looked so remarkably like Mary. Baltimore! She had heard of the thriving city and knew it was near the capital of the young republic. How could Mary give up the life she must have known there to live in this desolate fort so far from civilization?

"Excuse me."

Rebecca whirled around startled by the soft-spoken voice. It came from a doorway she suspected led to the kitchen for it seemed to be where the mouthwatering aromas originated.

"Lona," Mary smiled. "Please come in. I want you to meet Rebecca Winslow. Rebecca has just arrived on the *Victoria* from England."

"It's a pleasure to meet you, Miss Winslow," Lona said politely in flawless English.

Standing before Rebecca was the young woman she had seen Lance Logan talking with a short time ago. *Talking with?* He had been holding her hand in full view of the fort, and she was even lovelier up close with her dark, slanted eyes.

Rebecca had no doubt that she was an Indian yet she

was quite different in appearance from the women cooking over the open fires outside the walls of the fort. Her long blue-black hair wasn't straight nor was it braided. Thick and heavy it seemed to ripple down her slender back, curling under where it ended several inches below her narrow waist. She was tall and moved with the fluid grace of meadow grass swaying in the gentle breeze. Her olive complexion was satin-smooth much like Davey's though her cheekbones were more rounded and not so high.

"I've made fresh coffee and thought you might like some," Lona said with a gentle smile which further enhanced her exotic beauty.

Rebecca was annoyed when the scene she had witnessed outside the gates of the fort continued to nag at her, the image of Lance Logan touching the exquisite maiden in a manner she could almost term "intimate."

"That sounds wonderful," replied Mary motioning Rebecca toward the open doorway.

Rebecca followed the two women into a large airy kitchen where a breeze fluttered the ruffled curtains at the windows. A rough-hewn wooden table stood in the center of the room, and though serviceable, she was certain it had not been among the furniture imported from Baltimore. Still Rebecca felt comfortable as she seated herself in a straight-backed chair and thanked Lona for the steaming cup of coffee she placed before her. There was a homey atmosphere about the room. It seemed the perfect place for women to sit and share confidences.

As they chatted, Rebecca found herself hard pressed to keep from staring at the young Indian who sat across from her seeming much at home in her surroundings.

"Lona lives with us and I can't imagine what we would do without her," Mary smiled, and Rebecca blushed hoping her curiosity had not prompted the friendly woman's comment.

"Lona is the daughter of the Calusa cacique, Chief Nokomis," added the colonel's wife.

Rebecca choked spilling a goodly portion of the dark liquid over the rim of her cup and into the saucer. She had quickly reasoned that if Lona was the chief's daughter, then she was also the sister of Little Dove and the Indian brave, Chikiki. The news set her mind spinning. She remembered what Lance Logan had said about Chikiki being required by tradition to marry his sister. Somehow she could not imagine Lona, who seemed so comfortable in the world of the white man, adhering to such primitive customs, and she wondered if Little Dove had adapted as well to the life that had been forced upon her. It was at that moment George Brooke entered the kitchen.

"Good afternoon, ladies," he greeted them giving Mary a peck on the cheek and grabbing a handful of cookies as he spun a chair around and straddled it. Rebecca dimpled. There was something strangely boyish about the fort's commander sitting backwards in a chair munching cookies.

"Mary, I've invited Justin Wentworth to dinner this evening," George informed his wife as he reached for the cup of coffee Lona placed on the table in front of him.

"For dinner? But won't he be staying with us?"

"No. He said something about being intimidated by a house full of women."

Rebecca looked up in time to see the colonel wink.

"Now enough of your teasing," Mary chided swatting him with the damp towel she had been holding when she sat down.

"Honest, Mary. Justin wants to stay in the barracks with the other men. He wants to live like they do and I think it's a good idea. Maybe some of his enthusiasm for this land will rub off," George replied, concern showing on his handsome face.

Rebecca wondered fleetingly if there could be a morale problem among the soldiers here at the fort. She could readily understand how trying the isolation must be.

The back door burst open and a very excited Edward bounced in followed by Elizabeth and Davey.

"Becca, Davey's going to show us how to catch a fish! Can we Becca? Please say yes," Edward pleaded jumping up and down pulling on the puffed sleeve of Rebecca's green cotton gown.

Elizabeth appeared to have lost her original wariness and stood gazing at Davey with something akin to adoration.

"They'll be fine," Mary assured Rebecca. "As long as they take enough cookies to stave off starvation."

The children filled their hands with cookies then turned toward the door. Edward was nearly beside himself with excitement. Mary called to Davey who came back and stood beside her. She put her arm around the boy affectionately.

"Please tell your father we would like the two of you to join us for dinner."

"Yes Ma'am," came his smiling reply.

Rebecca watched the two small redheaded children

walking on either side of the dark-haired, slightly taller child. George rose from the chair and followed the children saying he looked forward to seeing them at dinner but must now be about his duties.

"Davey won't let anything happen to them," Mary assured once more when George had left the room. "He's a fine boy. Lance has a right to be proud."

At the mention of Davey's father Rebecca returned her attention to the two women seated across the table as Mary continued to speak.

"I hope when George and I have children we will be able to demonstrate as much wisdom as Lance has with Davey."

"Your children will not be Indians." Lona's words surprised Rebecca but Mary answered matter-of-factly.

"You're right, of course. But don't you see, the fact that Davey is half Calusa makes what Lance has done even more worthy of admiration. He has allowed his son to maintain his Indian heritage while offering him the advantages available in the white man's world."

Rebecca sat quietly pondering the things she had heard about a man she was unable to get out of her mind. The more she learned the more confused she became by the complexities of Lance Logan.

The three children stood on the mossy bank of the creek where huge oak trees formed umbrellas of shade above the seemingly calm water. Each held a long cane pole to which a cork was attached by a length of string. The corks bobbed listlessly on the water's surface.

"Witches' hair," Elizabeth whispered, staring at the

Spanish moss draped over the low hanging tree limbs.

"Shush!" Davey put a finger to his lips. "The 'grandaddy' won't come out if he knows we're here," he whispered.

Edward looked ready to explode with the effort it took to stand silently waiting. He knew that at any minute the enormous fish Davey called "the grandaddy" would be unable to resist the fat worm the Indian boy had taught him to put on his hook.

"Uh oh!" Elizabeth rolled bright blue eyes nudging Edward with her elbow. "That man is coming this way!"

Edward turned to watch Lance Logan's approach. Davey's father was taller than anyone Edward could recall, even taller than Captain Higgins. And in his fringed buckskins Lance did indeed look formidable as he came to a stop just behind the trio.

From out of nowhere a colorful dragonfly came to rest on the end of Edward's fishing pole.

"That's a lucky sign, Edward. You're bound to get a bite soon," Lance encouraged.

"Shush!" Davey hissed. Then realizing who stood behind him, he mumbled, "Sorry, Pa, but we're out to get 'the grandaddy,'" he explained.

Lance eyed his son suspiciously. "Davey, you know the big guy won't show himself when it's this hot."

Davey grinned up at his tall father. "Makes a good story though, doesn't it?"

"Yeah, son, I guess it does," he laughed, affectionately roughing Davey's dark hair. He thought back to the day he first told his son the story of the legendary fish that lurked just out of reach among the undergrowth near the edge of the creek.

"Now are we here to fish or cut bait?" Lance asked squatting down and taking the pole from Davey then lightly flicking the cork so that it bobbed breaking the smooth surface of the water.

Edward and Elizabeth didn't know what he meant, but were fascinated by the way he maneuvered the pole as Davey looked on proudly. Moments later the cork disappeared beneath the water. Elizabeth squealed! Lance traded poles with Edward just as a hungry bass broke the water trying unsuccessfully to spit the hook from its mouth.

Edward was elated when he managed to land the fish after following step-by-step instructions from Davey. He watched with satisfaction as it flipped and flopped upon the bank.

"Poor fish," Elizabeth sighed sympathetically. "Can't we put him back?"

"We will eat the fish, Elizabeth," Davey stated, his voice brooking no argument. "We only kill to eat," he added emphatically.

Lance hid a smile as he listened to his bright young son repeat what he had been taught by both his father and his grandfather, for this was one of many things upon which he and Nokomis agreed.

As Davey lectured the two English children, Lance noted how Elizabeth hung on his every word. Her dislike of the father obviously did not extend to the son. He was grateful that the young seemed unaware of any differences between them, unaware of the segregation which too often existed in the adult world. If they were allowed to grow up with their own values how much easier it would be to live peacefully with one another.

Davey competently removed the still lively fish and rebaited his hook as Edward stepped back dangerously near the edge of the creek.

"Careful, Edward," Lance warned. "Don't stand so near the water."

"I can swim," Edward announced proudly. "Becca taught me. There's a lake where we live. Becca swims real good."

Lance was surprised by the boy's words. He found it hard to envision the prim Miss Winslow splashing about in the water teaching a child with Edward's exuberance to swim.

"Hear me well, Edward," he said sternly but not unkindly. "A creek is much different from a lake. It looks calm enough but the water is steadily being pulled toward the bay. Below the surface there is an undertow that is nearly impossible for even a strong man to swim against. If you fall in, the current will suck you right out to sea."

Edward listened solemnly staring up at the man towering above him.

"I will be very careful, sir," he promised somewhat awed by this man who could catch fish and explain creeks.

Elizabeth moved closer to Lance and away from the water's edge, never doubting his words. She was still intimidated by his size and she had not forgotten his ferocity when they had arrived so unexpectedly, but she knew with a child's intuition that she had no reason to fear him.

"Tell me about your home in England, the one with the lake," he said smiling down into her serious round face with its sprinkling of freckles. It surprised him to discover he was genuinely interested in these two children of Andrew Townsend.

"Our manor house is big and it's so beautiful," Elizabeth exclaimed, her blue eyes sparkling excitedly. "There are gardens of flowers and miles and miles of land where we ride ponies, and we really do have a lake!"

"I didn't doubt it for a minute," Lance assured her.

Edward interrupted not liking the attention his sister was getting. "It's not our manor house, silly. It belongs to Becca."

"I know that, Edward, and I'm not silly," Elizabeth insisted,

Lance raised his eyebrows but made no comment as the children bickered back and forth. He wondered how the impressive English estate being described to him had become the property of Rebecca Winslow.

"And did you always live in the big house?" Lance asked, taking advantage of a lull in the argument.

"Oh yes, Mr. Logan. We were born there," Elizabeth replied, ignoring her brother for the moment. "We lived with our father and grandparents and Becca," she continued, counting by holding up fingers as she listed each member of her family. "Then everybody died!"

Lance started, remembering how he had felt upon learning of the deaths of his parents and sister.

"Not everybody died, Elizabeth. Why do you always have to exaggerate?" Edward asked disgustedly. "Our father isn't dead, and Becca isn't dead, and we aren't dead." His tone was scolding as Elizabeth stood studying her feet.

"But our mother and grandparents all died, and

papa left, and Becca didn't like us anymore so it seemed like everybody died," Elizabeth stated. She firmly defended what she had said, and added to the picture Lance was forming of Rebecca Winslow as a spoiled, self-centered English aristocrat who wanted only to rid herself of the responsibility of the two innocent children looking up at him so angelically.

But she had taught Edward to swim and the children had stayed close to her, clinging to her skirts as they stood on the beach. Why would they say she didn't like them? It didn't make sense.

One thing was certain. Lance knew it was time to steer the conversation away from the talk of death. "You must be anxious to see your father again," he said with purpose.

"We don't remember him, sir." Elizabeth seemed a little nervous about the upcoming meeting with her father. "He left when we were very young, you see."

Lance was becoming more and more puzzled. He knew Andrew Townsend well and Andrew did not seem like the kind of man who would desert his children.

"I'm sure your father will be delighted to find you here when he returns," he said confidently.

"One thing is certain, sir," Edward piped up. "He sure will be surprised!"

Lance frowned wondering what the outcome would be in the imminent confrontation between Andrew Townsend and Rebecca Winslow. The last thing the inhabitants of Fort Brooke needed was another war with the British—even if the only soldier facing them was one small, golden-haired Englishwoman!

Chapter 5

Rebecca sat on a large white boulder gazing with a decided lack of interest out over the gently swelling blue-green water as sturdy tri-hulled boats moved rapidly away from the beach to where the *Victoria* lay at anchor in the deep natural channel of the bay. The oarsmen returned at a much slower pace hampered by the weight of the cargo they were transporting from ship to shore.

Rebecca had been secretly relieved when Mary declined her offer of assistance to help prepare the evening meal. Instead Mary suggested that she might enjoy watching the activity at the waterfront where supplies were being unloaded. She wondered if Mary Brooke suspected that her culinary skills went no further than handing Cook a written menu each morning. Not that it mattered. At least she had been spared the humiliation of demonstrating her ignorance in the kitchen. Actually she didn't give a fig about what the "natives" thought of her. Their opinion had nothing to do with her petulance.

No, indeed! What made her want to snarl and gnash her teeth was betrayal! The disloyalty of her own flesh and blood. For hadn't she seen them with her own eyes as she came through the gates? Edward and Elizabeth were walking, one on each side of that arrogant rogue, looking up at him as though he were omnipotent!

Damnation, Andrew! Why couldn't you be where you were supposed to be so I could go home where I belong? Her tiny foot began tapping a rhythm against the hard-packed sand.

Rebecca watched as the huge distorted image of a man cast a shadow in front of her. She turned slowly wondering how someone so large could approach so quietly. She jumped in surprise as she saw Lance Logan standing only a few feet behind the boulder on which she sat.

"You look like a rose in a weed patch," he said in way of greeting.

"How poetic, Mr. Logan," she replied disdainfully. "Is that supposed to be a compliment?"

"Not at all. It's another way of saying you don't belong here."

Embarrassment at her misassumption and anger over the man's audacity tinted Rebecca's smooth ivory cheeks a blushing pink as she rose slowly to face him.

"Funny, isn't it? I was thinking precisely the same thing when you so rudely intruded upon my privacy," she retorted with eyes blazing.

"The beach is hardly a private place when a ship is in port, Miss Winslow."

Oh, how she longed to wipe the smug expression from his face as she searched her mind for a suitable reply. Why did the man infuriate her so?

"Make no mistake, Mr. Logan. If my brother-in-law were here I would be aboard the *Victoria* right now counting the minutes until she sailed for England!"

"Ah, but she doesn't sail for England, my lady. From here the good Captain Higgins journeys to New Orleans." His derisive manner was so enraging Rebecca wanted to spit!

"I have no objection to returning to England via New Orleans," she replied haughtily. "Being aboard ship is vastly preferable to being stranded in this pest hole!"

"What? No fear of the dangerous pirates that roam the waters of the Gulf?"

Rebecca assumed a bored expression which prompted Lance to say, "Complacency is most unwise, my lady, for Gaspar would find you a rare and tempting morsel. No question about it!"

Rebecca had had enough of Lance Logan's unprovoked sarcasm.

"Stop calling me 'my lady'!" she demanded. "My name is Miss Winslow, and just who is this Gaspar?"

Rebecca was aware of the serious edge in Lance's tone when he answered. His gray eyes no longer held the hint of perverse humor she had seen in them moments ago.

"Jose Gaspar is a vicious parasite . . . a scourge to the human race. I will not offend your innocent ears by describing the atrocities he has committed. Suffice it to say, you would not want to run across him in open waters."

Rebecca was taken aback by the sudden change in his manner. It was difficult to carry on an intelligent conversation, if one could call it that, when he pivoted from humorous bantering to somber warning so rapidly.

She turned away from him and let her eyes roam over the men busily working with the cargo.

"I once read a book about a pirate." It was one of the scandalous tabloids she had borrowed from Amy Dickerson. "The pirate captain was the hero, you see. When the heroine's evil guardian pushed her into the ocean to prevent her discovering that he had squandered her fortune, the pirate rescued her. They sailed the seven seas together and lived happily ever after."

Rebecca could not suppress a dreamy sigh remembering the handsome pirate and his beautiful lady love. But she was quickly snatched from her reverie as Logan grasped her by the shoulders and whirled her back around to face him.

"Of all the childish, naive, harebrained . . ." His eyes were like molten steel drilling into hers. Then, as if suddenly realizing what he was doing, he dropped his hands. Rebecca used the opportunity to take several steps backward.

His next words, though he ceased to shout, seemed more reprimanding than his rantings and ravings.

"Lady! You are so stupid you're dangerous!"

Rebecca was angrier than she had ever been in her life. Never had anyone spoken to her in such a deprecating way. She longed to lash out with words but could not form them. She wanted to do the man bodily harm but knew her feeble strength would be no match against his. So great was her need to vent her spleen that tears welled up in her snapping, gold-flecked eyes.

But Lance was angry, too. He felt no regret over the

things he had said, only contempt for the dimwitted little chit. He leaned down within inches of her face.

"Hear me and hear me well," he commanded through clenched teeth. "For over thirty years, Jose Gaspar has victimized the ships sailing the Gulf. He and his villainous band of cutthroats ruthlessly loot, burn, rape, and murder their helpless prey and they feel no remorse over the destruction they leave in their wake!"

Rebecca put her hand to her mouth willing the tears in her huge, horrified eyes not to spill.

"Oh, and one more thing," Lance added as he straightened to his full height. "Gaspar is an ugly old man of near sixty years!" He thrust the final barb. "How does that strike your romantic fancy, lady?"

Rebecca could stand no more. Failing to stifle the sob that rose in her throat, she skirted around him and ran toward the gates of the fort as if the devils of Hell were nipping at her heels.

As Lance watched her flight, twice nearly tripping over the hem of her gown, a persistent voice chimed in his head, *Are you satisfied now, Logan? Are you proud of yourself?*

And standing alone on the white-sand beach, the mighty man hung his head in self-reproach.

A meal with the Brookes and their friends was unlike anything Rebecca had ever experienced. She barely tasted the dainty portions of glazed ham, sweet potatoes, and green beans she had selected from the vast array of dishes which had been placed side by side on the linen-covered table.

Fascinated by the extraordinary seating arrangement, she allowed her gaze to move from one person to the next. Mary and George Brooke sat beside each other, George at the head of the table. This in itself seemed unusual to one accustomed to seeing master and mistress at opposite ends.

The stout Captain Higgins sat across from Mary, his plate piled so high Rebecca worried that something might slide off to stain the snowy white cloth. To the Captain's left was Lance Logan still wearing his buckskins, with Davey at his side. The twins sat one on each side of Rebecca opposite Lance and Davey, while Justin Wentworth was seated at the other end of the table across from the Colonel. But the biggest surprise came when after helping Mary bring the food from the kitchen, the Indian girl, Lona, moved to take the empty chair beside Justin who rose swiftly to assist her.

Rebecca had assumed Lona to be living with the Brookes in a domestic capacity. Apparently she had assumed wrong for those present treated the girl like a member of the family and no one took exception when she seated herself at the table.

At home dinner had always been a subdued affair. Servants offered one course at a time, removing each at exactly the proper moment. Since the death of her parents, Rebecca always sat at the head of the table with Edward on her right and Elizabeth on her left, but there had been a minimum of conversation, especially during the weeks just prior to sailing.

Once Rebecca made up her mind to return the children to their father, her feelings had continually vacillated. She wavered between relief that she would no longer be solely responsible for their welfare, a responsibility she felt ill-equipped to handle, and guilt at the prospect of uprooting Elizabeth and Edward from all that was familiar, thrusting them into an unknown, unsettled wilderness inhabited by strangers.

There were times when her eyes would mist as she looked down at the two redheads bent over their plates eating small bites of food with precisely the right utensils, napkins neatly folded in their laps just as they had been taught. They seemed so small and vulnerable. How could she bear the thought of losing them?

Then she would remember their antagonism toward William and the childish, but effective, ways in which they had made their feelings known. She would then angrily renew her determination to see that they were safely placed into their father's keeping.

Time and again she had mentally justified her decision. But there was no escaping that gnawing feeling in her stomach that made those last meals together at the manor house most indigestible.

"Becca?" Rebecca was brought back to the present by Edward's gentle, but persistent, prodding of her arm with his elbow.

"What is it, Edward?" she asked looking at the boy whose wide blue eyes were focused on the bowls and platters of food threatening to break the table.

"Can I have more?" he whispered hopefully.

As her nephew turned his expectant freckled face toward her, Rebecca realized that he had never seen such a banquet as was set before him at this moment. For Edward had been brought up the same as she in a household where servants regulated their portions and removed their plates when they felt the proper time for ingesting each course had elapsed.

Rebecca watched the people seated at this table, with the exception of Lance Logan whose eyes she refused to meet. Lamplight replaced, but could not compete with, the light of the sun now setting on the western horizon, a red ball in the cloudless sky barely visible as it sank behind the walls of the fort. Everyone seemed to be talking at once, often disagreeing in what could be called polite argument. But conversation continually flowed even as arms reached out to pass dishes. Plates were filled and refilled.

How could people eat so much? Rebecca wondered, shaking her head.

Looking up at her, Edward assumed the negative shake of her head meant he could have no more to eat.

"But, Becca," he pleaded. "I'm still hungry. And how do they make potatoes taste like dessert?" he added, as his eyes rested longingly on the sweet potatoes baked with sugar and rich creamy butter.

Rebecca appeared to consider his questions most seriously but she could not hold the pose long as her green eyes sparkled with humor and her mouth curved into a smile.

After a lengthy pause, she astounded the boy by saying, "I really don't know, Edward."

Edward's mouth gaped open. Surely he must have misunderstood what his aunt just said. "You don't know?"

"Elizabeth!" he hissed under his breath.

Elizabeth looked up, not believing her eyes, for her brother was leaning rudely in front of Becca at the dinner table.

"Elizabeth," he repeated, "Becca doesn't know something!" He moved even closer to his sister waiting for this monumental pronouncement to sink in.

"Oh, Edward! That's impossible," Elizabeth retorted tossing back her bright red curls. "Becca knows everything," she stated matter-of-factly.

At this point both children were leaning toward each other pushing Rebecca as far back as possible in order to carry on their whispered conversation. The rungs of the hard wooden chair pressed uncomfortably against her spine as Edward continued melodramatically, for the youngster loved an audience, even if it was only his sister.

"Actually, I'm not sure what she doesn't know," he confided, trying to keep his voice low. "Either she doesn't know if I can have more to eat, or," he stared at Elizabeth whose turned-up nose was now nearly touching his, "she doesn't know why the potatoes taste so good."

A deep rumble of laughter came from across the table and Rebecca's eyes flew up to be caught and held by those of the man seated opposite her.

"Little did we suspect, Miss Winslow, that seated in our midst was a lady so highly acclaimed for her indisputable knowledge."

Lance Logan's sarcasm was punctuated by the equally cynical expression on his face.

Edward and Elizabeth sprang apart as they realized their whispered conversation had been overheard by at least one other. This enabled Rebecca to take a deep breath for the first time since the twins had begun to close in on her some minutes before. She took another for good measure and as she exhaled amber flames ignited in her eyes nearly eliminating any trace of green.

"Perhaps, Edward," Rebecca suggested, her fiery eyes never straying from Logan's face, "it would be best to ask Mrs. Brooke about the propriety of taking another portion of potatoes for since we are strangers here, we are unfamiliar with what is proper and what is not."

No angry retort could have served Lance such a setdown as the softly accented words spoken by the delicate young woman staring at him as though she would like to cut out his heart and eat it for breakfast. Without raising her voice she had managed to make him feel like a spiteful little boy.

Regardless of her stupid reasons for venturing halfway around the world and endangering the lives of two innocent children, not to mention her own, the fact remained that she and the twins were here and would be here until the *Victoria* returned from New Orleans on its way back to England. Deliberately antagonizing another human being, worse yet, a new arrival to the territory, was beneath contempt. And Lance was man enough to admit that that was exactly what he had been doing since he had first laid eyes on Rebecca Winslow.

"Becca?" Elizabeth looked up, a puzzled frown creasing her forehead. "I didn't think you wanted anyone to find out."

"Find out what, Elizabeth?" Rebecca asked perplexed.

"You know. About your being a 'lady.'"

"Ssh! Eat your dinner!" she admonished, glancing across the table, relieved to find Lance laughing at something Justin had just said.

"Edward, dear, you may have as much as you would like to eat. Please help yourself," Mary smiled turning toward the twin sitting between Rebecca and herself.

She had been listening to Jeremiah and her husband discuss the supplies that had been unloaded from the *Victoria* that afternoon so she was unaware of the tense drama taking place between two of her guests. She had, however, heard Rebecca's last words to Edward and was anxious to make the child feel not only welcome but replete.

Edward's blue eyes lit up with pleasure, but before he could reach for more, the front door was thrown open slamming against the inside wall then swinging back toward the bewhiskered bear of a man standing in its frame. The men at the table were on their feet in an instant.

"I'm sorry, Colonel. I couldn't stop him," a young soldier apologized from where he stood on the porch for it was impossible to get past the huge, barrel-chested man blocking the opening.

"Ezra!" George exclaimed moving toward the intruder.

The front of the man's shirt was covered with blood, but George could see no sign of a wound to account for it. Rebecca and the twins sat staring in stunned silence as Ezra looked at those in the room.

"You," he shouted, pointing a finger at the colonel, "are suppose to protect the settlers in this territory! Instead you are here entertaining at your fancy table while those bastard savages murder my wife and daughter!"

"Oh, no!" Mary cried as Rebecca shrunk back in her chair pulling Edward and Elizabeth close to her, seeking to protect them from the fanatic hatred she saw in the eyes of the man standing in the doorway.

"Ezra, please," George pleaded. "Tell us what's happened." He tried to take a step closer but the burly man warned him back.

"Stay away from me!" he yelled. "I'll tell you what happened, but don't come near me for you are evil! All of you!" His mad searching gaze seemed to include everyone in the room, and Rebecca held her breath fearing for the safety of the children.

"While I was away from the cabin hunting food for my family, the heathen murderers attacked. It wasn't enough that they killed my woman and baby!" his voice thundered in their ears. "They remained long enough to perform their sadistic rites over the bodies!"

George and Lance knew what the man meant. Both men wondered briefly why Ezra would have left his family unprotected for what had to be a considerable length of time but neither voiced the question.

Ezra's outstretched arm moved to point the accusing finger directly at Lona. "And while that 'spawn of the devil' committed his atrocities against my family, his sister, that harlot, sat eating at your table!"

Blood drained from the Indian girl's face turning her olive complexion quite pale.

George tried again to calm him. "Ezra, you can't blame all Indians for the acts of a few," he reasoned.

"But I can and I do! They are rabid animals, a blight on the world the Lord created!" he roared shaking his fist in the air. "God has ordered their destruction and the destruction of all who choose to defend them. In the name of the Almighty, I curse this Fort!" he screamed demonically. "Its walls will crumble and all within will reap the vengeance of the Lord!"

With that, he turned and ran toward the open gates

before anyone could stop him, running as if he feared the punishment he foretold would begin before he could reach safety.

Rebecca clutched the twins tighter and sighed with relief as the man disappeared out the door.

"Lance! Get the men mounted!" But the tall scout was already heading toward the barracks with Davey at his heels before George could finish issuing the order.

"I'm going with you, Colonel," Justin spoke up.

The commander searched the determined face of the young Englishman. "Are you sure, Wentworth? This is hardly the way to initiate a new recruit."

Justin's gaze never faltered. "I'm sure, sir."

Without another word the two men walked out into the now dark night where not even a sliver of moon appeared to light their way.

No one spoke for some minutes after the men had taken their leave. Mary moved to the chair next to Lona but said nothing nor did she reach out to touch the girl for she knew her sympathy could not be appreciated.

It was Lona, herself, who finally broke the silence. "They will not find them," she stated without emotion.

Mary turned toward her and replied in a tired voice, "Probably not. But perhaps they will find a clue as to who is supplying Chikiki with rifles."

"Perhaps." But both women sounded doubtful.

"Please," Rebecca interrupted. "I don't understand what has happened. Who was that man?" Her eyes looked warily toward the door Jeremiah had closed and bolted behind the departing soldiers.

"His name is Ezra Holcomb," Mary answered with

undisguised dislike. "His cabin lies twenty miles north of the fort and he claims to be a minister of the gospel." She gave a snort of derision. "What he preaches is hatred and prejudice. He says he is an emissary of God sent here to wipe out all Indians. Up until now his threats have been harmless but after what has happened, I don't know," she shook her head.

"Why did Mr. Holcomb choose to settle his family so far from the protection of the fort?" Rebecca asked then continued not waiting for an answer, as was her habit. "What reason could he have for jeopardizing his family's safety?"

Had Lance Logan been there he would have quickly pointed out that she had taken precisely the same risk in bringing Edward and Elizabeth to Fort Brooke.

"Ezra refused to allow Sarah or little Lizzie near the fort," Mary explained. "He said he would take care of his own without any help from the 'Devil's Disciples' who provided sanctuary to the 'heathen enemy.'"

She shook her head. "Lizzie was such a beautiful child. It's hard for me to believe such a brutal, unconscionable man could have conceived her. She was only five years old."

"Brutal? Surely Mr. Holcomb did not mistreat his wife and child!"

Mary looked at her thoughtfully. "I can't say that Ezra ever caused Lizzie physical harm although it was common knowledge that he had little regard for womankind. According to the 'Gospel of Ezra Holcomb' women were put on this earth to serve the needs of men. However, he clearly blamed poor Sarah because he had no son, no miniature prophet to carry on his deranged commission. What she suffered at his hands, no one can say for certain. But if ever someone might have preferred death . . ."

"A more defeated woman you cannot imagine," Lona spoke up. "I saw them only a few times—Sarah and little Lizzie—so lonely they seemed waiting patiently in their old buckboard some distance outside the gates while Ezra traded for necessary supplies.

"Funny, isn't it?" she laughed hollowly. "Ezra never considered that the goods he took with him might be as contaminated as the people within these walls."

Rebecca shuddered at Lona's grim humor.

Captain Higgins cleared his throat. "Mary, my dear! Is there anything I can do?" He was decidedly embarrassed knowing he could not join in the pursuit for his prowess was aboard his ship, not trekking through the woods on horseback searching for renegade Indians. But it unmanned him being left behind with three women and two small children.

"Oh, Jeremiah! Forgive me!" Mary rose to her feet and held her hands out to the frowning sea captain who grasped them in his own and looked worriedly into her pretty upturned face.

"There is nothing we can do but wait," she replied. "Please don't concern yourself. There are plenty of soldiers left to protect the fort and Lieutenant Kearny and his men should be back from patrol any day."

Jeremiah seemed uncertain what to do next as he stood there holding Mary Brooke's hands in his.

"If you are sure you will be safe," he floundered, "I really should return to oversee preparations." He was torn between his responsibility for the ship and its crew and his concern for the lovely woman standing before him.

"Men! Spare me from their sense of duty!" she chided.

Jeremiah tried for a smile. Mary Brooke was one fine lady. He prayed George could keep her safe from harm as he hugged her gently then turned to unbolt the door.

"You will lock this behind me?"

"Of course," Mary responded. "And, Jeremiah," she hesitated wondering as always if she would ever see this beloved friend again for life was chancy at best in this new territory, on land as well as at sea. "Godspeed!" she bade him softly.

"Wait!" Rebecca jumped from her chair startling the half-asleep twins who had been leaning against her.

Belatedly it registered that Captain Higgins and Mary Brooke were saying their farewells.

"Captain!" she implored. "Surely you are not leaving!"

Hope died with his reply. "My dear Miss Winslow. I have delivered the cargo bound for Fort Brooke and must now depart for New Orleans with the morning tide."

Rebecca knew that she and the twins were part of that cargo to which Jeremiah referred and with the departure of the *Victoria* would go any remaining link with her home. She had never felt so alone.

Noting the distress on the face of the beautiful Englishwoman whose frightened, sea-green eyes seemed to plead for something he could not give, he placed a workworn finger tenderly beneath her chin holding her gaze. "The *Victoria* will be back in a matter of weeks, a month at most." His smile lit up his bearded face and his blue eyes twinkled.

"If you still want to go, there will always be a place

for you aboard my ship." He laughed jovially, stepping aside to hug Mary one more time before he disappeared through the doorway.

Damnation! Captain Higgins talked as though he thought she might not wish to return with him to England. Such a preposterous notion brought a weak smile to her rosebud pink lips. Why, by the time the *Victoria* came back to Fort Brooke, Rebecca would most likely swim to the ship before the anchor was dropped!

"Mrs. Brooke." It was Elizabeth's timid voice which claimed their attention. Huge, frightened eyes stared up at Mary.

"Yes, honey," Mary replied moving back to the table then bending down to where the little girl still sat.

"The soldiers . . ." she stammered. "I mean, will they take Davey with them?"

Tears threatened to spill on freckle-stained cheeks. "I think it must be dangerous to chase Indians who kill people," she whispered softly. The hero worship Elizabeth felt for the young half-breed was plain for all to see.

Mary put her arm around the child's small shoulders. "Now don't you worry your pretty head about Davey. Lance Logan isn't about to do anything to endanger that boy of his. Not for one minute," she smiled reassuringly. "Though you can bet Davey would do everything in his power to convince his father to take him along."

"But, Mrs. Brooke?" Doubt was still evident in Elizabeth's voice as she continued to question the kindly woman. "If Davey didn't go with the soldiers, where is he?"

Mary chuckled. "If I know Davey, and believe me I do, he's probably at home kicking everything that isn't nailed down and cursing a fate that will not allow him to grow into a mighty warrior as quickly as he would like. That boy has his father's own temper! Never doubt it! It takes a lot to get either of them riled, but once you do, look out!"

Horse feathers! Since when did it take a lot to get Lance Logan riled? Rebecca wondered. All she had to do was stand within ten feet of the man!

Chapter 6

Dawn was just breaking the eastern sky when the small patrol led by Lance Logan and George Brooke arrived at the Holcomb cabin built in a small clearing beside a gently flowing stream. The first ten miles had been relatively easy as they headed north along the well-worn path to Fort King. But all too soon the soldiers left the beaten track and painstakingly made their way through heavy forest and dense underbrush in the pitch black of a moonless night in order to reach the secluded spot where Ezra Holcomb had chosen to settle with his wife and child.

Their progress was necessarily slow as men and horses felt their way through the darkness. But it mattered little how long it took, Lance thought to himself, for he knew what they would find when they reached their destination. Two fresh graves, one considerably smaller than the other, and a burned out cabin which had never offered much in the way of amenities.

His predictions proved depressingly accurate as his

gaze fixed on the clearing where logs that had once housed the Holcomb family now smouldered and turned to ash before his eyes. Not far away two moist mounds of earth intruded above a thick carpet of lush green grass.

The men sat motionless upon their horses, not one daring to speak as Lance dismounted and began circling the camp for some sign as to the direction Chikiki and his warriors had taken.

"Well?" George Brooke questioned, a frown etching furrows in his handsome face as Lance returned to the small group of men waiting silently at the edge of the clearing.

"They've headed due north but their trail is hours old," Lance informed his commander. "Damn it!" he continued angrily, "I know them too well! The bloody savages will take refuge in the swamps making tracking impossible."

Lance Logan was a good scout—one of the best—and he knew it. That the Indian rebel could continually best him stuck in his craw. There had to be a way to capture Chikiki and put an end to his destructive rampage against the whites attempting to settle the territory.

George Brooke shared Lance's frustration. "Their trail may lead north," he said shifting in his saddle, "but they've proven to be wily in the past and I feel uneasy leaving the fort virtually unmanned for any length of time. They could circle back without our being aware of it."

Suddenly George wanted nothing so much as to hold his wife in his arms again.

"Men! We're returning to the fort." As he voiced his

decision he turned his horse and began slowly retracing their earlier route. At least on the trip back they would be able to see where they were going.

The rider pushed his horse hard and fast down the hundred mile trail between Fort King and Fort Brooke. He had to get back to the fort as quickly as possible. The news he brought wasn't good! Chikiki and his followers had burned, looted, and murdered settlers within a thirty mile radius of Fort King and all signs showed they were headed in a southwesterly direction straight for Fort Brooke. He had to get there first!

His shoulder-length hair, now more blond than red, bleached by exposure to the relentless tropical sun, was blown back by wind created from the speed of his flight. He raced down the path on a spring day when not a leaf fluttered. Beneath a healthy tan, freckles still marked his round face giving him a boyish appearance despite his twenty-eight years. His look of youth and inexperience had caused more than one man to underestimate his strength and drive. Those men had lived or, in a few cases, not lived to regret it!

Though only of average height and rather lean of build, the strength that lay in the well-developed muscles of his arms and his legs had enabled Andrew Townsend to best men of far greater stature. In addition, as Colonel Brooke was quick to recognize, Andrew was smart—"Army Smart"! He had the inherent ability not only to strategize offensively but to undermine a defensive attack. He was precisely what was needed in this raw, undeveloped land.

But it was much more than strength and intelligence that pushed Andrew beyond the limit of a normal man's endurance. He had fallen in love with everything about this virgin wilderness from its moss-covered trees and bushes, to its lakes and rivers, the wildlife, even the Calusa whom he had come to respect, if not understand. He saw only beauty in this land, untouched and unclaimed.

Just like Amanda when he had first seen her lying unconscious beneath a tree by the stream—untouched and unclaimed! His eyes stung. He wondered if Mandy had ever realized how much he loved her and if somehow she could feel, wherever she was now, how much he missed her. If only she were here so that they could share this magnificent country.

He knew it was a dream that could not happen! But his children, Edward and Elizabeth, were real. What would they look like after nearly five years? He hoped they were both small replicas of his soft, beautiful Amanda. Soon, he promised himself, they would be with him. Very soon.

He had wept upon receiving Rebecca's letter telling of her parents' tragic death for he had loved both the Lord and his Lady. Then drying his tears he proceeded to soundly curse his father-in-law, whom he had formerly admired as a man with the courage and daring to do exactly what he desired to do regardless of censure. Now he condemned Lord Winslow's actions as foolish and reckless for while driving his carriage at breakneck speed it had overturned causing not only his own untimely death, but also that of his beautiful, gay-hearted wife.

Andrew felt no little guilt over burdening Rebecca

with the care of his children. Yet he never for a moment doubted that they were in very capable hands. He was one of the few people who recognized Rebecca as the strength behind the Winslow family, even though she seemed unaware of it.

Andrew had watched as she contrived to steer her father away from his more foolhardy daredeviltry. Rebecca was clever. She had a good head for figures for he had seen her working at the huge desk in the Lord's study straightening out his accounts. She had a good head for people, too. He remembered the times she had managed to calm the flustered housekeeper when her Ladyship disappeared somewhere with Lord Winslow. It was Rebecca who soothed the woman's ruffled feathers and competently gave the instructions which kept the household running smoothly.

Even Mandy depended on the wise counsel of her younger sister, asking advice on her choice of gowns, her coiffure, then going so far as to seek her opinions on the various aspects of child-rearing after learning that she was soon to be a mother. Rebecca had always come through offering sensible solutions to problems far beyond her limited range of experience.

No wonder her family depended on her for she was so damnably good at everything she did!

He thought back to the day he had announced that he was leaving. Amanda's father and mother did not understand his need to start a new life for himself far away from the memories he could not escape in England. They had looked skeptical when he assured them that he would send for the children once he had established himself.

It was Rebecca who had understood and had

promised him that no harm would come to Edward or Elizabeth. And he had left England certain that his children would be well taken care of, but determined to bring them to the New World as soon as possible. It had taken nearly five years of long hours and hard work to establish himself here and now that he was in a position to send for the twins, damned if the territory wasn't on the brink of an Indian uprising.

Andrew sniffed the air then saw the smoke spiraling upward some distance west of the trail he followed. "Oh, hell!" he said out loud as he pulled back on the reins. He had to get to the fort as quickly as possible. Every instinct told him to continue riding straight ahead. His duty was to reach Colonel Brooke and deliver his dispatches from Fort King. Chikiki and his band of renegades were somewhere in front of him and nothing, but nothing, must sidetrack him now.

Such were Andrew's thoughts as he reined in his horse then turned west away from the main trail heading in the direction of the tiny ribbon of gray-white smoke rising to blend and become a part of the cloudless blue sky.

He picked his way slowly through the dense underbrush using the trees to conceal his approach. When he reached the clearing by the river he looked around cautiously. It was quiet . . . deathly quiet. Even the birds had ceased their endless chirping. The scene was all too familiar yet as he felt his stomach lurch he knew he would never get used to the results of an Indian massacre.

Smoke still drifted upward from the burned-out wagon, and the bloody remains of a man and woman lay sprawled in the grass not far away.

Andrew, knowing he would be greatly outnumbered, circled the camp carefully not wishing to surprise the murdering band of savages. He felt reasonably certain that they had taken the spoils they were after and were by now miles away but it didn't pay to take chances.

He had reached the opposite edge of the clearing when he heard a soft moan coming from beyond the perimeter of the trees. With pistol drawn he inched forward.

"No!" he whispered. "It can't be happening again!" Andrew shook his head disbelievingly. It wasn't possible!

He quickly holstered his gun and ran forward to where the girl lay on her stomach, her face turned away. As he went down on his knees beside her he half expected to see Mandy just as she had looked the day he found her thrown from her horse.

He knew better, of course, for Mandy's hair was the soft golden-blond color of sunshine and daffodils. The young woman he looked down upon had unbound curls as black as a moonless night contrasting sharply with the green of the grass across which it spilled around her.

He carefully touched her shoulder and felt her body quiver beneath his fingers.

"Easy, love. I won't hurt you." His softly accented voice was reassuring as he turned her over to lie on her back upon the grass-covered ground where sunlight filtered through the branches of the tall cypress high above them.

Andrew sucked in his breath as he looked into the clearest, most arresting pair of sapphire blue eyes he ever expected to see this side of Heaven. A large knot, already beginning to discolor, marred the smooth, pale skin of her forehead but only detracted slightly from her angelic features.

I'm lost, he thought, still bewildered by the strange, memory strewn sensation which had begun the moment he set eyes on the injured girl.

"They're dead, aren't they?"

He drew back, surprised by the depth of her husky voice when she spoke through full pink lips, yet the sensuous sound seemed in keeping with the rest of her beautiful body.

"I'm sorry," he replied, dreading the tears he expected but which did not come.

"I was walking in the woods," she went on, her voice showing no emotion. "I ran toward the clearing when I heard the rifle fire, but I tripped and everything went black."

Thank God! Andrew thought, shuddering at the picture of what would have happened had she been seen by the Indians.

Andrew suspected that the girl, for he judged her to be no older than Rebecca, must be in shock. Though he had never known how to comfort a weeping female, he knew from experience that it was not healthy to keep one's grief bottled up inside.

"We must bury them." There it was again. That soft, husky, emotionless voice.

Andrew was worried about her. "I'll take care of it," he said, determinedly, "but not until I've seen to you, love."

When Andrew stood up she made no move to follow. He dampened his kerchief in the nearby river then folded it into a soggy square and returned to where she lay, gently placing the cool pad against the rapidly swelling knot on her forehead.

"What is your name?" he asked as he held the wet cotton lightly. He couldn't seem to concentrate on anything beyond the brilliant blue of her eyes.

"Rachel," she answered, wincing in pain, trying to pull away as he pressed the cold cloth against her skin. "Rachel Jordan," she completed.

"Well, Rachel Jordan," he smiled, "you just lie still and keep this compress in place. I'll be back."

With that, he turned and disappeared among the trees, but Rachel knew what he was about, knew that he was doing what had to be done. Her head hurt dreadfully while the rest of her body felt numb. *Odd,* she thought. *It's as if my mind was up in the trees overhead looking down. Eerie, really! This feeling of disembodiment.*

Rachel closed her eyes trying to concentrate on the handsome young man with the ready smile that made the lines beside his light blue eyes crinkle.

He wouldn't leave her. She was certain of it, and the knowledge gave her comfort as nothing else could. Her greatest fear at this moment was in being alone!

Andrew buried the Jordans beneath a shady tree not far from the clear waters of the river, then returned to the spot where he had left Rachel. She was still there. He hadn't imagined her.

She was sitting now with one leg drawn up beneath her full gray-striped skirts, her arm resting upon her knee. Vacant blue eyes starred unseeingly into the dense woods surrounding them, eyes that didn't even blink when he approached.

Squatting down to face her he smiled, "My name is Andrew Townsend." Rachel turned to look at him blankly. "I'm an army scout," he went on. "Tomorrow I'll take you to Fort Brooke where Mary will know what to do."

Andrew frowned, concerned by the girl's continued remoteness. "I'm going a little further into the woods to find us something to eat. The Indians are gone now, Rachel," he said as much to reassure himself as her. He stood up and patted her shoulder awkwardly. "I won't be gone long."

He didn't expect any response so was not disappointed when none came.

Rachel nibbled on a piece of the rabbit Andrew had shot and then cooked over a small open campfire near the river but out of sight of the two fresh graves. Though accustomed to the solitude of the trail, he was uncomfortable in the presence of the seemingly mute young woman seated across from him. She had not spoken a word since she had told him her name.

Andrew talked quietly while they ate, describing life at Fort Brooke and the people she would meet when they arrived. He could not tell whether his words were penetrating the wall Rachel seemed to have erected to block out her horrific memories of what had taken place in the early afternoon.

As the sun faded behind the branches of the tall cypress trees, Andrew gathered dry pieces of wood and fed the dwindling fire leaving a pile of sticks close by to be used during the night. He took his bedding and blanket from behind his saddle and spread it on the soft ground within the circle of warmth given off by the fire. He removed the saddle, placing it against the base of a tree on the opposite side of the campfire.

Andrew gave his horse a good rubdown, fed him several hands full of the grain he always carried in his saddlebag, then staked the animal within reach of the clean, cool water. He knew that a strong, healthy horse was vital to survival in this wild, untamed land where life often depended on how fast one could move.

"Get some rest," he told the girl motioning toward the pallet and blanket. "It's still a long ride to the fort."

Seeing the wary look she leveled on him, Andrew's mouth quirked up and his blue eyes twinkled. Luckily it was too dark for Rachel to see his expression. *I wonder,* he thought to himself, *if she is worried about what might be lurking out there in the woods or about where I plan to sleep?*

Whatever had caused the fear he saw in her eyes, Andrew sought to put her mind at ease. He seated himself on the other side of the fire, leaned back against the saddle with his rifle across his lap, then giving her one last steady look he pulled the wide brim of his hat forward leaving his face in shadow.

It was some minutes before Rachel stood up cautiously, glancing toward him like a frightened doe poised for flight. She finally tiptoed to the makeshift bed and lowered herself upon it. Andrew could tell that she was as taut as a bowstring even as she pulled the blanket beneath her chin.

The hours passed slowly as he sat wondering about the girl whose remarkable blue eyes were now closed in sleep. Only the rustle of the night animals disturbed the quiet of the woods. He allowed his own eyes to close knowing he would awaken instantly at the merest hint of danger. But a short time later it was the earpiercing scream of a woman that brought him to his feet, his heart thumping madly in his chest.

Rachel was sitting up wringing the blanket with her hands. Her huge eyes were filled with terror as Andrew gazed into the surrounding darkness trying to determine what could have frightened her so badly without waking him. But nothing seemed amiss.

He circled the campfire slowly then stooped down laying the rifle aside. He was at a loss as to how to reassure her when she seemed as much afraid of him as of any prey that might be stalking them from the underbrush.

"What is it, love? What did you see?" His gentle concern proved to be her undoing. Tears brimmed in gemlike eyes then began rolling down her rose petal soft cheeks. And once the dam holding back her emotions cracked and broke away, there was no end to the floodtide unleashed.

Rachel reached out and gripped the strong muscled arms beneath Andrew's shirt pulling him toward her. In a voice choked with sobs she cried out, "You left me! I dreamed I woke up and you were gone!" She gasped out accusingly. "I was here all alone, and," she continued pathetically, "I don't even know where 'here' is!"

His arms went around her drawing her tight against his hard chest. "It was a dream, love, just a bad dream! I'm right here," he said pushing back slightly so that she could look at his face, then gathering her close once more.

Andrew felt the salty wetness soaking his shirtfront as she sobbed out her grief over the violent death of her parents and her fear of what lay ahead. He rubbed her back and spoke words that made no sense, words meant to calm and soothe her battered spirit. Never did he loosen his hold on her. She was so small, so vulnerable, and so incredibly lovely Andrew wanted only to protect her and keep her close to him always.

At last, too exhausted to weep anymore, Rachel hiccuped then closed her eyes resting her head against his sodden shoulder. Andrew eased her back upon the pallet then lay down beside her, pulling the blanket up to cover them. He drew her against him aware of her body heat through their layers of clothing.

"I feel safe with you," Rachel murmured sleepily. Then she roused herself to ask, "Who is Mary?"

Before he could answer, her eyes closed once more and she drifted off to sleep.

So she had heard at least part of what he had told her earlier about the people at Fort Brooke. Andrew chuckled even as he felt the deep ache of longing begin to manifest itself within his loins. "Let's hope your faith in me is justified, love," he whispered to the still figure beside him. "After all, I'm only a man!"

A shudder ran through him as he thought how nearly he had decided to ignore the distant smoke he had seen that morning. He hugged Rachel Jordan's small form, her head resting trustingly upon his shoulder, and said the first prayer of thanks he had uttered in many years.

As the soldiers headed back toward Ft. Brooke, Lance remembered the promise he had made to himself to look into the background of the young Englishman, Justin Wentworth. On the surface, he had to admit a grudging admiration for the newcomer who had uncomplainingly managed to keep pace with the more experienced soldiers threading their way through the dense forest.

As the path widened Lance dropped back until he and the young recruit were riding abreast. Justin cut his eyes suspiciously wondering why the rugged frontiersman would single him out for attention.

"So, Wentworth! What decided you to venture to these rugged shores?" Lance asked without preliminaries.

Justin knew better than to respond flippantly as he had with Miss Winslow. "I wanted to see what England had fought so hard for and lost," he replied without hesitation.

Lance gave the man beside him a piercing look.

"And what is your opinion thus far?"

"I believe, sir, that England has forfeited a very rich prize."

Lance Logan laughed as he leaned over to clap the young man on the back nearly unseating him.

As he rode Justin spoke of the family he missed, his parents, his older brothers, their wives along with many nieces and nephews. Without any pretense toward boasting, it soon became apparent that Justin Wentworth came from a titled English background and it obviously caused the young man no end of embarrassment. Justin found it difficult to explain to the tall scout the need that drove him to seek out his future in this fresh new land where nothing was given but had to be earned. Yet Lance understood and with each passing moment he felt more certain that Justin would soon find what he was looking for here in the territory of Florida.

He was impressed with the Englishman's knowledge of the history and politics that had formulated this independent young country.

Then Lance startled himself by asking, "And were you also acquainted with the Winslows when you lived in England?" *Now why in hell had he brought the Winslows into the conversation,* he wondered disgustedly, even as a pair of flashing green eyes drifted through his memory.

Justin seemed not to have noticed the big man's irritation. "Unfortunately, no," he replied. "Though the Winslow family is well-known, I was never privileged to meet Lord or Lady Winslow before their tragic accident, nor did I have the pleasure of knowing their daughter or the twins prior to the voyage."

Lord and Lady Winslow! Good God! A flicker of surprise appeared in Lance Logan's eyes quickly replaced by a cynical expression which he hid beneath hooded lids. So the prim and proper "Miss" Winslow actually deserved the title he had used to annoy her! No wonder she was anxious to quit Fort Brooke. Its raw young inhabitants must sorely test her sensibilities.

That he could be wrong in his assumption never crossed his mind. Nor did he stop to wonder why Rebecca chose not to use her rightful designation.

"Let's get one thing straight, Wentworth!"

Justin looked into gray eyes as frigid as a winter's day.

"Here we don't hold much with titles and such. This country was founded on the premise that all men are created equal! Understand?"

"If you say so," Justin replied, shrugging his shoulders nonchalantly.

"What do you mean 'if I say so'?" Lance growled.

"It's just that I find it puzzling about 'equality,' I mean. I understand it and you understand it," he paused tilting his head to one side. "But I can't help wondering, sir, if the Indians understand it."

"Damn it! Will you please stop calling me 'sir'?" Lance shot back angrily, all too well aware that the words "liberty and justice for all" had a hollow ring for some.

As they came within sight of the main trail between Fort King and Fort Brooke, suddenly, above the plodding hoof beats of the small patrol, Lance heard the drumming sound of a single horse swiftly approaching the junction just ahead. He raised his hand and the soldiers immediately became silent as he dug his moccasin-clad heels into his horse's flanks.

Just south of a sharp bend in the road the soldiers positioned themselves side by side forming a human barricade. Motionless they sat with rifles cocked and ready as the thundering hooves of the lone horse bore down on them.

Rachel had awakened to the aroma of fresh brewing coffee bubbling in a small pot over the open fire. She came awake slowly, knowing that some terrible occurrence had taken place yet willing her mind to remain encased in the protective oblivion sleep offered. But all too soon the devastating events of the day before intruded, and she sat up with a pitiful moan as she tightly clutched her blanket and pulled it beneath her chin.

Andrew swung around from where he sat beside the

fire drinking strong black coffee from a battered metal cup. He had been staring into the flames wondering if Rachel Jordan's eyes could possibly be as blue as he remembered. When he turned he discovered they were even more brilliant, for at the moment tears brimmed threatening to spill again onto her flushed cheeks.

"Mornin', love," he smiled and moved toward her, offering the cup of steaming brew as he knelt beside the pallet.

"Thank you," she said quietly, her husky, sensuous voice arresting him in mid motion.

How can such youth and innocence arouse my male needs with only a glance, he wondered. Especially when she sat before him fully clothed in her wrinkled gray gown? As she reached to grasp the hot cup gingerly with both hands, she let go of the blanket. Andrew found himself following the descent of the covering as it fell to her waist revealing full luscious breasts straining against the well-worn material of her dress.

With no little effort, he tore his eyes away from the sleep-dazed beauty hoping she had not seen the desire he found difficult to hide. Rachel needed time to heal. She certainly didn't need to be frightened further by a lonely man's uncontrollable longings. Yet he wanted nothing so much as to take her in his arms and comfort her as he had done hours earlier.

"Is Mary your wife?" Those fascinating eyes peered at him from above the rim of the cup she held.

"Why, love, I could have sworn I told you who Mary was when I described the people to you at Fort Brooke."

The pink blush which added an attractive tint to

112

Rachel's pale cheeks was caused more from the tingling sensation that overtook her whenever Andrew Townsend called her "love" than from any embarrassment over her faulty memory.

"I'm afraid I wasn't paying much attention to what you told me last night," she apologized feeling unaccustomed heat beneath her skin.

"Understandable," Andrew sympathized, "but as to Mary . . . no, she is not my wife. In fact, she is the wife of the commander of Fort Brooke, Colonel George Brooke. You'll go far before you meet a finer couple," he finished, his admiration for the Brookes readily apparent.

"I'm anxious to meet Mrs. Brooke and her husband, but do you have a wife?" Rachel asked shyly lowering her eyes to study what remained in the cup. Thick black lashes fluttered as she held her breath waiting for his answer.

"I was married once and I have two children to prove it!" Andrew berated himself for his sharp reply. His words had a defensive ring to them. But sometimes even he doubted the brief interlude when he had loved and been loved. It seemed so long ago and so far away.

Rachel could feel his pain. Although she didn't understand all that was behind it, her heart went out to the man before her, the knight who had come to her rescue. She longed to relive the time when he had held her in his arms protecting her from the terrible dreams that had come in the night. She hoped she might find a way to help him banish his demons, whatever they might be.

Rachel rode astride behind Andrew, her arms clinging tightly around his waist as they headed south toward Fort Brooke. Though her position was precarious as she bounced up and down roughly, her full skirts hiked above mid-calf, she voiced no complaint even as she felt her exposed skin rubbed raw against the hide of the horse. Andrew had explained his urgent need to deliver the dispatches he carried to Colonel Brooke and she was determined to cause him no further delay.

As they rounded a bend in the trail, she felt Andrew's muscles tense as he pulled back sharply on the reins, the bit cutting painfully into the horse's tender mouth. Rachel screamed, burying her face against his shirt. She did not want to see death coming and she was certain the savages had returned to finish what they had begun the day before.

As the frightened animal lurched sideways finally coming to a halt beside a thicket of sharp-needled bramble bushes, Andrew yelled, "God almighty damn! What are you jacklegs trying to do? Kill us?"

Andrew was very angry but there was no fear in his voice. Slowly Rachel raised her color-drained face and peeked over his shoulder. Enormous blue eyes nearly burst from their sockets at the awesome sight before her.

Uniformed soldiers formed a line blockading the path and each man held a rifle aimed directly at them. Heading the group was the largest, most ferocious-looking man she had ever seen. That he wore tanned buckskins and Indian moccasins made him even more outstanding among the men in uniforms.

While she continued to stare, the men lowered their weapons and smiles replaced the stern expressions of a moment ago when the soldiers had been prepared for battle. Even the big man looked less fierce as the patrol moved toward them.

"Welcome back, Townsend!" several of the men shouted as they reined their horses in beside the young couple and gazed with undisguised admiration at the raven-haired beauty.

"It seems Fort King has come up with a new way to send dispatches." The deep baritone voice of the man in buckskins was unexpectedly gentle as his silver-gray eyes fixed upon Rachel where she sat still clinging to Andrew Townsend who was rapidly becoming her lifeline in a topsy-turvy world.

The men chuckled while Andrew scowled darkly at his friend.

"It takes awhile to get used to Lance's humor . . . or lack of it," laughed the handsome officer seated on a horse beside the man wearing buckskins. "Both of my scouts seem to have forgotten their manners, miss. I'm George Brooke, commander of the fort toward which you are heading," he said extending his hand along with an ingratiating smile to Rachel.

As the men dismounted, Andrew raised his hands to encircle Rachel's narrow waist. When he lowered her to the ground he held her a moment longer than was necessary, meeting her eyes reassuringly. While he introduced her to the men and briefly explained what had happened the day before, a story all too familiar to the men listening, he kept one arm possessively around her. Lance couldn't help wondering at the bond that seemed to have formed between the young scout and Rachel Jordan who had known each other less than a day.

His musings were interrupted as he heard Andrew

say, "I'm sure you haven't ridden ten miles just to welcome me home, especially since you had no way of knowing when I would return."

"Unfortunately, you're right," George returned gravely. "It seems Chikiki paid a visit to the Holcomb place before he attacked the Jordans. Ezra's wife and daughter were killed."

At the news, Rachel drew closer into the shelter of Andrew's arm, a shiver of fear running through her body.

"Damn!" he swore loudly as he ran his hand up and down her sleeve in an unconscious gesture of comfort. "It doesn't make sense, Colonel. Chikiki was spotted heading south toward Fort Brooke. He was within twenty miles when he hit Ezra's homestead then he turned around and attacked Rachel's family ten miles further north. What the devil is he up to?"

"Chikiki hasn't got the manpower to attack the fort and he knows it," Lance reasoned. "But in a territory this size there's not a lot we can do to protect the settlers in the outlying areas."

"By God, there's one thing we can do!" Andrew burst out explosively as he hugged Rachel closer against his side. "We can kill the murdering bastard!"

Ah! But we have to catch him first, Lance thought to himself as the men remounted.

Chapter 7

Rebecca was up before the sun, and had dressed in a full-skirted pink and white candy-striped muslin gown which she hoped would look cool even if she were not. She saw no reason to expect anything other than the same blistering heat she had experienced yesterday. Mary had suggested that she dispense with her petticoats as a concession to the humid weather assuring that the lightness and freedom would offset any notion of immodesty. She had even offered to assist Rebecca in hemming any gowns should they be too long. But even as Rebecca admired the ease and grace with which both Mary and Lona moved about, she knew she would feel quite naked without her underskirts.

Glancing around her at the beautifully appointed bedroom she shared with Elizabeth, her admiration for what Mary Brooke had accomplished here rose even higher. The canopied bed in which Elizabeth still slept burrowed beneath a green and yellow flowered quilt, her red curls tousled about her head, was crowned with a

117

yellow ruffled fabric. Matching yellow curtains framed the two windows facing south where above the high stockade fence Rebecca could see the blue waters of Hillsborough Bay in the distance. Even now the sun was peeking over the wooded shorelines sprinkling the water with diamonds.

The door to the smaller adjoining bedroom had been left open and Rebecca moved quietly across the moss-green carpet to peek in at Edward curled on his side hugging his pillow.

Suddenly Rebecca spun around. "Oh, no!" she cried, racing back to the window.

"What's wrong, Becca?" Elizabeth asked sleepily.

"It's gone!" she exclaimed, leaning out the open window as tears welled up in her eyes.

"What's gone, Becca?" Elizabeth had tumbled out of bed, and now stood barefoot in her long, white, cotton nightgown beside her aunt. Trying to rub the sleep from her eyes using both little fists, she repeated, "What's gone?"

"The *Victoria,*" Rebecca moaned in despair.

Last night she had hoped, then prayed, that something would happen to prevent the ship's departure until Andrew returned. But the harbor was empty. Now everything familiar was gone. Rebecca felt as if her past had disappeared while she slept and at this moment her future was too frightening to contemplate. She willed herself not to cry biting down hard on her lower lip.

"Becca?" A small warm hand clasped hers and she looked down with surprise to find that Edward had come in unnoticed to stand at her other side. But he wasn't looking at her. Edward was staring intently out the window. He released her hand moving closer to the opening.

"Becca! I think they're coming back!"

Rebecca stepped forward placing her hands on the small boy's shoulders as she peered expectantly toward the channel where the bay flowed into the waters of the Gulf.

Visible in the distance were the billowing white sails of a ship slowly making its way toward the harbor, and for a moment Rebecca dared to think it might be so. But all too soon her hopes were dashed for bearing down on the inadequately staffed fort was a mighty warship, heavy cannon lining the main deck, a man of war proudly flying a flag of red, white, and blue, emblazoned with stars and stripes.

They watched the ship's approach from the window of the upstairs bedroom. No one else within the fort seemed unduly concerned by the brig's advance though several of the soldiers stood on the beach attending the progress of the floating arsenal.

Edward and Elizabeth soon became bored with the ship's sluggish headway and the lack of excitement it engendered. When Davey appeared beneath the window a short time later with fishing poles in hand, seeming to have forgotten the events of the previous evening, the twins dashed down the stairs and the trio headed toward the open gates.

Rebecca, unable to bear the silence that followed the children's departure, soon followed suit only to find the first floor of the house deserted and eerily quiet. She walked out onto the porch then down toward the entrance to the fort hanging back within the shadows still alarmed by the heavily armed ship preparing to drop anchor in the channel of the bay.

She had never given much thought, actually none at all, to what men faced when they went to war. It was accepted as part of an Englishman's life. Unless, of course, you could pay someone to accept your commission, as William had done. He had explained it as a charitable practice among the aristocracy for it gave men born beneath the elite the opportunity to rise above what the English class structure normally allowed. If a soldier proved himself in battle, whether he was a commoner or lord, he was proclaimed a hero, a man who could control his own destiny regardless of his humble beginnings.

To Rebecca, William's explanation had seemed perfectly logical at the time. But as she stood staring at the monstrous gray hulk looming out of the water, good sense suggested a less benevolent reason for seeking out a substitute. Surely no one in his right mind would want to challenge so formidable an enemy.

From where she stood just inside the gates, Rebecca could barely make out the letters etched on the bow of the awesome vessel *U.S.S. Enterprise.* And she could well imagine that like its name this mighty craft stood always ready to engage in daring action.

Rebecca was surprised to see Mary standing at the water's edge, her hands outstretched in welcome to the imposing figure of a man just stepping from the longboat.

"Lawrence! Welcome back!" Mary greeted the handsome young man in the uniform of an American naval officer.

Lieutenant Kearny frowned as he squeezed Mary's hands warmly at the same time studying the quiet all but deserted fort. "What has happened here, Mary? Where are George and the men?" Alert chestnut brown eyes continued to take in the outlying area searching for any sign that the fort had been under attack during his absence. He could see nothing amiss except the noticeable lack of soldiers.

"We're fine here," Mary quickly reassured, then hastened to explain what had happened during his absence. "Chikiki and his warriors attacked Ezra Holcomb's place yesterday. They killed his wife and daughter."

Lawrence Kearny shook his head somberly. "I'm sorry to hear it, but Ezra was strongly advised not to build his cabin so far north of the fort. He just wouldn't listen. And now it has cost him his family. Such a waste!"

"Ezra is a stubborn man."

"Mary, there's more to it than that and you know it! Ezra Holcomb is a fanatic! A madman who justifies cruelty and inhumanity in the name of religion!" he returned heatedly. "Holcomb is as dangerous in his way as Chikiki!" He paused for breath. "I suppose George and Lance have given chase."

"Yes," Mary nodded. "But you know the odds against catching them. What makes them so elusive? How can they continue to disappear without a trace?"

"Chikiki knows this territory like the back of his hand and besides that they're fast. Too damned fast. By the time the soldiers hear of an attack the band is already miles away."

"Lawrence," Mary could not disguise the fear in her voice. "How in the world are the renegades able to get rifles and ammunition?"

Kearny gazed off into the distance. "It has to be white men who are supplying Chikiki and his followers with the arms necessary to pull off these raids."

"But who would do such a thing?" Mary found it hard to believe it was her own kind providing the band of cutthroats with the instruments of destruction.

"Not all white men are as anxious as we are to see this territory settled peacefully," Kearny tried to explain. "George and Lance have begun to suspect that some of the trappers may be in league with Chikiki and his bunch of murderers, men who are afraid that civilization will bring regulation to what has always been a wide open hunting ground."

Mary sighed, trying to understand. "But game is so plentiful here! It doesn't make sense."

"Plentiful for now, but seeing their way of life and possibly their livelihoods threatened can make men desperate," he reasoned.

"And what of your mission? Any sign of the pirates?"

"Not a trace!" Disappointment threaded his voice. "We sailed north along the coast. But the Gulf was as quiet as a sleeping babe. We passed the *Victoria* this morning. Jeremiah should have a smooth trip to New Orleans."

"At least that is good news!" Mary smiled wistfully as she thought of the kind-hearted sea captain.

"Gaspar and his rabble seem to have holed up temporarily. I'd like to believe they are at the bottom of the sea feeding the fish, but I doubt the old devil will make my job that easy," he shrugged returning Mary's smile.

Mary liked Lawrence Kearny. She knew that he was a dedicated naval commander well respected by his men. He had supreme confidence in his ability to get the job done and it was, perhaps, that confidence that gave him an unfailingly optimistic outlook on life. There was something very reassuring about the young lieutenant.

"What will you do next, sir?" Mary laughed up at him prettily.

"What will I do next?" He repeated her question scratching his head as if searching for an answer then looked steadily over Mary's shoulder, his gaze intent on the area just inside the stockade.

"Hmm. I believe what I will do next is ask you to introduce me to that enchanting bit of peppermint candy standing behind the gate watching us!"

As the army patrol headed by George Brooke and Lance Logan resumed their journey south toward the fort, Andrew lifted Rachel up in front of him gently cradling her within his arms. He had handed over the dispatches he carried from the commander at Fort King which the Colonel scanned briefly, the frown on his tanned brow deepening before he folded the documents and carefully tucked them inside his coat.

His mission complete Andrew no longer felt the urgent need for speed especially since all signs indicated that Chikiki and his followers were again headed in a northerly direction. For his part the young scout wished to prolong the time he had to hold the precious burden in his arms before relinquishing her to Mary's keeping.

Rachel allowed her head to rest against Andrew's shoulder, feeling safe and secure despite the dangers she knew could be lurking in the dense woods or waiting to surprise them around the next turn in the road. How much better it was riding in front of her protector. With each jolting motion of the horse beneath them she became more and more aware of Andrew's manhood growing rigid against her hip. Her entire body began to tingle until even her toes curled inside her sturdy little boots. And, innocent though she was, she felt the strongest desire to lean back harder into the man seated behind her.

As Andrew inhaled the delicate fragrance of the soft, black strands of hair blowing against his face, he too was aware that his manly needs were becoming apparent. It was definitely time to channel his thoughts elsewhere before he embarrassed himself.

Colonel Brooke had briefly introduced Andrew to his newest recruit, Justin Wentworth, saying that he had recently arrived on the *Victoria*. Andrew forced himself to concentrate on the young Englishman. Perhaps he knew of the Winslows. Not likely, but at least he could find out how things fared in faraway England.

Justin, riding just behind Lance Logan and George Brooke, studied the backs of the two men. One was tall and lean with neatly trimmed blond hair beneath a wide-brimmed military hat; the other had immensely wide, muscular shoulders which threatened to burst the seams of his buckskin shirt each time his long arms moved to give emphasis to what he was saying. Logan wore no hat allowing his shaggy brown hair to blow back from his head just as the fringe blew from his tanned shirt and tight-fitting breeches.

Justin was puzzled that no mention had been made

to Andrew Townsend about his sister-in-law and his children's arrival at the fort.

"Mind if we join you, Mr. Wentworth?" Andrew asked smiling as he pulled up beside Justin.

"Not at all," he answered amiably while admiring the crystal blue eyes of Rachel Jordan. He noticed how they sparkled when she looked up adoringly into Andrew Townsend's round, lightly freckled face.

"What part of England are you from?" Andrew's query held more than polite interest and Justin understood why.

He again eyed the backs of the two men riding ahead of him as he replied, "My family home is in Kent."

Though he had no intention of eavesdropping, Lance could not help but overhear the two young men behind him. He knew that sooner or later the name Winslow would enter the conversation and he felt a twinge of guilt as it dawned on him that Andrew Townsend was yet unaware that his family anxiously awaited him at Fort Brooke. But Lance certainly didn't feel it was his duty to enlighten his young friend. Besides considering the unusual circumstances surrounding their unanticipated meeting, there had been little time for more than the briefest of explanations before Colonel Brooke ordered the men to mount up and make haste for the fort. Still, Lance knew that postponing the telling would in no way lessen the shock he felt certain the young scout was bound to experience.

Andrew looked eagerly toward the Englishman hoping for news that would somehow make his children seem closer as he replied, "I lived in Warwickshire for a short time. Would you happen to know the area?"

Lance could feel Justin Wentworth glaring at him.

"Though I've never been to Warwickshire," the Englishman answered curtly, "I have heard much about it in recent weeks."

Andrew stiffened, caught off guard by the man's terse reply.

"I'm afraid I don't understand," he replied giving Justin a puzzled frown.

Lance turned in his saddle and seeing the appeal in Wentworth's eyes, he felt constrained to come to his rescue.

"Now you've done it, Townsend!" Underlying the harshness of his words, his deep baritone voice was laced with humor. "You've forced us to spoil the surprise we have waiting for you at the fort."

"What surprise?" Andrew asked suspiciously, unaware that he had tightened his hold on Rachel. His reaction was purely reflexive for past surprises had rarely proved pleasant.

"Wentworth wasn't the only passenger to disembark when the *Victoria* arrived at Fort Brooke," Lance went on, amusement turning his gray eyes to silver.

"Spit it out, Logan! What's this all about?" Andrew was rapidly losing patience as Rachel looked nervously from one man to the other.

"Seems there's a couple of red-haired, freckle-face kids waiting at the fort who claim you're their father." Lance watched as Andrew's mouth fell open and though he tried to speak no words would come.

"That's wonderful!" Rachel exclaimed when after several minutes Andrew continued to stare speechlessly at the man in buckskins.

"That's impossible!" Andrew bellowed seeming suddenly to find his voice. Rachel quickly covered one ear with her hand. "And if this is your idea of a joke, it's not a damned bit funny!"

Even Lance had underestimated the effect his words would have as blue eyes fixed on him with unbridled fury. Andrew had never shared with anyone at the fort his dream to bring Edward and Elizabeth here. No one knew the battle that raged within him as the need to be with his children once again fought with his desire to guarantee their safety. That anyone could make sport of his dilemma was intolerable.

By this time the patrol had come to a halt and Lance had turned his horse so that he sat facing his irate comrade.

"Have you ever known me to jest about a man's family, Townsend?" his voice was quiet, his tone sympathetic.

"He's telling the truth," George confirmed. Though he was completely bewildered by how such a thing could have happened, Andrew realized that neither man had any reason to lie to him.

"I don't understand," he murmured, slowly shaking his head. "Edward and Elizabeth are supposed to be in England with Rebecca."

"Oh, the children are with Miss Winslow all right," Justin volunteered. "Only they're at Fort Brooke."

As the realization began to penetrate his initial dismay, Andrew experienced a feeling of euphoria he hadn't known in nearly five long, lonely years. His children, Edward and Elizabeth, were a scant ten miles away. A wide grin covered his face as he let out a resounding whoop of joy hugging Rachel so tightly she was certain her ribs would crack, but she smiled happily ignoring the pain.

As they moved forward once more, Andrew plied Justin with questions wanting to know everything he could tell him about Edward and Elizabeth: what they looked like, how they behaved, every small happening during their ocean voyage.

Rachel was horrified when Justin described Edward's attempt to climb to the crow's nest and Rebecca's heroic rescue of the boy. Andrew howled with laughter once he knew the incident had not ended in disaster. She felt an even greater admiration for the unknown woman who was the sister of Andrew's wife as Justin admitted that he had recognized the Winslow name from the beginning and had known that Rebecca deserved to be addressed as Lady Winslow. But when Edward and Elizabeth confided in their childlike way that their aunt did not want to be a lady, he had immediately understood what they could not and he had respected her wishes.

When the Englishman had exhausted every minute detail he could remember relating to Rebecca and the children, Andrew began to regale Rachel and Justin with tales of his life with the Winslows. Brief though the time had been, he had an endless store of humorous anecdotes about the derring-dos of the Lord and his lovely Lady.

While laughing at the outrageous antics of the senior Winslows, it soon became apparent to those listening that the younger daughter, Rebecca, only fourteen at the time, was mature far beyond her years. She had provided the steadfast force which enabled the wealthy, aristocratic family to continue living in the manner that

128

generations of Winslows had lived before them.

Lance tried unsuccessfully to block out the conversation going on behind him. Grimly he thought to himself if Andrew Townsend told just one more story of how Rebecca Winslow had saved her stupid parents from their own folly he was going to be sick. Lady Winslow! Hell, he was surprised they didn't call her "Saint Winslow" the way they were carrying on.

Just as he made up his mind to fall back and ride rear guard until the two men tired of heaping plaudits on the young woman, he heard Andrew remark disgruntledly, "I suppose Rebecca is still infatuated with that milksop, William Pennington."

It was a comment more than a question but Justin responded with a chuckle. "Miss Winslow never mentioned a gentleman by that name but I wonder if he could be the same 'Frilly Willy' Edward and Elizabeth often giggled about? Mind you, they never spoke the name in front of their aunt," he added.

Lance suddenly lost interest in assuming the rear guard. Could it be, he wondered, that there was a flaw, however slight, in the paragon of virtue?

"Damn! So the fop is still around!" Andrew's tone was exasperated. "Rebecca is the most sensible young woman I have ever known except when it comes to her infatuation with William Pennington!"

"But who is William Pennington?" Rachel ventured to ask.

"He's 'the boy next door' in a manner of speaking," Andrew answered still thoroughly annoyed. "Only he's not a boy any longer. His parents own the estate adjoining the Winslows. Young Pennington is their heir though considering what it costs them to continually buy the rounder out of trouble, there may be little left to inherit when the time comes. Drinking, gambling, women . . . especially other men's wives, you name it! That's what life is to William Pennington. Not just sport, mind you, but life itself!" Andrew shook his head as he finished his diatribe.

"Why would Rebecca have anything to do with so worthless an individual?" Rachel couldn't reconcile the Rebecca Winslow she had come to admire just from hearing Justin and Andrew speak of her with a woman who could be so naively taken in by a useless rogue.

"Rebecca has thought herself in love with Pennington since she was in nappies," Andrew explained. "Everyone thought she would grow out of it, that she would eventually see him for what he is, and maybe she does."

"How do you mean?" Justin asked.

"Rebecca's intelligence is exceeded only by her stubbornness," Andrew explained raising his eyebrows at an unintelligible sound made by the man riding directly in front of him. "You see," he went on as he stared at Lance Logan's back, "for years Rebecca has been told by her friends, her parents, her sister, even by me that Pennington is no good. He just uses her as a cloak of respectability. Without her he would be shunned by polite society. Even if she has come to recognize the irascible fellow's faults, it would be difficult for someone of Rebecca's temperament to admit that she was wrong."

The noise which could only be described as a snort came again causing Andrew to wonder what Rebecca could possibly have done to earn Lance Logan's disdain on so short an acquaintance.

"From what you and Mr. Wentworth have said about your sister-in-law, I think she will come to her senses before she does anything foolish." Rachel felt it unfair of the men to speak disparagingly of Rebecca when she was not there to defend herself.

"I wonder," Andrew smiled thinking how true the old adage was that women stuck together even when they had never met. "As I've said, remaining loyal to Pennington has been the only foolish thing I have known Rebecca to do. Up until now. But she had better have a damn good reason for bringing Edward and Elizabeth to the territory with the Indian situation the way it is. The least she could have done was to write and let me know they were coming."

"I rather think Miss Winslow made her decision to bring the children here during a moment of anger then set her plans into motion before she had an opportunity to consider her actions rationally," Justin offered.

"Doesn't sound like the Rebecca I remember," Andrew said doubtfully. "Did she tell you that?"

"No, but I spent a great deal of time with Edward and Elizabeth during the crossing and was greatly enlightened by some of the stories they told." Justin had to smile at his understatement, remembering the outlandish tales with which he had been entertained, tales made even more enticing because he was certain that they were true. "I've yet to meet two six-year-olds with such inventive minds," he laughed, then sobered. "They certainly detested 'Frilly Willy.'" Justin colored slightly, embarrassed that he had unthinkingly used the childish derogative.

Andrew chuckled. "If the shoe fits . . ." he shrugged

anxious for Justin to continue.

"It seems the children sought to discourage Pennington's courtship with their aunt, if it could be called that, by playing pranks on the man. Harmless, but annoying nonetheless. You know the sort of things. Pepper in his snuff box, adhesive on his saddle . . . Of course, that did cost him a pair of breeches," he added thoughtfully. "But no matter what deviltry they tried, the dolt kept coming back for more. They were terribly afraid he was on the verge of declaring himself. So, desperate to discourage his suit, they came up with a scheme to surpass anything they had attempted thus far."

"I'm not sure I want to hear this," Andrew grimaced rolling his eyes.

"One afternoon," Justin continued ignoring the remark, "Edward and Elizabeth overheard Miss Winslow telling her maid that Mr. Pennington was taking her rowing on the lake. Just before the scheduled outing, the twins drilled a small hole in the boat."

"Oh, dear!" Rachel exclaimed.

"They knew that their aunt was a strong swimmer and naturally assumed Pennington could also take care of himself. Unfortunately, the fool could not so much as keep himself afloat. When the couple reached the middle of the lake and the boat began taking on water, Pennington became hysterical, screaming and flailing his arms like a bedlamite. Luckily, just before the small boat overturned, he fainted thus enabling Miss Winslow to tow him ashore."

Lance's shoulders shook with silent laughter as Wentworth reached the climax of his tale. He could scarcely imagine a man's mortification at having to be rescued from drowning by a mere slip of a girl. For the tough frontiersman such a situation was inconceivable.

"To make a long story short," Justin concluded, "William Pennington swore he would never come near Miss Winslow again as long as the children remained in her care, and before Edward and Elizabeth realized what was happening, arrangements had been made for the journey to America."

"Good God!" Andrew exclaimed. "I have scant regard for the man but, damn, the little buggers could have killed him! What kind of children are they?" He was horrified at the ends to which the twins had gone in an attempt to achieve their objective.

"Now just a moment, Townsend!" Justin's voice was stern as he held up his hand to halt Andrew's tirade. "I think I know Edward and Elizabeth a little better than you do!"

The words hurt, but Andrew could not argue with the truth in them.

Justin continued giving Andrew no chance to reply. "I would say they are the kind of children who love their aunt very much. The kind of children who have a keener insight into human nature than most adults. In short, Townsend, they are the kind of children a man should be proud to call his own!"

Andrew let his eyes drift down to the hard dirt packed trail and for some time the horses' plodding hooves were the only sound disturbing the quiet of the woods. Then he raised haunted blue eyes to meet those of the Englishman riding beside him. "You're absolutely right. Please accept my apologies for that unwarranted outburst."

He extended his hand which Justin grasped unhesitantly for he had instantly regretted his reminder of the man's lengthy separation from his children.

As Andrew brought his arm back, Rachel squeezed it encouragingly longing to assure him that he would not be alone at the forthcoming meeting which she was sure would prove awkward for all parties involved.

He smiled into her luminous sapphire eyes. "Perhaps, love, you would feel safer riding with one of the soldiers. After what's happened my spunky little sister-in-law is liable to shoot me on sight."

"I'll take my chances." The look of tender affection she turned upon him caused Andrew's heart to skip a beat.

"Don't worry, Miss Jordan," Justin interjected. "Though the fool lad may deserve such a fate, I doubt it would be at the hands of Miss Winslow. She is one fine lady." His words were sincere, wistful, as they came out almost on a sigh.

She's one fine lady, Lance mimicked to himself. *Damn it! There was that word again. "Lady" this and "Lady" that! Who gave a rat's ass anyway? Fort Brooke had no need for "ladies"! Not that Mary wasn't a lady, for she was. Lona was working at it by trying to imitate everything Mary did. But that was different. Mary was just Mary! No fancy frills, no fancy titles. She was real, down-to-earth. . . .* He searched for a word. *Mary was American! There! That was it!*

And what gave Wentworth the right to speak as if he had known Rebecca all his life? Hell, he'd only known her since they left England. There was something insidious about a woman who had men rushing to her defense on such short acquaintance. Wentworth was nothing but a poor besotted ninny, Lance decided.

Thank God Lance was immune to Rebecca's dubious charms.

His thick dark brows drew together in a frown. At what point in his musings had his mind unconsciously switched from thinking of her as Miss Winslow to thinking of her as Rebecca? Funny that her given name felt so comfortable.

"There it is!" Andrew shouted as they came through a break in the trees and saw the gray log walls of Fort Brooke in the distance.

Giving an ear-piercing yell, he nudged his horse in the flanks and it pulled ahead of the others, running for home with nostrils flaring. Rachel clung to the saddlehorn with both hands staring speechlessly at the formidable bastion looming ever larger before them.

Chapter 8

Rebecca was seated in a comfortable high-backed rocking chair on the Brookes' wide front porch shaded by the leafy arms of the mighty oak, chatting amiably with Mary and Lieutenant Kearny. Without warning the tranquillity of the lazy afternoon was shattered by a shrill outcry that brought her instantly to her feet.

"The children!" she shrieked certain that the renegade warriors were attacking while the twins and Davey fished beside the creek cut off from the protective walls of the fort.

But her two companions showed no signs of alarm. Though both had risen from their chairs, they stood impassivley watching the open space between the gates.

"Mary! Lieutenant! For the love of God! Do something!" Her voice mirrored her terror and confusion. Damnation, she thought. How could they just stand there waiting to die? Could anyone, even these intrepid colonists, face their enemies so stoically?

Mary looked over at Rebecca nonplused then moved to her side as she observed the sickly pallor of the young Englishwoman's face.

"Rebecca, there's nothing to fear," she soothed. "Why, honey, I thought you'd be happy."

Rebecca blinked twice thinking she must have misunderstood. Happy? Of course she was happy! Who wouldn't be happy when faced with the prospect of being mutilated by savages! She felt her hysteria rising and willed herself to remain calm.

Mary's concern suddenly turned into a weak smile as she studied her new friend's blood-drained visage. "But of course, Rebecca, you couldn't know."

"Know what!" she demanded in a shaky, high-pitched voice as she struggled to maintain her control.

"Well, if I'm not mistaken, that banshee war whoop means your brother-in-law, Andrew Townsend, has returned."

If anything, Rebecca's face blanched still more. The moment of truth had arrived and suddenly she felt less sure of herself than she ever had in her life. What could she possibly say to Andrew to justify her rash actions? Now that she had seen this rugged territory and borne witness to its merciless violence, she realized the stupidity of her coming here. And she knew that the danger to which she had exposed Edward and Elizabeth was unforgivable.

Before she could finish berating herself she heard the charger's pounding hooves and saw the dust rising in its wake. The horse did not slow its speed until it was within a few feet of the bottom step. Only then did Andrew pull back hard on the reins causing the animal to skid to a halt kicking up clods of green turf.

Rebecca fixed her eyes suspiciously on the man before her. This was not the thin pale Englishman to

137

whom she had bid farewell that misty morning on the docks of Southampton. This man was dark-skinned with white crinkly lines forking out beside sky-blue eyes. Yes, the eyes were the same, she marked with something akin to relief. She noticed how light his hair was now, tawny rather than red as if the unrelenting tropical sun had stripped its natural shades.

He was powerfully built, the muscles of his arms and chest bulging beneath the cotton material of his shirt, his thighs and calves stretching tight-fitting, buff-colored britches where his legs gripped the belly of the horse.

She noticed only briefly the beautiful, raven-haired woman Andrew held so possessively in front of him as she tried to see in this stranger the one she had looked upon as a brother. Her brow knitted as she studied his inscrutable features wondering what he could be thinking, but he gave her no clue, his face a mask hiding any show of emotion. Then she saw the uncertainty in his eyes and realized with a start that he was as much at a loss for words as she.

Suddenly all of the acid sermonettes she had rehearsed during the past months, discourses aimed at making him feel guilty for shirking his duty, flew right out of her mind. For regardless of the physical changes the years had wrought, this was Andrew! The same Andrew her sister had loved beyond all others.

He seemed to sense the exact moment when her barriers began to crumble. He lowered Rachel gently to the ground then dismounted to stand beside her. As if on cue, Rebecca bounded down the steps and into his arms hugging him as if she would never let him go.

She could not say how long they stood beneath the

138

broiling afternoon sun locked in an embrace. Despite his immigration to the new world, Andrew represented a part of the life she had left behind and Rebecca was loath to let him go.

Little by little she became aware of a tingling sensation running the length of her spine, a stimulating reaction to something that had nothing to do with the man to whom she was clinging.

Standing on tiptoe she peered over Andrew's shoulder directly into a pair of glaring gray eyes, eyes that bore into her with such intensity she felt as if they could see to her very soul. Artlessly she smiled at Lance Logan still sitting astride his big black stallion, a saucy dimpled smile that caught him completely off guard.

Damnation, she thought turning quickly away. *How can I be glad to see the arrogant rogue?* As illogical as it seemed, she had to admit to herself that for some inexplicable reason she felt safer knowing that he was back within the walls of the fort.

Rebecca was bewildered by the strange feelings that shook her whenever she came near the glowering army scout. She had no time to ponder the turmoil his presence generated for just as the question started to take shape in her mind everyone began speaking at once . . . except Mary Brooke.

Mary, who was torn between her desire to rush into her husband's arms and the need to welcome Rachel Jordan and put her at ease, stood on the porch uncertain, her eyes darting from one to the other. Meanwhile Andrew's words were scarcely coherent as he tried to explain Rachel's circumstances and ask after his children in the same breath. Rebecca, making no more sense than her brother-in-law, intermingled her explanation for being here with apologies for her imprudent behavior. Over the babble of voices, Lawrence Kearny was attempting to hear what Lance Logan and George Brooke had to report on their pursuit of the Indians.

Finally with one arm draped proprietarily around Rachel's shoulders, while the other encircled Rebecca's small waist, Andrew leaned down and fairly shouted into her ear to make himself heard over the cacophony of noise.

"Edward? Elizabeth? Why aren't they here?"

Undeniable concern mixed with the excitement and anticipation of a small child about to receive a long-promised treat proved just how much he had missed his offspring.

Smiling, Rebecca answered in an equally loud voice. "The creek! They're fishing with Davey!"

An embarrassed blush tinted her smooth heart-shaped face as she glanced around and realized that everyone had stopped talking the moment Andrew had bellowed his question. Her trumpeted response seemed to linger in the air as all eyes focused in her direction. But the indignation which quickly rose to overshadow her discomposure stemmed more from the cynical smirk she saw on the wide, tantalizing mouth of Lance Logan than from the fixed attention of the other people standing close by. Never again would she smile at the ill-bred lout she promised herself fuming inwardly as her foot tapped a steady beat and her chin tilted defiantly upward.

With hands fisted she forced herself to repeat what she had said in a more circumspect tone of voice even as sparks of amber fire flared up in her incensed sea-green eyes.

"Edward and Elizabeth are fishing at the creek. Come," she urged tugging gently on his hand. "Let's go find them for they are beside themselves awaiting your arrival."

She flushed guiltily knowing she had greatly exaggerated the twins' enthusiasm. As she cast a smoldering look at Lance, the need to put as much distance as possible between herself and the churlish provincial outweighed her self-reproach.

"Wait!" Andrew released his hand from her grasp then held her by the shoulders at arm's length. "If you don't mind, I would like to go alone." His voice was apologetic but determined.

It had never occurred to Rebecca that Andrew might prefer to meet the children without her beside him to lend support. The fact that he neither wanted nor needed her on this auspicious occasion was disappointing in the extreme. After all, Edward and Elizabeth had been her responsibility for what seemed a very long time.

This line of thinking quickly brought her up short. For hadn't she dreamed of the day she could return the little hoydens to their father? It made no sense to feel ill-used when freedom was at hand. Yet now that the moment had arrived, she felt empty and a little bit afraid, instead of the delight she had anticipated.

Damnation! What has come over me lately? she wondered disgustedly. Hadn't she always taken pride in her unflagging self-assurance? It was this place! Ever since her arrival in this untamed wasteland her sanity

141

had been in jeopardy. So, why should she be surprised at her illogical reaction to Andrew's perfectly reasonable request?

She straightened her shoulders and stood as tall as her diminutive height would allow.

"Of course you should go alone." She managed an encouraging smile as she saw Andrew waver momentarily.

"You're sure? I mean . . . you don't think they'll be afraid of me, do you?" His anxious blue eyes pleaded for reassurance.

"Posh! Neither ogres nor ghosts could frighten those two scamps," she teased pushing him toward the open gates.

"I won't be long," he called over his shoulder grinning with renewed confidence in Rachel's direction.

Only one person in the small group left standing inside the fort read the emotions that played across Rebecca's face. Puzzled, Lance Logan could not ignore the stab of pity that softened his heart as he watched her narrow shoulders slump dejectedly.

"Damnation!" Elizabeth muttered under her breath repeating the word Rebecca often used when she was disgruntled and thought no one would hear.

"Boys! Who cares what they think! Damnation!"

She dug the toe of one tiny booted foot into the hard-packed earth that formed a path running beside the creek as she watched the orange-billed coots dart in and out of the weeds on the far side of the stream. The woods were alive with the sounds of nature. Barking squirrels set birds aflight as they scampered from tree to tree. Frogs croaked while crickets chirped hidden within the heavy grass growing along the water's edge. But Elizabeth, weighed down with self-pity, found no delight in her surroundings. She couldn't help that she was born soft-hearted, at least that's what Becca said. And it didn't bother her when Edward called her "soft-headed" laughing at her sensibilities.

She flicked the cork attached to her line and watched the ripples spread in circles disturbing the deceptively calm-looking, gray-green water which flowed half-heartedly several feet below the bank. Her eyes filled with tears as she cast a glance toward Edward and Davey standing a good distance away near a point where the creek made a sharp bend to the right.

Elizabeth had wandered down the path to be alone unable to bear Davey's impatience with her. It was all because she had begun to cry as he inserted the nasty old hook at the end of her pole into the helpless wiggling worm. How could he be so unfeeling toward the unfortunate little grub and toward her? With obvious irritation he had explained that you could not catch a fish without bait . . . as if she didn't know that already. Did he think her a ninny for goodness sake?

His voice had been gruff and unsympathetic while she had felt like an accomplice to murder . . . or perhaps the murderer, herself. For if the poor creature hadn't already died of its wounds, she was bound to drown him. And to make matters worse, she was standing here wishing—yes, wishing—she could catch the biggest fish Davey Logan had ever seen which would definitely seal the worm's fate!

"Oh dear!" she frowned as she remembered what

Becca had told her more times than she could count: "Be careful what you wish for because sometimes wishes come true, and you wish you hadn't wished for what you wished for!"

Well, that wasn't exactly the way Becca had put it, but her meaning was clear which led Elizabeth to wonder if you could unwish wishes. The last thing she really wanted was to have an unsuspecting fish attach itself to her innocuous little worm.

Just as she had made up her mind that even the opportunity to be in Davey's company was not worth the agony of guilt she must contend with, Elizabeth heard a rustling in the dry grass behind her. Her blue eyes widened in horror as she looked down to see a long black snake slither out of the weeds onto the path directly in front of her feet.

At the same moment she felt a mighty tug on the end of her pole. Elizabeth had time for only one panic stricken scream as she lost her balance and tumbled backward to disappear beneath the water's surface.

Andrew Townsend was actually trembling as he made his way toward Davey Logan's favorite fishing spot. What would his children think of him? And how could he possibly bridge a gap of nearly five years?

So much was happening all of a sudden. After years of loneliness he had his children again. And then there was Rachel Jordan. Perhaps it was too soon to contemplate a future which included Rachel, but for the first time since Mandy's death it seemed he might have found someone with whom he could share his life. Having so much to look forward to was a bit disconcerting. He had become so accustomed to merely existing rather than looking forward to awakening to each new day. It would take time to emerge from the dark clouds which had blotted out the sunshine overhead.

A smile of amazement lit his face as he stopped to watch the two boys standing with their backs to him. So much for hoping Edward would take after his beautiful mother he thought wryly as the sun glinted down illuminating the smaller boy's bright russet hair.

As he stood staring in fascination an unexpected movement downstream caught his attention just before a violent scream rent the surrounding silence. Andrew caught only a brief glimpse of the small figure flying over the bank and through the air to land in the water with a resounding splash, but he had no doubt as to the identity of the imperiled youngster for the brilliance of her red-gold curls proclaimed her to be his own. Heart pounding, Andrew raced toward the spot where Elizabeth had disappeared and without breaking his stride dove cleanly into the water.

Those within the fort, having heard the child's shriek, rushed outside the gates in time to see Andrew hurl himself into the stream. The men ran ahead while Rebecca, Rachel and Mary hurried along as quickly as possible hampered by their full skirts.

Lance and George, with Justin at their heels, dashed past Edward and Davey who watched helplessly searching the water for any sign of Elizabeth or her would-be rescuer. The boys stood rooted to the spot where she had gone over the embankment, but the men knew that *if* Andrew managed by some miracle to conquer the creek's treacherous undertow he would come up further downstream.

They came to a halt fifty yards away, each holding

145

his breath trying to gauge how long would be too long as the women moved in behind them; shock enabling them to do no more than watch silently.

Their cry of relief came in unison as Andrew broke the water shaking his head to send droplets raining out in all directions, clearing the wet hair plastered over his eyes while he choked and sputtered trying to fill his lungs with air.

Rebecca closed her eyes tightly, her body beginning to shake with delayed reaction as she saw that Andrew had Elizabeth in tow. The men were in the water now helping to drag the seemingly lifeless burden to shore.

"Please God!" Rebecca prayed, but could find no other words.

"What the hell!"

Rebecca recognized the booming voice and her eyes flew open.

Andrew sat on the edge of the bank with Elizabeth across his lap as he pounded on her back until a goodly amount of water spewed from her mouth. She coughed and struggled to catch her breath.

Lance, wanting to do something of use, leaned down to pry the small fingers loose from the end of the fishing pole still clutched in her hand. With a snap of his wrist he jerked the line upward then let out an astonished oath as he gawked at the weighty black bass flopping about at his feet.

Having rid herself of the foul-tasting water she had swallowed, Elizabeth turned her head to peer up at the man holding her. Identical blue eyes met and held for what seemed an eternity. Then without hesitation she croaked hoarsely, "Papa!"

Andrew caught her to him and the moisture dripping

from his hair mingled with his tears as he clung to the daughter he had found to nearly lose again.

Looking up Andrew spotted Edward standing apart from the crowd around them, speechless for once and seemingly bewildered by what had taken place. Smiling tenderly he held out his hand toward the boy. Happiness flooded Edward's face as he crossed the short space that separated him from his father and flung himself into the man's arms.

Lance cleared his throat feeling awkward in the presence of such emotion. He glanced around to see Mary smiling affectionately at the three as they embraced each other. Rachel's tears were flowing freely down her cheeks as she reached out to smooth Elizabeth's damp curls then squeeze Edward's shoulder.

But the one Lance sought was nowhere in sight.

147

Chapter 9

Seated on the sun-warmed boulder Rebecca gazed at the western horizon where an azure blue sky dotted with downy gold-rimmed clouds met the aquamarine waters of the bay. She cursed the fates who had allowed Andrew's ill-timed arrival. Had he been but a few hours earlier she would be watching this breathtaking spectacle from the deck of the *Victoria* enroute to New Orleans and from there, home. Home to England and the man she loved.

She tried to summon forth William's image in her mind but to her vexation an insolent, rough-chiseled countenance superimposed itself over the likeness she yearned to see. She heard no footsteps yet she knew without moving that the object of her chagrin was standing right behind her.

"So, Mr. Logan, have you come to gloat over my misfortune?" Still she did not turn but continued to stare straight ahead.

Lance guessed that she was thinking of how narrowly she had missed sailing with Captain Higgins and he was rankled by her determination to quit this land of his.

Ignoring her question, he asked one of his own. "How did you know it was me?"

Rebecca slowly spun around, her captivating face alight with wonder.

"I really can't explain it," she replied, genuinely baffled by her cognizance.

"Could I be so lucky as to suppose you might have been thinking of me? Just a little?" he qualified.

His voice held none of the arrogance she had come to expect. He seemed instead shyly hopeful which confused her still more.

"When horses can fly, Mr. Logan," came her sassy rejoinder but she softened her impudence with a dazzling smile that caused Logan's heart to skip a beat.

He knew he should never have come looking for her. She was a dangerous entanglement that he did not need. But he couldn't help himself. And when he had found her sitting alone and vulnerable on the shell-strewn beach, the impulse to speak to her again easily won out over his better judgment.

Now he could think of several reasons why he should get the hell out of here, not the least of which was his desire to lift her up and enclose her delectable body within his arms. He could almost feel her perfectly rounded buttocks beneath his hands, feel her firm generous breasts pressed against his chest. Damn! He was getting as horny as Kearny's sailors.

"Are you woolgathering, Mr. Logan?" Rebecca's enchanting laughter brought Lance back to attention as she rose gracefully to stand before him.

"Here in the territory we tend to avoid formality,

Rebecca, so perhaps you could just call me Lance."

His use of her given name without permission did not escape Rebecca's notice, but she decided there was little to be gained by arguing the finer points of etiquette with a native.

"I suppose it could do no harm ... Lance." She spoke his name hesitantly but found it not objectionable.

"Contrary to what you may believe, Rebecca, I am not quite the ill-mannered bumpkin I appear to be. Please forgive my impropriety but I could not bring myself to address you as 'Lady Winslow.'"

Rebecca looked so flabbergasted Lance could not stifle the laughter that rose in his chest then exploded like thunder on a stormy day.

"How ever did you find out about that?" she asked warily.

"More important, why did you allow me to tease you with a title you justly deserved?"

It was most bothersome the way he always answered a question with another question, but still he had given her the perfect opening to voice her opinion regarding the pretentious absurdities practiced by the English. She was not one to miss such an opportunity.

"It is my understanding that titles of nobility mean little in this new world of yours. I have no intention of giving the people here a reason to resent me. Besides in this regard I could not agree more with American ideals. Such distinctions are useful only to those who are too indolent to succeed on their own merit."

This time it was Logan's turn to be dumbfounded.

"What a strange speech for a Britisher," he remarked searching her candid green eyes.

"Not so strange really, but then you don't know *this* Britisher very well, do you, Mr. Logan?" Rebecca lifted her pert little nose in the air.

"Lance," he reminded, "and there is a quick remedy for such an oversight, my lady. Why don't you sit back down on your throne," he suggested motioning toward the big rock, "and regale me with tales about your life in merry old England."

Rebecca giggled at his foolishness and wondered what had become of the melancholy mood that had cast a shadow over her just moments ago.

"Ladies do not sit on thrones. Queens sit on thrones. But queens never entertain. They summon their jesters who perform for *their* amusement."

Caught up in the levity of their conversation, Rebecca guilelessly played with an escaping lock of hair wrapping it loosely around her finger. She was unaware of the effect her youthful lightheartedness was having on the man standing so close to her.

Lance could not remember a time when his body had been so completely in control of his brain. If he knew what was good for him he would turn and walk away from this enigmatic sprite without looking back. But even as his common sense argued in favor of such action, he felt his manhood awakening with a need too long denied and he knew it was not just any woman he craved. But damned if he could figure out what made this hoity-toity little minx so special.

Striving to gain some semblance of control, he asked solemnly, "And what if the queen is not amused?"

Green eyes sparkled with mischief as Rebecca replied knowingly, "Oh, one way or another the queen is always amused for there is nothing so funny as a headless jester!"

Her tinkling laughter bubbled as Rebecca twirled gleefully around in circles unmindful that her full skirts and petticoats were billowing out to reveal slender ankles and calves.

The consequence of her efforts to shock Logan's sensibilities with her farcical narrative differed greatly from what she had anticipated. Without warning she was snatched up by two powerful arms and propelled across the sand in an exaggerated travesty of a dance. Around and around they whirled making their own music as they moved together across the glistening white beach.

It ended as abruptly as it had begun. They stopped on cue as though hearing the final strains of a waltz, but Lance did not release his hold. He pulled her closer enfolding her in his mighty arms as he bent his head to taste the nectar from her honeyed lips.

His lips were warm, his touch gentle, undemanding. Yet Rebecca was swept up in a tidal wave of emotion that threatened to inundate the essence of her being. Certain that she was about to drown in a tumultuous sea of passion, she wrapped her arms around Lance clinging as though he were a buoy keeping her afloat.

It was Logan who at last broke the spell that locked them together in a feverish embrace. Though it was not without considerable regret, he knew that if he did not stop he would be unable to resist the temptation she offered until he had satisfied his unquenchable thirst for the trusting young innocent clutched in his arms. The price of his greed would be her virginity.

As soon as Lance loosened his hold, Rebecca came plummeting down to earth wishing the ground would open up and swallow her whole. Mortified by her unseemly behavior she kept her eyes hidden beneath thick brown lashes until he gently raised her chin with his fingertip. His heart lurched at the tear-bright emerald orbs looking up at him.

"So much for my life story," she said glumly as a cheerless smile curved her rose-pink lips. "Now you know all there is to know about me. I am a wanton!"

His unrestrained laughter earned him a truculent glare as amber sparks lit up her eyes. Lance knew without looking down that her foot was tapping a staccato rhythm beneath her skirts.

"I hope you realize that you caught me unaware, Mr. Logan. That kiss meant nothing," she declaimed obstinately bracing her hands upon her hips.

"My name is Lance, and of course it meant nothing," he agreed with an audacious smile that made her long to smack his ruggedly handsome face.

"Damnation! You are the most arrogant, obnoxious, loathsome, overbearing. . . ." Rebecca stamped her dainty slippered foot. "Words simply fail me, *Mr. Logan!*"

"You could have fooled me," he chuckled. "Having heard more than enough of your 'failed' words, *Miss Winslow,* I can only conclude that you are indeed *no lady!* You really should learn to control your . . ." he deliberately paused for effect, ". . . tongue, Rebecca."

Rebecca could scarcely contain her fury as taunting silver-gray eyes smiled down at her.

"Ooh! You, sir, are a cad of the first water!" she hissed. And with that she stomped off in the direction of the fort.

"Seems we've played this scene before, lady!" His

153

words were softly spoken for his ears alone. He smiled remembering how she had felt in his arms, the way in which the sun had turned her glorious hair to spun gold. The air still held a hint of her perfume.

As he strolled along the beach away from the fort, Lance was inordinately pleased with himself. As he kicked at a loose shell his laughter rang out over the calm blue water. He hadn't felt this good in a long time!

"Your cousin is insane, Leon! Why will you not admit the truth?" Ramona shouted at the man seated at the small table holding his head in his hands.

"Hush, Ramona! He will hear you?" Leon Gaspar looked apprehensively around the small room.

"He will not hear me," the woman countered petulantly. "He is much too busy tormenting his child-slave."

Pitiful moans could be heard penetrating the thin walls of the identical thatched houses built side by side, one of which Leon Gaspar shared with his woman, Ramona. Leon placed his hands over his ears trying to block out the sound.

"We should have fled Boca Grande with the rest of the brothers when we had the chance," the black-haired, sallow-skinned woman harped on as she paced the small confines of their quarters.

"Not all of the brothers have deserted. There are still some who remain loyal to Jose." For just a moment his expression held defiance.

"Aye, and what kind of men are they, I ask you?" She did not wait for an answer. "They are men like him, Leon. Men too blind to see that this way of life is over."

"He has been good to us, *querida*. We are rich beyond measure because I chose to follow my cousin and he allowed it!"

His black eyes snapped with anger as he looked upon the woman he had lived with for over twenty years. Past her prime and pounds heavier than the comely señorita she had been when first she caught his eye as she hawked her wares in the marketplace of Madrid, she was still capable of igniting the flames of desire within him then dousing the heat of his ardor with earthy abandon.

Only when she played the shrew, as she was doing now, did he consider setting her aside. But he knew in his heart he could never do such a thing. Whatever the future might bring they would face it together.

"Rich we may be, you foolish man, but what good to us are chests of gold if we are dead?"

Ramona threw matted strands of coarse black hair over her shoulder, then stopped her pacing to fix Leon with a belligerent stare.

Her face softened as she sat down across from him and pulled his hands from his face holding them within her grasp.

"Can't you see that times have changed, Leon?" Her voice begged for understanding as did the pleading look in her ebony eyes.

"Since the Americans have taken over this area it is no longer a safe haven for us. They have driven out Laffite. We no longer have him to rely on for smuggling our goods into New Orleans. Our storehouses are filled with treasure that we have no means of marketing."

Seeing that she had gained his attention she took advantage of the opportunity to say more, hoping to convince him that they should leave with all speed.

"When first we came here Jose plundered only the vessels of Spain. I could understand this for he was unfairly treated by our countrymen. But now no ship sailing the waters of the Gulf is safe from attack. And what of the women he holds in the compound?"

Leon shifted uncomfortably.

"His ransom notes promise the prisoners will be returned unharmed if his demands are met. Lies! All lies!" she shrieked, standing again to move restlessly about the room like a caged animal.

"Those poor women are at the mercy of Jose and his murderous cutthroats, and mercy is one thing they know little of!"

It had always amused Leon the way Ramona set him apart from his cousin and the other members of the brotherhood as though he had never taken part in the vicious raids or cold-bloodedly wielded his sword against their hapless victims. True he had taken no part in despoiling their captives but for this he credited Ramona who never failed to welcome him home with such robust enthusiasm he had no need to look elsewhere for his pleasures.

Just the thought of her eager lovemaking aroused desire in the aging pirate and when Ramona passed within arm's reach, he grabbed her wrist and hauled her down upon his lap to nuzzle his chin in the musky hollow of her neck.

Her irritation swiftly dissolved into a need only he could fill as she felt his manhood thrusting up against her buttocks. But caressing his cheek she determined to try once more to make him see reason before giving herself up to her own carnal pleasures.

"Nanette Dubois. . . ." she whispered the name as her tongue darted in and out of his ear. "Her family will bring us much trouble for I doubt she can survive much more of your cousin's abuse."

"It is his obsession with the blonde woman that is making him crazy," he explained as his hand disappeared beneath her skirt to massage her inner thigh.

"Bah! Who knows such a woman even exists outside his demented mind!" She reached inside his shirt to finger the dark swirls of hair upon his chest.

"She exists. Never doubt it for I have seen her with my own eyes."

And when Leon took her on the dirt floor of the tiny hut, his thoughts were not of his mistress writhing shamelessly beneath him, but of a beautiful golden-haired goddess poised like one of the mythical Furies ready to take flight.

The days following her encounter with Lance Logan passed slowly for Rebecca. With her limited domestic skills, she found little to do but walk along the well-worn path beside the creek or stroll down the white sandy strip of beach stopping occasionally to study a pastel-colored shell left behind in the wake of a receding wave.

The mornings were warm and humid as the sun rose toward its zenith; the afternoons blistering hot with heavy storm clouds rolling in from the west to deluge the land with cooling showers of rain. Soft evening breezes brought a welcome respite from the heat of the day.

Rebecca was loathe to admit that there were any

redeeming qualities to alter her first opinion of this oppressive jungle, but in all fairness she had to concede that the sunsets which followed the cloudbursts were awe inspiring. Never had she seen such a kaleidoscope of changing colors as resplendent specters of gold, blue, and pink gradually faded to more subtle hues of honey, primrose, and hyacinth.

She was fascinated by the spindly-legged sandpipers who raced the waves to unearth coquinas burrowing beneath the wet sand and by the unwieldy pelicans as she watched them home in on a defenseless school of mackerel.

Life teemed all around her. Exotic fish splashed in the surf. Colorful birds flew overhead. Rabbits and field mice scuttled in and out of the tall rough-edged saw grass. Rebecca seemed to be the only creature among the animals, human or otherwise, who had nothing to do, and she quickly learned that time without purpose meant time to think.

Her thoughts vacillated between romantic dreams of what the future would hold for her when she returned to England and the all too real image of the huge empty manor house which awaited. And no matter in which direction her thoughts turned, they always came back to *that* kiss! Why couldn't she forget? Hadn't he told her it meant nothing? No, actually she had told him it meant nothing . . . but he had agreed!

She could still feel his warm, sensual lips pressed gently against hers. Her body had betrayed her with its willing heated response. And he had known it! Oh yes, he had known! For a few moments she was certain that he felt something, too.

His touch had been tender, his eyes soft and

searching. Then he had set her aside laughing at her shame. What was worse, she suspected he may also have been laughing at her naivety and ineptitude for she was confident that he had known many women. Lance Logan was an incorrigible bounder! No doubt about that!

He believed she lacked the fortitude it took to become a part of this vast unsettled territory. Well, so what? She was an English lady and she had never claimed to be anything else!

But ever since that moment when he had held her in his arms what confounded her to the point of restless days and sleepless nights was her stubborn determination to prove him wrong!

Chapter 10

Elizabeth still shared Rebecca's bedroom but Rebecca saw little of either twin during the day. They were forever off on a picnic or swimming in the warm undulating surf with Andrew, Rachel, and Davey. Not that they didn't invite her to accompany them, for Andrew and Rachel always sought her out telling her where they were going and enthusiastically urging her to join in their fun.

It was becoming more and more difficult to find a plausible excuse with which to beg off. And try as she might she could not justify her ungracious behavior even to herself.

She truly liked Rachel whose sweet affable nature endeared her to everyone. Edward and Elizabeth adored her for she was not only a willing listener interested in their incessant chatter but someone who could answer their endless questions with knowledge and wit as well.

That Andrew loved her was obvious and Rebecca expected to learn any day that he had asked Rachel to become his wife. Rebecca was genuinely happy for she felt that they were a perfectly suited couple and she knew that Mandy would approve Andrew's choice of a mother for their children. This in no way accounted for her low spirits.

"Damnation! I've got to rid myself of these blasted doldrums," she declared glumly as she sat hidden within the umbrella branches of a willow tree idly plucking the petals from a daisy.

Rebecca realized she was no longer alone when she heard a familiar gruff voice just beyond her hideaway.

"What am I to do with you?" Lance Logan demanded forcefully.

She shrank back against the trunk of the tree wondering how he could possibly see through its thick leafy boughs.

"And why must you do anything with me?" came a haughty feminine reply.

Rebecca wasn't aware that she held her breath until she expelled it with a sigh of relief. This was one time the man's anger was not directed at her. At least not yet as she realized the precariousness of her position concealed beneath the tree. She had no intention of eavesdropping on an argument between Lance and some unknown woman, yet to make her presence known might prove even more awkward. She tried to still her rapidly beating heart while wishing herself invisible.

"You aren't my keeper, Lance Logan!" The person with whom Lance argued was vehement in her denial. "Why can't you get that through your thick head?"

"I'm only trying to protect your foolish hide, Lona!" Lance shot back.

Lona? So that's who it is! Rebecca was surprised for she had never heard the gentle Indian girl raise her voice, but she was certainly raising it now . . . and to the formidable Lance Logan of all people.

She could not repress the smile that played across her lips. But the smile was wiped away in the next moment.

"You know how much I care about you." His words were soft and pleading now, tender like those of a lover, Rebecca thought crestfallen.

She felt herself flush feverishly then shiver as a chill swept through her body. What a simpleminded idiot she had been to imagine the man might have some feeling for her. Of course he loved the beautiful Indian maiden. They were two of a kind, hearty and rugged like this untamed land in which they lived.

If only she could be any place but here listening to their lover's quarrel. She bit her lower lip between her teeth hoping they would leave so that she could tuck her tail between her legs and slink back to the fort unseen.

"You have no right to care! My father gave you Little Dove, not me!" Lona's words came out fast and furious then hung in the sudden unearthly silence that permeated the air.

Rebecca carefully crawled on her hands and knees to a spot where she could peek through the thick green foliage. Just as her eyes focused on the two people standing less than a dozen feet from where she knelt, Lona gasped and hurled herself into Logan's arms.

"I'm so sorry," she wept against his shoulder. "I should never have said such a thing. Can you ever forgive me?" Her words came out in broken sobs as she

162

clung to the full-muscled army scout.

"It's all right, Lona," he soothed holding her close and smoothing her hair. "I understand and there's nothing to forgive."

"But there is. I should never have lashed out at you that way. It's just that I cannot bear to be locked within the walls of the fort."

Lance laughed holding her at arm's length so he could look down into her distraught face. "You're hardly a prisoner," he answered patiently. "I just don't want you to wander so far from the fort unescorted. Is that so much to ask?"

"And who should I invite to escort me?" she queried, a streak of mischief lighting her dark moisture-glazed eyes. "One of Lieutenant Kearny's sailors?"

Lance frowned then grinned crookedly, glad that she suffered no lasting ill-effects from her recent attack by Kearny's men.

"You may joke about it if you like. I'm just trying to make certain no one else has the last laugh."

"I know you are, Lance, and I do appreciate your concern," she returned leaning up to run her hand across his lean clean-shaven cheek. "I'll be careful. I promise."

He pulled her close again cupping her cheeks with his two powerful hands, his lips just inches from hers. Rebecca wanted to look away but her eyes remained glued on the figures before her. She felt as if she were watching a scene from a play, an unwilling audience to what was taking place on stage.

"Damn it! I keep seeing her lifeless body there in the woods. Raped! Beaten to death! No one should have to die like that! No one!"

With his outburst Lance released Lona and turned away rubbing his hand across his eyes as if he could obliterate the nightmare that refused to go away.

Rebecca knew instinctively that he was talking about Little Dove. She now knew how she had died. The anguish in Lance Logan's voice evidenced the all-consuming guilt that was growing like a cancer within him. She was unaware of the tears trickling down her cheeks as she looked on helplessly wanting to ease his pain but sure in her own mind that it was the comfort of the woman standing at his side that he most desired.

"Never forget, Lona, the fiends that killed your sister are still out there someplace." Lance scanned the impenetrable line of trees beyond the brook. "And until I find them, no woman is safe away from the protection of the fort."

His words echoed in Rebecca's ears like a promise. "Until I find them. . . ." She shuddered to think what Lance, powered by his inexorable hatred, would do to the person or persons responsible for the ruthless murder of Little Dove.

"It wasn't my brother," Lona spoke defiantly, daring anyone to dispute her.

"Of course it wasn't," Lance readily agreed. "Chikiki wanted to marry Little Dove to fulfill the ancient laws of the tribe. He would have done anything within his power to get her, but I know he would never have done her harm."

Rebecca remembered the story Lance had told her, a tale of incest which required the Indian chief and his sister to marry. That such a thing could be allowed in this age of enlightenment was inconceivable.

"I know Chikiki was not responsible for the crimes against Little Dove," Lance repeated gravely. "But accept the fact that you are now the only means left by which he can carry out the dictates of the prophets. And he's close by, Lona. I can feel it!" The intensity with which he spoke sent chills down Rebecca's spine.

"I feel it, too." Lona shivered glancing nervously behind her, then straightening to give him an impish grin. "I won't do anything foolish, Lance, for I have come to like the comforts of the white man's world."

Their shared laughter as they turned back along the trail on which they had come piqued Rebecca. Her heart felt weighted beneath her breast and fleetingly it crossed her mind that she had just lost something she never had. She shook her head at such a silly notion. After all, what was Lance Logan to her?

It was just another example of how irrationally her mind seemed to be working lately. But as she moved from the shelter of the willow tree she found it impossible to ignore the nagging premonition that something catastropic was about to happen ... something that would change all of their lives.

The next morning Rebecca entered the cheery kitchen to find Lona beating eggs in a large wooden bowl while Rachel sliced generous slabs of ham onto a platter. She poured herself a steaming cup of coffee and sat down at the table.

She felt tired and irritable blaming Logan for yet another night spent tossing and turning. How she longed to wipe the man from her mind, but as soon as she closed her eyes he was there to haunt her with memories of that forbidden kiss. His quicksilver eyes stole into her dreams and she awakened damp with perspiration, her legs drawn up in a fetal position as if to protect her body from an invasion she could not fathom.

"Where is Mary?" she asked coming out of her stupor for the colonel's wife was always in the midst of the hustle and bustle that went into preparing the substantial breakfast her husband, like all the men at the fort, seemed to require.

"She must have overslept," Lona answered frowning slightly for she knew better than any how unlikely that would be.

The three women turned toward the door as they heard a girlish giggle coming from the other side. The door swung open and George and Mary Brooke entered. George had his arm draped lightly over his wife's shoulders and was grinning from ear to ear while Mary's smile could only be described as radiant.

"Well, don't you two look like cats that ate pigeons?" Lona observed as she continued to whip the eggs briskly.

"Good morning, ladies," George beamed, "and the expression, my dear, is 'swallowed the canary' not 'ate the pigeons,'" he corrected good humoredly, tweaking Lona's cheek as he passed her heading toward the back door.

The Indian girl stared after him wondering if the very proper colonel had taken leave of his senses.

"Well," she said, "are you going to tell us what makes you so smug and him," she motioned in the direction George had taken, "so very pleased with himself?"

Mary opened her mouth but no words came out. Her eyes held a bemused expression.

Finally she uttered, "I . . . I'm going to have a baby."

Her voice was filled with wonder as she lovingly laid a hand over her stomach.

With a squeal of delight both Rachel and Lona ran to hug Mary, dancing around with joy-filled elation while Rebecca stood watching but taking no part in the merriment.

"Rebecca?" Mary questioned. "Aren't you happy for me . . . for us?" she corrected not understanding the other's indifference.

Rebecca, realizing that her feelings about the news would hardly be appreciated, rose from her chair forcing a smile and embraced Mary warmly.

"Of course I'm pleased for you and the colonel."

But Mary could sense Rebecca's reserve. She drew back to study her more closely.

"George and I have waited so long for this child. It seems a miracle that the whole world should be celebrating. What is it that upsets you?"

"I'm sorry, Mary. But the truth is I don't understand why anyone would want to bear a child in a godforsaken place like this!" she exclaimed.

Rebecca was immediately ashamed of herself. It was none of her business and she would never intentionally hurt her kindhearted hostess. The other two women were shocked speechless by her outburst and she would have given much to recall her words.

"Never believe God has forsaken us here, for he hovers quite close. His Spirit abounds in this great land reaching out to protect his creations. Without His acquiescence this fort would be no more than a dream," Mary smiled as she replied.

Rebecca lowered her eyes as Mary continued.

"Where better could one bring new life into the

world than in this fresh unspoiled wonderland. The sons and daughters of the Florida territory will grow up strong and independent unhampered by obligations to tread in the footsteps of their forebears. They will charter their own course and it will be something to see!"

Rebecca wasn't sure when she had raised her head during the woman's discourse but she found herself staring into Mary's ginger brown eyes. They were so filled with promise for the future that she too became caught up in hopeful anticipation.

The approach of horsemen and the commotion which ensued brought an end to their conversation as they rushed out onto the porch to welcome their visitors. Rebecca noticed how quickly Mary's and Lona's smiles faded to grim disappointment.

"It's Martin and Brady. I hope Lance can keep a rein on his temper," Lona said to no one in particular.

Rebecca studied the two men curiously as they drew to a halt outside the supply depot. That they were rough-hewn she could see, but it was a different kind of roughness than the unequivocally masculine description she applied to Logan. There was something sinister and furtive in their expressions that made her feel vulnerable.

Colonel Brooke, with the scowling army scout at his side, greeted the visitors as they dismounted.

"Martin? Brady? What brings you to the fort?" His voice was neutral, neither friendly nor hostile, merely questioning.

"We're in need of some supplies, Colonel. Just thought we'd trade a few skins for some of those staples a man can't live without."

168

It was the one called Martin who answered and though he spoke to the Commander, Rebecca was alarmed to see how his beady black eyes darted toward Lona. He was tall and lean with the narrow, skulking face of a rodent. His sallow skin bore deep disfiguring pock marks and his body reeked of many days' accumulation of sweat and dirt.

"Get what you need and get out," Lance growled in a voice as hard as granite. His eyes were the cold gray color of gunmetal and Rebecca wondered what Martin had done to earn such undisguised hatred.

"Now wait just a minute, Logan. Who do you think you are giving orders around here?" It was the short fat man called Brady who questioned the authority of the angry mountainous man towering over him.

He took off his mangy beaver hat and swatted it against one filthy pant leg causing a cloud of dust to rise. Rebecca suppressed a giggle when she saw that he was completely without hair on the top of his head but had allowed the remaining fringe along the sides and back to grow well past his shoulders stringing down like dark greasy filament.

He presented a comical figure when seen in the midst of a crowd but she would not wish to be caught one-on-one with the balding buffoon.

"I'm the man who's going to kick your butt to hell and back if you don't get what you came for in a hurry and head back to whatever stinking hole you crawled out of!" The inflection of Logan's words was like tempered steel and served to quell Brady's bravado. But his equally foul-smelling sidekick was not yet ready to buckle under.

"Back off, Logan! You got no call giving us orders!

169

We've as much right as any other white man to trade here at the fort!"

With hands braced defiantly on his hips, Martin let loose an ugly tobacco-brown stream of juice that splattered in the dirt just inches from Logan's right foot. Rebecca had to give the man his due for though Martin stood a head taller than his stocky little friend, the massive bulk of Lance Logan left no doubt in her mind as to who would be the winner should their war of words lead to fisticuffs.

Lance started forward, his jaw clenched in rage.

"Hold on, Logan!" Colonel Brooke issued the command as he grabbed Lance's arm.

Lance jerked free but stayed where he was, the muscles in his chiseled face contorting with the effort to control his fury.

George Brooke had no more liking for the two unsavory characters than Lance did and he was equally certain that Martin and Brady were up to their dirt-encrused ears in illegal gun-trading with the renegades, but he had no proof. And without proof he could not allow one of his men to beat the offensive bastards to a pulp, though it went against the grain to see the villains go unpunished.

"Get what you came for and make it quick, boys, or I might hear nature calling and be forced to excuse myself for a short time," he warned frowning toward the women gathered on the porch. Had they remained inside the house he might not have been so anxious to protect the low-life scum from Logan's wrath.

As the disreputable pair approached the entrance to the dark windowless storehouse where the supplies were kept, Brady was careful to keep his partner between himself and Lance while Martin strode cockily past the glaring man as if daring him to object.

The four women breathed a sigh of relief and reentered the house to continue their preparations for breakfast while Lance, George, and a handful of soldiers waited impatiently for the two men to conclude their trading.

They emerged a short time later with heavy sacks of flour, salt, coffee, and meal.

"If that's all you need we'll bid you good day, *gentlemen*," George said brusquely.

"Reckon we got all we came for, Colonel, unless you'd consider trading that little Indian gal for some prime bear skins. Be interesting to see which keeps a man warmer on a cold night!" Martin guffawed showing stained yellow teeth.

Before he could wipe the smirk off his face he was flat on his back seeing stars that weren't there. Lance reached down grabbing the front of his shirt and hauled him roughly to his feet then threw him toward his horse.

"Get the hell out of here you son of a bitch before I cut off your tongue and a few other parts I find offensive!"

With Lance's threat hanging in the air Martin struggled into the saddle of his nervous mount, then turned to glower maliciously. "I'll get you for this, Logan. And when I'm through with you I'll be back for that half-breed *puta*," he snarled viciously as he wheeled his horse around and beat a path toward the gate leaving Brady to choke on his dust.

* * *

171

Later that day Rachel, Rebecca and Mary sat in the shade beneath the outstretched arms of the giant oak. Mary held a metal pot on her lap, her fingers dexterously removing the shells from young spring peas as she stared off into space dreaming the dreams of an expectant mother. Rachel, too, seemed in a world of her own and Rebecca knew she was thinking of Andrew who was among the small patrol of men following Martin and Brady to make certain they did not stop until they were well away from the fort.

Try as she might, Rebecca could not seem to conjure up a single daydream worthy of note. Her mind still drew a blank when she tried to call forth a visual image of William which was probably just as well. At least she wasn't seeing him dripping wet and ready to kill as he rode away spouting ultimatums after their boating misadventure. But she couldn't understand why she thought of him less and less frequently as each day passed.

"Spring! What a wonderful time of the year!" Mary enthused looking up at the cloudless blue sky visible through the thick leafy branches.

Rachel giggled, "Spoken like a mother-to-be. Perhaps, Rebecca, we should write down such a profound observation lest it be lost for all time."

Rebecca dimpled joining in the lighthearted laughter. She liked these two women who had seemed so foreign in the beginning.

"Call me silly if you like, but I happen to think life is rather grand right now," Mary retorted good humoredly.

"And well you should," Rachel replied. "But Lona was right. You do look smug sitting there with your lap

172

full of peas. I just couldn't resist teasing. What will you do in a few months when you have no lap on which to hold a pot?"

"Why I'll just let Rebecca do the shelling," she answered airily.

The three women broke up in laughter at the unlikely picture of Rebecca doing anything so domestic. Rebecca started to remind them that she would be back in England by then but decided to let it go. After all they were only joking.

But Mary misunderstood her changing expression. "Don't worry, honey. Peas will be out of season in a few weeks."

She was so serious in her reassurance Rebecca and Rachel once again dissolved in mirth.

As the army patrol returned through the gates of Fort Brooke, Lance Logan looked toward where the women were sitting and felt a lump lodge in his throat as his attention focused on Rebecca doubled over in laughter. She looked as fragile as a china doll and just as perfectly put together in her crisp yellow cotton dress patterned with golden jonquils and bright green leaves. One could mistake her for a happy carefree child, he thought, then changed his mind as he observed her low form-fitted bodice.

Lance, George, Andrew and Justin separated their mounts from those headed toward the stables and rode over to join the women. George dismounted and stepped to Mary's side leaning down to give her a gentle possessive hug.

"Well, ladies, you seem in fine fettle this afternoon. Care to share the joke? A little humor would not go amiss about now," he smiled amicably.

"Female witticism, darling," Mary explained. "I'm sure you men would find our source of merriment quite absurd."

George cocked a blond eyebrow at his sparkling wife, equally certain he would find the source of their amusement most entertaining.

Rebecca regarded Justin Wentworth sitting astride his horse hunched forward holding the reins loosely in his hands while his arms rested upon the saddle horn. He had adapted to the ways of the western world with remarkable alacrity. No one would believe the self-confident young man wearing the uniform of the American Army was, in fact, a newly arrived English aristocrat. She wondered how William would fare in this rugged land but did not pursue the thought.

"And how have you spent the afternoon while I've been away, love?" Andrew asked as he dismounted and came to stand behind Rachel.

Rachel leaned her head back and batted her thick black lashes in his direction. "Ah, my knight! I have spent the hours pining away longing for your return."

"I noticed your wretchedness immediately upon my arrival." Andrew couldn't resist planting a quick kiss on her delectably sensuous lips which brought a blush to Rachel's cheeks and a chuckle from those surrounding them.

Rebecca stole a look at Lance still mounted upon his majestic black stallion then caught her breath in wonder as she realized he was smiling at her. Not the cynical you-don't-belong-here kind of smile she had come to expect but a warm genuine smile that was mirrored in his smoke-gray eyes.

She felt herself responding as white-hot flames coursed through her, causing every nerve in her body to tingle with such blazing emotion she wondered why no one else seemed aware that she was on fire. She willed him to look away, to break the spell he was casting over her. But he didn't. For what seemed an eternity he held her clear emerald eyes locked with his, finally releasing her to let his gaze travel the length of her body then return to rest languidly on her heaving breasts. When their eyes met again the derisive expression was back in place making his ruggedly handsome face seem more familiar but disappointingly out of reach.

Rebecca glared, grinding her teeth as the flames that had threatened to consume her died and turned to ashes. Only in her eyes did golden sparks remain to leap about like dancing devils as her foot tapped furiously beneath her skirts.

Damnation! Why do I always behave like a moonstruck featherbrain around the big oaf? she scolded herself silently. *Will I never learn?* Why, for a moment, she had been fool enough to believe the blighter was actually glad to see her? She deserved his scorn for being such a goose. But even now she longed to see some sign of tenderness on his face that would ease the yawning emptiness she felt inside.

Instead his words were harsh with urgency. "Where is Lona?"

Rebecca felt as if the wind had been knocked out of her. To allow herself to believe even for a split second that Lance Logan cared about her was the height of folly.

Mary answered surprised by his curtness, "She

probably went for a walk. You know how she dislikes being cooped up in the stockade."

Without another word he jerked his horse around preparing to ride out in search of the missing girl only to draw up short as Lona appeared walking with her usual easy grace in their direction, Davey and the twins at her side.

As soon as Edward and Elizabeth saw that their father had returned, they broke into a run eager to share their latest discoveries. Davey and Lona approached at a more leisurely pace. If the Indian maiden was aware of the harried look on the face of the man staring down at her, she gave no indication.

"Where have you been?" Lance barked out sharply, and only then did Lona give him more than a brief glance.

She responded with both confusion and annoyance but no sign of fear which earned her Rebecca's admiration. Rebecca found herself thoroughly intimidated while simply standing on the sidelines of the confrontation.

"I went for a walk with the children. I sought you out to gain permission but you were nowhere to be found," Lona's voice fairly dripped with sarcasm.

Rebecca felt the corners of her mouth lift as Logan fought to control his temper, seeming suddenly to remember that they were not alone.

"We will talk of this later," he stated firmly, his expression daring the young woman to defy him.

But defy him she did. And quite commendably to Rebecca's way of thinking!

"We have already talked! The subject is now closed! Final! The end! *Comprende, mi hermano?*"

Lance knew better than to argue for lapsing into her mother's native tongue was evidence that Lona had tolerated all the high-handedness she would allow. He shrugged his wide shoulders accepting temporary defeat. But he promised himself that one way or another he would make the stubborn girl understand the danger she courted by venturing out alone.

Chapter 11

"Riders approaching!" came the shout of a sentry standing guard along the northeast wall.

The men looked questioningly at one another recognizing the pounding hoofbeats of perhaps a dozen horses.

"Soldiers?" George wondered aloud.

"Most anyone would be more welcome than our last visitors," Mary volunteered, linking arms with her husband as they stood before the fort's open gates.

As the noise of the riders grew louder Lance stepped in front of Rebecca so that she had to lean around him to see. As she started to move to his side a broad arm shot out to stay her, a protective gesture that took her completely by surprise.

She looked up into Logan's firmly set face but he didn't spare her a glance, his attention centered on the unknown horsemen coming ever closer.

The soldiers rode through the gates in a flurry of dust then pulled up before the small group of watchers.

Andrew Townsend immediately stepped forward.

"Sergeant Reed," he greeted. "What are you fellows doing so far from Fort King?"

"Townsend," the burly sergeant acknowledged, switching a stubby cigar from one side of his wide mouth to the other. He squinted his eyes as he blew out a puff of smoke. "Been trackin' redskins. Lost 'em when they took to the swamp 'bout twenty miles north."

Rebecca stared disbelievingly as the cigar again changed sides in the man's mouth while both of his hands remained folded across the saddle horn.

"So close. Decided to drop in." Having explained his unexpected appearance to his satisfaction, Reed reached out to shake the hand Colonel Brooke extended while Rebecca concluded that the dour sergeant was a man of few words.

As George introduced his wife and friends, Rebecca eyed the young soldier at Reed's side. He was dressed like the other men in the party and had obviously ridden just as long and hard for his uniform was powdered with dust and his boots were caked with dried mud. But there was something different about him, something Rebecca could not quite put her finger on. The word "soft" came to mind, but then again that wasn't exactly right for he seemed to equal the others in stature and stamina. Serenity! That was what Rebecca saw in the soldier's face that set him apart. There was a gentle peace about him that seemed out of place in this naked, savage land.

When George finished acquainting the sergeant with those present, he stood waiting for the patrol leader to do likewise.

Reed nodded his head in the general direction of the

man at his side. "Marsh," he grunted as Rebecca, paying little heed to the formalities, watched him do the cigar trick yet again. "New recruit. Shouldn't be here," he grumbled clamping his teeth down hard on the butt end of the smoking cylinder.

"Robert Marsh, sir," volunteered the recipient of the sergeant's scowling countenance. "I've only recently been assigned to Fort King and I wanted to see more of the territory, so against his better judgment the sergeant allowed me to tag along."

His warm smile was infectious. "I'm afraid Sergeant Reed doesn't believe a chaplain can pull his weight on the trail."

"Chaplain! You mean to say that you're a preacher?" It was Andrew who spoke out with more than a little excitement threading his voice.

Robert Marsh laughed heartily.

"Soldiers don't sit still for no preachin'," Reed interjected disgustedly.

"Unfortunately, that is so," Robert agreed. Then he turned toward Andrew with a grin. "But I can give their souls a real nice ceremony when they go to meet their Maker."

"Never mind the funerals," Andrew interjected, hardly daring to ask the question. "What about weddings?" He rushed on too impatient to wait for a reply. "Are you a real minister . . . legal, I mean? One that can marry people?"

"Newly, but duly ordained," Marsh assured glancing around at the ladies wondering which of them had won the heart of the boyishly exuberant frontiersman. His eyes rested first on Rebecca standing with her mouth agape, but the stunned look in her wide green eyes

180

seemed at variance with that of a woman who had just been given the opportunity to marry the man of her dreams.

Then he looked at Rachel Jordan. There was no mistaking the love on her face as she smiled, not at Andrew, but down upon the two red-haired children standing at her side, each a small replica of the man before him.

"Am I to assume you wish a wedding performed, sir?" Robert Marsh asked teasingly.

Mary Brooke took Andrew by the arm and turned him to face her. "Perhaps," she stated firmly, "the young lady in question might have something to say in the matter."

Andrew's expression swiftly changed from joyful anticipation to trepidation as he realized he had yet to ask Rachel formally to become his wife. What an idiot he had been to plunge ahead with his plans before he had discussed the matter with his intended. He held his breath certain that his heart had ceased to beat in his chest as he looked at the only woman who could fill the void in his life.

"Indeed, I have something to say," Rachel replied shyly. Her heart was in her eyes leaving no doubt as to the depth of her love. "Yes," came her soft response.

Andrew remained motionless for a long moment fastening his gaze on the calm beauty who belonged to no one but him. Then he let out a mighty whoop that could be heard halfway to Fort King as he rushed to gather Rachel, Edward and Elizabeth in a tight embrace. *His family.* He knew that he had to be the luckiest man alive as the others offered their congratulations and best wishes.

"No time! Can't stay!"

Everyone froze in place then glared up at the stern-faced sergeant. Andrew's look was murderous. No way was this cryptic son of a bitch going to thwart his chance for happiness.

Before he could take action, Mary stepped forward. "We understand completely, Sergeant," she acceded graciously giving the startled soldier her most winning smile. "Why, heavens! You and your men have the grave responsibility of seeking out those who threaten the safety of every settler in Florida. How could we be so selfish as to detain you from your duties for something so inconsequential as a wedding?"

She scoffed at such a preposterous idea while Reed's chest swelled visibly.

"Why don't you come up on the porch out of the sun while the horses rest a spell," Mary cajoled. "Surely you have time for a cold glass of lemonade and maybe a piece of fresh fruit pie."

All eyes followed the two as Mary led the bemused sergeant toward the house. George and Lance looked at each other speculatively.

"Thirty minutes," George predicted.

"Five dollars says it will only take her fifteen," Lance countered.

"You're on!"

With that both men turned to clap a still fuming Andrew on the back.

The wedding took place the next evening. The rapid, efficient manner in which Mary Brooke supervised the preparations down to the most minute detail had Rebecca's head swimming.

All day the kitchen was filled with bustling activity.

182

For hours Rachel had stood on a small wooden stool clad in a lustrous full-skirted ballgown of deep indigo blue which enhanced her sapphire eyes making them glimmer like the purest of gems.

The dress was one Mary had worn the night she attended President Monroe's inaugural celebration; the night she was introduced to the handsome army officer, George Brooke. She knew there would be no occasion to wear it at the fort, but she could not bear to leave it behind.

Now pushing sentiment aside as she pinned and stitched, altering the lovely creation to fit Rachel's slimmer figure, she was only too pleased to know that the dress would be put to use for another happy celebration.

Mary reminded Rebecca of a sandpiper darting back and forth; one minute poking pins into poor Rachel who remained stoic and uncomplaining; the next moment running to peek at some delicious smelling concoction baking in the oven.

Before long the heat in the kitchen was sweltering. Eventually Rebecca had stuffed her damp handkerchief into her apron pocket employing a dish towel to mop the perspiration from her brow. But she was proud of the small contribution she had made peeling vegetables, turning the spit where succulent chunks of beef roasted, and stirring the numerous pots set to simmer. It had actually been fun, she thought many hours later, as she soaked in the heavy metal bathtub which had taken two soldiers to carry to her bedroom.

She closed her eyes thinking back to when they had all gathered at the table the previous night. It was much like the first dinner she had shared with the Brookes except that a glowing Rachel Jordan sat in Captain Higgins's place. And, thankfully, there had been no interruption by the demented Ezra Holcomb.

Amid much laughter and lighthearted banter they had lifted their goblets of wine to toast the engaged couple. During the course of the meal, Lance Logan suggested that the soon-to-be newlyweds make use of his cabin until they could see to building one of their own. It would be a wedding present, he insisted, adding that he and Davey would be quite comfortable in the barracks where the soldiers slept.

Rebecca had seen the Logans' home, a sturdy log structure situated in a clearing on the bank of the creek not too far from the fort, but outside its restrictive enclosure. It was a picturesque setting. A perfect place for lovers. But it was not Rachel and Andrew she envisioned in the secluded honeymoon retreat. Her vivid imagination took flight reconstructing scenes of Lance and his beautiful "gift" clutched in each other's arms upon a soft featherbed. They were nestled warmly beneath a bright-colored blanket much like the ones she had seen the Calusa women weaving on their looms.

The thought made Rebecca go cold inside for she still found it impossible to accept the practice of rewarding a man's deeds with the life of another human being. But she knew her chilled emotions were not brought on by her repugnance to what she considered the ultimate in heathen customs. It was knowing that within the walls of the small cabin Lance Logan had slept with Little Dove. He had caressed her with his big callused hands. Little Dove had known Lance intimately as Rebecca had never known a man, and Lance had planted a seed within the womb of his Indian mistress. It resulted in the creation of the beautiful child seated across from her.

Had Lance truly loved her? He must have, for she had heard the anguish in his voice when he spoke of Little Dove? She remembered, too, his vow to avenge her brutal murder.

Knowledge of the depth of his feelings for the woman who had been taken from him so cruelly caused such an ache in the pit of Rebecca's stomach that the food on her plate lost its appeal. She became afraid she might humiliate herself by losing what she had already eaten. Only by sheer determination had she been able to remain at the table pretending a cheerfulness she did not feel.

Edward, ever alert to the possibility of new adventures, had pounced on the idea of sleeping in the barracks with Davey and his father. Logan had assured Andrew that he would be no bother after which Edward could scarcely remain in his seat until the meal was over. Only his father's stern reprimand prevented him from rushing to pack his belongings and to move at once.

It was not difficult for Rebecca to convince the happy couple that Elizabeth should continue to share her room temporarily. In truth she was relieved that she would have her niece's companionship for a little while longer.

As Rachel Jordan promised to love, honor, and obey Andrew Townsend until death did them part, Rebecca allowed her attention to wander. Her sea-green eyes riveted around the large living area taking in the garlands of greenery strung along each wall in loops

185

attached to the ceiling. Vases and bowls of fresh spring flowers in every conceivable color adorned the decorative tables scattered about while two tall white candles in gleaming silver holders flanked the pine boughs lining the mantel.

The glittering opulence of the London ballrooms which she had once thought impressive now seemed gaudy and pretentious when compared to this simple rustic dwelling where people gathered together because they truly cared about one another.

Rebecca couldn't say exactly when the differences between the two worlds had separated themselves so clearly in her mind. But gradually during the past twenty-four hours, she had come to realize that the effort these people had put forth to make tonight a joyful occasion for Rachel and Andrew was done out of love. It was done unselfishly and with their whole hearts.

How artificial and insincere the members of the *ton* appeared in retrospect as she recalled the feigned gaiety of resplendent soirees. Jealous women competed for attention by recounting spiteful tales about one another while pompous powdered gentlemen judged a man's worth by the number of fancy folds in his cravat.

She watched George and Mary standing together smiling as the ceremony continued. The colonel hugged his wife closely against his side. Earlier George had proudly predicted that his son would be the first white child born in the area. Rebecca secretly thought he was taking an inordinate amount of credit for the accomplishment. One would think his wife was but a witness to the historic event. However, since Mary seemed content to allow her husband to exaggerate his role in propagating the territory, she decided to keep her own counsel.

Elizabeth stood beside Rachel holding a nosegay of wildflowers clutched in her hands while Edward, standing next to his father, scuffed his booted feet and shifted his weight from one leg to the other. He obviously found the proceedings tedious in the extreme.

As Rebecca wiped a tear from her eye, clearly accepting the fact that the children were no longer her responsibility, the future loomed empty before her. Empty without the twins and so very, very quiet. She felt incredibly lonely in spite of the friendship of the people around her. She wondered what it would be like to be one with these rugged Americans whose vitality and lust for life she grudgingly admitted she had come to admire.

Lance had not taken his eyes off Rebecca since Robert Marsh had begun the service which would unite Andrew and Rachel in holy matrimony. He was fascinated by the changing emotions that played across her lovely face, enchanted by the way each delicate, perfect feature revealed the workings of her mind.

He was bewitched by her mercurial green eyes as he watched flickering bits of amber infuse with rich deep-colored emerald, thick lashed eyes first wide with wonder then somber and misty. He suppressed a grin as her dainty little nose wrinkled, twitched, and finally sniffed softly. Her expressive rose-tinted mouth made his loins ache with need. He remembered the taste of her sweet sensuous lips and wished he had prolonged that one moment when he had held her willingly in his arms.

She reminded him of a fairy princess in her iridescent gown, a rainbow of colors and ever-changing hues brought to life by the twinkling light of the candles. Her golden hair rose in a crown of curls atop her head. She needed only a magic wand to make the alluring picture complete.

As he gazed upon the creamy white swell of Rebecca's breasts rising above the lace-edged bodice of her gown, he became aware of her rapid breathing. He raised his eyes to meet hers. Only then did he realize his own breath was coming in a similar quick, irregular fashion. For a moment as they stared at one another from across the room he was sure his heart had stopped beating. The spell was broken as Robert Marsh solemnly intoned, "I now pronounce you man and wife."

The wedding feast was held outside beneath the stars. Everyone at the fort was invited to join in the celebration. It was a boisterous group made up of soldiers from both Fort Brooke and Fort King, Kearny's sailors, and the four greatly outnumbered women. The Indians preferred to ignore the noisy festivities.

The mounds of food spread upon several long cloth covered tables was quickly devoured along with a good amount of wine and ale. And when one soldier whipped out a harmonica from his pocket and began to play, others joined in with banjos and guitars. A drum beat was added when an inventive young sailor turned over an empty wooden bowl and began tapping out a rhythm with a pair of large serving spoons. The result was surprisingly melodious and Rebecca found herself smiling and clapping in time to the music.

But not for long. Soon she was swept up by a high-spirited soldier who whirled her in circles then right into the eagerly awaiting arms of one of his comrades. Rebecca laughed uninhibitedly as she saw Mary swirling among the throng, trying to maintain her balance while avoiding having her toes trounced upon by her husband. Justin and Lona circled near, nodded gaily, then spun away amid the foot-stomping on-lookers. Even Edward and Elizabeth joined hands and frolicked about doing their own interpretation of the dance.

Rebecca lost count of her partners. She only knew that she was having a thoroughly wonderful time twirling lightheartedly and carefree from one pair of arms to another. It was fortunate that there always seemed to be someone to catch her for she felt too dizzy to stand alone. But she didn't care. Tonight she would ignore her gloomy forbodings. She was young and full of life. The future could take care of itself. For now she wished only that the music could go on forever.

She closed her eyes as yet another dancer took the lead, but this time something was different. The strong arm encircling her waist tightened, pulling her possessively against a rock solid chest. As they moved together the music faded into the distance until the chirping of crickets became the orchestra accompanying the couple lost among the shadows.

Rebecca knew who held her for she had been in his unyielding grasp once before. They stood still now as she clutched his powerful arms and felt the muscles ripple beneath her touch. She fought to clear her head but she was no longer certain what caused her giddiness. It was too dark to see his eyes but she could feel the heat of his desire, and she knew Lance was going to kiss her.

Time stood still as his warm lips covered hers gently at first, then fiercely, hungrily, as though he intended to devour her mouth. His tongue forced its way between her teeth to mate and become one with hers. As her body melted against him, his long arms clasped her buttocks drawing her closer still.

Rebecca felt the heat begin at her toes where they curled inside her soft slippers. The flames quickly ignited spreading upward to center in a burning coil at the juncture where her thighs met. Their bodies were molded together in a fervid embrace as Logan's tongue performed an erotic dance. It thrust then withdrew until Rebecca knew her throbbing heart would burst from the intoxicating sensations he was creating within her.

Her body arched against her tormenter as her arms lifted to circle his neck. As he cupped one full breast, his thumb brushed the hard peaked nipple. Rebecca experienced a need so intense, so new to her, she could not identify what it was her body craved. But she longed for something that would put out the fire threatening to consume her.

Lance was stunned by the passion he had unleashed within Rebecca. Never would he have suspected that the prim and proper young Englishwoman was capable of returning his embrace so enthusiastically. The old adage came to mind that one should never judge a book by its cover. At the same time in some shaded corner of his brain reason tried briefly to assert itself. *What the hell do you think you are doing?* a small voice questioned. But how in God's name could a man be expected to think rationally when he was being ravished by an angel whose hair smelled as fragrant as the flowers in springtime and whose lips tasted as sweet as honey fresh from the comb?

"Ah, so sweet," he murmured against her ear, one hand tracing the length of her spine while the other continued to tenderly knead her breast.

Rebecca felt as if she were being swept out to sea, drowning beneath waves of pleasure, lashed by a storm of emotions she could not control. She begged silently for Lance to cease his assault on her oversensitive body even as she longed for him to fulfill the aching need that was driving her insane. She could feel the evidence of his desire as his hardened manhood pressed against her stomach and his lips once again claimed hers. She knew they must end this madness before it was too late, but her traitorous body was responding with a will of its own.

Much to her chagrin it was once again Logan who summoned the necessary restraint to bring her out of her dream world and back to reality just as he had during their encounter on the beach. As he released her and took a step backward she wondered if his boundless self-control was an indication that he found her lacking in feminine appeal. It was very confusing the way he seemed attracted one minute, repelled the next.

"Correct me if I'm wrong, but it would appear her Ladyship found some pleasure in our provincial merrymaking."

Logan's voice was husky and Rebecca wished it weren't so dark where they stood. If she could see his eyes she could more clearly judge his mood.

Assuming from their past confrontations that he was being sarcastic, she replied sharply, "Don't call me that!"

"And why not, may I ask? Having earned the title, are you ashamed to wear it?"

Certain now that Lance was mocking her, she could not hide her irritation, annoyed as much with her own lack of discipline in curbing her physical responses as with the fact that what had occurred between them seemed to mean nothing to the cold-hearted rogue.

"No matter in what context you use the term 'lady,' it seems I have forfeited the right to be addressed as such by allowing myself to be mauled by a conscienceless barbarian without so much as mounting a defensive!"

"Spoken like a trooper," Logan observed, his deep rumbling laughter further infuriating her.

"I find nothing humorous in being made to look the fool," she retorted fighting down the urge to cry.

"You are no fool, Rebecca, and you could never be less than a lady."

She blinked back her tears as she heard the sincerity in his voice with no hint of ridicule. But his sudden turnabout from teasing banter to serious affirmation tended merely to confound her already muddled emotions.

"Come," he said quietly, groping in the dark for her hand. "We'd best be getting back to the others before we are missed."

Chapter 12

Jose Gaspar bolted upright on the cot, black eyes wide with terror, one hand immediately clutching his throat. It was the dream again, the recurring nightmare that had plagued him for months.

"The blasted infidels will not hang Gaspar!" he vowed as he rose hurriedly from the damp, sweat-soaked mattress and rushed to the door.

He clumsily unloosened the strap that closed off entry to the thatched hut and pushed it aside, stepping out into the starry night where he breathed deeply of the balmy, salt-tinged air. He could still feel the rope tightening around his neck cutting off his air to choke the very life from him.

"No! It will not end that way!" he ranted into the darkness.

"It is Leon and his bitch, Ramona, that fill my head with doubts," he declared looking around at the sleeping village.

This was his empire where he alone ruled. He had built his stronghold amid the vermin-infested mud flats where none but the savages dared to intrude. For years he had been left alone, free to revenge himself against a despotic Spanish government that had forced him to abandon a promising military career. He was rich beyond his wildest expectations, but what good did his caskets of gold and jewels do him when his markets had been cut off by those usurping, upstart Americans?

The long arm of the Spanish tyrants had stretched across an ocean to thwart him once again, he thought, bemoaning the fates that would allow such a thing.

Until a few years ago, he had wreaked his vengeance by plundering the ships of his homeland without thought of retribution. With the help of his friend and ally, Jean Laffite, he had sold his ill-gotten goods, both human and otherwise, for a healthy profit in New Orleans. But as if to spite his efforts, Spain had had the gall to sell the Florida territory to the United States and Laffite had been driven from the area. As if that wasn't enough, the country's new young navy seemed bent on ridding the Gulf of every remaining pirate that sailed its waters.

Unconsciously Gaspar rubbed the weathered skin around his neck and sighed as he looked down the hard-packed dirt road lined by fifty or more identical thatched huts. Many were deserted now that the weaker of the brethren had taken their shares of the treasure and fled to safer shores.

Perhaps this time Leon was right and they should follow suit, he considered as his gaze focused on the three warehouses where his booty was stored then traveled out along the dock made of palm trunks to where the *Dona Rosalia* rocked serenely upon the water. He was a wealthy man. He could sail to the Isle of Pine where no one would trouble him and he could live out his days in peace and luxury. The idea seemed suddenly not so untenable for, in truth, he was tired and the dream was making him fearful.

"Yes," he decided, as he watched the light of the moon illuminate the white foam left along the beach's edge by the gently receding waves. His eyes narrowed as his thoughts turned inward. "Yes," he repeated. He would leave this refuge and seek another safe haven thus defying all who sought to destroy him. But he would not go alone.

He laughed mirthlessly as a sinister plan took shape in his mind. One final prize would be his. He would sail with the golden-haired goddess at his side and together they would find paradise in each other's arms. He would share with her all of his riches and in return he would lay claim to a treasure whose worth could not be measured.

The heat of late morning was more oppressive than usual as Rebecca made her way toward the gates of the fort thinking to take a walk along the shady path beside the creek where the air might be some degrees cooler outside the walls of the compound.

Dark circles beneath her eyes attested to another sleepless night. She had lain awake for hours after the festivities had ended and only the night sounds disturbed the peaceful tranquility of the slumbering garrison. Trying to sort out her jumbled feelings had accomplished little, save to bring on a headache which had persisted even as the first rays of dawn cast shadows about the room and outlined the small figure of Elizabeth tucked up under the covers beside her.

Rebecca was riddled with guilt remembering the way she had melted in Lance Logan's arms. How could she have again allowed herself to respond to the caresses of that colonial knave with such blatant disregard for propriety? Surely, if she cared nothing for her own reputation, she owed it to William to remain pure and unsullied. She had made this arduous journey in order to remove the obstacles impeding their pursuit of happiness, yet here she was undermining all that she had worked to achieve for a few stolen moments of bittersweet passion with a man who obviously wanted only to toy with her affections. In England she would not have thought twice about one as ill-bred as he.

And what of Lona? Lance appeared to care deeply for the girl, but was he capable of forming a lasting attachment for any one woman? Certainly few gentlemen of her acquaintance remained loyal to their wives once assured of an heir. That their spouses had an equal proclivity toward indiscretion was not at issue. Only one thing was clear to Rebecca at the moment. She must return home as quickly as possible, and until she was safely back aboard the *Victoria* she would simply have to avoid Lance Logan at all costs.

Pausing at the fort's entry she gazed westward where far out over the Gulf ominous gray-black clouds boiled heavily meeting a rough, whitecapped sea. The afternoon thundershowers appeared to be forming earlier than usual but directly overhead the hot sun blazed down form an azure sky dotted with downy puffs of white. Not so much as a hint of breeze stirred the leaves in the nearby trees.

She stopped to watch a group of Indian children at play sending up swirls of dust as they took turns batting a rounded object back and forth within a large circle. Each child had a stick which he used to propel the ball from one player to another while apparently trying to keep it inside the ring of participants. The children squealed in delight and shouted encouragement to each other in a language that sounded harsh and guttural to Rebecca. Then loud and clear, amidst the strange ejaculations, she heard an all-too-familiar young voice.

"Damnation, Edward! You let the bloody thing roll right between your legs!"

A small gasp escaped as Rebecca's mouth flew open for there stood a most indignant Elizabeth in the center of the fray, hands on hips as she made clear her opinion of her brother's athletic prowess.

"You do not approve of the children playing together?"

Rebecca was startled by Lona's softly spoken question for she had not heard the Indian woman step up behind her. She spun around quickly, surprise easily recognizable in her wide green eyes.

"On the contrary," Rebecca smiled. "I am indeed happy to see Elizabeth and Edward adjusting so readily to their new surroundings."

"Yes," Lona agreed solemnly. "The young ones are in many ways more adaptable than the old. That is good since they have so little control over their lives."

Rebecca wondered if Lona's comment was a subtle criticism of her decision to bring the twins to America. But surely she could see that Rebecca had made the right choice. Andrew and his children belonged together and now, with Rachel for their mother, they would have the guidance and affection of two loving parents.

"If by 'the old' you mean me, you are absolutely right," Rebecca stated deciding to meet the challenge head on. "As your friend, Mr. Logan, has pointed out on numerous occasions, I do not belong here."

"I would not take the things Lance says too seriously," Lona advised, a gleam of mischief lighting her eyes. "One who doesn't know him well might see Lance as totally self-assured, completely invincible, when the truth is he fears his own feelings."

Rebecca creased her foreheard aware that the prickling of annoyance she was feeling toward the woman stemmed partly from the knowledge that Lona knew and understood Logan as few others did. Intimately? She wondered.

"But perhaps afraid is too strong a word," Lona continued staring off in the distance as if having trouble defining her thoughts. "Lance is distrustful of his own sensibilities. Everyone he has ever loved has been taken from him so he has erected a barrier around his heart. If he doesn't care for a person, he can't be hurt when that person is no longer with him. Or so he thinks."

She now held Rebecca's gaze with her own and Rebecca sensed that she would like to say more but hesitated. Insight into Lance Logan's personality as revealed by the Indian maiden caused an uneasiness she found difficult to explain. Rebecca sought to channel the conversation away from the man whom she now considered a real threat to her well-ordered plans for the future.

"Be that as it may, it hardly concerns me," she replied with a toss of her head. "Mr. Logan's problems are his own and I have a feeling he prefers to keep it that way."

"Too bad." Lona's statement was barely audible. Rebecca cut her eyes at her olive-skinned companion whose face had become inscrutable but refused to ask what was meant by her strange pronouncement. She decided not to be drawn into further discussion of the very person she was trying to expunge from her thoughts.

Instead Rebecca used the dainty handkerchief she held in her hand to pat the moist skin exposed above the high neckline of her rose and white dimity gown. Her several layers of petticoats captured the heat, making her feel as if she were being steamed alive. She envied Lona who wore a full, bright-colored cotton skirt which flowed straight down to her bare feet unhampered by numerous undergarments.

"It is not so hot in England?" Lona asked noting Rebecca's discomfort.

She laughed at the understatement of the other's query. "Good heavens, no! I'm beginning to wonder if even Hell is as hot as Florida!"

Rebecca blushed remembering that this province was the Indian woman's home and Lona might very well take exception to her candid assessment of the place. But rather than being offended, Lona giggled girlishly.

"Come," she whispered conspiratorially. "If you wish to be cool I will take you to my secret place." She glanced around as she spoke making sure no one overheard.

"Secret place?" Rebecca repeated dumbly. She was

curious but she was also wary knowing that Lance had warned Lona against leaving the fort. Of course she could hardly bring that subject up without explaining how she had unintentionally overheard their exchange as she sat hidden beneath the willow tree.

Instead she asked skeptically, "Where is this 'secret place'?" She doubted that such a haven existed. On the other hand if there were even the slightest chance that Lona actually knew of a refuge from the sweltering heat Rebecca would be foolish to pass up such an opportunity.

"I will show you," she said, taking Rebecca by the arm and steering her in the direction of the creek.

Since that had been Rebecca's destination to begin with, she shrugged resignedly and allowed herself to be led away from the fort. At least she wouldn't chance running into Lance Logan.

"Now where do you suppose *they* are going?"

Lance straightened from where he leaned against the solid trunk of a tall gray-barked cypress tree talking with Lawrence Kearny about the latter's attempt to rout out Gaspar and his iniquitous pirates. He followed Kearny's gaze and caught a brief glimpse of Rebecca and Lona just as they disappeared into the dense foliage along the creek bank.

Frowning, Lance studied the threatening black clouds still well out over the Gulf waters moving slowly but inexorably toward them.

"Whatever they're up to they had better be quick about it," Lance growled. "Looks like a bad storm heading our way."

"You're right about that and I don't mind telling you I prefer to be on dry land when it hits. I'm rowing out to the *Enterprise* now to make sure everything's battened down," Kearny informed as his eyes scanned the gently swelling waters of the bay then rested proudly on the formidable warship anchored in the channel. "Care to join me?" he invited, looking back at Logan in time to catch him staring at the spot where they had last seen the two women.

"Thanks, but I'd better see if they need any help here," he answered absentmindedly still contemplating the tangle of brushwood across the open field.

"That's one pretty lady," Kearny laughed clacking his tongue as he slapped his friend on the back before turning toward the waiting longboat.

One pretty lady, thought Lance shaking his head. *That was the whole problem in a nutshell! Why the hell did Rebecca Winslow have to be a damned 'Lady'? Why couldn't she just be a regular person? Not that she put on airs or anything.*

Her title seemed unimportant to her and, in itself, it was unimportant to him. Yet it was a constant reminder that she came from a different world. A world where life was so far removed from that of the settlers at Fort Brooke that there could be no common ground on which they could meet. Rebecca simply wasn't equipped to do even the simplest chores most women took for granted, like cooking for instance!

Lance shuddered then chuckled to himself imagining Rebecca left on her own to prepare a meal. Her poor husband would likely starve to death. The thought sobered him even as he felt his stomach churn, and he knew the knot in his gut was not caused by visions of Lady Winslow turned loose in the kitchen. He was picturing what it would be like to be the husband of such a woman, to possess her, to have her in his bed each night. He knew that the last thing on his mind would be food.

He had stirred the passion she tried valiantly to hold in check beneath her prim and proper exterior. The fleeting moments when he had tasted her honeyed lips had only whet his appetite for more. He hungered to see her golden hair flowing unbound in all its lustrous glory, to feel her silken skin beneath him, to see the flames of her need ablaze in those dazzling emerald eyes.

Lance realized where his lustful thoughts had taken him when he felt his breeches stretch to accommodate his burgeoning manhood.

"Good God! I'm acting like an infatuated school-boy," he said aloud as he ground his teeth in disgust and fought to regain control of his profligate imagination.

Again he wondered where Rebecca and Lona had gone as he studied the ever darkening clouds moving in upon the coast. He debated whether or not he should try to follow their trail then shrugged it off as a foolish idea. Lona wouldn't dare risk his wrath by straying too far away after repeatedly warning her of the danger.

With that certainty he turned and whistled to Davey and the twins motioning them toward the fort where hurried preparations were underway to safeguard those within against the approaching storm.

Rebecca was not without misgivings as she followed Lona along the tree-shaded path. She had never ventured this far from the fort and every instinct told her they should turn back. Just as she was about to suggest the same to the Indian girl forging ahead of her with a confidence that led her to believe she had traveled this way often, Lona stopped abruptly. The track appeared to end at a natural barrier of thick underbrush growing across the footpath. Lona smiled mysteriously as she waited for Rebecca to catch up. Then, without a word, she grasped the scraggly branches and pulled them aside to reveal a sight so breathtakingly beautiful Rebecca thought she surely must be dreaming.

In front of her was a lake of crystal clear water surrounded by a variety of trees she had never seen before. Their slender, reedlike branches covered with tiny leaves stretched out over the pool to form an arbor which blocked out the sun and allowed only dimly filtered light to enter. No grass grew along the bank. Instead the ground was covered with a thick carpet of spongy green moss.

To Rebecca it was an oasis in the desert. She gasped with delight taking a tentative step closer to peer down at her reflection. It would not surprise her if the scene disappeared before her eyes. Who could have imagined such a bewitching oddity hidden away as it was in this sheltered glen?

"I can't believe it!" Rebecca marveled turning just as Lona unloosened her skirt and let it fall at her feet then pulled her round-necked cotton blouse over her head tossing it carelessly aside. She shook her long mane of jet black hair about her slender shoulders until it covered her bare breasts like a velvet mantle.

Rebecca stared at the young Indian who stood on the bank, her sleek, flawless body the image of an artfully sculpted Venus gilded in bronze. Then before Rebecca could find her voice, Lona dove cleanly into the air slicing a path through the pure tranquil pool, seeming as at home in the water as any fish.

As her head broke the surface some distance from the bank Rebecca admired the lithe young native who might have been a water nymph so much did she seem a part of this fairy tale setting.

"Come on," Lona called, laughingly waving Rebecca forward.

Rebecca glanced around at the thick vegetation which gave the appearance of an impenetrable barricade against the outside world. She could think of several good reasons not to remove her clothing and join Lona in the pool. But as she began enumerating each in order of importance she could almost feel the fresh water washing over her perspiration-drenched body. And as the list continued to grow, her arms reached behind to begin unhooking the many fastenings of her gown. Soon clad only in her lacy white chemise, she followed Lona's example executing a perfect dive into the crystalline basin. The shock of the unexpectedly cold water brought her swiftly to the top gulping for air.

"Where does it come from?" she sputtered as they tread water too deep for their feet to reach the sandy bottom they could see below.

"From an underground spring," Lona explained. "Do you like my secret place?"

Rebecca sighed lifting her feet until she was floating on her back. "It's a little piece of Heaven!"

"In the midst of Hell?" Lona teased laughingly.

"Oh, Lona. I apologize for what I said back at the fort. It's just that I was feeling so miserable."

"I can understand how you must feel. I'm sure I

204

would freeze to death in your England," she vowed with an exaggerated shiver.

They swam to the other side of the pond then back again swooping and splashing like two playful porpoises. Finally they climbed up onto the mossy bank exhausted but rejuvenated by the cool water of the spring. Lona draped her skirt casually around her shoulders covering her body against the chill.

Rebecca smiled to herself as she wondered what those in England would think if they could see her sitting here next to a naked Indian with her wet chemise plastered to her body hiding little of what was beneath. Strangely enough, she thought as she dangled her feet in the water, this risqué divertissement seemed quite natural and pleasant. She realized with some surprise that an improbable friendship was beginning to manifest itself between the two of them.

"Lona? Would you tell me what it was like when you were a little girl? You know, before you came to live at the fort?" She turned to face her companion, genuine interest plainly visible in her expressive green eyes.

Lona leaned back bracing herself on her arms, her face lifted toward the cloak of leaves shrouding the sunlight overhead.

"There's not much to tell. My mother was Spanish. A real lady like you, Rebecca."

Rebecca recognized the pride in the girl's voice.

"She was aboard a ship bound for Havana to marry the man her family had chosen for her. The ship was caught in a fierce storm and blown off course. It broke up on a coral reef close to the islands they call The Keys. My father, Nokomis, found my mother clinging to a piece of wood even after the waves had washed her upon the rocky beach. She was near death but he carried her to his camp and willed life back into her."

Already she had gained Rebecca's full attention for the story had all that makings of a fairy tale unfolding as she herself sat within an enchanted wonderland.

"My father fell in love with her, of course. She was so beautiful." She paused caught up in her memories. "Do you think it odd that Indians love?"

Rebecca didn't know how to answer the unexpected question. She hesitated then replied honestly. "Actually, I've never given it much thought."

Lona's laughter was a melodious, tinkling sound. "I only asked because there are those who do not believe Indians capable of experiencing the feelings others take for granted." There was no rancor in her voice. Rebecca wondered how one could accept such closed-mindedness.

"How can you be so matter-of-fact about those who have taken the land of your people, those who treat the Calusa with such disdain?" she demanded, sparks of indignation igniting her eyes.

"I've learned to laugh at their ignorance because I know the truth. No one could have loved my mother more than my father did. And my mother loved him with equal fervor."

Lona's face took on a dreamy expression then she giggled girlishly. "My father is a great chief, you know, respected by our people, feared by our enemies. My mother . . . she was so small and as fragile-looking as a piece of Mary's fine china. Oh, but she was not just a pretty ornament to set on the shelf and admire. She was well educated. She was also most stubborn and willful. No one would dare argue with her once she made up her mind about something."

She laughed again with gentle humor. "Father ruled the tribe but mother ruled him. They were married in the traditional tribal ceremony and from then on she fought just as hard as the bravest warrior to see that no harm came to her adopted people."

Rebecca tried to imagine what it must have been like to wake up in a foreign land surrounded by unfamiliar faces, a land where customs and language would not be understood by an unfortunate castaway. Lona's mother must have been a very courageous woman.

"You speak English well and yet your mother was Spanish."

"When I was young I spoke only Spanish and the language of the Calusa. Later David taught me to speak English."

"David?"

"David Grayson. He was a missionary of sorts. Not like Ezra Holcomb or those that had come before preaching against our gods and calling us heathens. David didn't try to change or discredit our beliefs. He just wanted to teach us the ways of the whites because he knew we would have to learn to share our land with others or face annihilation."

"He sounds like a remarkable man," Rebecca commented as she idly plucked the leaves from a piece of fern growing nearby.

"That he was," Lona agreed wistfully. "He died when the fever swept our village. The same fever that took my mother from us."

"I know that Little Dove was your half sister. How did she feel when your father remarried?" Rebecca knew she was treading on dangerous ground by bringing up the woman whom Logan had taken to wife in all ways save marriage, and she wondered if she might have a penchant toward self-flagellation.

"My mother treated Little Dove and Chikiki as her own children. Little Dove loved and respected her above all women."

"And your brother?"

As seconds stretched into minutes and no answer was forthcoming, Rebecca decided she had overstepped the bounds of propriety by broaching a subject the other did not wish to discuss. Then slowly, choosing each word carefully, Lona replied, "For my brother the old way is the only way." There was a melancholy resignation in her voice as she pulled the makeshift cape tighter about her shoulders. "Chikiki will never accept what he sees as the intrusion of the whites upon the land of the Calusa. No, Rebecca," she answered heavy heartedly, "he neither loved nor showed respect for my mother. To him she was a usurper unworthy of being the wife of the mighty chief. His unyielding hatred toward anything he saw as a threat to the way of life he understood caused both of my parents great sorrow."

It was not like Rebecca to so boldly pry into what was clearly none of her business but she felt an irrepressible need to understand. Lona was an enigma. How easily one might tend to dismiss her as irresponsible and flighty especially after overhearing Lance reprimand her as a father would a naughty child. But Rebecca knew better. The woman spoke three languages fluently. Her cultural background was an unlikely blend of refined European and primitive native. Yet from the two she had emerged as a lovely young maiden on the brink of womanhood who had earned a position of respect among the colonial settlers at Fort Brooke.

Yes, Rebecca concluded observing from beneath thick-fringed lashes. *Lona was like the clear water of the pool which deluded an unsuspecting swimmer into thinking he could touch its illusive depths.*

Thunder rumbled in the distance as the umbrella of leaves sheltering the two women stirred overhead in a sudden gust of wind. Neither Rebecca nor Lona took notice, separated as they were from any view of the darkening sky.

Rebecca found Lona's account of her parents' unusual love story fascinating but she wanted to hear about Logan and Little Dove.

"Logan told me that he once saved your father's life." She hoped this opener might lead to more information concerning the alliance between the girl's sister and the silver-eyed rogue who continued to haunt her dreams.

"It is true." Lona's reply evidenced the devotion she felt toward the multifaceted army scout. "If it weren't for Lance, I would have no one left."

Rebecca wondered if she meant that her father would be dead if Logan had not saved him or if her words were an indication that Lance now belonged to her.

"My father had gone fishing one day alone. As he stood on the branch of a tree far out over the river, spear in hand, the limb cracked without warning hurling him into the water. Before he could swim to shore a hungry gator slid into the river cutting off his escape. Lance was hunting in the nearby woods and witnessed what was happening. Just as the alligator

209

was about to clamp his jagged teeth around my father's leg, Lance shot the vicious reptile right between the eyes."

Lona related the tale with breathless excitement as she spoke of the man who had snatched her father from the jaws of death.

"I can understand why you and your father are grateful. Logan's marksmanship certainly saved the day," Rebecca acknowledged, knowing that her inane rejoinder scarcely befit the magnitude of the deed. It did seem more a matter of luck than true heroism. To her way of thinking Logan just happened to be at the right place at the right time.

Annoyed by the Englishwoman's apparent lack of understanding, Lona replied impatiently, "I'm not talking about Lance's skill with a rifle for goodness sake! The point is that he saved the life of an Indian. Not many white men would have done such a thing."

Rebecca hurried to make amends realizing that her ignorance had again upset her sensitive companion. "It is difficult for me to believe that anyone would think a man's life is not worth saving because of his ancestry. I'm glad it was Logan who was there when your father needed help."

"Lance has done so much for us," Lona sighed feelingly. "He has saved my life as well. It was Lance who arranged for me to live at Fort Brooke. It is he who protects me from my brother who would compel me to abide by the ancient laws of our people."

Lona smiled impishly. "At least he tries to protect me," she amended looking more child than woman at the moment. "Sometimes my foolishness makes the task difficult and he threatens to return me to my father, but he won't for he knows that I prefer living at the fort. Lance Logan is the kindest man I've ever known. I guess that's why I love him so much."

How unpretentious the words sounded, yet to Rebecca they rang like a bell of doom. Pulsing vibrations pounded inside her head: *You knew you fool! You knew the truth but you would not accept it!* The beat seemed to echo her thoughts until she feared her skull would split with the sonorous throbbing. The rest of her body was numb and she knew her legs would not hold her weight if she tried to rise. And that was exactly what she wanted to do. She wished to jump up and run away from the reverberations that continued to chant *You fool! You fool!* She longed to escape the woman who had unashamedly admitted her love for the man who had held Rebecca in his arms, touched her willing lips with his own. The man who had aroused in her a frenzy of desire she never knew existed and still did not fully understand. She knew only that the pleasure she had found during the brief idyllic afternoon had been destroyed in less than the beat of a heart.

"Rebecca? What is it?" The hand Lona placed on her arm pulled Rebecca back from the dark abyss into which her tortuous thoughts had taken her.

Blinking back tears she fought hard to hold in check, her reply came softly. Even so she was unable to disguise the telltale catch in her voice. "Th-that's wonderful." The words formed around the bile that rose in her throat leaving a bitter aftertaste.

Lona looked confused. "What's wonderful?" she asked, a frown drawing her dark brows together.

Rebecca was equally bewildered. She felt as if they

were carrying on two distinctly different conversations.

"It's wonderful that you love Logan, of course, since he so obviously returns your affection."

Lona looked at Rebecca in disbelief then bent her head as she slapped her hands against her knees not trying to hide her bubbling laughter. She laughed until tears flowed down her cheeks. As she swiped at them with the hem of her skirt she struggled to regain her composure.

"I have heard that you British have a peculiar sense of humor. Now I know it's true."

Looking at Rebecca who sat regarding her in stoney-faced silence, she broke up again as peels of mirth joined with a loud clap of thunder that boomed directly overhead. Lona sobered instantly.

"We must return to the fort at once. There's a storm coming."

"Not so fast," Rebecca commanded, grasping Lona's arm. "I refuse to budge one inch until you explain what I said that you found so amusing!"

"The storm, Rebecca! We have to go!" Alarm showed in the girl's face but Rebecca refused to loosen her hold. "All right," Lona acquiesced sensing it would be useless to argue. "It was what you said about Lance and me. I love Lance the way I wish I could love Chikiki as a big brother. And he loves me like the little sister he once had. We do not think of each other in the man and woman way. Not in the way he thinks about you! Now we must go quickly," she finished jerking her arm free and rising to search for her discarded blouse.

Rebecca remained where she was, unmoving. Lona's words and their implications refused to penetrate her muddled brain. "Not in the way he thinks about you," she repeated dizzily.

A bolt of lightning flashed, followed by a cannonade of thunder that seemed to go on forever. Suddenly the urgency of their situation bore in on her, but as she made ready to stand, she heard an ominous click and felt the touch of cold metal against her back. She swiveled around to find Lona held tightly in the clutches of the pudgy little trapper called Brady, one grimy hand covering her mouth while his other arm locked about her slender body making her struggle for escape futile. She was not surprised when she looked up into the evil, leering face of the man she knew only as Martin. When the foul smelling bully prodded her once again with the rifle he held, the cold fingers of fear washed over her bare skin blanketing her with gooseflesh just as the skies opened up to unleash drenching torrents of bone-chilling rain.

Chapter 13

Lance, too, felt the cold fingers of fear. They had been searching for hours calling the women's names only to have their cries sucked up by the gale force winds which howled around them bowing tall trees and sending clumps of spidery Spanish moss soaring through the air to land in rain-soaked heaps upon the ground. He shivered as a steady stream of frigid water ran off the wide brim of his hat and down his back, a shiver brought on by apprehension rather than the dropping temperature or the chill of the rain.

Where the hell could they be? He knew of no place they could have taken shelter, but why for God's sake hadn't they returned to the fort? Lance shook his head sending a spray of droplets flying but he could not shake off the despair that wrenched harder at his gut as each minute passed without a sign of the pair.

Perhaps they had lost their way for it had grown so dark that even he had to depend on instinct for direction as he sloshed along the muddied trail running beside the fast flowing creek. But he knew Lona could find her way through the woods blindfolded.

At last Lance was forced to consider the most likely explanation. Lona and Rebecca had been prevented from returning to the fort! But by what or whom? God, don't let it be Chikiki, he prayed unconsciously seeking consolation from above. But the only answer forthcoming was yet another jagged flash of lightning illuminating the tunnel of dank, dripping foliage ahead followed by an earth-shuddering clap of thunder that threatened to shake the trees from the ground.

Lance reacted to a loud warning crack overhead, jumping back into the brush just as a heavy limb came crashing to the ground landing where he had stood just seconds before.

"Logan!" came a shout in the distance.

Lance waited hoping whoever hailed him had found the women safe. His hopes were dashed as Lawrence Kearny came into view struggling to maintain his balance on the slippery trail. Kearny was alone.

"It's no use, Lance! We'll never find them in this!"

Standing so close their hat brims touched, Kearny still had to holler to make himself heard over the roaring of the wind. "Best we return to the fort and start again after the storm subsides!"

Lance knew his friend was right, but how could he sit high and dry inside Fort Brooke when Rebecca was somewhere out here probably being held against her will. If Chikiki had her . . . he let the possibility blow away with the wind. For, in truth, he had no idea what the angry young warrior would do with the golden-haired Englishwoman.

Rebecca, his lady! Yes! *His lady,* he finally admitted without regret. He desired this woman who had wormed her way into his heart with her prim and proper ways and her innocent sensuality more than anything he had ever wanted in his life! Love? Perhaps it was too soon to put a name to his emotions. He only knew he had to get her back. Fate could not be so unfair as to once again give and then needlessly take away before they had had an opportunity to discover whether the tenuous bond that drew them together was strong enough to overcome their differences.

Chikiki would not hurt Lona. Not physically at least. For he needed her to carry out the age-old laws of the Calusa. And though Lance was repulsed by a tenet that sanctioned incest among its leaders, it was Rebecca's safety that caused him to heatedly take exception to his friend's sensible suggestion.

"Take the men and return to the fort if you must, but I'm not giving up yet!"

The lieutenant understood and sympathized for he was not unaware of the attraction between Lance and Rebecca.

"Lead on!" he directed gesturing toward the muddy path ahead. He still felt that fighting the unrelenting elements to continue the search at the height of the gale was foolish, but the determination he had seen in the other's slate-gray eyes convinced him of the futility in arguing further.

Lance clapped him on the shoulder grateful that they would not have to waste more time debating his stubborn resolution.

"I want to check out Lona's secret place."

"Surely she wouldn't have taken Miss Winslow so deep into the forest," Kearny reasoned.

Lance shrugged. "We've looked everywhere else."

He pulled his hat lower over his face and plunged ahead leaving Kearny to wrestle with the branches that snapped back in his wake.

Everyone at Fort Brooke knew about the secluded lake Lona called "her secret place" and they respected the Indian woman's occasional need to commune with nature away from the confines of the garrison, where finding a private spot to be alone was all but impossible.

Lance pushed aside the heavy underbrush that hid the lake from view and burst into the clearing with Kearny on his heels. Even here the wrath of the squall could be seen as whitecaps rolled upon the pool's usually mirrored surface washing fallen leaves against the spongy bank.

With a leaden heart Lance stooped to lift the mud-splattered pile of petticoats that peeked out from beneath a bushy shrub apparently kicked carelessly aside. Shaking the delicate lace-trimmed garments out one by one he hugged them against his waist unaware of the comical sight he made, the dripping, grimy lingerie falling barely to his knees. He knew that nothing short of disaster would have persuaded Rebecca to dispense with the cumbersome under-things.

Silently the two men circled the water; neither willing to voice the terrible misgivings that battered their hopes as surely as the wind and rain hammered away at their bodies. Where the dense forest met the mossy bank on the opposite shore, Lance knelt to examine the mud-filled outline left by the hoof of a horse. Running his fingers very lightly over the damp depression, he looked up at Kearny ignoring the drops of water pelting his face and rolling down his cheeks like tears. His eyes glinted in the dusky light giving forth some small measure of encouragement.

"This horse was shod." He wiped his hand on the leg of his buckskin breeches as he spoke.

"That means it's not Chikiki," Kearny nodded. "But if not Indians, then who in hell could have taken them. And why?"

"Damned if I know," Lance admitted, his features turning hard and ugly. "But I intend to find out!"

"We'd better round up the men and get the horses," his partner reasoned. "It'll take a fair bit of tracking to find them now."

"I'll find them," Lance vowed grimly. "And when I do, I plan to kill the bastards!"

As they turned back toward the fort Kearny was relieved to know that it was not his trail Lance Logan would be following.

Damnation! She was going to be sick! She couldn't be sick! To throw up now meant strangling to death on her own vomit. God help me, Rebecca pleaded knowing with a certainty there was nothing she could do to help herself.

It had been hours since the diabolical rat-faced trapper had forced her to don her gown before tightly binding her hands and feet despite her efforts to kick his shins and scratch his evil beady eyes. A fetid kerchief promptly put an end to her furious delineation of her captor's transgressions. Rebecca was then flung unceremoniously across his saddle with no more consideration than if she had been a sack of grain.

The curtain of falling rain had drilled into her back pricking with needlelike sharpness. Her arms and legs grew cold and numb dangling from either side of the horse as it plodded through the thick waterlogged forest where no trail seemed to point toward their destination.

Rebecca tried to protect her face with her arms as thorny underbrush raked her tender skin and tangled painfully in her hair. Blood pounded in her head as she fought against the waves of nausea that threatened to surface with each jolting step the animal took. She knew that Lona had been trussed up in similar fashion and was being supported by the slow-witted Brady on the horse following behind. Obviously Martin was in command for when he barked out orders his potbellied partner was quick to obey.

Through her fear and pain, Rebecca tried to sort out what had happened. Clearly they had been kidnapped by the two unprincipled trappers, but to what purpose? Perhaps the blackguards planned to hold them for ransom. But she was a stranger, unknown to the two. They could not count on her being of any value to the inhabitants at Fort Brooke. It made even less sense to think that Lona's return would fetch a high price. Didn't most white men consider the Calusa to be of little worth?

Rebecca remembered the way Martin had darted his shifty rodent eyes at Lona when he arrived at the fort to replenish his supplies. No one could mistake the undisguised lust in his regard. Had his need been such that he would kidnap two women merely to sate his sexual desire for one of them? Somehow she doubted it. There had to be more behind their evil deeds.

Something worth risking the retribution of the United States Army.

It was impossible to piece together the answers to such a puzzle while suffering the indignities of her present position. But at least her efforts to think had temporarily quieted her rebellious stomach. It seemed that the only way to prevent the queasiness from overtaking her was to stay mentally alert. Frightened though she was, she was determined to channel her thoughts in a positive direction.

Immediately the image of Lance Logan took shape in her mind. She found it curious that he was not standing on his head in her mental picture considering that she herself was upside down. Logan, of course, would never stand on his head. He would hold himself proudly erect, as tall as a tree, muscular legs braced apart, broad shoulders thrust back, powerful hands fisted upon lean hips. Naturally his handsome face would be scowling. She felt her brow crease in a frown. She wondered when his face became handsome rather than roughly chiseled as it had first appeared to her?

She thought of what Lona had said. Did he really look at her differently than he did other women? Thank God he couldn't see her now, sprawled across a saddle, her hair streaming down in wet disarray collecting an assortment of nettles and twigs as the ends swept the path. And as a final humiliation the monster who held her prisoner had spirited her away without her petticoats!

Logan would be angry when he learned she had been forced to accompany these unconscionable miscreants. Of that she had no doubt! She wondered if he would come after them. Common sense told her that even an experienced tracker like Logan would be unable to follow their trail. The storm had most likely washed away any trace of their abduction. Besides if Lona's secret place was really a secret, no one would know where to begin the search. Yet, beyond the realm of logical thinking, a small inner voice kept insisting that Logan would find them and that he would make everything right again.

How odd it seemed to place all hope for her future in the hands of the man she had once dubbed the biggest blighter of them all. Where had her sudden faith come from? She pondered for only a moment before the answer dawned like a glorious sunrise. Her faith in Lance Logan came straight from the heart!

She must have lost consciousness for when Rebecca became aware of her surroundings the rain had stopped and night had descended upon the forest. The mount beneath her moved at an even slower gait than she remembered and turning her head slightly she wondered how the animal could find its way enfolded as they were in a solid cloak of darkness.

The damp dress clung to her skin and the slight breeze that rustled the leaves overhead held a chill. Unlike the cool fresh air around the pool, the dank, musty atmosphere of the woods reminded her of a tomb and she hoped that the analogy was not a forewarning of things to come.

"The clearing's just ahead," Martin called over his shoulder, his voice sounding unduly loud against the absolute silence of the night.

"Think they'll be there?" questioned his partner from behind.

"Hard to tell. The storm could have held them up. If

so, we wait."

They? So the two men planned to meet someone. But why would they schedule a rendezvous in the middle of nowhere on this dark and gloomy night? And what part did she and Lona play in these strange happenings? Rebecca's mind whirled with unanswered questions.

Just then the clouds shifted enabling the feeble light of a haze-covered moon to illumine a wide break in the dense foliage. This must be the clearing the men spoke of, Rebecca decided as the horse blew steam from its nostrils and came to a halt. Her eyes widened as her captor put a hand on her back pressing her stomach painfully into the saddle in his effort to dismount.

Clumsy jackass! she fumed. Oh, would she singe his ears if he were foolish enough to remove the blasted gag from her mouth.

He grabbed her legs pulling her to the ground. Then, without so much as a "by your leave" he gave her a shove that sent her flying against the trunk of a cypress tree where she crumpled in a heap at its base. Meanwhile Brady half dragged, half carried Lona to a spot beside her, then stood grinning down at them like a mangy tomcat with two cornered mice.

"Take off the gags but leave them tied," the leader commanded.

As the filthy cloth was torn away, Rebecca took a deep breath preparing to launch a verbal attack on the two. But before she could begin Martin spun around and pointed a finger at her face.

"Shut up!" He didn't shout the order as one might expect. It was, in fact, the menacing calm of his voice contradicted by the heated fury in his hard black eyes that caused her to clamp her teeth tightly around the

222

words she had planned to say.

It was Lona who found the courage to ask the question.

"Why?" she whispered staring up unflinchingly into the obsidian eyes of her captor.

His reply was something between a sneer and a growl. "I don't answer the questions of a *puta* bitch that thinks she's better than me!" His thin lips curled upward in a sinister grin. "You'll find out soon enough why we've brought you here."

Rebecca shivered at the way Martin looked at the Indian girl with barely restrained lust and wondered if his desire had, indeed, been the motive behind their abduction.

"You'll find out soon enough," "Bald Brady" parroted rocking back and forth on his heels snickering gleefully like a small child who is bursting to tell a secret. "When do you think they'll get here?" he asked turning to the taller man while he continued to rock nervously.

"They'll be here when they get here. Now shut up!"

Something behind the leader's gruff manner led Rebecca to believe he was not completely at ease with the situation.

"I was just thinking—" the little man began.

"Don't do that! It's dangerous!" Martin barked, cutting the other off in midsentence.

"I was just thinking about how you been wanting under that Injun's skirts. Maybe if we got time you could stick it to her while I have a little fun with her friend."

The idea made Rebecca's skin crawl as the loathsome creature turned his attention on her. Before she could react Martin drew back his arm and sent his fist plunging into Brady's doughy stomach, doubling him over as air swooshed from his lungs like a punctured balloon.

"You gnat-brained son of a bitch! You want to ruin the biggest deal we've ever made? Touch either one of them and I'll cut off that thing you're so proud of and feed it to the gators!"

The tension was palpable. While Brady gulped air and tried to straighten, he was held in check by the other's frenetic glare.

Then he whined half to himself, "You didn't think nothin' of it the other time. We both had our fill of that purty little Injun gal before she went and died on us. I like it when they put up a fight so's you have to hit 'em." He snickered, his empty eyes suddenly alive with remembrance.

Dear God! Little Dove! Rebecca waited soundlessly to see who would make the next move, hoping the ruthless man's anger would not steer off in her direction. The move when it came was totally unexpected and took place so fast Rebecca scarcely had time to flinch.

Brady opened his mouth but whatever he had been about to say was lost in the roar of a rifle fired from the bushes at the edge of the clearing. The fat little trapper made a gurgling sound as he pitched forward, a bullet lodged in his throat. Spinning around in stunned disbelief, Martin had no time to draw his pistol before a second bullet found its target right between his evil rodent eyes.

Then all was quiet. Deadly quiet. Tightly bound and shaken by what had taken place, the women could do no more than stare at the lifeless bodies of their kidnappers and wait for their rescuers to show themselves. Somewhere in the back of Rebecca's fog-clouded brain the thought occurred that Lance and the soldiers had made remarkable time in finding them.

As the eerie hush continued and her mental processes began to function once more, Rebecca grew uneasy but fought the urge to call out. There had to be a reason why their liberators chose not to reveal themselves, though it made little sense to her. Her patience was strained as she remained seated on the wet ground tied hand and foot. Surely the danger was past.

Several more minutes went by with nothing stirring save the leaves overhead and an occasional small animal scurrying about in the underbrush. Then as Rebecca made up her mind to throw caution to the wind and shout for help the bushes parted. The shout turned into a scream when she saw the huge hairy figure looming before them. At first she thought it was a giant bear. But though she'd never seen a bear, she doubted one carried a rifle cradled in its arms or clothed its body in tattered rags.

"Ezra Holcomb!" Lona's voice as she spoke the man's name held both fear and scorn despite the fact that he had probably saved their lives.

Peering more closely, Rebecca found it hard to believe that beneath the layers of filth and grime there could be a human being. Then their eyes met and she knew she had come face to face with the fires of hell stoked by an inextinguishable inferno of hatred and intolerance. Demonic eyes glowing red in the blackness of the night led Rebecca to wonder if their emancipator might present an even greater danger than that from which they had been delivered.

She had not missed the alarm in Lona's voice as she identified the wild man now standing over them. And wild he was with his long, unkempt hair blowing in the breeze and his face, except for the blazing eyes, entirely covered by a thick tangled beard and bushy brows. A dark shredded cape hanging loosely about his gargantuan shoulders completed the picture of a disciple wandering in the wilderness . . . until one looked closely. For the eyes of a true believer, unlike Ezra Holcomb, reflected inner peace and an absence of malice. Not so the eyes of the grisly preacher who advocated enmity, bigotry, and murder. But surely he would see fit to set them free and point them in the direction of the fort.

Then Rebecca realized the import of her own analysis of Ezra Holcomb's character and panic shook her anew. For here was a man with a raging obsession to wipe out every Indian who had the misfortune of crossing his path. And she knew that his animosity extended to anyone he considered an ally to the "heathen" for she had witnessed his demented ravings the night of her arrival at Fort Brooke. To Ezra Holcomb's unbalanced mind, she and Lona were the enemy. Why had he bothered to save them from the two avaricious trappers?

"Mr. Holcomb,'" she began unsteadily in the face of the man's menacing scrutiny.

"Silence!" came the harsh command reverberating through the shadowy woods. "I am *Reverend* Holcomb, God's ambassador sent down to rid the earth of all who pledge allegiance to the prince of darkness. It is

I who will pave the way for the second coming of the Messiah!"

As he railed at her shaking his weapon as though it were a staff with the power to rain down fire and brimstone, Rebecca knew her worst fears had become reality. She could expect no mercy from the deranged evangelist who instead of being their savior would undoubtedly serve as their executioner. The knowledge that she might die at any moment did little to curb her growing irritation toward men in general.

Damnation! First there was Lance Logan who had continually treated her with chauvinistic disregard. Then within the space of a few hours "Meanminded Martin" had told her to shut up and now this pox on society was demanding her silence. Enough was enough! After all a genteel young lady of her sensibilities deserved to be treated with courtesy and respect. In an effort to make the *Reverend* understand that such was the case, Rebecca dared to defy his mandate.

"One question, please," she implored most sedately. "Why in the name of Heaven did you save us from Martin and Brady if you plan to shoot us yourself, you empty-headed lout?"

Her voice had risen considerably by the time she finished speaking. Holcomb gaped at her in open-mouthed astonishment while Lona sucked in her breath and tried to move closer to the tree seeking protection from the explosion she knew was imminent.

Every muscle in the man's body tensed. His features, what could be seen beneath the covering of hair, were clearly apoplectic as he lost the battle to bring his fury

227

under control.

"You handmaiden of the devil!" he thundered. "You sorceress of Satan! Those fools had no intention of killing you! They were going to sell you to the vipers that plague this land! And in her," he nodded toward Lona, "the accursed seed of the serpent would be planted!"

Vipers? Rebecca wrinkled her brow trying to gain some meaning behind the rantings of the crazed fanatic. Before she could think it through, the madman stepped back and raised his gun pointing it at Lona's head.

"It is the Lord's will that you both shall die by my hand!"

Rebecca squeezed her eyes shut and waited for the inevitable. The report of the rifle came as expected and tears wedged their way between her tightly closed lids. She knew there would be little time to mourn the loss of her friend before she, too, would be facing the timelessness of eternity.

Two things happened simultaneously. There was a mighty thud that shook the ground as though a tree had been felled. At the same time someone sounding very much like her dead companion uttered a cry of dismay.

Rebecca opened her eyes slowly. At her feet lay Ezra Holcomb who would spread his malignant doctrine no more. Forming a semicircle around the bodies now littering the forest were endless pairs of dark-skinned legs and moccasin-encased feet. She allowed her gaze to travel upward. Above the sinewy thighs breech-clouts barely concealed the wearers' most private parts. Lean chests devoid of hair and long muscled arms were decorated with a multitude of crude, brightly colored designs; some of animals, others of symbols she did not recognize. A dozen hawklike faces were marked with wide ribbons of paint, red, white, blue, yellow. Twelve pairs of dark eyes, alert but empty of emotion, focused on the spot where she and Lona sat.

Hysterical laughter rose in her throat as Rebecca contemplated the irony of it all. Martin and Brady. Ezra Holcomb. And now this! No one had to introduce her to the latest in what seemed a long line of captors. She knew without being told that she was now in the hands of the cold-blooded renegade warrior, Chikiki.

Resigning herself to whatever the fates had in store for her, Rebecca did something she had never done before. She fainted!

Jose Gaspar cursed in both English and Spanish as he held tightly to the rail of the storm-tossed *Dona Rosalia* and watched the shadow of the crippled English ship disappear behind the solid screen of rain, making good its escape. He had savored the taste of victory as the heavily laden British vessel floundered in the turbulent gulf waters, cannon shot having ripped asunder its main mast. Then the unpredictable gale-force winds had shifted, driving the pirate galleon away from its helpless quarry. By the time Gaspar and his motley crew brought their own ship under control it was too late. To find their prey again in the violent thunder squall would be sheer luck, and Gaspar finally admitted what his cousin Leon had been saying for many months. Fortune no longer smiled on the rapscallion pirate.

To make the pill even harder to swallow, the buccaneer leader knew that in all likelihood the badly disabled merchant ship would soon sink to the bottom of the sea taking its valuable cargo with it.

Jose shouted orders to set a course for Gasparilla Island. Yes, the time had come to move on. He would take his booty and seek sanctuary on the tropical Isle of Pine where he could live out his days in peace. Under gently swaying palm trees he would walk the smooth white sand beaches and bathe in the tranquil green waters with his golden goddess by his side. He would leave behind his troubled days and dream-plagued nights.

But he would not go alone.

Chapter 14

She was dead! Rebecca knew that she had crossed over into the dark void beyond life on earth when she opened her eyes to inky-black nothingness, a neutral zone of tranquil oblivion. Death had been surprisingly painless. One minute she was sitting beneath the tree; the next she was floating about in this silent abyss where she could close her eyes and sleep forever.

She smiled realizing that in all likelihood she would do just that. Somewhere around the middle of eternity she would probably become bored in her lightless dreamland but she would worry about that a few million years from now. For the present she was content to drift peacefully toward whatever celestial sphere lay ahead.

Her eyes flew open! Something was wrong! Dead people didn't open and close their eyes and they definitely didn't smile.

Rebecca stretched tentatively testing her arms and legs then groaned as galvanizing sensations jolted her body but at least she knew her appendages were still in place. So were the ropes!

"Rebecca?" A ragged whisper echoed in the opaque cavern then all was quiet once more. Had she only imagined another presence? Then the sound came again.

"Rebecca! It's me. Lona. Keep your eyes open so they will adjust to the darkness," the spectral voice directed.

Rebecca forced her eyelids to remain open as she tried to penetrate the blackness surrounding her. After several minutes of intense concentration she was able to make out the dimly shadowed figure of the Indian girl on the other side of what appeared to be a tomb. The air was cool and musty smelling, and panic swept over her along with the fear that she and Lona had been buried alive.

Hoping she had the courage to meet her fate bravely she dared to ask, "Where are we and how did we get here?"

"We're in a cave not far from the clearing. After you fainted we were brought here by my brother and his men."

Too vividly Rebecca remembered the death and destruction she had witnessed.

"How long have we been here," she queried, "and where is your brother now?" She glanced around nervously, surprised to find that their latest victors were not standing guard over the spoils.

"We've been here perhaps an hour," Lona answered, her voice hardened by anger. "As to Chikiki, I hope he's in Hell which is no less than he deserves. Look around you, Rebecca. Observe the willful betrayal of one's own people."

232

As her eyes grew used to the vague light, Rebecca noticed the numerous objects crowding the floor of their prison, others nesting in shelved indentures along the smooth rock walls. She could scarcely believe the dazzling array of beauty she beheld. Hand-decorated pottery and intricately designed wooden carvings rested side by side with priceless urns and goblets of silver and gold which were encrusted with precious jewels.

Gazing in awe, Rebecca murmured, "Oooh! What is this!" Her words were hushed much the same as when she had first entered the hallowed halls of Westminster Abbey.

"It is the treasure of the Calusa," Lona answered gravely, "handed down from generation to generation for hundreds of years. The pottery and wooden carvings are the work of our own craftsmen, most long dead. The Spanish invaders brought with them silver and gold when they invaded our land. Those who were not killed fled the territory leaving behind rich prizes to be added to the highly cherished objects housed in the sacred temple."

Rebecca studied the varied works of art hidden in the gloomy chamber. "But how did the treasure get here?"

"For some time now things have been mysteriously disappearing from the temple. Lance suspected that Chikiki was responsible but my father refused to listen to his accusations. He could not believe his own son capable of such deception and dishonor."

"But why would your brother do such a thing?"

"Lance thinks Chikiki is planning to trade our heritage for guns and ammunition so that he can wage war on the whites. With enough weapons at his disposal my brother believes he can rid the territory of invaders just as our ancestors did. I imagine Martin and Brady were his means of getting the treasure to unscrupulous dealers in the north who are willing to exchange weapons and lives to enhance their own wealth."

"And their greed cost Martin and Brady their lives," Rebecca added as pieces of the puzzle rapidly fell into place.

Lona nodded. "It was no more than the vermin deserved. I suppose their final act of treachery was to deliver me into my brother's hands. I wonder how much silver and gold would have been exchanged for my freedom? We've got to get out of here before they come back. Chikiki is in a rage now that Ezra Holcomb has eliminated the men who could supply him with arms. There's no telling what he might do when he returns."

Rebecca trembled all too aware of their danger and decidedly uncomfortable in the cryptlike atmosphere of the cave. She refused to let her mind dwell on tales of the atrocities for which the savages were known.

"Why would your brother want to harm *me?*" she argued breathlessly.

"Two reasons," came the frightening answer. "You're white and you're here!"

"But I'm not white! I'm English!" Realizing the ridiculousness of her words, she amended quickly, "I mean of course I'm white, but I'm not colonial and I'm certainly no threat to your brother. I refuse to become a pawn in a game where I don't even understand the rules!"

Rebecca was more than a little miffed to think that

she might unwittingly serve as a catalyst in increasing hostilities between the two opposing forces. "It isn't fair," she complained tugging painfully at the ropes that bound her wrists.

"Fair or not," reasoned her companion, "our only hope is to escape. We must return to the fort at once and bring the soldiers back so that they can restore the birthright of my people."

Giving up on the ropes, Rebecca sighed. "And just how are we to bring about this miraculous escape? Have you perchance a knife hidden beneath your skirts?"

"You are the one who can set us free," Lona replied ignoring the sarcasm directed her way. "Look! A few feet to your right is an *adz.*"

Rebecca glanced down at the peculiar-looking object the other had indicated with a nod of her head. It appeared to be some sort of primitive tool. From the carved wooden handle about twelve inches long protruded a socketed blade half that length, its shiny roughened edge winking in the dim rays of light filtering through the tunnel.

"An *adz* is an implement used for digging," the Indian girl explained. "The blade has been serrated to break through the hard ground. It is an old-fashioned tool, but it will easily saw through the ropes."

Even as she listened Rebecca began inching her way along the wall at the same time giving thanks that the unconventional cultivator had gone unnoticed by their captors. When she finally had the instrument within her numb grasp she debated how to go about positioning the tool to her best advantage.

"Hurry, Rebecca! The sun is rising and my brother

will not leave us unguarded for long."

The urgency in Lona's plea spurred Rebecca to hasten her efforts. She squirmed around until she had the handle of the *adz* firmly planted beneath her buttocks, the blade pointing upward behind her. The deceptively sharp edge bit into her flesh more than once but she refused to give in to the pain even when she felt blood trickling down her hands as she continued to saw clumsily at the stubborn ropes. At last she felt the cord give and snap. As she rubbed her hands together, circulation began to return bringing stabbing needle pricks and burning sensations to her chaffed wrists and self-inflicted abrasions.

"Hurry!" hissed Lona from where she sat propped against the far wall.

Pushing aside her discomfort Rebecca tore the restraints from her ankles and crawled on hands and knees to free her companion. Leaning against each other, they stood up clinging together to keep from falling. They crept soundlessly toward the mouth of the cave listening for any sign of the returning warriors.

Once there Lona, who had taken the lead, hesitated then pointed toward a barely discernible path leading into the dense woodland not far from where they stood.

"Take that trail," she pointed. "Run and keep running! Don't stop for anything!"

"What about you?" Rebecca cried, paralyzed with fright at the thought of exposing herself to whatever might be lurking behind the bushes.

"I must return to the cave. I have to take something back as proof of my brother's treachery. Proof that even my father cannot deny!"

"No! You must come with me! Please!" Rebecca

begged. She was horrified to think that Lona would risk her life to gain the damning evidence of Chikiki's deceit. "We can send the soldiers back to get the treasure," she implored tugging on the other's arm.

Lona wrenched loose and gave Rebecca a firm shove propelling her into the sunlight beyond the tunnel.

"Run, Rebecca! I'll be close behind you," she promised as she disappeared back into the dark opening.

Given no alternative Rebecca took a deep breath and bolted toward the shelter of the forest, fleeing as though the demons of Hell were at her heels. Just as she reached the treeline she heard the guttural shouts of the devil band returning to the cave.

Damnation, Lona! Where are you? her mind screamed as her lungs threatened to explode within her chest.

Rebecca followed the narrow winding trail setting a rapid pace for herself heedless of the barbed branches that reached out to clutch at her skirts and yank on her hair like fiendish apparitions in the worst kind of nightmare. On and on she ran, blood pounding in her head, her heart hammering against her ribs. She thought she heard the drum of footsteps behind her, but she wasn't sure.

Descending a slight incline she dared one quick glance over her shoulder. When her eyes left the trail ahead, she collided full force into an immovable object that seemed to have risen out of nowhere to block her path. The impact would have sent her sprawling had not two powerful arms with hands like steel bands reached out to grab her pulling her forward against a massive chest.

"Rebecca!"

She lifted her head and looked up into the silver-gray eyes of Lance Logan.

Overwhelmed with relief, Rebecca longed to remain where she was, locked in the safety of Logan's protective arms. But she knew Lona was somewhere back in the forest and that they were far from out of danger yet. Purposefully she thrust herself away from the man whose mere presence represented security.

"Lona!" she gasped, moving to his side and extending her arm in the direction from which she had come.

As she spoke the Indian girl came sprinting over the hill and down toward them. Above her the bloodthirsty renegade halted his pursuit. Black eyes gleaming with hatred, he raised his rifle aiming the weapon at the heart of the fearless army scout. Rebecca screamed as Lona hurled herself into Logan's arms at the same moment her brother pulled the trigger. Everyone froze suspended in place as the explosion thundered in their ears.

"Nooooo!" Logan's tortured denial roared through the forest while the face of the Indian warrior registered shock at the result of his action.

Then, as if on signal, the woods erupted with gun shots. The soldiers, who had remained mounted while Lance studied the trail, took off in pursuit of the fleet-footed rebels.

Rebecca stood by helplessly as Logan placed Lona gently on the ground. She felt the bile rise in her throat when she saw the amount of blood spreading across the girl's slender back and coating the hands of the man she had saved by throwing herself in the path of the bullet.

Lance knelt touching the pulse in the girl's neck with his huge callused hand.

"She's alive, but just barely." A troubled frown creased his wide forehead.

He hurried to where the big black stallion stood patiently cropping grass along the path. Snatching a bundle of white cloth tied behind the saddle he returned to where the unconscious girl lay and tossed the material to Rebecca.

"Tear some strips I can use for bandages," he directed kneeling once more as he pulled a knife from his belt and carefully cut away the blood-soaked fabric around the wound.

As Rebecca began to rip apart the familiar lace-trimmed garments she gave little thought to why Logan had been carrying her discarded petticoats. Right now time was of the essence for already he was reaching for a piece of the soft cotton which he folded into a square pad and pressed firmly against the torn flesh.

In the distance the sound of rifle fire became more and more sporadic and by the time Lance had done all he could to stem the bleeding, the others had returned.

"How is she?" Justin Wentworth was the first to ask as he knelt down and took Lona's limp hand in his.

Rebecca knew that Justin was fond of the beautiful Indian girl but she was surprised at the depth of emotion his voice could not hide.

"She's lost a lot of blood and the bullet's still in her. We've got to get her back to the fort."

Colonel Brooke came to peer down at Lona's still form. "We got about half of the red devils, Lance, but the rest made it to the swamp." He hesitated then added, "Chikiki was among those that got away."

Logan seemed not to have heard.

"Lance?" Rebecca spoke his name softly. When he looked up she wished there were some way to erase the torment in his eyes. "The Indians were holding us in a cave not far from here. It's full of priceless artifacts Chikiki stole from his people."

Scowling impatiently Logan snapped, "Do you think I care about that now? We've got to get Lona to the fort so Doc Murphy can get the bullet out of her back!"

As he turned away Rebecca touched his shoulder, drawing his attention once again.

"The treasure was very important to Lona," she insisted understanding the reason for his brusqueness and taking no offense. "She went back into the cave after we had managed to escape. She wanted to take her father proof of her brother's crimes."

Their eyes met. Hers sympathetic, his deadened by sorrow. Then he looked beseeching toward his commanding officer.

"Don't worry, my friend. We'll see that the treasure is brought to the fort before the bastards have a chance to get their hands on it again," George vowed.

As the soldiers aided by Lawrence Kearny disappeared into the woods, Lance lifted Lona taking care not to jostle her as he mounted the stallion. He held her cradled against his hard chest as if willing a portion of his strength into her weakening body. Justin, who had chosen not to accompany the others to the cave, set Rebecca upon his horse then climbed up behind.

The need for haste in getting Lona back to the doctor at the fort had to be balanced with caution so as not to

240

complicate her injury. Their progress was further impeded by the tangled vegetation along the way making the return journey seem endless to Rebecca.

Lance spoke not a word while Justin swore a string of oaths then settled down to devising hideous punishments for the Indian renegade once he was caught. The Englishman's inventiveness made the hairs rise on the back of Rebecca's neck.

When at last they entered the gates of Fort Brooke, Mary took immediate charge leading Lance with his burden up the stairs to Lona's bedroom and dispatching Justin to the barracks for Sergeant Murphy.

"Put some water on to boil," she flung over her shoulder at Rebecca who was grateful for something useful to do.

A few minutes later the back door opened and Justin hurried in followed by a fresh-faced young man who couldn't have been much older than Rebecca herself. Except for the black satchel he carried he looked like any of the other new, youthful soldiers. Neither spoke as they moved quickly through the kitchen, the sound of their booted feet against the wooden stairs echoing hollowly in the solemn stillness.

Justin reappeared almost instantly.

"How is she?" Rebecca asked as he took the heated water from the stove and started for the door.

"Too soon to tell," he replied gravely. Then he was gone.

She put another pot of water on to boil in case it should be needed, then poured herself a cup of strong black coffee and sat down at the table to wait. Soon she was joined by Justin and Lance. After handing them

241

each a mug of the hot brew she sat back down with her elbows braced on the table resting her chin in her palms.

Logan stared sightlessly out the window. He looked as if he carried the weight of the world on his broad shoulders, and Rebecca ached to share his load. Seeing him brought so low in spirit scared her more than trappers, preachers, and Indians put together. If only she could see some flicker of the self-assured arrogance she thought she despised. Anything but the all-consuming guilt and despair that rested on him now.

"Sergeant Murphy seems terribly young to be a doctor," Rebecca commented trying to draw Lance from behind the wall he seemed to have built around his emotions.

"He's young but he's a good doctor. Up on all the latest techniques. He'll do as much as any physician can." He heaved a sigh adding, "Pray God it's enough."

A short time later George Brooke and Lawrence Kearny entered the kitchen.

"How is she?" came the familiar question.

"Too soon to tell," Justin Wentworth answered.

Rebecca looked at her young countryman sharply. His white-hot anger was a clear indication of the depth of his feelings for the unconscious girl upstairs.

"We've put the stolen goods in the supply house," informed Lieutenant Kearny. "They'll be safe there until Nokomis can take them off our hands."

"Rebecca?" It was the first time the colonel had used her given name. That plus his businesslike manner made her wary. "We found the bodies of Martin and Brady. Ezra Holcomb, too. We can guess part of it," he continued twirling his cup in slow circles, "but I'd appreciate it if you would tell us exactly what happened."

Rebecca glanced at Logan slumped in his chair, his long legs stretched out before him. He seemed lost in his own thoughts paying no heed to the conversation. She took a deep breath then launched into a detailed account of all that had occurred from the time the two trappers accosted them beside the pool until she had literally run into the search party in the woods.

Finishing her recital she leaned back and then nearly bounced out of her chair as Logan's ham-sized fist slammed against the table overturning two of the empty cups. Silver sparks shot from his eyes as he pinned her with a furious glare.

"Haven't you left something out of your little tale?" he snarled, his teeth clenched in his square jaw, a muscle working in his temple.

Her eyes widened. She knew he wouldn't attack her with the other three men present, but he sounded so menacing. His rage seemed so volatile she pressed herself against the back of the chair crossing her arms over her breasts.

At last she stammered, "Wh-what do you mean?"

He rose and stood over her, the muscles of his brawny arms rippling under the buckskin as he leaned upon the table. He spoke with a deadly calm Rebecca found more threatening than his shouts.

"What the hell were you and Lona doing at the pool in the first place?"

He waited, challenging her to come up with a plausible reason for being so far from the fort when a storm was brewing. Rebecca bristled, beginning to get her own back up as he loomed over her. He was a self-appointed magistrate who deemed the defendant guilty before the evidence was heard. What gave this backwoods colonial the right to put her on the defensive? The air was charged with tension as amber flames battled icy slivers of granite.

All eyes turned to Sergeant Murphy as he strode into the room, his face impassive. Lance straightened to his full, formidable height and looked at the young doctor.

"Well?"

Rebecca recognized the entreaty underlying the gruff demand.

"I got the bullet out easy enough but she's lost a lot of blood. She may not regain consciousness for a few days." Murphy watched Lance solicitously and Rebecca felt certain the army doctor had purposely refrained from adding "if at all."

"She's in good hands. Mary knows what to do and I'll stay close by," he assured them.

Before the man finished speaking the back door banged loudly, rattling the windows in their frames. Rebecca swung around but Lance Logan had gone.

Chapter 15

By the third day after their return to the fort, Lona had not regained consciousness. The doctor assured them that this was to be expected. While the body worked to heal itself, the mind also needed time to recover from the shock of what had occurred. Still it left the inhabitants of Fort Brooke anxious and, in the case of Lance Logan, as testy as a pup with a burr in its tail. What few words he spoke came out in a straight-lipped growl accompanied by a deeply furrowed frown encouraging Rebecca to avoid him as much as possible.

During the past two days the soldiers had worked diligently erecting a two-storied house, a slightly smaller replica of George and Mary's home, for Andrew and Rachel within the confines of the stockade. The newly married couple had moved in the previous evening without the festivities that usually marked such an occasion in the territory. Under the circumstances no one felt like celebrating.

Lance had thrown all of his energies into the building project doing the work of three men and causing

Rebecca to wonder if he were impatient to return to his own cabin with its memories of lost love.

As she sat on the Brookes' wide front porch surveying the activities of the men working in the compound, Elizabeth came bouncing up to join her.

"Becca! Becca! Guess what? Mrs. Brooke gave me a pink coverlet to put on my bed, and she and Rachel are going to make pink lace curtains for my room. Can you believe it? My very own room just like back in England!"

Rebecca smiled dimpling prettily as Elizabeth spun around in circles, her clear blue eyes sparkling with excitement.

"I can hardly wait to see it," she replied with as much enthusiasm as she could muster, remembering how much she had missed Elizabeth's companionship as she had climbed into her empty bed the night before.

"I would say you are a lucky little girl."

Elizabeth stopped her spinning and walked over to where Rebecca was seated.

"I'm not a little girl anymore, Becca. Rachel said I am a young lady and Papa said they would have to find me a husband soon. Only when Papa said the part about finding me a husband Rachel told him to shush. Do you think finding a husband for me is supposed to be a surprise?"

It was all Rebecca could do to keep from laughing aloud as she looked at the serious but bemused expression on the face of the six year old twin. She hugged Elizabeth to her enjoying the feel of the child's small, warm body.

"I hope it's Mr. Logan," Elizabeth said, pulling out

of the arms that held her to twirl once more across the porch.

Rebecca arched her eyebrows. "You hope what is Mr. Logan?"

"I hope he's who they pick to be my husband. I like Mr. Logan." Elizabeth's tone made Rebecca wonder if she had sensed a certain hostility between Logan and herself.

Rebecca decided it was time to change the subject.

"Well, if I were you I would wait a few years before I thought about getting married. After all, you haven't had a chance to enjoy your new house and your new bedroom yet."

"Or my new mother," Elizabeth beamed proudly.

Rebecca was glad Elizabeth had so readily accepted Rachel. She pushed aside the aching loneliness that came each time she thought about returning to England without the twins. And why was it that with the thought of going home came the uninvited image of a rough-spoken giant? A man with the strength and necessary courage to tame this wild back country. A man whose dedication of purpose was tempered with compassion and respect for the people who had made this land their home since the beginning of time.

And then the answer came to her with all the clarity of a shooting star arcing across a midnight sky. She knew suddenly what had caused her restless days, her sleepless nights, the sensations that weakened her joints and filled her stomach with butterflies.

The conventional and prudent Lady Rebecca Winslow had fallen head over heels in love with an unpredictable, stubborn colonist whose heart belonged to a woman gone but not forgotten.

Rachel emerged from her new house, looking every bit the radiant bride as she smiled and waved to them. Bounding down the stairs Elizabeth raced across the yard toward her stepmother. Rebecca felt a stab of envy as Rachel put her arm around the small girl's shoulders and together they disappeared through the doorway.

But as much as she missed the little magpie's chatter, Rebecca was glad for time alone to accustom herself to the awakening of desire for a man who could not love her in return. How could she live without him? How could she leave knowing she would never see the handsome rogue again? Her emerald eyes misted, a single tear escaping to roll down her smooth pale cheek. Just the thought of Logan made her stomach turn somersaults and her heart beat faster. Thrump! Thrump! She marveled at the steadily increasing pulsation hammering within her breast. The drumming came louder and louder. It seemed as if the very boards beneath her feet were vibrating.

Damnation! The boards beneath her feet *were* vibrating.

She cocked her head to listen. It sounded like a herd of horses was approaching. Yet the noise was different, muted.

The soldiers recognized what Rebecca could not. The hoofbeats of many unshod mustangs. Without an order being given, they quickly exchanged tools for rifles and assumed battle formation outside the open gates.

What in the world were they doing? If they expected an attack they should be inside the fort with the gates closed. If they didn't, then why the need for arms?

As Rebecca stood pondering their strange behavior, Mary rushed out of the house drying her hands on her apron.

"The fat's about to hit the fire," she said as she hurried down the steps and headed toward her husband and Lance Logan now standing in front of the soldiers waiting for the oncoming riders to appear.

As she followed in Mary's wake, Rebecca asked herself what could possibly happen next.

On reaching the gates, she felt she had dared fate by asking. Several hundred horses were stampeding toward them, their nostrils flaring, carrying an equal number of Indian braves clad in buckskin breeches and little else. Some held lances, others clutched rifles. None were smiling.

They drew to a halt in front of the unwavering line of soldiers sending clods of dirt flying through the air. Rebecca looked on as silent minutes went by during which the Indians and the men of the fort remained motionless each waiting for someone else to make the first move. Finally one of the warriors gigged his mount and moved forward.

Even on horseback Rebecca could tell the man was at least a head taller than average. She was sure his moccasined feet could touch if he wrapped his long legs around the mustang's belly. He was thin for all his height, rawboned, yet the hard sinew of his hairless chest and arms marked him as a man of unquestionable strength. His face was narrow reminding Rebecca of a hawk; the resemblance accentuated by high cheekbones, dark hooded eyes, and a beaked nose.

He was some years past middle age, his brown face

leathery and crinkled. Wings of gray hair blended into coal-black, were then gathered in a topknot and secured to his head with a circle of beads. There was a regal bearing to the man as he sat his horse looking down haughtily at those on the ground below.

"Does my daughter live?" His gravelly voice was controlled and as icy as a winter snowstorm. His words confirmed Rebecca's premonition. The arrogant Indian was none other than Nokomis, mighty chief of the Calusa.

"Your daughter lives." Logan's clipped answer carried the same lack of emotion as that of the chief.

Wordlessly the Indian dismounted causing Rebecca to suck in her breath. The formidable-looking chieftain had to be seven feet tall . . . discounting his topknot! Even Logan seemed dwarfed in comparison.

"Thank God he isn't wearing war paint," she whispered to no one in particular as she stared up at the towering figure facing them.

Mary smiled over her shoulder at the awestruck Englishwoman.

Nokomis continued to glare at Logan obviously expecting the scout to say more. When it became apparent that Logan had said all he intended to say, George Brooke interceded.

"The doctor thinks Lona will be all right given a little time. She's still unconscious but Sergeant Murphy assures us that is to be expected."

Nokomis's deep set eyes continued to stare at Logan. Frowning, the commander tried once more to gain the Indian's attention.

"We have the objects taken from your temple."

The chief shifted his hooded gaze to the colonel.

"We found the treasure hidden in a cave not far from where your daughter was wounded." George hesitated wishing he could spare the guileless chief the pain he knew his words would bring. "Chikiki stole the sacred relics of the Calusa. He planned to trade them for guns and ammunition."

"You lie, white man!" came Nokomis's rasping denunciation. "You dare to call my son a thief? You dare to accuse him of bringing dishonor to his people?"

Rebecca retreated a step for in that moment the Indian chief looked every bit the savage ready to murder with his bare hands.

"He speaks the truth." Logan's voice was hard and unyielding as he confirmed the colonel's allegations though his heart bled all the while for the old warrior. He feared the news would be the final swell in a sea of disappointments that would break the man's unconquerable spirit. Nokomis had accepted the intrusion of the whites on his land knowing that to do otherwise would mean the destruction of his people. Lance doubted if even the great chief who had earned his complete admiration could bear the burden of knowing his only son had betrayed him.

From his pocket Lance withdrew a silver chain. Attached to the chain was an intricately carved amulet. He held it in his outstretched hand. When Nokomis made no move to take the necklace he let it dangle loosely from his fingers, the charm swinging like a pendulum.

"Lona was wearing this pendant when she was shot," Logan went on. "She risked her life to get it, going back into the cave where Chikiki had held her prisoner. She was determined to bring you proof of her brother's foul deeds."

Nokomis slowly reached out and took the necklace from Logan's hands. He turned it over studying the object from every angle.

"This was my wedding gift to Lona's mother. It was supposed to keep her safe from evil spirits. Its powers were not strong enough to ward off the fever that took her from me."

Recognizing his sadness, Rebecca knew Nokomis had loved his wife beyond measure and still mourned her loss. She remembered Lona's description of her parents' devotion to each other and forced herself to swallow the lump in her throat. However, his next words erased all traces of pity she felt for the downtrodden Indian as he focused his scrutiny once more on the solid form of Lance Logan who had remained uncommonly passive throughout the confrontation.

"I trusted my daughters into your keeping. I believed you would protect them as I no longer could. Now Little Dove is dead and Lona lies gravely wounded." He paused so that what came next was all the more dramatic. "If Lona dies I will no longer call you 'brother'!"

In the charged atmosphere that followed Rebecca waited for Logan to strike back, to defend himself against the unwarranted indictment made by the tribal leader.

"So be it," Lance replied soberly without debating the chief's unfair censorship.

As Nokomis made his way through the throng of soldiers that separated as he turned in the direction of the Brooke house, Rebecca watched Logan walk away toward the lonely isolated cabin he had shared with Little Dove. It broke her heart to see those broad shoulders slumped. But sympathy soon gave way to anger. What right had Nokomis to saddle Lance with the responsibility of protecting his daughters then lash out at him with undeserved criticism seeming to forget that it was his own son who had fired the shot that struck Lona? Such a flagrant injustice was not to be tolerated!

Rebecca was waiting on the porch, hands on hips, tiny foot tapping when Nokomis stooped to clear the door frame and walked out into the bright sunshine with Mary Brooke at his heels. She was too angry to notice their smiles or to be intimidated by the nearly two foot difference in her height and that of the Indian overlord.

"Shame on you!" she shouted, looking up and up into his dark startled face. Sparks flared in her eyes as she brazenly poked his bare chest with her finger. "You may be the *mighty* chief of the Calusa but let me tell you one thing," she thundered, "you don't have the brains of a *pissant!*"

"Rebecca!" Mary squeaked in alarm.

"Hush, Mary! I'm not yet finished with this jolterhead!" she commanded, never taking her fiery eyes from those black orbs scowling down at her in bewilderment. "Lance Logan is twice the man you will ever be! He's forthright and courageous, and he would die before he shirked his responsibilities. I have heard him admonish Lona time and again to stay near the fort. I never knew your oldest daughter but I have come to know and love Lona like a sister, and I can tell you nothing short of tying her up would have kept that girl

253

out of mischief."

Rebecca was so incensed it did not occur to her that despite her peculiar accent she sounded more like a stalwart pioneer than a titled peer of the realm.

Nokomis turned to Mary who stood with her mouth opened in horror, her arms crossed as if to shield her slightly rounded stomach.

"Who the hell is this woman?"

"Rebecca Winslow," Mary croaked. "Rebecca is from England," she explained as though that would excuse her outburst.

The chieftain's laughter rumbled deep in his chest taking Rebecca by surprise. Then before she could regain her aplomb he caught her beneath the armpits and lifted her slight frame, bringing her eye to eye with him.

"You remind me of my second wife," he chuckled lowering Rebecca once again. He swung himself off the porch with the litheness of a young buck. "Logan's gonna have his hands full with that one," he predicted still chortling as he headed for his horse.

"Well, I never," sputtered Mary after expelling a sigh of relief. "What do you make of that?" she asked her young visitor.

Rebecca hadn't the slightest idea.

Chapter 16

The Logan cabin stood about a quarter mile northwest of the fort in a clearing beside the creek. Moss-strewn cypress and pine trees shaded the neat log structure. Trumpet vines crept up the stone chimney while lilies and wild orchids grew here and there adding color to the gray-green landscape.

The fiery red ball of late afternoon sun was just drifting below the treetops as Rebecca made her way carefully along the trail of crushed grass leading to the front porch. She focused all of her attention on where she placed each slippered foot, otherwise she might have second thoughts about what she was doing. There was no logic to her determination to go to Logan. She doubted he would welcome her company. Still she was drawn like a moth to flame.

Davey and Edward had not yet tired of life in the barracks among the soldiers, and the thought of Lance alone in the cabin chastising himself not only for what happened to Lona but Little Dove as well compelled Rebecca to seek him out. Surely even a man as self-reliant as Logan needed someone to talk to in times of trouble. Or did he?

"There's only one way to find out," she reasoned squaring her shoulders as she stepped up onto the narrow covered entrance and rapped sharply on the sturdy wooden door before her courage deserted her.

When there was no response she knocked louder. Against the pressure of her closed fist the door swung inward. The interior of the cabin was gloomy, the furniture casting vague shadows across the single room. Rebecca stood framed in the door silhouetted by the waning rays of the sun while her eyes adjusted to the dim light. Then she saw him standing beside the fireplace, one arm resting upon the mantel as he stared into the cold grate.

"You don't belong here, lady!" he said without looking around. His words sounded hollow in the shadowy, unlit room and she wondered how he had known who was there. At the same time she realized that his sarcastic use of her title no longer raised her ire.

"You've become quite adept at telling me where I *don't* belong," she responded briskly.

His laugh lacked humor. "It's good to know I can still *do* something well."

Rebecca moved further into the room.

"If there's one thing I loathe, Mr. Logan, it's self-pity, so I will say what I have come to say then leave you to wrestle your demons."

Lance turned toward her then folding his arms across his massive chest. Though she couldn't see them, Rebecca could feel the glare of his steely gray eyes.

"Of course, if you want to be a martyr in the true sense you should don a hair shirt," she goaded. "In this heat that should provide enough penance for a lifetime of sins."

"If you've said what you came to say perhaps it would be better if you return to the fort now," he advised coldly.

"Well actually I haven't said what I came to say. I just decided to throw in a little advice about the hair shirt since I was here," she said nonchalantly while inside she was quaking. Preferring anger to indifference she wondered how far she would have to go to make him lose his temper completely. She hadn't long to wonder.

"Enough, Rebecca!" he lashed out. "Tell me why you're here then leave me alone!"

How could she tell him why she had come? How could she say that she was here because she loved him and she couldn't stand to see him hurting. That the only place she ever wanted to be was by his side. That she wanted to kiss away every heartache and wipe out all of the pain he had known in the past. If she told him the truth he would laugh and call her a naive little fool to think her love could ever mean anything to him. From the beginning he had made it clear that she was a misfit. Why should he feel any different now? She had been nothing but trouble to him since she stepped out of the longboat.

Despite her resolve to remain aloof, she felt tears well up in her eyes and she knew she had to get away from this man or suffer the embarrassment of allowing him to see her cry. With a sob in her voice she delivered the message she had used as an excuse for coming.

"Lona regained consciousness while her father was with her. She's going to be all right."

She spun around and sprinted for the door but Logan was quicker. Catching her from behind he hauled her back against his hard-muscled chest locking his arms around her so forcefully she felt the air whoosh from her lungs. It was too much! Rebecca simply didn't have the strength to fight Logan and hold back her tears at the same time. All of the fear, uncertainty and loneliness of the last few days surfaced bringing with it great racking sobs that Rebecca could no longer keep inside.

Lance didn't know what to make of it when he felt her body convulse in tears. Without letting go of her slight form he pivoted her around and buried her face against his shirt cupping her head in his huge hand while he massaged her neck gently.

"Rebecca, sweetheart, I'm sorry. I didn't mean to hurt you. Please, honey, stop crying."

His sudden shift from harsh words to tenderness made the tears flow harder.

"Please, darlin', don't cry. I didn't mean to hurt you. I'd never hurt you, sweetheart."

Logan's pleading endearments finally brought Rebecca's head up.

"Y-you didn't hurt me," she stuttered hiccuping.

"Then why are you crying?" He placed his finger beneath her chin when she tried to conceal her tear-streaked face against his damp shirt.

"I-I'm crying because I'm sad," she answered keeping her eyes downcast.

"And why is my lady sad?"

"Because you're sad," came her nearly inaudible reply.

"That doesn't make sense," he said softly erasing a

tear with his finger.

Rebecca raised her moist emerald eyes to his. "It does if I love you." The words were out before she could stop them and she felt the heat of humiliation flood her face.

An astonished Lance held her at arm's length studying her so intently she felt as if he looked into her very soul. When he was able to speak he asked in a hushed whisper, "And do you love me, Rebecca?"

"I'm afraid so," she admitted wondering how she could bear the shame if he laughed at her.

Instead he picked her up in his arms as if she weighed no more than a feather and carried her to where a large cushioned rocker stood before the fireplace. He lowered his big body into the chair cradling her like a baby. He leaned back and pushed against the floor, setting the rocker into motion. Rebecca closed her eyes content for the moment just to snuggle into his protective embrace.

"What am I going to do with you?" he murmured nuzzling his warm lips against her neck.

Rebecca jerked forward nearly tumbling out of his lap before strong arms pulled her back to safety.

"You needn't worry yourself about me, Logan! I am perfectly capable of taking care of myself!" she retorted hotly. "Besides the last thing you need is the responsibility of *another* woman!"

"Hey! Pull in your claws, little kitten."

He brought her hand to his lips and kissed each fingertip lightly. Every nerve in her body screamed for release when he put her finger into his mouth and began to suck gently.

"Lance?"

"I'm making progress," he smiled still swirling his velvety tongue around her finger creating a dull throbbing ache between her legs.

"Progress?" A puzzled frown creased her smooth brow.

"In the space of a few minutes we've gone from 'Mr. Logan' to 'Logan' to 'Lance.' At this rate I may be 'honey bunch' before the evening is over."

"Honey bunch?" Surely no man in his right mind would wish to be called something so absurd. Still natives were a strange lot.

"Try it again," he teased. "But this time put a little more passion in your voice."

Laughing eyes betrayed the jest.

"You are a silly goose!"

Rebecca nudged him in the ribs with her elbow. Lance was fascinated by the deep dimples that appeared in her cheeks when she laughed. He had rarely seen her laugh; one more thing for which he could blame himself.

"Silly goose? Lacks the ring of 'honey bunch' but it beats the hell out of 'Mr. Logan.'"

"Lance! Do be serious!"

She felt his body stiffen.

"I'm afraid to, my lady."

Rebecca could feel his heart beating against her breast and she knew that he was no longer joking.

Lance rose abruptly setting her back down on the rocker as he moved away to light the lamp on a table nearby. As the glow fanned out dispelling the shadows, Rebecca got her first real look at the inside of the cabin. It was a large room, the walls covered with smooth dark paneling. The furnishings were sparse, a bed pushed against one wall, another chair similar to the one in which she sat, and a bookcase filled with bound volumes. Behind her was a hand-hewn table and six matching chairs. Shelves holding dishes and a few small pots were attached to the wall above a wider wooden work bench. Stairs led to a loft overhead where she assumed Davey slept.

Unlike Mary's imports the few pieces of furniture looked to be of local vintage. There were no knick-knacks, no keepsakes on the mantel nor doilies on the table. Even the bed lacked the bright patterned spread she had imagined, covered instead with a nondescript brown blanket most likely army issue. If Little Dove had added any feminine touches to this stark uninviting chamber they were no longer in evidence.

Lance remained standing with his back to her and Rebecca flushed as she remembered how she had boldly professed her love for him. At times he had seemed as cold and empty as this room in which he lived but she knew better. She had seen the gentle compassionate side of him. She had watched his silver-gray eyes turn smokey with desire when he looked at her. He had held her with a need as fierce as her own. Oh yes! Lance Logan wanted her just as much as she wanted him. Now she must find a way to break down the shield he had built around his heart.

"Thank you for telling me about Lona. I'll go and see her at once." He seemed ready to ignore her declaration but Rebecca would have none of it.

"That may not be so easy," she laughed. "When I left the house Justin was standing guard outside her bedroom door daring anyone to disturb her."

Lance frowned disbelievingly. "Justin Wentworth?

Do you think he has designs on Lona?"

Musical laughter trilled through the dreary room. "If by 'designs' you mean is Justin in love with her, I would say yes!"

"Damnation!"

"Hold on, Logan! That's my word!"

"You shouldn't swear!"

"Don't tell me what to do!"

Lance shook his head. "Somebody better! What's the matter with you English? Do you always fall in love with the wrong people?"

Rebecca's temper soared. "Are you talking about me or Justin?"

"Both! And why in hell's name can't we be in the same room for five minutes without shouting at each other?" he shouted.

Rebecca bowed her head meekly. "I cannot understand it, Logan. I am the most even-tempered, mild-mannered, easy-to-get-along-with—"

"In a pig's eye," he roared.

Grabbing her by the wrist he pulled her out of the chair and into his arms clutching her tightly as he gazed down into her lovely laughing face. Her slender hands were splayed across his chest and as he bent toward her irresistible satin lips she raised up on the tips of her toes to meet him halfway. His mouth touched hers, gently at first. Then as her arms looped around his neck he deepened the kiss, forcing her lips apart until his tongue could enter the forbidden paradise and he could quench his thirst for the sweet nectar within.

As Rebecca's knees turned to jelly and buckled beneath her, she leaned more heavily into Logan aware of his rigid manhood pressed against her stomach. He felt it too and tried to pull away but she refused to let him go.

"Why are you afraid of me?" Her lips were a scant breath away from his.

Gray eyes clouded with painful memories. "I'm not afraid *of* you, sweetheart. I'm afraid *for* you. Everyone I have ever cared about has been taken from me."

He told her how his parents and sister had died of the fever in Charleston, of the guilt and anguish he had suffered when he discovered the ravished body of Little Dove in the woods.

"And now, Lona . . ." He let the words trail off. "Don't you see, Rebecca? I am afraid my love would destroy you and I simply can't take that chance."

"Balderdash! I suppose next you'll tell me you believe in curses and death heads! Do you really think you have some divine power over life and death? Spare me anymore of this nonsense, Logan! You sound more like Ezra Holcomb every minute!"

Rebecca was spitting mad to think Lance would believe himself responsible for the tragedies in his past.

"You're not the only person to lose loved ones who should have had years of living left! I lost my parents and my sister, too. Little Dove died because she refused to heed your warnings. Lona was wounded for the same reason. Besides, it was Martin and Brady who killed Little Dove. They bragged about it just before Reverend Holcomb shot them. But none of that was your fault and I won't allow you to throw away our happiness because of superstitious nonsense!"

By the time Rebecca finished her tirade she was exhausted and on the verge of weeping again. Never quick to cry she had suddenly become a regular watering pot. She glanced up to see if she had gone too far in her vehement defense of this man she loved. His grip on her arms grew tighter and she knew a moment of fear as raw anguish changed his handsome face into that of the ruthless savage she had first thought him to be. Then he released her and appeared to collapse, reaching toward the fireplace where he leaned against the mantel burying his head in the crook of his arm.

"Damn them to hell!" His hatred was a tangible thing as he whirled to face Rebecca, his ragged words ripping through the silence. "I knew it! Damn it, I knew they were the ones! It should have been me who killed them but instead I gave those sons of bitches the benefit of a doubt. I had to have proof!"

Rebecca was at a loss as to how to deal with Logan in his present frame of mind. A vein throbbed in his temple and he seemed ready to explode. Suddenly he turned and beat his fist against the solid cypress lintel. "It should have been me who killed them. Death came too easy to the bastards. They didn't suffer as I would have made them suffer," he lamented continuing to pound the heavy wooden beam.

Finally Rebecca could stand it no longer. She grasped his arm and with some effort turned him toward her once more.

"The man that I love could not mistreat another human being, no matter what he might have done to deserve it." She hoped she was getting through to him, but although he had calmed, his look was far away. It was impossible to tell what he was thinking. Somehow she had to bring him back to her. "No matter the circumstances, Martin and Brady are dead," she hesitated, "and Little Dove is dead."

As she stared into his smoke-gray eyes she could see him gradually returning from a hell to which his conscience had resigned him. "It wasn't your fault, Logan. Are you going to reject my love as penance for a sin you didn't commit? Please," she pleaded as tears streamed unchecked down her cheeks, "come back to me. I know you loved Little Dove, but let her rest in peace."

Lance looked at her for long moments as if wondering if the miracle of a lasting love were possible for him. Then he enfolded her in his embrace. Putting her from him at last, he sought to explain. "I know now that my feelings for Little Dove were more those of a protector than a lover. Certainly I cared about her but mostly I felt responsible for keeping her safe. You see, in her heart she was more child than woman and she never cared for the things other women hold dear like a home and family. The only time she seemed truly happy was when she was riding like the wind across the meadows and through the woods. I could have stopped her and I did warn her again and again, but even knowing the dangers I could not bring myself to forbid her the freedom that kept her spirit alive."

So that was why the cabin held no mark of its previous mistress. Rebecca, while relieved to hear of his true feelings for the beautiful Indian woman, knew too how weighed down with guilt he must have been when he learned of her brutal death. She sought for words of consolation but could find none worthy of so poignant a moment. So she simply held him close and waited. She felt his heart beating rapidly against her breast and she longed to infuse him with her love, a love so strong it would wipe out every painful memory in his past.

As his breathing steadied, he bent to search her face looking for answers only she could give.

"I have to know the truth, Rebecca. Do you love me enough to give up your dream of returning to England, give up your title and all that it entails? Could you be content as the wife of a bad-tempered army scout, mother to a half-breed little scamp? Think about it carefully, sweetheart," he cautioned, "for the only thing I have to offer you is danger and uncertainty."

"And love," she sighed against his lips. "I don't have to think about it. I love you more than life itself. It isn't important where we live or under what circumstances as long as we are together. Please, Lance, let me exorcise your ghosts."

He gave her a smile so full of love and hope she knew that nothing could ever take the place of the happiness they had found in each other. Finally she understood what Amy Dickerson had tried to explain when she talked of how her husband made her feel. Thinking of Amy brought to mind William Pennington. How odd that she could scarcely remember what he looked like. She hadn't thought of him for days. But she really must write to him tomorrow and explain that she would not be coming home. She was already *home*.

Her thoughts returned to the present as Lance drew her closer, his hands playing up and down her spine.

"Have you any idea what you're getting yourself into, lady?" he whispered against her ear.

Rebecca smiled up at his strong, handsome face.

"Surprise me," she challenged nibbling the corner of his mouth.

"Ah, sweetheart, if you knew the depth of this weak man's need you would turn tail and run as fast as those gorgeous legs could carry you." It was more than the wanting in his voice that convinced her of his sincerity as he pulled her against him. "How I long to take you to my bed and make love to every inch of your beautiful body until you beg me to stop."

As he played with a golden ringlet that had escaped the pins holding her silken hair, she smiled seductively. "I am the one who is weak, for I would gladly join you in your bed."

Gone was the proper-minded young miss who had placed such store in the rigid moral standards dictated by a hypocritical society. She was a woman in love, and as she rubbed her palm against the shadowed stubble on his cheek Rebecca wanted nothing so much as to become one with this man who had taken possession of her very being.

It was Lance who found the strength to resist the temptation to make her his own in the fullest sense of the word.

"I love you, Rebecca, and although letting you out of my sight is the hardest thing I have ever done, I won't have your reputation tarnished just to satisfy my own needs."

"But they're my needs, too," she half pleaded, green eyes smoldering with passion.

To love and be loved in return was a new experience for Lance. It frightened him to know that he belonged to this tiny, enchanting creature body and soul, while at the same time he welcomed the idea of laying his heart at her feet. He vowed to let nothing spoil their future together, a future that promised to be stimulating given his forceful personality and her intractable nature. He kissed her adorable turned-up nose and held her at arm's length.

"Don't make it more difficult for me than it already is," he implored. "I have to return you to the fort before George sends out the troops. But tomorrow I will ride to Fort King at first light and bring Robert Marsh back with me. At gunpoint if necessary. In two days' time we'll be married. Then let anyone try to keep us apart! You're mine, lady. And soon you'll understand exactly what that means."

His leering look made her giggle. "You, sir, had best conserve your energy for we British are known for our stamina."

Hand in hand they walked back to the fort. A half moon illuminated the path and cast a glow about the lighthearted couple. Too soon they reached the gates.

"Oh! I almost forgot to tell you something," Rebecca apologized as they stopped beneath the sheltering arms of the giant oak. "I don't think Chief Nokomis is angry with you anymore. I believe he is sorry for the things he said."

Some of the joy went out of Logan's face as he remembered the Indian's bitter words. "What makes you think so?"

"He and I had a little talk," she evaded.

Lance looked at her suspiciously. "And just what did you say to change the way he felt?"

"I don't think it was what I said. It was how I said it,"

she replied innocently. "He told me I reminded him of his second wife."

"It figures. I've heard she was a real hellion!" Lance feigned a shudder which Rebecca ignored as her hands glided up his shirt front and around his neck.

"And I've heard she was completely devoted to her husband," she countered demurely touching her lips to his with soft butterfly kisses. "I wish you didn't have to leave." Her impassioned sigh was nearly his undoing.

"Soon, my love, nothing will keep us apart," he promised folding her into his arms. "For now, go to bed and dream of me. I'll see you before I leave in the morning."

Logan reluctantly let her go and hurried toward the gate cursing his gallantry. Then the compound echoed with his laughter as her lilting voice called to him from out of the darkness.

"Goodnight . . . honey bunch!"

Chapter 17

The eastern horizon was painted with streaks of palest pinks, blues and lavenders, the only hint of the sunrise to come, as Rebecca stole across the dewy ground. A sleepy guard yawned as he pushed open the heavy gates to greet the new day. He nodded a good morning when she passed but made no move to prevent her departure nor did he question her reason for leaving the post unescorted at such an early hour.

Making her way down to the sandy beach where waves lapped softly against the shore, Rebecca perched upon the boulder she had come to regard as her thinking place. But today she no longer felt the restless discontent that usually plagued her when she sought out this particular spot. She knew she had found what she had been waiting for all of her life.

This morning she saw only beauty surrounding her. Even the screeching of the greedy gulls diving for their breakfast was music to her ears. As the brilliant red-orange sun crested the treetops adding pigments of vibrant gold and purple to the pastel sky, Rebecca wondered how she could ever have thought of the Florida territory as ugly and uninviting. Surely it was the most glorious place on earth. Lifting her nose to inhale the pungent salty air she wanted to shout to the world how wonderful it was to be alive.

To Lance hidden in the shadows cast by the needled branches of a tall slash pine, everything else paled in comparison to the beautiful lady seated on the rock gazing at the sunrise. Dressed in a gown the color of meadow grass with her head tilted to catch the light, she was beauty personified. Her delicate features were in perfect proportion to her dainty form. She wore her thick golden hair loosely tied with a green ribbon, the gilded ringlets cascading down her slender back.

His heart skipped a beat as he watched her waiting patiently for her lover. That he was that man seemed too good to be true but he pushed aside his vague ill-feelings that such a stroke of luck could not last.

Rebecca felt rather than heard his approach and rose, turning to be caught up in his welcoming arms. He squeezed her tightly for it seemed more than a few short hours since he had held her.

"Has a good night's sleep restored your sanity, my lady?"

Rebecca was not fooled by his teasing manner. She could see the doubt written on his face. He was wondering if she had changed her mind and knowing that she held the key to his heart and happiness in her hand was both exhilarating and frightening at the same time.

Rebecca dimpled, her eyes sparkling in the early morning light.

"My mind is quite sound," she replied leaning up to

brush her lips against his. "And I love you very much," she added, tears misting her eyes as she saw the relief her words brought to him.

He held her close, breathing in the floral scent of her hair, rubbing his thumb gently along one satin-smooth cheek. He longed to keep her locked in his embrace forever. His desire for her was so compelling it threatened to overpower his common sense. Maybe she had been right in thinking him uncivilized for he wanted nothing so much as to lower her to the sand and make love to her on the beach regardless of who might be watching.

"Whoa, sweetheart! If you keep kissing me like that I'll say to hell with the preacher and show you what a shameless rogue I really am."

Rebecca blushed thinking how much she had changed since coming to this violent untamed land. Throwing herself into a man's arms and kissing him was hardly accepted behavior for one of good breeding. Yet it seemed right and natural to express her love in such a way and Lance didn't seem the least offended by her forwardness.

"I wish I could go with you. Now that I've found you I don't want to let you go." She gave him a weak smile. "I'm afraid you'll remember what a useless piece of baggage I am and decide not to come back."

Rebecca was only half joking for she knew there was much she had to learn about being a pioneer wife and she could only hope Lance had an inordinate amount of patience. She looked so small and scared Lance quickly hugged her against his big solid body. He placed his fisted hand beneath her chin and tenderly raised her head until their eyes met.

"I love you, Rebecca, as I never thought I could love any woman. You're everything I want and need to make my life complete. But there's a lot I don't know about loving a woman and being a good husband. Why don't we make a pact to help one another learn the things we need to know?"

Rebecca marveled. Could this gentle giant be the same man she had once thought cold and unfeeling?

"Pacts should be sealed with a kiss," she stated firmly.

"An old British tradition, I suppose."

"The start of a new Logan tradition," she purred seductively.

He touched her lips lightly then deepened the kiss, his tongue sought the honeyed sweetness within. Rebecca felt giddy, drifting in a sea of dreams, soaring above the tallest trees. Surely no one else had ever been as happy as she. Lance said he had never loved another woman the way he loved her. That must include Little Dove and the knowledge added to her joy. She had worried needlessly about the depth of his feelings toward the woman who had borne him a son. Now she knew that not even a ghost could come between them.

At the sound of the sentry's shout they sprang apart, looking first toward the fort then to the west in the direction the guard was pointing. Far out to sea the straight stretch of horizon was broken by what appeared to be a tiny gray specter in the distance. Rebecca clutched Logan's arm standing on tiptoe as if the few added inches would enable her to identify whatever had gained the soldier's attention.

"What is it?"

"I can't be sure," Lance answered squinting to see

273

beyond the blinding reflection of sun upon the water, "but my guess is it's Kearny and the *Enterprise* returning from patrol, and if I'm not mistaken he has another ship in tow."

As they watched along with the crowd that had quickly gathered on the beach when the alarm sounded Logan's guess proved to be correct. Inching ever closer the indistinct image gradually materialized as two separate vessels. The mighty *Enterprise* led the way clearing a foam-glazed path through the sun-kissed waters of the bay. Dwarfed by the awesome man-of-war was a bedraggled merchant ship minus its main mast. Heavy braided ropes connected the ships and as the smaller of the two listed awkwardly from side to side Rebecca wondered how it had managed to stay afloat. Just above the waterline a gaping hole decorated the port side resembling the bull's eye of a target. The deck was littered with debris and cheering sailors obviously relieved to be within shouting distance of dry land.

Rebecca jumped up and down excitedly tugging on Logan's arm.

"Look, Lance! They're British!"

Even without a flag flying there was no mistaking the white ducks and striped jerseys of the men lining the rail.

As the longboats brought load after load of men ashore, the beach became a jubilant madhouse. The sailors celebrated their narrow escape by dancing upon the hardpacked sand, their cockney accents blending with the screeching protest of the annoyed seagulls. Rebecca laughed delightedly at their antics as a feeling of familiarity spread through her for these were her countrymen and she rejoiced that they had arrived safely at Fort Brooke.

The last boat brought the Captain ashore, a dour, stern-faced individual not at all like the affable Jeremiah Higgins. Before Colonel Brooke could greet the captain properly the man launched into a diatribe about the lack of protection the Americans offered those on whose trade they depended. He demanded that they do something about the barbarous pirates who had had the affrontery to attack his ship.

"You may be sure the Minister of Trade will have a full report regarding your lackadaisical attitude toward the riffraff that roam these waters practically within sight of this fort."

Rebecca felt the corded muscles beneath her fingers stiffen but Lance held his temper in check. She, on the other hand, had no qualms about disputing the red-faced captain's unfair allegations.

"Rubbish!" she snorted taking a step toward the spluttering Englishman. With hands on her hips and fire in her eyes she made no effort to disguise her indignation. "You make it sound as if you are doing this poor upstart young country a tremendous favor by bringing your precious cargo to our shores when in fact the crown will reap a healthy profit from merchandise that will fill your hold on the return voyage!"

Lance could barely contain his laughter as his feisty lady berated the astonished ship captain, and he nearly burst with pride when she said "our" shores. She was rapidly becoming one of the territory's staunchest defenders.

"My word! You are an Englishwoman!"

If Rebecca had been in less of a temper she might

275

have found humor in the man's disparaging tone. Instead she snapped back, "And you, sir, make me ashamed of that fact!"

"I believe you've made your point, Rebecca," Lance grinned as he pulled her back against his chest and wrapped his arms around her in a possessive gesture that left no room to doubt that she was *his* woman.

George took the opportunity to introduce himself leaving Captain Horatio Cavendish slightly mollified with his assurances that the pirates plundering the Gulf would soon be a thing of the past.

"Mistress?" Captain Cavendish frowned as he once again addressed Rebecca. "Would you by chance be Lady Rebecca Winslow?" he asked skeptically looking her up and down from the spray of freckles across her pert little nose to the loose-flowing skirt of her cotton gown no longer padded with numerous stiff petticoats.

Rebecca hesitated then replied warily. "That's correct, but how did you know?"

"This . . . gentleman," the captain paused to look haughtily at Lance, not a particularly smart move, Rebecca thought smugly, since the captain had to look up a considerable distance to express his disdain. "This gentleman called you Rebecca. That plus your manner of speech led me to wonder if you might possibly be the woman to whom this missive is addressed."

As he spoke he reached inside his coat to withdraw a wrinkled white envelope extending it toward her dubiously for he still could not reconcile the young woman before him with his mental picture of what an English lady should look like.

For her part Rebecca stood staring at the letter making no attempt to take it. She was aware of a

276

sinking sensation in the pit of her stomach for she was sure it was from William. How she wished she had written to him first letting him down easily as she explained the happiness she had found here. She did not want to learn that he had missed her and anxiously awaited her return for it would make her response all the more difficult.

A subtle nudge in her back brought her out of her stupor. She reached for the letter begrudgingly murmuring her thanks to the arrogant Captain Cavendish as she tucked the envelope into the pocket of her skirt. Later would be soon enough to read its contents.

But as the others moved toward the entrance to the fort, Rebecca hung back. She pressed her hand against her hip and heard the paper crackle. Knowing there was no point putting off the inevitable she strolled down the beach in the opposite direction pausing beside a leafless gumbo limbo bush. As she examined the well-worn wrapper she recognized the small neat script as that of her lifelong friend, Amy Dickerson not the expected scrawled handwriting of William Pennington. Opening the letter she smiled with relief then vowed to write William without delay for to do otherwise would be unconscionable.

Her smile faded quickly as the words blurred before her eyes. She reread the brief message in which Amy apologized for being the bearer of bad news then negated the apology by assuring Rebecca that she was better off without the cad.

Lance cleared his throat to announce his presence. He had not intended to intrude on her privacy but the simple truth was he could not bear to let her out of his sight. Their love was new and tenuous. They had much to learn about each other and deep down Lance still found it hard to believe Rebecca was his and that she was willing to give up all she had in England to stay here and make the territory her home. He had to be certain that whatever news the letter held would not change her mind about marrying him. If he could see her face he would know one way or the other.

He had held his breath as she ripped open the envelope and unfolded the single sheet inside. But he had not been prepared for her reaction. The blood drained from her face leaving her ghostly white. Her hands shook as she looked up at him with dry dazed eyes.

"He's dead."

Lance knew about William Pennington even though Rebecca had never mentioned his name. Through things Edward and Elizabeth had told him he had pieced together a fairly accurate picture of an arrogant dandy who cared only for himself. He had spared little thought for the man secure in the belief that Rebecca's feelings for Pennington were merely infatuation. Now he wondered.

He fought the urge to draw her into his arms and kiss away all memory of the dead Englishman who had not deserved this extraordinary woman's love. Instead he waited for her to make the first move, praying silently that she would come back to him. He hadn't long to wait. She let out a long sigh then melted into his arms.

"My dearest love," she whispered. "How fortunate I am to have found you." Her heart was in her beautiful emerald eyes.

Lance swallowed the lump in his throat as he clasped

her fragile body tightly to him and wordlessly thanked a benevolent God.

Hand in hand they walked along the shore until Rebecca pulled free bending to pick up a perfectly formed scallop shell, its russet ridges contrasting sharply against a background of white. She kept her eyes lowered appearing to study the incrustation resting in her palm. When she spoke her words were barely audible above the sound of the waves and the splashing of mullet playing in the shallow water.

"He was killed in a duel by a jealous husband. The man came home from his club earlier than expected."

Her faint laugh held a note of bitterness that made Lance wish he could get his hand around the bastard's throat. Rebecca was too good for the likes of Pennington but that would not take the sting out of her humiliation. She still did not raise her eyes to meet his.

"Don't shut me out, sweetheart," he entreated as he caressed her arm.

Rebecca could feel his callused hand through the thin sleeve of her dress.

"Did you love him, Rebecca?"

She gazed into eyes the color of polished metal, eyes that held sympathy and concern for her.

"I thought I did until I discovered real love. Now I know that my determination to marry William was a form of childish rebellion. Everyone said he wasn't right for me so, of course, I had to have him. You may not believe this, Lance, but I used to be quite willful."

She was absolutely serious and so adorable Lance decided not to laugh though it was no easy effort. He was glad she had wasted no tears on the unfaithful son of a bitch.

"Are you going to be all right now?"

"Honestly, Lance. I have never felt better," she assured. "I just wish you didn't have to go away."

"I don't."

"You don't what?"

"I don't have to go away."

"But Lance? I thought you wanted to marry me."

Rebecca was thoroughly confused and filled with dread at the prospect that he might have changed his mind. Shameful as it was to admit the shock of William's death had been accompanied by a sense of relief and release. But the thought of losing Lance was too devastating to contemplate. He took her in his arms and kissed her soundly.

"Don't frown so, my lady. I am totally committed to making you my wife but I can do it without going to Fort King."

Her expression proved she still did not understand and Lance hurried to explain.

"Captain Cavendish," he enthused. "A ship's captain has the authority to perform marriages."

Her mien changed instantaneously from perplexity to horror.

"Captain Cavendish?" she shrieked.

Reading her thoughts, Lance went on to remind her of their options.

"Of course we could wait until Captain Higgins returns. He should be back from New Orleans in two or three weeks. A month at most. Or I can leave within the hour for Fort King."

He allowed none of the suspense churning inside him to show as he gave her time to mull over the alternatives.

"What if Captain Cavendish refuses to perform the ceremony? I don't think he sees me as a shining example of the English aristocracy."

Lance relaxed knowing he had won.

"If he balks at the idea, I'll tell him you're in a family way," he teased.

Rebecca punched him playfully.

"Last night protecting my reputation was your major concern. Today you threaten to tell a total stranger that I'm pregnant!"

"By tomorrow it could be true," he reminded and Rebecca found the idea most appealing.

"Let's go talk to the good Captain. I'll race you to the fort," she challenged hiking up her skirts as she sped back the way they had come.

Shells crunched beneath their feet as startled sandpipers took flight. The morning sun smiled down on the carefree couple running against the wind, their hearts soaring in wild anticipation of a bright future ahead.

Chapter 18

Lance scowled as he assisted Rebecca across the litter-strewn deck of the *HMS Bountiful*. She tried to stifle her giggles by coughing delicately into her handkerchief and just missed tripping over a broken timber.

"Damn it!" Lance growled steadying her. "I should have gone to Fort King like I planned. The man is a fiend! He blames us because the damn pirates shot up his damn boat and this is his revenge!"

"Shush! If Captain Cavendish hears you call his ship a boat he may refuse all together," Rebecca warned. "Besides he might have been telling the truth when he said he could only perform a marriage ceremony on his boat . . . I mean ship."

"Like hell! It's revenge, pure and simple!"

Rebecca looked up coyly. "We can always tell the Captain we've changed our minds and you can leave for Fort King in the morning."

"No chance, lady." The beginning of a smile played

on Logan's lips, the first hint of a smile since their confrontation with the pompous ship captain.

His ill-humor had begun when they politely asked the disdainful gentleman if he would conduct the service that would unite them as man and wife. He had answered with an exaggerated sniff and a bored expression; then suggested that they wait for a proper preacher.

When Rebecca unthinkingly blurted out that they couldn't possibly wait for it might be months before a "proper preacher" passed by, the arrogant ass had looked pointedly at her stomach and replied with a loud "Harrumph!"

Only after Lance threatened to set him adrift in a longboat with no oars did Captain Cavendish reluctantly condescend. He then cast a pall over their victory by insisting that the marriage would not be legal unless it was performed aboard his ship.

It had been a colorful parade of small boats that brought the wedding party and their guests to the battle scarred *Bountiful*. Rachel looked like a peacock in the dress she had worn at her own wedding blending prettily with Mary's gown of rose pink and Elizabeth's green organdy ruffles. The men were dashing in their elegant military garb trimmed with braid and numerous badges of honor.

Rebecca had been struck dumb when Lance appeared in a uniform much like that of Colonel Brooke weighed down with at least as many medals. The coat molded his huge frame as though it had been made expressly for him which surely must have been the case. Apparently Logan wore buckskins and rode scout for the army because he preferred to do so and he obviously had sufficient rank to get away with such eccentric behavior. Rebecca smiled as the point was brought home to her that she still had much to learn about this man who would soon be her husband.

The bride looked like an angel in a full-skirted gown of lavender overlaid with delicate lace of an even lighter shade. On a whim she had packed the dress in the bottom of her trunk, never dreaming she would have occasion to wear it. Now she was grateful for her impetuousness. The glossy curls piled atop her head, held in place by a tiara of wild orchids, shimmered like spun gold in the late afternoon sunlight. But it was the radiance of her smile that accounted for her ethereal beauty. Had her ensemble included a pair of gossamer wings, Lance knew she would have ascended into the puffy white clouds hovering overhead.

"I'm sorry, sweetheart. This is hardly the kind of wedding girls dream about."

He looked so angry and so glum Rebecca searched for the right words to reassure him.

Cupping his clean-shaven face in her small hands she replied, "Do you think me so shallow that I would care where our wedding took place?"

Before he could answer she went on, "Would saying our vows before the Archbishop in St. Paul's Cathedral bind us any more securely or make our marriage any more lasting than making those vows before God surrounded by his most wondrous creations. Here we are standing beneath an infinite blue sky upon a boundless sea. There could be no more fitting place to consecrate our never-ending love for one another."

Her simple words spoken with unquestionable sincerity gave Lance a feeling of joy he never thought possible.

"Oh, my love. You make me believe in miracles," he confessed squeezing her hard. She tingled with anticipation knowing that there were many more embraces to come.

At home aboard his vessel, despite the wreckage, Captain Cavendish quickly took charge. First he ordered Davey and Edward to come down from the bridge where Edward had been spinning the steering wheel while Davey took a look at everyone on deck through a long telescope. He then proceeded to position each of the witnesses as well as the prospective bride and groom where he thought they should be, seemingly oblivious to the fact that all but him were facing directly into the relentless afternoon sun.

From behind Rebecca came Mary's soft voice. "Don't worry, honey. We'll have a real celebration when we get back to the house."

Encouraging Lance to whisper smugly, "She's wrong. We'll have a *real* celebration when we get back to the cabin."

And so the solemn service began with Rebecca blushing while trying not to choke on her bubbling laughter.

A full moon hung low suspended in the clear tropical sky embellished by a million twinkling stars as Lance and Rebecca made their way along the familiar path toward the dark cabin.

"Oh, Lance! Wasn't it the most wonderful party?" Rebecca enthused gaily. "I'm at a loss for words to describe it."

"Try endless," Lance suggested with a groan gaining him an elbow in the ribs.

"Ingrate!"

"Surely you didn't expect gratitude from an uncivilized *native.*"

She looked at his handsome profile silhouetted in the moonlight.

"Yes . . . well . . . actually I'd like to talk to you about that."

"About what? My barbarian manners?" He chuckled pulling her against his side as they walked. "I hope, Mrs. Logan, you don't intend to try and make me over now that we're married. I'm afraid I am what I am," he breathed in her ear causing chills to run down Rebecca's spine.

"That's the whole point," she retorted pausing and tugging at his arm until he turned to face her.

She flicked her forefinger disarranging one of the medals decorating his jacket. "Just what are you? This uniform belies the backwoods impression you strive so hard to give."

Logan's laugh came from deep in his chest. "Now there's where you're wrong, sweetheart. The last thing I have ever tried to do is impress anybody."

Rebecca stamped her foot. "Don't bandy words with me, Logan. You know exactly what I mean."

"Of course I do," he replied taking her in his arms. "But I can't resist teasing you. You look so cute when you're riled."

Even in the semi-darkness he could see flames spark to life in her vivid green eyes.

"All right," he conceded knowing better than to push her too far. "While I was in Charleston I attained the rank of major in the army. Officially I'm still Major Lance Logan. But I abhorred the regimented behavior the service demanded and I didn't like ordering men around, especially since following those orders could get them killed."

He paused tilting his head thoughtfully. "I had made up my mind to resign from the army and try another line of work though God only knows what that would have been. Anyway about that time I was asked to come to the Florida territory to scout around for strategic locations to build forts. My family had just died in the fever epidemic and it seemed like the perfect way to escape what I didn't want to remember. It worked almost too well for by the time the forts were established I'd become so accustomed to my 'uncivilized' way of living I balked at resuming my duties as a conventional soldier."

He stopped, seeming to think his explanation sufficient but Rebecca refused to be put off.

"Let me guess the rest. Refusing to resume your assigned duties, you were court-martialled and shot at dawn," she finished, her tone indicating a satisfactory conclusion to his story.

"Fortunately not, you bloodthirsty, wench! The government and I reached a compromise. As long as I continued to do their scouting and caused them no undue embarrassment, I could live and dress as I pleased. The arrangement has worked well for everyone concerned."

Rebecca had become so engrossed in her husband's

narrative she didn't notice that they had reached the steps leading to the porch.

"I'm glad they didn't shoot you," she remarked laughing up at the enigmatic rogue. "And I'm glad you wore your uniform for our wedding. Knowing now how you dislike 'dressing up' I am most grateful. As I recall," she laughed lightly, "this conversation began with the subject of gratitude and here we are again."

"Yes, here we are," Lance agreed looking at the wooden structure before them. "And to prove your gratitude I feel it is only fitting that you help me take this damn thing off."

With that he scooped her up in his powerful arms and carried her across the threshold of her new home.

Lance released her legs letting them glide to the floor, but he held her close molding her slender body to his. He ran his hands along her spine, cupping her rounded buttocks as he drew her against his male hardness.

"Somehow I knew you would have no fear of coming to my bed."

There was satisfaction in the words he murmured next to her ear as Rebecca collapsed against him rather than resisting his nearness.

"I warned you of my wantonness," she replied demurely as she wiggled and stretched to fit the contours of her body to his.

Rebecca knew she was far from the self-indulgent creature she claimed to be. Up until she met Lance Logan she had felt no great desire to be touched by any man. On the rare occasions when William had held her hand or kissed her, though she had not been repulsed, she had never experienced the rapturous ecstasy described by the heroines in the books she read. Surely, she had decided, such emotion must be the figment of an author's overactive imagination. Now as she ached with longing for Logan's tender touch she realized how wrong she had been.

Reluctantly he let her go, moving to light the lamp. As its warm glow dispelled the shadows he began to shrug off his heavy braid-trimmed coat but stopped in mid-motion when Rebecca rushed to his side.

"Wait!" she demanded smiling seductively as she reached to pull the jacket from his wide shoulders and slide his arms free. "I believe this is my job."

She let the garment fall to the floor as she reached around him to run her hand across the corded muscles of his broad back feeling them ripple beneath her fingers.

Slowly, wordlessly, they undressed one another until they stood in naked splendor within the subdued light of the lamp. There was no false modesty between them as they studied one another. Lance had the well-honed body of a jungle cat, proud and sleek and incredibly masculine. Rebecca's small flawless figure with its gently rounded curves begged to be caressed.

Logan allowed his gaze to roam freely from the rich gold coronet of curls atop her head to the toes of her tiny feet, his silver eyes smoldering with passion.

"Promise that you'll always be *my* wanton lady," he beseeched as they came together once more in a languorous embrace, the coarse dark hair of his chest brushing the rounded globes of her pearly white breasts.

289

Her luminous green eyes radiated the love and desire she felt for the rugged frontiersman.

"I promise," she pledged placing her dainty hand against his lean dark cheek. "And what of you, sir? Will you always crave the affections of your shameless wife?"

"Even when the infirmities of old age slow this randy body to a snail's pace, I will hobble after you with lust in my eyes."

He took her laughing lips with his. Pulling the pins from her hair his breath caught in his throat as the thick ringlets, gilded by the light, cascaded down her back to cover his hands. Lifting her he walked to the narrow bed and gently laid her atop the cover, watching admiringly as the shimmering tresses fanned out upon the single pillow.

He stared at her rose-tipped breasts illuminated against her smooth white skin. Rebecca quivered with excitement as the mattress sagged beneath his weight. She moved to give him room but as he unfurled his long frame his arms clasped her to him wrapping her within his warmth. Rebecca inhaled the totally masculine scent of musky male desire. She could hear the strong rapid beat of his heart even as her own raced erratically, setting her blood to pounding.

She raised her face to offer him her slightly parted lips. His mouth came down on hers, his tongue entering to taste that for which he thirsted. His hand closed over one breast, kneading tenderly as her nipple hardened to a taut peak. Rebecca moaned as warm lips traced a path down the curve of her neck to replace his hand, his tongue teasing her engorged nipple, his mouth pulling and suckling until she arched her back crying out.

His skillful hand dipped lower to stroke her flat belly as he shifted to begin his stimulating assault on the other trembling mound. Rebecca felt as if she were balanced on the crest of a gigantic wave in a turbulent sea rushing toward the beach only to be dragged back by an undercurrent that kept her from reaching the final destination.

Lance plied her lips with kisses once more, his tongue thrusting and withdrawing in the age-old mating ritual as she writhed, clasping her arms tightly around his neck. The heat of his arousal singed her hip as his exploring fingers found the moist softness of her most private place. Shock turned to pleasure as she dug her nails into his back giving herself up to the surge of emotion threatening to drown her in a storm of passion.

"My beautiful ladylove," Lance crooned, his breath coming in ragged spurts. "I must have all of you. I can't wait any longer."

His big body quaked as he lifted himself above her. Rebecca was too consumed with need to be afraid. Her thighs parted naturally to receive his rigid manhood. He forced himself to go carefully, fighting the urge to enter her quickly and bury his shaft to the hilt in the tight warm shield of her womanliness. He was a large man in every sense of the word. He knew he had to hurt her and he wished there were another way but such was not the nature of things.

Rebecca was so incredibly small. Lance shuddered and almost withdrew when he felt the barrier of her maidenhead. He wasn't sure he could purposefully

291

inflict the pain he knew she would feel when he broke through the layer of tissue safeguarding her virtue.

Nearly incoherent with wanting and sensing Logan's hesitation Rebecca took the matter out of his hands. With supreme effort she reared up grabbing hold of his firm buttocks, pulling him down upon her unresisting body. Caught off guard there was little Lance could do to cushion her against the force of his driving staff except to smother the scream of agony he knew was inevitable.

He captured her mouth just as huge green eyes flew open and the air expelled from her lungs in an uncontrollable gasp.

Rebecca lay motionless blinking back tears as she waited for the searing pain to cease while she wondered if there were a cure for a body ripped apart.

Lance braced himself on his elbows as he remained deeply embedded within her. The anguish on his face as he watched the tears flow down her cheeks was a horrible thing to see.

"God, Rebecca! Are you all right?" His voice, tormented by her suffering, sounded like that of a stranger.

"I didn't know it would hurt so," she panted weakly.

Despite his concern, Lance had to quell his anger at her for the grief she had brought upon herself.

He shook his head sadly. "It wouldn't have hurt so badly, sweetheart, if you had shown a little patience."

"I'm afraid I wasn't thinking too clearly at the time," she answered meekly lowering her eyes, her thick lashes wet and spiky upon her colorless cheeks. "I thought you were going to stop."

"You've a lot to learn about men," he sighed rolling his eyes upward. "I couldn't have stopped if my life depended on it, but I could have made it easier for you. I would get up but I'm afraid I'll hurt you more if I move."

Lance was at a loss as to what to do. He could feel his still hard shaft pulsating for release which was unthinkable under the circumstances. Yet to withdraw could cause her greater misery than to remain where he was.

As he pondered Rebecca discovered that the burning sensation between her legs had eased considerably to be replaced by a yearning need that was growing stronger by the minute.

"So then, have I married a quitter who cannot finish what he has begun?"

As she challenged with words, she moved tentatively beneath him. To her relief, she discovered not the smarting discomfort she had expected but an aching need to experience the fulfillment of being one with this man.

Lance eyed her doubtfully. "I don't want to hurt you any more, sweetheart," he said, giving her time to reconsider even as he felt the perspiration of his unsated need break upon his forehead.

Rebecca answered by raising her hips against the pressure of his arousal. He began very slowly to move inside of her; his eyes locked with hers, determined somehow to stay his lust should he see her flinch. Instead he looked into emerald eyes burning with uninhibited desire. Together they moved, Rebecca matching the rhythm of his strokes.

Crying out her love, Rebecca clamped her legs firmly around Logan's quivering hips as she felt him give one final thrust, spilling his seed deep within her. He shifted to take his weight from her but took her with him as he turned aside. Rebecca lay contentedly locked in his embrace waiting for her heart to return to its normal beating as Logan's heaving chest pressed against her breasts.

She looked up at him eyes wide with wonder.

"I never knew loving a man could be so beautiful," Rebecca sighed. "But then I love a beautiful man."

Lance chuckled kissing the tip of her turned-up nose.

"You, dear wife, should have told me before we wed that you were amaurotic. I only hope you will be as blind to my faults."

"Hmm. Have you so many?" she questioned quirking a brow as she twined her fingers around the swirls of crisp dark hair matting his solid chest.

"Innumerable," he murmured rubbing his foot up and down her calf erotically.

"One particularly acrimonious critic once told me I was brash and overbearing."

"Imagine that." Rebecca was finding it difficult to concentrate as Lance traced the contour of her ear with his tongue.

"She accused me of being an insufferable dolt!"

His hand was working its magic in featherlight strokes across her shoulders and down her back, creating a tingling sensation all the way to her toes. Rebecca suddenly became alert rearing up on one elbow, bumping her head hard against Logan's chin. Only one word penetrated her passion-clouded brain.

"She?"

"Ouch!"

Lance worked his jaw back and forth gingerly.

"Just a tiny slip of a thing but that gal was sure full of piss and vinegar."

He gazed at the far wall seeming to recall a memory while Rebecca massaged her sore head feeling as if she had just been dashed with a bucket of cold water.

"I didn't take offense though even when she continued to insult me." His words oozed with magnanimity setting Rebecca's teeth on edge.

"I'm surprised you didn't just feed her to the crocodiles."

"Alligators," he corrected. "We don't have crocodiles here."

Rebecca, who was in no mood for a lecture on reptile habitat, gave Lance a scathing look. Ignoring the amber flames springing to life in eyes of green crystal, he stared at the ceiling and continued in a voice infused with self-assured arrogance.

"I knew from the beginning that she was crazy about me, but she was too stubborn to let her feelings show so she cloaked her ardor behind a venomous tongue."

Rebecca retorted indignantly, "I would call her perceptive rather than stubborn."

"Then you would be wrong for the lady herself once told me the English were known for their stubbornness."

Rebecca looked blank for a moment. Then as Logan's mouth twitched she smiled in spite of herself. She would rather be the target of his jest than hear him talk about another woman in any regard, especially in

295

their bed.

"You are incorrigible, Logan," she laughed roughing his hair.

"Ah! Yet another word of praise to add to the ever growing list."

He pulled her closer clasping her tightly to his hungry body. She thrilled at the evidence of his need as his manhood pressed hard against her smooth flat belly. Giving herself up to the pleasurable onslaught of emotions evoked by his touch, Rebecca cried out softly as they came together once again. The two lovers soared above the highest clouds into a heaven of their own making.

Chapter 19

"Hello, Elizabeth. Why so glum?"

Lance had been watching the little girl for some time as she walked forlornly along the beach kicking shells with the toe of her tiny booted foot.

"Oh! Hello, Mr. Logan."

Lance smiled as Elizabeth squinted up into the sun, her round pixie face liberally sprinkled with freckles. There was no answering light in her melancholy blue eyes and he wondered what had caused the usually high-spirited child to look so sad. Lance knelt down balancing himself on the balls of his feet.

"What's this? Pretty young ladies shouldn't go around with frowns on their faces."

"Becca says frowning gives you wrinkles."

"Your aunt is a wise woman. Perhaps you should mind what she says," Lance advised.

Elizabeth shook her glossy red curls.

"I have good reason to frown, Mr. Logan. You see, Edward and Davey went fishing and they wouldn't let me go with them."

The serious little face puckered as tears welled in blue eyes the color of the sky on a clear day. Lance affected an equally sober mien.

"Well now, Elizabeth," he said thoughtfully, "I can certainly understand why they wouldn't want you along."

"You can?" Elizabeth sniffed then crinkled her nose regarding him questioningly.

"Of course I can. It's because you are the champion. The first time they took you fishing you caught the prize and no one has landed a bigger fish since."

"But, Mr. Logan. I nearly drowned catching that fish and I haven't caught another fish since," she replied unconvinced.

"Ah! But the point is you bested them once and they're afraid you might do it again. It's a matter of pride," he explained. "We men simply can't handle being bested by a woman."

"Do you really think that's why they didn't want me to go?" Her hopeful expression tugged at the big man's heart.

"Absolutely." Lance was relieved to see a smile tease the corners of her rosy lips. He stood up taking her by the hand and together they strolled down the beach.

Seagulls squawked overhead as the dark shadow of a huge gray pelican blocked out the sun. They watched the unwieldy bird dive head first into the shallow surf then rise triumphantly, a long white fish clamped firmly within its viselike bill.

"Elizabeth? About this 'Mr. Logan' thing. Don't you think since we're family now you might call me something a little less formal?"

Elizabeth cocked her head mulling over the idea.

"I suppose so, but what should I call you?"

Lance rubbed his smooth chin with his free hand appearing to give the matter considerable thought. "Since I am married to your aunt perhaps 'Uncle Lance' would be appropriate."

"Uncle Lance. I like that," she said beaming with pleasure. "I guess you will have to let Edward call you 'uncle,' too." She sounded disappointed.

"It would be only fair," Lance reasoned.

Elizabeth stumbled but Logan's firm grip on her hand kept her from falling. She squatted down to study the large irregularly shaped shell partly embedded in the sand which had caused her to trip. Lance reached down and dislodged the shell wiping it off on the leg of his breeches then holding the open side to his ear. Elizabeth watched in fascination.

"It's a Queen Conch," he said handing it to her. "If you place it against your ear you can hear the roar of the ocean."

Elizabeth's eyes grew wide with wonder as she listened to what sounded like waves washing onto the beach.

"Can I keep it, Uncle Lance?"

"Why sure, little one."

She skipped around in circles clutching the shell in her small hands finally coming to a halt at Logan's side. She gazed up at him with mischief in her eyes reminding Lance of Rebecca when she was up to something. Then she giggled lightheartedly.

"I think Edward is going to be sorry he went fishing."

"And why is that?"

"Because I found a magic shell *and* because I got to call you 'Uncle Lance' first!"

With that she turned and skipped ahead singing a nonsensical song about magic shells and wedding bells, making up words as she went along. Lance grinned watching her cavort across the sand. One of these days, he predicted, Elizabeth was going to give some young fellow a run for his money. Again the image of his wife came to mind and he felt an ache in his loins that seemed to come whenever she was out of his sight.

"You've got it bad, you randy goat," he said to himself shaking his head ruefully but smiling inanely none the less.

Lance sat down upon a large boulder to watch Elizabeth cautiously follow a receding wave as it folded back into the sea. She turned with a squeal as another foam peaked breaker rolled in to take its place, chasing her from the damp sand to where the waves could not reach. There she sank to her ankles in loose white granules. When she tired of the game she plodded through the sand coming to a stop as she wedged her small body between Logan's long legs and balanced herself by bracing her arms against his knees. As she peered up at him, her eyes mirroring her trust, Lance hoped with all his heart that he and Rebecca would soon give Davey a sister just like this little freckle-faced imp.

"Uncle Lance? Can I ask you something?"

She wrinkled her pert nose plucking at the fringe decorating his buckskin breeches.

"Of course, little one," he answered picking her up and settling her on one knee.

Elizabeth squirmed looking down, suddenly shy, then continued hesitantly. "I was just wondering . . .

since you are my uncle does that mean Davey and I are related?"

Now that she had given voice to the question Elizabeth raised her eyes to his, waiting expectantly yet not quite certain what answer she wanted to hear. Lance stiffened for he, too, wondered what answer the child sought.

Lance loved his son more than life itself and he knew that Davey would someday grow into a man to be reckoned with. Proud and strong with an understanding of the two distinct cultures from which he came, Davey would be the kind of man this young country needed to meld the ways of the Indian and the white man together so that they could live in peace. He also knew that his son would have many obstacles to overcome. Obstacles not of his own making. Some would see only the Indian and think him a savage in a savage land. Lance had witnessed prejudice in its cruelest form and he wished there were a way to shield Davey from the pain of rejection he knew was inevitable. But such was not possible. Instead he must strive to instill in him the wisdom to recognize intolerance as ignorance and the strength to subdue any who might threaten his right to exist in whichever world or combination of worlds he saw fit. Always protective where the boy was concerned, he wondered if this small innocent on his lap had recognized a difference between Davey and herself and felt repulsed at the idea of kinship. Lance studied Elizabeth's features as she awaited his answer but he could not guess what thoughts lay behind the clear blue eyes staring into his.

Tentatively he asked, "Would it be such a bad thing if you and Davey were say . . . cousins?"

He held his breath willing her to assure him that it would not matter but he was doomed to disappointment.

"Oh, Uncle Lance! That would be dreadful!"

His heart plummeted to the pit of his stomach. He had been so certain that Edward and Elizabeth had accepted Davey regardless of the differences in their backgrounds.

"And why would that be such a dreadful thing, Elizabeth?" It hurt but he had to know.

Elizabeth touched her tiny palm to his chiseled jaw in a surprisingly grown-up gesture.

"Don't you see, Uncle Lance? If Davey and I are cousins then we could never get married!"

Lance found the explanation which seemed perfectly logical to Elizabeth so different from what he had expected to hear he could only gape. She leaned toward him, her tone confidential.

"You were my first choice," she whispered. "But Becca needed you and besides I am just a child. So after I thought it over I decided that the best thing to do is wait a few more years then marry Davey."

Lance chided himself for jumping to conclusions and vowed not to do so in the future. He had defensively assumed the worst when it came to Elizabeth's feelings toward his son and that made him as closed-minded as those he was so quick to criticize. As he had argued so often, perhaps the younger generation would find their own solution to the problem of living together.

He squeezed Elizabeth's thin body setting her on her

feet as he rose towering over her protectively. Gracefully he bowed toward her.

"I am most honored that you considered me first, little one. And I believe Davey is most fortunate to have you for a friend."

Elizabeth smiled a satisfied smile. "So Davey and I don't have to be cousins. We can just be friends. What a perfect way to start," she declared.

Yes, Lance thought to himself as he glanced around at the rich and verdant land. *What a perfect way to start!*

"Go on now. Do you take me for a fool?"

"It's the truth, Edward. I swear!" Davey insisted as the two walked slowly along the path beside the creek, a string of small brim dangling from the shorter child's hand. "I tell you I've seen it!"

Edward's blue eyes were wide with wonder. "Just imagine an island made entirely of shells collected by your grandfather."

Davey guffawed. "Edward, you are funny. I didn't say my grandfather built the island. I said our *ancestors* built it. It was started hundreds of years ago and took several generations to complete. Men and women gathered the shells from the shallow waters in baskets made of woven palm fronds."

"But with so much land to live on why did they want to build an island?" Such an unnecessary expenditure of energy made no sense to Edward.

"My people were fishermen. They had to be near the water to survive but when storms came many drowned because the land near the water was low. They could not bury the dead because the graves would fill with water. So they decided to build a place where even the flood waters could not touch them."

Pride in the ingenuity of his forebears was evident in the boy's explanation and Edward felt a stab of envy wishing he could relate an equally impressive tale about his own predecessors.

"And you've actually been to the island, Davey?"

"Of course," Davey replied affecting a superior attitude. "My grandfather took me to see the treasure of the Calusa and to teach me the ways of my people. Calusa means brave and skillful and that is what I must be if I am to become a mighty chief."

Edward could not picture his friend filling the shoes of his ferocious looking grandfather but he knew better than to voice his doubts for he understood that Davey's dream was to someday be a leader among his people. Instead he begged to hear more about the mystical island built of shells.

"The island is very big and mounds rise toward the sky like pyramids with terraces at different levels which serve as steps to reach the top. At the peak of the highest mound is the temple which houses the treasure."

They paused to watch a flock of brightly colored birds fly overhead then land in the trees a short distance away chirping and singing to one another. But Edward's mind was still on the city of shells.

"Where did the treasure come from?" he asked eagerly.

In his excitement Edward had forgotten the fish they had worked so diligently to catch and two of the pathetic creatures were coated with dirt where he had allowed them to drag on the ground. Davey reached over and took the stringer from his hand giving it a vigorous shake before answering.

"Most of the gold and silver came from the Spanish invaders who tried to conquer the Calusa and make us their slaves. But as they soon learned, such a feat was impossible."

Davey's chest swelled. He spoke as though he had been among the fierce warriors who more than three hundred years ago had chased away the foreign usurpers. For a moment Edward could visualize the tall, dark-skinned youth in such a light as his near-black eyes gleamed with the triumph of long ago victory.

"Ah, small warrior, but it is a different world today."

Both boys jumped at the sound of the deep sonorous voice behind them.

"Grandfather! You still have the padded feet of the mountain lion," Davey complimented the elderly chief while Edward stared agog at the enormously tall Indian with the deep hooded eyes.

He was sure the strange-looking man could hear his heart beating madly within his chest as he fought down the urge to run to the fort where people looked like people were supposed to look. Not like some wild apparition stalking the jungle!

"And what does a lad from 'the land of flowers' know about mountain lions?" the chief teased in a manner Edward found surprisingly human.

Enthusiastically Davey replied, "My father has told me of the furtive cat for he has seen it, but only because the animal chose to make his presence known."

"Sometimes it is wise to remain hidden until you know whether those close by be friend or foe," his grandfather advised somberly, motioning his head in Edward's direction.

If not for the fact that he had seen the fearsome chief wink at his grandson as he spoke, Edward would have fallen into a swoon.

"I can vouch for Edward. He is my friend," Davey countered without hesitation.

"But he is a white man bent on making this land his home."

Edward was elated by the chief's description, but Davey frowned struggling for the deeper meaning behind his grandfather's words.

"And, unless I am gravely mistaken, you were just bragging to your *friend* that the Calusa would never allow strangers in their land," Nokomis went on unrelentingly.

The furrows in Davey's brow grew closer together while Edward was left to wonder what they were talking about. As the boy gazed up at his grandfather the air became still. Even the birds ceased their incessant chatter. Edward realized he was holding his breath but could not say why. It was as if the world had paused in its spinning. Then he heard Davey let out a long sigh and, as if on cue, life returned to normal. Birds sang, frogs croaked, and fish splashed in the creek.

"I understand, Grandfather."

With the smile of a tutor who has seen the light of knowledge suddenly dawn in the eyes of his prized pupil, Nokomis faded soundlessly into the dense foliage.

"It's all very well to say you understand," Edward

grumbled peevishly. "But would you be so kind as to explain it to me, because I haven't a clue as to what you and your grandfather were talking about."

Davey put an arm across Edward's shoulders in a conciliatory gesture. "My grandfather told me that it is good to remember the past but that times change and that I must change with them. We agreed that some outsiders are acceptable and should be made welcome in our land like my grandmother and my father. And you, of course," he added as an afterthought. "We also agreed that it is important to live together in peace."

Edward jerked to a standstill. "You and your grandfather said all that?" he asked incredulously. "How could you say so much in so few words?"

Without so much as a hint of a smile, Davey replied solemnly, "Sign language!"

Nanette Dubois huddled in the corner of the thatched hut trying not to draw attention to herself as the dark shadow of a man stooped to enter. Like a small frightened animal who knows the futility of attempting to elude the stalker she drew up her knees and buried her face in the remnants of her once fine gown, taking what comfort she could in the fanciful notion that if she couldn't see him he wouldn't see her.

What difference did it make really? She had already reached the depths of despair and degradation. Having been forced to endure and commit the most unspeakable and humiliating acts of degeneracy conceivable, she thought herself inured to anything he might now demand. Yet a thread of rebellion persisted, a tiny fiber of hope which held onto the belief that if she could just

307

forestall one more attack, rescue would come.

Up until now, her logic, if it could be called such, had proved not only faulty but excruciatingly painful. The man did not like being thwarted and her continued abhorrence to his touch had resulted in punishments ranging from beatings to starvation to forced participation in perverted acts of copulation. But she sensed that something in his manner was different tonight. He seemed distracted, lost in his own evil thoughts, and she found respite in being ignored.

He paced the small confines of the dimly lit room then sat down abruptly on the filthy cot Nanette had too often been forced to share. He ran his hands through oily salt and pepper-streaked hair. Giving a disgruntled sigh, he rested his elbows on his knees letting his head droop forward. Nanette strained against the murky light in an effort to read the expression on his detestable face but could see little in the fading dusk.

"Come here!"

She cringed when the order came, feeling the familiar numbness of defeat.

"Come here!" he barked again. Realizing the uselessness of refusing to obey the command, she slowly crossed the room to stand meekly before Jose Gaspar.

"Sit!"

As she turned to take her place beside the villainous pirate her trembling knees buckled, causing her to land hard upon her bruised buttocks. She managed to hide her discomfort refusing to give him the satisfaction of knowing that the welts he had raised with his thick leather belt still burned, a constant reminder of the price one paid for disobedience. Her stomach rolled as his unwashed hand brutally squeezed her thin thigh but again she refused to acknowledge the pain. She knew she would eventually beg for mercy but it had become a sort of self-flagellating game she played to see how much torment she could endure before crying out.

"The ransom? When will my father deliver the gold for my release?"

He was surprised when she dared to ask, for rarely did she speak in his presence except to recite the despicable words he made her say, obscene verbalizations that served to stimulate his arousal. He leaned back against the wall picking his teeth with a dirty fingernail. His obsidian eyes took on a feral glow as he studied his captive. Her brown hair had grown dull and lank in the weeks he had held her prisoner and she had lost weight to the point of emaciation.

"What makes you think anyone would part with a chest of gold for a skinny ugly slut like you?" he taunted.

Her eyes flared with resentment as she fought down the urge to remind him whose fault it was that she had been brought so low. Instead she answered with an assurance borne of desperation.

"My father will pay whatever you ask to get me back."

His derisive cackle raised the hairs on the back of her neck.

Flicking an imaginary morsel from the end of his finger he replied sarcastically, "I'm afraid that is something we'll never know."

Nanette froze in place. "What do you mean 'we'll never know'? Surely you have contacted my father telling him of your demands!"

His hand had worked its way up to the apex of her legs but she scarcely noticed as she sought an explanation for his enigmatic words.

"You must understand, my little whore slave, how offended your father would be if I took his money in exchange for such a worthless piece of goods. Just look at yourself! Why, a scullery maid would seem a queen in comparison and you smell as if you bathed in a slop bucket."

He wrinkled his nose for emphasis then shook his head while the painful pressure of his hand made her wince.

"As much as it annoys me to lose the gold I might have gotten from your father, I fear if I gave him what I see before me now he would not consider it a fair bargain. No," he said rubbing his grizzled chin, "I think it best if we let him continue to believe you were drowned in a storm."

Nanette was too shattered to speak. All these weeks she had lived with the certainty that the greedy pirate had made contact with her father and that he would gain her release before it was too late. Her eyes swam with tears as she envisioned the sadness her dear papa must feel over the loss of his only child while the hopelessness of her situation bore down with the weight of a collapsing fortress burying her beneath a bulwark of crumbling stone.

"I should have left you on *Captiva* and sent the ransom demand," he hissed in her ear as he jerked her closer, roughly grasping one breast. "I am sick of you and your whining ways!" He glowered at her and even the absence of light could not obliterate the madness reflected in his eyes.

"Soon, very soon, I will have no further need of you," he gloated taking pleasure in her bewilderment. "I shall have my beautiful golden-haired goddess. One worthy of being Gaspar's woman!"

Nanette was too frightened to wonder who such a woman might be. Through quivering lips she asked, "What will become of me?"

His sinister laugh rang like a death toll. "I am sure my men will enjoy what little you have left to give," he sneered heartlessly.

Thoughts of the unsavory band of followers caused the bile to rise in her throat. Surely even a man as debauched as Gaspar could not toss her like a bone to his hounds. But his next words made clear his intentions.

"Enough talk! Let me see if I have taught you well enough to please my men. Make me ready for you, little whore!"

Every instinct rebelled against what was being demanded of her even as Nanette reached inside the opening in the pirate leader's breeches to take hold of his limp staff, massaging and stroking as he had instructed until it became hot and distended. At last he rolled her onto her stomach and raised her skirt to her waist pausing long enough to savagely knead her sore cheeks. Then raising her hips he plowed into her like a rutting beast.

When his lust had been sated he reared back and applied several hard slaps to her already bruised posterior. He stood up muttering curses as he adjusted his pants then left her alone in the inky blackness.

Nanette lay with her head cradled in her arms

knowing that only a miracle could save her now. Sometime later it occurred to her that for the first time she had submitted to the ravishment of her body without so much as a word of protest. Only then did her bitter tears fall, for yielding without a struggle must surely signify that her soul was dead!

Chapter 20

Rebecca's eyes widened. Breathing deeply she filled her lungs with air as she felt herself being pulled beneath the surface of the water. Down and down she went into the darkness her legs pinned together making it impossible to kick against the force dragging her toward the bottom of the pool. Above she could see sun rays penetrating the cerulean blue water, speckled with powdery granules drifting lazily to and fro. She watched in fascination as iridescent bubbles of air escaped her to float slowly upward. Then without warning her legs were released and she was able to thrust out propelling herself once more toward the light.

She broke the surface gasping and laughing at the same time. As Lance shot up beside her one arm made an arc across the water spraying him with droplets.

"I fear I have met the monster that guards Lona's secret place against unwelcome visitors," she sputtered as she threw her arms around her husband's neck while he tread water using his powerful arms and legs to keep them both afloat.

Lance kissed her cold wet lips. "What self-respecting sea monster could resist a mermaid such as you?" he defended, enjoying the feel of her small curvaceous body next to his.

Rebecca wrapped her legs provocatively around his waist as his feet touched the sandy bottom close to shore. They had been married a whole week and for Rebecca the days had passed swiftly. It had been a wondrous time of exploration, a time for learning everything there was to know about this big, virile man who now belonged to her. She had traced her fingers over every inch of his magnificent male body familiarizing herself with the rugged contours of his wide muscular shoulders, feeling the tremors in his rock-hard arms and thighs. She thrilled to the discovery that she could caress his nipples to hardness just as he could hers and arouse his need from across a room with just a look. It was a heady feeling knowing the extent of her power but it was no more absolute than his over her. She had become attuned to every nuance of his movements and expressions. She found it disconcerting at times, for he had become so much a part of her that she wondered if she had lost her own identity. At the very least she knew that she could never again feel complete without him.

"And what will the sea monster do when he catches the mermaid?" she asked coquettishly, locking her feet together at his back, squeezing him around the middle.

Standing waist-high in the water Lance cupped her buttocks in his huge hands pressing her against his hardened manhood. "First he would nibble her ear," he answered huskily demonstrating by gently tugging

314

on her lobe with his teeth. "Then he would carefully lick the water from her skin."

Rebecca tingled from the inside out as he lowered his head to blaze a trail down her neck, over the hollow curve of her shoulder, then lower still stopping to give attention to first one taut globe-shaped breast and then the other with his raspy tongue. He raised her into the air as though she weighed no more than a feather and continued his sensuous path downward to her navel.

Still suspended above Logan's head Rebecca could feel her heart pounding in her ears. Breathless with anticipation she asked, "And what would the monster do then?"

Lance cocked his head thoughtfully to one side. "He would take her for a ride, a wild tumultuous ride. The way would be rough and she would have to cling to him tightly to keep from falling. But he would take her beyond this world to his kingdom beneath the sea, a place of shimmering light and inconceivable beauty. A place where only two bound together by love can ever go."

Logan's gray eyes smoldered with passion as he gazed up at her.

"Take me," Rebecca begged. And he did.

Lowering her with remarkable tenderness for a man his size, he eased himself into the moist, welcoming core of her womanhood as she entwined her legs about him once more. Together they rocked back and forth slowly, at first buoyed by the water around them. Lance took her mouth, deepening the kiss as his tongue thrust in and out matching the rhythm of their bodies. Soon their actions became frenzied as Rebecca arched her back frustrated by the lack of leverage that made it impossible for her to grip him tightly enough to satisfy her longing.

Lance waited until she was writhing and sobbing with unfulfilled desire, her damp heavy hair swaying from side to side like a silken curtain as she twisted in his arms. Only then did he grasp her firmly about the hips and take her to the summit where the world exploded into a million fragments of ineffable light and color. Together they went over the edge of the precipice. Rebecca cried out glorying in the ecstasy of the moment while Lance trembled clutching her to his massive frame. As their breathing slowly returned to normal he released her to slide down the length of his body. Rebecca shivered in the aftermath of love.

"Come on, Mrs. Logan," he urged afraid the late afternoon breeze had turned too chilly for her comfort. "You're turning blue and the color clashes with your lovely eyes."

He pulled her from the shallow water up onto the mossy bank where they dressed quickly then sank to the ground beneath a leafy sycamore tree. Rebecca leaned against its narrow trunk as Lance stretched out on the ground resting his head upon her lap.

Suddenly their solitude was interrupted by a discordant cry that could only be described as something between a squawk and a whoop. Rebecca shrieked as two huge, long-legged gray birds with bright red faces glided out of the sky to land on the far side of the pool. Oblivious of the two lovers watching, they performed a balletic dance, dipping and bowing to one another then stretching their thin necks upward.

Rebecca, never having seen anything like them, looked at Lance questioningly.

"They're sandhill cranes and are among the tallest birds in the world," he described laughingly.

"Oh, how lovely they are," she whispered not wanting to scare them away for she found the pair a delight to watch.

"Sandhill cranes are unique in that they mate for life and are very attentive to their offspring," Logan informed. "Quite a rare thing among birds."

He reached up to run his hand along the curve of her cheek sending tremors of anticipation through her body. "Their arrival is a good omen I think. Like the cranes, I intend to love you for the rest of my life, and I can't wait to fill the cabin with brothers and sisters for Davey."

Leaning down to kiss the bridge of his nose Rebecca sighed, "I love you, Logan," somewhat awed by the intensity of her feelings for this giant among men.

"Of course you do," he replied nonchalantly plucking a fallen leaf from the ground then twirling it to tickle her chin.

Her perfectly arched brows drew together. "Mighty cock-sure of ourselves today, aren't we?" she retorted tilting her head haughtily.

Lance closed his eyes looking for all the world as though he were preparing to drift off to sleep. Rebecca eased her knees up slowly then straightened her legs without warning, causing his head to bounce against her thighs.

"Surely, my lady, you can't expect humility when for the past week you've spent every waking moment telling me how wonderful I am!"

Lance turned his head to gaze at the trim ankles peeping from underneath Rebecca's skirt.

"Remarkable," he muttered staring downward.

She eyed him suspiciously. "What's remarkable?"

He raised up twisting his body to the side as he wedged her legs apart with his elbows placing his chin in the palm of his hand. He continued to study her lower extremities until Rebecca became impatient. Leaning forward to peer over his shoulder she repeated, "What is remarkable?"

He circled her neck with his free arm pulling her down until their lips were a breath apart. "You are the only woman I know who can tap her foot when it isn't even on the ground," he chuckled taking her mouth with his, his tongue tenderly seeking her velvet softness.

"Damn!" Lance jerked back as Rebecca bit him none too gently.

Jeweled eyes sparked with mischief. "Are you familiar with the feet of a sufficient number of women to judge mine 'remarkable'?"

He looked over his shoulder at the appendages in question. "I've seen my fair share, but perhaps I had better study the objects in question more carefully."

Before Rebecca could blink, Lance shifted his body so that he lay with his head at her feet half straddling her as he began a thorough examination of each tiny toe. Cradling one foot and then the other with both hands, he nibbled and sucked each delicious digit slowly working his way upward. Rebecca felt her body growing hot beneath his ministrations. Her breasts swelled and her nipples grew taut. Never had she felt so wanton. Her fingers tangled in his dark hair lending impetus to his seductive progress along her aching, wanting body. Of their own volition her legs parted.

His tongue raked the essence of her being as Rebecca shuddered drawing him deeper, encouraging him to quench his thirst at the springhead of her desire. When he knew she had gained release he pulled her down upon the lush, green turf to seek his own pleasure. In doing so he sent her spiraling to new heights only a favored few could ever hope to reach.

At peace with the world they rested side by side concealed beneath a sunscreen of thick foliage, their hands entwined. Idly Rebecca rubbed her face against Logan's chin where a scant prickle of beard brushed the surface.

"Do you think Lona will mind our coming to her secret place?" she asked languidly evoking a rumble of laughter from deep within her husband's chest.

"I doubt it will register even if you tell her," he answered still chuckling. "Lona has been 'in this world but not of it' ever since she agreed to marry Justin, or haven't you noticed?"

Rebecca giggled. "I will admit she has seemed a bit light-headed of late."

"Light-headed, my sweet, is not unusual for Lona," he rebutted. "She has lately progressed from light-headed to completely muddled!"

"Surely you exaggerate," Rebecca defended.

"Would you call it exaggerating after tasting the black-eyed peas with clotted cream she served for dessert the other night?"

Rebecca shrugged indifferently. "It seemed perfectly normal to me."

"That, my dearest heart, is because you don't know a black-eyed pea from a Black-eyed Susie," Lance chided laughingly.

Snubbing her nose, Rebecca refused to take offense. "Perhaps you wilderness people are not as daring as I thought. Frankly, I found the offering unique though I did think it strange that I was the only one eating."

Lance hugged her close. "Have I told you lately that I think you are adorable?"

"Yes!" she answered nudging him away to straighten her skirts. "Now let's be serious!"

Caressing the smooth curve of one breast outlined beneath the bodice of her rumpled gown, he muttered huskily, "I'm always serious when I'm with you."

"I mean *really* serious," she explained pushing his hand aside. "I know Justin loves Lona but do you think she loves him? It took a lot of persuasion on his part before she agreed to marry him."

"Not every woman who meets the man of her dreams recognizes him right off. You just happened to be more astute than most," he replied managing not to laugh aloud as he thought back on their fiery courtship! His efforts won him a poke in the ribs.

"This is no joking matter, Logan!" Rebecca admonished.

"You're right, my lady, so let me put your mind at ease. Lona loves Justin."

"How do you know?" she persisted. Because she cared about the young couple she longed for assurances. Their backgrounds were even more diverse than those of Logan and herself. Lona, half Spanish, half Calusa; Justin born into the world of the uncompromising English aristocracy. Putting any physical attraction aside she wondered if they would be able to find a common ground on which their love could grow.

320

"Lona had doubts about her feelings to begin with," Lance explained. "She wants so much to be a part of the white world that she questioned her motives; whether by marrying Wentworth she was using him as a means to an end."

"Then what convinced her that she really cared for him?"

"Lona kept telling Wentworth that Indian women didn't marry Englishmen. Quite a reversal. Usually the argument is the other way around. At any rate, Justin became so desperate that he went to Nokomis and asked if he would make him a blood brother to the tribe."

Rebecca's eyes grew wide. "And did he?"

"Hell, no!" Logan snorted. "Men have been known to die going through a ritual like that. When Lona found out how far Wentworth was prepared to go in order to have her she realized she really loved *him,* not just his way of life. And she certainly wasn't willing to risk their future by allowing Wentworth to go through a primitive ceremony that might get him killed. So she said yes," he concluded matter-of-factly.

So much for uncompromising Englishmen, Rebecca thought marveling at Justin's tenacity.

They were silent for some time each lost in his own contemplations. It was Rebecca who finally broke the tranquil hush of the forest. Keeping her eyes downcast she confessed, "You know, Logan. When I first arrived I thought *you* were in love with Lona."

He looked at her skeptically. "Why on earth would you think that?"

Rebecca went on to tell him how she had inadvertently overheard the conversation between Lance and

Lona the day she had sought refuge beneath the willow tree. Lance pulled her close trailing feathery kisses over her face. He remembered his heated argument with Lona and knew how easily his words could have been misconstrued.

"Rebecca," he breathed against her lips. "I love Lona the way I loved my sister. I feel responsible for her, protective toward her. There was never anything more between us." He tipped her chin with his forefinger. "And let me assure you I look forward to relinquishing all responsibility for the little hellion once she marries Wentworth. I have as much as I can handle keeping you out of trouble," he teased.

Before Rebecca could think of a suitable retort Lance sobered abruptly. The change brought with it a palpable sense of foreboding that caused gooseflesh to rise on her smooth skin.

"Lance! What is it?"

He tried to smile but failed miserably. "Sweetheart, I brought you out here today for more than the obvious reason of wanting to make love to you. There is something I have to talk to you about that I thought might be easier discussed here."

Rebecca gave him a worried look but waited for him to explain. She was certain whatever he had to say would not be to her liking. Seconds ticked by before Lance went on apologetically, "Andrew and I have to go to Fort King for a little while."

"Noooo!" Her mouth formed a perfect "O" as she cried in dismay.

Lance pulled her close burying her head in his shoulder as he whispered soothingly, "It's just for a little while, a few days or a week at most, sweetheart.

It's not the end of the world. I'll be back in no time."

But Rebecca was not appeased. She knew the dangers that could befall one riding the trail. Hadn't Rachel's parents been killed along that very same stretch of road? What was meant to be a few days' separation could result in a lifetime of loneliness and despair.

Suddenly she drew away from him, anger flashing even as tears brimmed in accusing green eyes.

"You don't have to go! You are an officer! Playing scout is just a game! You could send someone else!"

Lance shook his head willing her to understand. "No, I can't, sweetheart. This is more than a matter of riding scout. Governor Duval has called a legislative council meeting in Tallahassee this fall. Despite the distance between here and the capital, the people of Florida have to unite together to form a workable government if we ever hope to gain statehood. Andrew and I are meeting with others concerned with the future of this area to prepare recommendations to present to the council."

As he spoke his excitement and enthusiasm gained momentum reminding Rebecca how much this untamed virgin peninsula meant to her husband. She knew that he wanted to take part in the formulation of a strong government that could withstand the test of time. As difficult as their parting would be, she could not fault his need to go.

"When do you leave?" she asked tremulously.

Lance interpreted her question as approval or at least acquiescence and beamed his appreciation.

"Tomorrow," he answered half-expecting more arguments at the suddenness of his departure, but she masked her disappointment behind a radiant smile.

He stood up taking her with him. When he held her lightly by the shoulders his sober countenance was back in place. "I want you to promise me that you will stay inside the fort with George and Mary while I am gone."

"Whatever for?" she asked bristling as she recognized the command behind his request. "Chief Nokomis said Chikiki and what is left of his renegades have joined a warring tribe far to the north. Surely we are no longer in danger of attack."

"Humor me, my lady. I will rest easier knowing you are safe inside the fort while I am away."

Lance saw no point in frightening Rebecca by mentioning the unpredictable hazards one might have to face at any time here in the territory. Better to let her believe she was merely cosseting him as long as he gained her promise not to leave the fort.

"Oh all right!" she agreed grudgingly and was rewarded with a kiss.

As they walked hand in hand back along the path toward their isolated cabin, Lance was determined to turn the conversation away from the parting that would come with the dawn.

"How are the cooking lessons coming?" he ventured in an effort to change the subject. "I'm looking forward to a hearty meal for I find myself quite spent from trying to satisfy my lady's more sensual appetites."

Rebecca, who was still miffed not only because their honeymoon was about to be cut short but also by the fact that Logan would not allow her to remain in their love nest while he was away, took advantage of an opportunity to retaliate for his overbearing attitude.

"I feel certain you will be astounded by my progress when you taste the delicacy I have prepared for you tonight," she assured him, looking up at Lance with demure innocence. She then ruined the effect by giggling.

"Oh, and just what is this culinary wonder called?" he asked suspiciously.

"Actually I can't pronounce the Indian name for the dish but it's an old family recipe of Lona's. She showed me how to make it this morning."

Lance was hard-pressed to imagine what the capricious Indian girl and his own novice chef might have concocted.

"But I can tell you what's in it," Rebecca went on looking very pleased with herself. "The dish contains eye of the eel sautéed with butter and mushrooms!" She paused to consider. "At least Lona thinks they are mushrooms."

Lance groaned having heard of cases where people died from eating toadstools they thought were mushrooms.

"Eye of the eel," he shouted. He had been so genuinely concerned about mushroom impostors it had taken a minute for the full impact of her recipe review to hit him.

Rebecca burst into peals of laughter at the horrified expression on her husband's face. Appreciating the jest, even if it was on him, Lance soon joined in.

"I may be forced to disprove the theory that man cannot live by bread alone," he sighed as they continued on their way.

"Speaking of bread," Rebecca interrupted excitedly, "Lona tells me the Indians make flour from cattails. I can hardly wait to try it!"

Lance fervently hoped Lona had gone on to explain that the cattails she referred to were the marsh plants whose roots could be ground into flour. For if she hadn't, he pitied the unsuspecting felines that roamed freely about the fort!

Chapter 21

Three long, lonely nights and nearly four endless days had passed since Rebecca bid Lance a tearful goodbye. Standing at the edge of the wide porch she watched the sun change from resplendent gold into a red ball of fire as it dipped ever lower toward the horizon where the sky and the sea came together. How she had looked forward to this time of day when she and Lance strolled down the beach arm in arm holding out crusts of bread to the hungry gulls who swooped down to grab the proffered morsels from their fingers. But now plagued with emptiness and worry for the one she loved, Rebecca wished there were some way to suspend the sun in place so that she would not have to face the solitary darkness she knew would follow.

"Rebecca, honey, come and sit down. Finish your coffee before it gets cold," Mary suggested from the rocker where she sat placidly knitting a tiny garment of pale yellow yarn.

Beside her Rachel held up a plaid shirt she was making for Andrew, critically eyeing the shoulder width and the length of one sleeve.

"Do you think it's too long?" she fretted measuring against her own slender arm.

Damnation! Rebecca fumed inwardly. *How can Rachel think about anything so mundane as shirt sleeves when Andrew and Logan might at this moment be lying injured along the perilous trail.* That something worse could have befallen their two brave scouts she refused to even consider. *How,* Rebecca wondered, *could Rachel carry on as usual at a time like this?* She knew that Rachel loved Andrew to distraction, and Elizabeth had confided earlier that she had awakened to hear her stepmother crying just the night before. Yet Rachel seemed adept at concealing her emotions when in the company of others.

Rebecca sighed wishing she had the temperament to emulate Rachel's self-containment. But she knew such was not the case. Her anxiety was plainly evident. Forcing herself to stop pacing she took her chair and reached for the delicate china cup resting on the table at her elbow.

"Stop worrying," Mary chided, never dropping a stitch. "Most likely Lance and Andrew will be home tomorrow."

Easy for you to say. George Brooke is safe within the fort and will be there to warm your bed tonight, Rebecca thought enviously as she sipped the lukewarm brew. She watched the flash of Mary's knitting needles interweave the yarn trailing around her fingers, her arms protectively circling the small rounded swelling in her lap.

It seemed more than a few weeks since she had argued the wisdom of giving birth to a child here in the territory so far from civilization. How could her views have changed so radically in such a short period of time? She smiled a secret little smile knowing the answer lay in her love for Logan. Involuntarily her hand went to cover her smooth, flat stomach as she wondered wistfully if even now Logan's seed might be growing deep within her womb.

Could it be possible? she wondered. *Damnation! She would wring the big looby's neck if he got himself killed before he even had an opportunity to hold his child in his arms.* Her indignation quickly turned to despair. What if something happened to Logan and she wasn't pregnant? She would never know the joy of bringing life, the ultimate symbol of their love. As tears of loneliness and self-pity rose in her eyes threatening to spill down her cheeks, Rebecca knew she had to get away from her two well-meaning friends or make an utter fool of herself.

The cup clattered against the saucer as she set it down clumsily then stood and walked toward the stairs. Mary and Rachel looked up in surprise as she descended the few short steps then paused uncertainly.

"Wait, Rebecca! I will come with you," Rachel volunteered starting to rise. Mary put a restraining hand on her arm, understanding Rebecca's need to be alone.

Rebecca turned giving them a weak smile. "I'm all right. I just want to go for a short walk," she assured drawing a deep breath.

Though Rachel didn't argue, she could not withhold a word of warning. "Remember what Lance said, Rebecca. Please don't go far."

Blast what Logan said! she fumed giving a noncommittal wave over her shoulder. *If Logan thinks I am in danger why isn't he here to protect me instead of playing political games at Fort King?*

In all fairness Rebecca knew that Lance was involved in important affairs involving the future of the territory. The decisions made at the council meeting would determine the future of all of central Florida and its inhabitants. But as each solitary day passed, she became less concerned about the years to come and more distraught over the nights ahead.

Just outside the gates she stopped to gaze across the wide expanse of water where the *Enterprise* lay at anchor in the deep channel of the bay. The awesome warship looked cold and threatening with her heavy cannon lining the deck. Rebecca shuddered. It was a relief to know the formidable vessel was on their side for she could imagine the fear its presence must strike in the hearts of the enemy. Alone the man of war stood guard like a silent sentinel protecting the fort against any who might invade by sea.

Having made minimal repairs to his ship, Captain Cavendish and his crew of British sailors had continued on their journey to New Orleans on the early morning tide. No one at Fort Brooke had been saddened by the dour man's departure. Perhaps his ship would pass the returning *Victoria* somewhere along the way. Thinking of affable Captain Higgins Rebecca smiled wondering if he would be surprised to find that she would not be accompanying him back to England. She thought not, remembering the knowing way he had looked at Logan and herself almost as if he could foresee the outcome of their stormy beginning. She hoped Logan would be here when Captain Higgins

330

arrived so that the man who had been so kind to her in his fatherly way during her voyage from England could witness their newfound happiness. Tomorrow she must collect her thoughts and prepare some letters for the good Captain to take back to her homeland. She would instruct her solicitors to close the manor house. She would need to include a list of the items she wanted shipped to her. Puckering her brows she cursed the fact that Logan wasn't here to help her decide how to handle her obligations across the sea. They had never discussed what was to be done with her holdings in England. Of course, Rebecca reasoned chuckling outloud, they had had little time to talk about business matters since their marriage. More immediate and infinitely more important pursuits seemed to occupy most of their waking hours.

"And," she said to a fat brown squirrel watching her from a low branch just ahead, "I think our priorities are in splendid order. Don't you?"

The tiny animal blinked twice before scampering further up the tree to fuss as she went by.

"You may argue now," Rebecca laughed, "but someday when you meet the right mate it will all make sense!"

As Rebecca continued along the familiar path paying little heed to the waning light, she began mentally to compose a letter to her best friend, Amy Dickerson.

Dear Amy,
    I know it must have caused you considerable grief to have to be the one to inform me of William's untimely, though self-precipitated, de-

mise. I want to assure you the shock was greatly assuaged by the events that have taken place since my arrival at Fort Brooke, the most significant of which has been my marriage to an American army scout named Lance Logan.

Perhaps a little more thought would be in order, Rebecca decided after picturing her dearest friend fainting as the pages of her missive floated dramatically down upon the carpet. Maybe she should impart the good news first, postponing her reaction to William's tragic expiration until the end. This would definitely take some thought! Now let's see . . .

My dear friend,

Surely you must realize that I had no way of understanding what you were trying to relate pertaining to your feelings for your husband some months ago. Truth to tell, I thought you were quite daft with talk of quivery legs and fluttering heart. You made love sound rather like a pudding. But let me assure you my perspicacity regarding said subject has increased ten-fold during the past few weeks. Here in a land I thought to be inhabited by savages I have found my own true love. A man who sets my blood on fire; a man who makes me tingle from the inside out; a man who makes my stomach churn with desire!

Damnation! All this talk about tingling and churning was making her rather nauseous. Rebecca sighed as she glanced at the deepening shadows hugging the path. Tomorrow would be soon enough to decide what she would say to Amy.

Her walk had brought her within sight of the cabin though it was still some distance away across the wide meadow. She knew she should turn back. It would be completely dark soon and the others would be worried. Yet the cabin drew her like a magnet. It was her home . . . hers and Logan's . . . where they had lived and laughed and loved. Oh how they had loved those few short nights they had shared together. With the memories came an aching need that began in Rebecca's loins and spread throughout her body until she thought she might die with longing. She needed her husband here with her now and knowing he was far away brought tears of frustration to her luminous green eyes. She wanted him beside her, to feel his touch and hear his deep resonant voice whispering in her ear. She began walking across the field toward the small deserted log structure that represented safety and security despite the lack of a welcoming lamp. Logan would be furious if he knew she had ventured this far from the fort with night approaching, but Rebecca felt compelled to return to the house that was her home if only for a few minutes. She wanted to stand in the dark panelled room and breathe in the masculine scent of her lover. She wanted to touch the covers that kept them warm at night and rub her fingers through the soft fur rug beside the hearth where they had explored each other's naked bodies giving themselves over to the desires of their heated flesh. Rebecca had to reassure herself that the rapturous fulfillment she remembered had not been a dream.

Rushing up the steps she threw open the door then made her way cautiously across the room to light the lamp and dispel the gloom. As the light gradually reached out to chase away the shadow Rebecca searched for the solace she could not find within the walls of the fort, even though she was surrounded there by friends who would keep her safe until Logan's return.

Frilly chintz curtains hung at the windows, a pleasant contrast to the cabin's dark walls. The drab blanket covering the bed had been replaced by a brightly colored quilt and the lamp now rested on a white lace doily. In the center of the dining table stood a vase of wilting wildflowers. Rebecca recalled how Logan had admired the first bouquet she had gathered saying that the clean sweet fragrance smelled like her hair. She had resolved then and there to see that a fresh arrangement of flowers always graced their table, ready to greet Logan when he came through the door. Tomorrow she would take Elizabeth to gather new blooms. They would have to start early for Logan could return at any moment.

"Oh, Logan! Where are you?" A sob caught in her throat as she cried out her anguish. Throwing herself across the narrow bed they had shared so briefly, she wept for the man who had stolen her heart. She feared he might never return, knowing that without him her life would no longer be worth living.

Mary stood wringing her hands and frowning as she

tried to penetrate the darkness beyond the gates.

"Where in the world could she be?"

Rachel did her best to hide her anxiety. "She said she was only going for a short walk but that was an hour ago." She was more worried than she cared to admit and found it impossible to hide her concern from the older woman. "She probably went a little further than she intended. You know how she misses Lance. I imagine she was so caught up in her thoughts she didn't realize how quickly the darkness comes upon us."

"Well, it's certainly dark now and not even a sliver of moon showing," Mary pointed out peering up at the starless sky. "She could be lost somewhere out there in the woods."

"Who could be lost?" Justin asked holding Lona's hand as they walked up behind the two women.

Rachel answered. "It's Rebecca. She went for a walk some time ago and hasn't returned."

"Damn! Lance gave her strict orders to stay close to the fort while he was gone."

"I guess some women just don't like taking orders," Lona commented knowingly, recalling how she had defied the man she thought of as a brother more times than she could count.

Rachel, too, understood how difficult Rebecca found the waiting. Keeping the young Englishwoman inside the fort was like trying to tie down a sunbeam. Rebecca was a stranger in a foreign land where not so long ago she would have been considered an enemy among the colonials. That she was willing to exchange the secure life of wealth and grandeur to which she was entitled for a future fraught with hardships and uncertainties proved to Rachel that she was not only self-sacrificing but deeply in love with the rebel army officer she had married.

"What the hell!" Justin craned forward as shouts rang out aboard the *Enterprise* and lanterns flared to life illuminating the deck then fanning out across the inky black waters of the bay.

Rebecca was forgotten for the moment as the four watched and waited to learn what had caused the sudden activity aboard the ship. Out of the darkness George Brooke and Lawrence Kearny appeared hurrying toward them.

Mary rushed forward. "George! What is it? What has happened?"

The colonel took his wife gently by the shoulders. "Nothing to worry about, my dear," he answered turning her toward the gate, urging her back inside with a firm arm about her thickening waist. "It must have been a trick of the light at sunset but we're going to check it out. I want you ladies to return to the house at once."

Mary came to a halt stubbornly digging in her heels as she whirled to face her husband. "George Brooke! I'm not taking another step until you tell me what you are talking about!"

The colonel complied knowing it would be useless to argue. "It's too absurd to take seriously but one of Kearny's men swears he saw a longboat manned by pirates rowing toward the beach just as the sun disappeared beyond the horizon."

"Pirates!" the women gasped in unison.

"It's a mistake," George repeated confidently. "The man admits that whatever he saw was too far away to

make out clearly and a handful of pirates could hardly hope to take the fort. The whole thing is insane. But just to be on the safe side I am going to take some men down the beach to where the sailor thinks he saw a boat land. And I want all of you safely inside while we are gone," he commanded sternly as he began herding the women into the stronghold. "Where is Rebecca?"

"Rebecca? Oh my God! I forgot all about Rebecca!"

Mary's horrified outcry brought Colonel Brooke to an abrupt halt.

Seeing Mary's distress Rachel hastened to explain, "Rebecca went for a walk and she hasn't returned. We were looking for her when we heard the commotion aboard the *Enterprise.*"

"You let her wander off alone in the dark?"

"Of course not," Mary defended. "It was daylight when she left. She said she would only be gone a short time, but she hasn't come back. We don't know in which direction she was headed."

The commander bit back any reminders he might have voiced concerning the dangers that could befall a woman alone even in broad daylight. He knew it was too late for recriminations and would only serve to increase their worry. Instead he instructed Kearny to round up the men and bring plenty of lanterns. The mysterious specter on the beach would have to wait. Right now they had to find Rebecca and bring her safely back to the fort, for he would not want to be the one to tell the formidable Lance Logan that they had misplaced his wife!

Rebecca sat up straight wiping her tears away, then

337

blew her nose before she tucked her handkerchief back into her pocket. *Some pioneer I turned out to be,* she remonstrated as she gave a final sniff and stood up a little shakily. *Logan would be ashamed of my sniveling. So much for the courageous spirit and independence he claimed to admire.* Glancing into the small framed mirror she continued to rebuke herself. *If Logan saw me now, he would probably put me on the first ship back to England! And who could blame him?* She winced at the puffy red eyes and sullen mouth looking back at her. *Enough!* she declared taking a deep breath. She would return to the fort and concentrate on her wifely duties. First she would write to her solicitors. There were so many handsome furnishings and knickknacks at the manor house that could add to the comfort of their home here in the territory. She would have to pick and choose carefully making sure she didn't diminish the cabin's raw natural beauty with overembellishment. But how satisfying it would be to complement her surroundings with treasures from her past. A smile curved her full lips as she planned the rooms they would add as their family grew.

With her usual optimism restored, Rebecca took a final look around the room then blew out the lamp. As she closed the door a half-moon appeared from behind the clouds to cast its pale light upon the clearing. Only then did she stop to think how concerned those at the fort must be over her long absence. She had not meant to cause them worry. She must return quickly and set their minds at ease. And maybe she could persuade her friends not to mention the imprudence of her coming here to her husband. Though she was confident he exaggerated the danger, she had promised to stay near the fort and her conscience pricked her with guilt.

Such were her thoughts as a sinewy arm came out of the darkness to clamp about her neck. A foul-smelling cloth closed over her face. As she drifted into oblivion, her last thought was how angry Lance would be when he discovered that she had disobeyed him!

Chapter 22

Lance and Andrew made record time in their return from Fort King, pushing their mounts recklessly along the trail giving scarcely a thought to the danger that might lie just beyond the next bend. But luck was with them and as the sun reached its zenith they rode through the gates, each man looking forward to the welcome he would receive from his waiting bride. Instead they found the fort in chaos with soldiers and sailors running over one another in what appeared to be preparation for battle.

"Andrew!"

As Rachel came flying through the Brookes' front door running across the compound to hurl herself into her husband's outstretched arms, Lance felt his first inkling of fear. *Where was Rebecca?*

Rachel's sobbing did little to assuage Logan's apprehension. He dismounted slowly, dread forming like a stone in the pit of his stomach. He stepped forward and stood a moment behind the weeping woman. Andrew gave him a bewildered look from over her quivering shoulder.

"Rachel," Lance spoke her name softly, repeating it several times before her shudders subsided.

"Rachel, where is Rebecca?" Lance held his breath as he awaited her reply.

Finally she turned toward him, her face ravaged with grief as she choked out the words. "Sh . . . she's disappeared."

For one interminable moment Lance felt his heart cease to beat. Blood drained from his head leaving him dizzy and disoriented. Then with a sudden surge the vital organ within his breast began to hammer so hard he could feel its throbbing pulse in his ears as wavy lines danced before his eyes.

"She's what?"

The birds took flight while small furry creatures scrambled for cover. The very earth trembled as Lance trumpeted his rage. His mood swung from jubilant anticipation to stunned disbelief to a fury so all-consuming he was ready to throttle the first man he could lay his hands on.

At that moment George Brooke and Lawrence Kearny appeared flanked by Mary, Lona, and Justin. They approached warily. The looks on their faces were all that was needed to convince Lance that Rachel had been speaking the truth.

Striving for control, he pierced Colonel Brooke with a glacial stare and waited for an explanation as to how the commander could have misplaced one small woman left in his keeping within the safe confines of the fort. George held his gaze briefly then dropped his eyes. To Lance no words could have more clearly emphasized the severity of the situation. In all the years he had known the man, George Brooke had always been able to look a man straight in the eye and say what was on his mind.

"Where is my wife?" Logan demanded through clenched teeth even as he felt his hands ball into fists. He still had to fight the urge to rip someone apart. *Someone would pay,* he promised himself but not until he knew who was responsible for Rebecca's disappearance.

"We don't know what happened," George admitted. "What we have been able to piece together just doesn't make sense. Come inside, Logan. Maybe together we can sort this out."

Lance paced the living room like a caged animal as he listened to the story unravel. When all that was known had been told, he paused to mull over the information in his mind.

"You're right about one thing," he said at last. "It doesn't make sense! Pirates? What would the goddamn pirates want with Rebecca?"

"Ransom?" Rachel suggested.

Lance ran his hands through his thick dark hair. "From whom?" he asked logically. "The pirates know there is nothing of value at the fort and how could they possibly know that Rebecca is an heiress?" Frustration threatened to defeat the rugged scout. How could fate be so cruel? Rebecca, with her love and understanding and even her feisty stubbornness, had managed to break down the barriers he had erected around his heart. She had wedged her way in through a chink in his armor and before he knew it she had become the life force that gave him a reason to go on. Through her he had found direction. He wanted to be a part of formulating the future of this territory he had come to care about so deeply. But how could he think of a future without Rebecca? His achievements would be meaningless? Life would not be worth living.

"We can only guess at the 'whys,' Logan." It was Lawrence Kearny who spoke. His voice brooked no argument as he stood with one leg crossed in front of the other, his elbow resting against the mantelpiece. "What we do know is that Rebecca was at the cabin early in the evening. The globe of the lamp was still warm when we arrived. There were signs of a struggle in the clearing out front and footprints leading into the woods. We followed the trail to the beach several miles west of the fort where we found the imprint of a boat's hull in the damp sand. One of my most reliable men reports sighting pirates rowing toward that section of beach a few hours prior to your wife's disappearance."

Kearny straightened to his full height, folding his arms across his chest as he surveyed the room's silent occupants. "Every shred of evidence points to one conclusion. Gaspar has her!"

His words fell like a prophesy of doom.

Rebecca was on a downward spiral. Strange, she thought from some vague recess of her mind. How was it she could breathe underwater as Lance teasingly pulled her toward the bottom of the pool? It hadn't worked that way before. He would let her go soon for he had no way of knowing she could continue to drift beneath the surface indefinitely. She stretched out her arm trying to touch one of the shimmering iridescent fish swimming by, but the elusive creature darted away and now she was alone. It was so peaceful floating along with the current. But as she continued her descent her surroundings grew dark and the temperature dropped dramatically. Truth to tell, it was freezing. Where had the warm sun gone? Only a moment ago its gold light had played upon the blue-green surface of the pond. Squinting her eyes, Rebecca could just barely make out Logan's angry shadow above her. Now what was he doing up there?

"Come back, Rebecca. Come back," he implored reaching his hand toward her but his voice sounded so far away. It was as if he were shouting through a tunnel.

She tried to assure him that she was all right but he didn't seem able to hear her. Then suddenly he was receding from her line of vision. She had to do something or he would be lost to her forever. But she was so tired. Her arms and legs felt weighted as she continued drifting downward into the ebony darkness.

"By God, you gave her too much, you brainless ass! You had better hope she comes around soon or you will be begging for a quick death!"

Damnation! What was Logan ranting about? She was really too fatigued to cooperate with one of his piques. Why couldn't he just lift her up into the light? She longed to feel his muscled body holding her, to feel the evidence of his need taut against her stomach. Suddenly she shivered and knew that only Logan could make her warm again.

"Please, sweetheart! I need you. I love you. Come back!"

High-handed dunderpate! Didn't he know she was trying. Could she help it that her limbs were leaden refusing to do as her brain directed?

Thick eyelashes fluttered as she struggled to lift her heavy lids a crack then closed the shutters tightly against the blinding light that made her head ache abominably and her stomach threaten to heave up its contents. She waited a few minutes then tested the action once more; this time managing with no little effort to keep her eyes open despite the fact that they failed to focus. She fought the urge to drift off once more into her quiet, peaceful sanctuary as the gentle swaying motion beneath her body lured her back into oblivion.

Then without warning her shoulders were seized by strong rough hands that shook her until her teeth rattled. Her already throbbing head swung back and forth against a pillow which felt as though it had been stuffed with solid granite.

In defiance of the ill-treatment she was receiving, Rebecca lashed out blindly pommeling the force that held her with her balled fists then clawing with her nails. When her fingers found their mark raking across a bewhiskered cheek, she was released abruptly. A string of obscenities and a sharp slap followed which set her head ringing.

"Perhaps it was better when my golden bird slept for her talons have the razor's edge," came a raspy whisper close beside her.

Neither of the two men within the small cabin altered their sullen expressions so much as a degree as their leader spoke.

"But Gaspar would not want a cooing dove. It is the free spirit of this wild and wondrous she-god that sets my blood afire. Together we will soar the skies, two birds of prey, devouring any so foolish as to fall beneath our shadow. We will nest at the end of the day atop the highest mountain peak closed within a world of our own making where mortal men dare not intrude."

Rebecca kept her eyes tightly closed willing herself to awaken from the hideous nightmare even as her smarting cheek bore evidence that this was no dream. Her stomach rumbled ominously as she listened to the lunatic ravings coming from somewhere just beyond her tightly closed lids. She felt the bile rise in her throat as her roiling stomach gave warning of things to come. Then the hands were on her again squeezing her upper arms with bruising force.

"Open your eyes, my treasure above all treasures, and look upon your destiny."

Though dreading what she would see, Rebecca felt compelled to obey. Disoriented emerald green eyes slowly widened as she concentrated her gaze on the face of the madman. Having ignored the lurches and rumblings that forewarned what came next, Jose Gaspar sat in frozen silence as Rebecca emptied the contents of her heaving stomach in his lap.

Neither Rebecca nor the nefarious pirate leader were aware of the devilish grins that suddenly replaced the saturnine expressions of the two buccaneers looking on.

"Damn it, man! We're not going to do Rebecca any good by going off half cocked," George Brooke reasoned as he tried to calm an overwrought Lance Logan. "After all, we're only speculating that Gaspar has her. Even if we're right we don't know where he may have taken her."

The look Lance turned on the colonel demonstrated the steely determination that had enabled him to survive in this untamed land prior to the coming of other white men. "If you think I will sit idly by knowing that Rebecca is in danger, think again, Colonel!" he roared turning to face the young lieutenant. "I'm warning you right now! I plan to take your ship with or without your permission. I'll search every inch of the damned Gulf if I have to, but I will find my wife and bring her back here," he vowed resolutely then added, "after I kill the low-life scum who took her!"

Lawrence Kearny raised his brows as he met the eyes of his enraged compatriot. He was not unsympathetic to the man's plight but he knew Logan was thinking with his heart and not his head.

"You're talking about a lot of water, my friend. Perhaps you have forgotten that my men and I have been searching for Gaspar and his crew of cutthroats for months. What makes you think you can find them when we've come up empty time and time again?"

Kearny's logic set Logan's teeth on edge. "Maybe I can't," he ground out. "But one thing's for certain. I'm not going to sit here and do nothing knowing she's out there somewhere."

"If only we could locate their stronghold," the naval officer mused. "But everytime we think we have them they seem to just disappear off the face of the earth."

It was Mary, standing silently by as the men discussed what was to be done, who first noticed the arrival of the tall tribal leader. "Nokomis. Come in, please," she bid warmly, knowing Lona's father felt uncomfortable inside the house.

He moved with caution glancing around nervously at the restrictive walls surrounding him. Nokomis was a man at home in the woods with the sky above him and the ground beneath his feet, out in the open where he could see his enemy's approach. He had been here only once before when his daughter lay gravely wounded in the bed upstairs. This was not a place he wanted to be and everyone in the room knew what it had cost him to come.

George held out his hand silently inviting the chief to join the small circle of men standing before the cold fireplace. Dark hooded eyes studied Lance as he glared back at the man whose life he had once saved. No hint of emotion was visible on the weathered face of the Indian, yet his presence said it all.

Several long moments passed in silence before Nokomis spoke. "I have heard that your woman has been taken." His words were directed toward the distressed scout. "I've come to help you bring her back."

Lance answered testily, his temper barely held in check. "Much as I appreciate your offer, right now I need someone who knows where that bastard pirate hides out when he's not kidnapping innocent women."

Nokomis chose to ignore Logan's curt rebuff.

"I repeat. I have come to help."

His words drifted in the air too far out of reach to readily penetrate the distraught minds of his listeners. Lance was the first to grasp what the chief was trying to say in as few words as possible. Alarms went off in his head creating a pounding in his temples that threatened to explode. His jaws clenched as he stepped forward and grabbed the taller man's muscled arms literally

348

shaking his top knot to and fro. The women gasped in horror as the men took a step backward.

Logan's voice was more bestial than human. "Are you telling me you know the location of the refuge used by that malignant flotsam?"

The imposing Indian looked down his hawklike nose at the man daring to interrogate him in such a fashion. For all Logan's strength Nokomis had little difficulty in removing the hands that held him. As the two men glared at one another, Lawrence Kearny stepped forward to demand impatiently, "If you know the whereabouts of Gaspar, why haven't you said so before this? You know we have been trying for months to end his reign of terror on the Gulf!" The naval officer was nearly apoplectic thinking that the answer to their search for the nest of vipers had unknowingly been so close at hand.

Nokomis turned to fix Kearny with a cold stare. "Why should I have volunteered to help you rout out pirates who have done my people no harm? For many years Gaspar has ruled the sea while I ruled the land and never has there been occasion for a confrontation. It is you colonials who have brought change to this territory. It is you who have forced the Calusa to adopt the white man's ways."

Lance held his temper as he listened to the justified argument Nokomis presented. He knew that to throttle the powerful chief, which was exactly what he itched to do, would not only exacerbate the situation but might also prove suicidal. That Lawrence Kearny had taken the affront personally was obvious in the way his chest expanded and his complexion mottled. But the exchange of accusations would not help Rebecca. It was time now for rational capitulation.

"Right you are, my friend," Logan acquiesced giving Kearny a meaningful look. Lance had too much respect for Nokomis to dispute what both knew to be true. He said instead, "Regardless of your reasons for withholding knowledge of Gaspar's whereabouts in the past, you seem willing enough to help us now. What has brought about this change of heart?"

He felt the unreadable hooded eyes observing him imperiously. The elderly Indian seemed in no hurry to answer and Lance fought to remain calm when every instinct urged him to beat the arrogant chieftain senseless in an effort to gain the information needed to go after Rebecca. But at last his restraint paid off. The barest hint of a smile curved the other man's thin lips as he replied, "I like your woman, Logan. She reminds me of someone I once knew."

Rebecca had told Lance about her encounter with Nokomis and his likening her to his Spanish wife. He knew that any assistance the man was willing to give in finding Rebecca would be because her courageous spirit was much like that of his long lost love, not because he felt any loyalty to the whites who had stolen the land of his people.

Lance was not one to beg. The very idea went against his nature and never would he have humbled himself for his own sake, not even if his life depended on it. But it was Rebecca whose life hung in the balance. Every moment she remained in the hands of the ruthless Gaspar brought her one step closer to death, for he knew she would never willingly submit to the blackguard's demands.

"There was a time when you called me 'brother.'"

Logan found it difficult to form the words around the lump in his throat. His gray eyes were as dull and muted as tarnished metal. "Please, help me find my wife," he implored unable to continue masking his desperation behind a facade of self-control.

Right now by refusing to tell them the location of the pirate refuge, Nokomis could exact his revenge for all the wrongs, real or imaginary, that had been done to the Calusa. And as he awaited the chief's response to his plea with gut wrenching uncertainty, he realized how little he understood the workings of the other's mind. Nokomis had volunteered his help yet when it seemed his offer might be rejected he had turned his wrath upon the group of settlers. If he refused to aid them now, Rebecca would pay the ultimate price in a contest of wills stemming from a long-fought battle in which she had taken no part. Beads of perspiration dotted Logan's forehead as his eyes locked with those of the man who held Rebecca's life in his hands. His heart plummeted as Nokomis pivoted and started toward the open door. But as the Indian chief ducked his head beneath its frame, he spoke without turning around.

"It's a long ride. We'd better get started."

Chapter 23

As the door of the hut was wrenched open, Rebecca found herself shoved roughly inside. Tripping against an unseen object, she fell face down upon the hard-packed dirt floor. It was that tenebrous time of evening following the sun's setting when the moon still yawned into wakefulness, its meager light casting the small room into shadowed obscurity. Making no immediate attempt to rise, she lifted her head to scan the room's dark interior as she waited for her eyes to adjust.

"Damnation!" she spluttered finally scrambling to a kneeling position.

The growling of her now empty stomach sounded overly loud in the stillness of her prison chamber, and her mouth tasted dry and sour. But for the moment her anger at the rude treatment she had received at the hands of the pirates overrode not only her hunger but her trepidation as well.

"Despicable vermin! I wouldn't want to be in your boots when Logan gets here."

She had spoken aloud only to assure herself that her

husband would not allow her kidnapping to go unpunished. Since she hadn't expected a reply, Rebecca came to her feet quickly when her words were met with a rustling noise from the far corner of the tiny structure.

"Probably infested with rats," she grumbled. "Vile rodents! Stay where you are!" she commanded swishing her full skirts for emphasis.

She nearly swooned when, instead of the scurry she had dreaded to hear, her order was met with the sound of a muffled sob. Rebecca froze in place then leaned forward into the darkness.

"Who's there?"

As minutes ticked by Rebecca began to think the strange events of the day had affected her imagination. Then without warning a cold, clawlike hand reached out and clasped her around the ankle. Her own hand went to her throat as she snatched her leg free from the clutches of her unknown assailant and stepped backward until she stood braced against the mud-packed wall of the hut. Rebecca was terrified. Her wildly beating heart threatened to burst in her chest while her head pounded like storm waves beating against the shore. At least when facing the dreaded pirates she had known her enemy. The thought of being trapped here in this lightless prison with an adversary she could not see nearly sent her over the edge. She tried to catch any alien sound that would signal the approach of her invisible attacker, but only her own ragged breathing disturbed the quiet night.

"Help me," came a whispered voice from the shadows.

Still paralyzed with fear, Rebecca thought surely her

ears were playing tricks on her. Then she heard it again.

"Please help me."

And this time there was no mistaking the pitiable plea of a human voice. She dropped to her knees just as two thin arms encircled her body clinging to her as if to a lifeline. Instinctively she ran her hand through the lank hair of the stranger weeping against her skirts, thinking at first it was a child unfortunate enough to be caught up in this escalating nightmare. Rebecca crooned soothing words as she continued to stroke the forlorn figure that seemed determined not to let her go.

By now she was able to make out the room's sparse furnishings. A cot covered with a rumpled quilt stood beside a rickety table, holding a porcelain pitcher and a single pewter mug. After a brief glimpse her gaze came back to the girl seeking shelter in her embrace.

Gradually the girl's sobs subsided into short hiccuping gulps. As she turned her tear-streaked face up toward the moonlight flowing through the single small window, Rebecca was surprised to see that her fellow captive was not a child at all but a woman no more than a few years younger than herself. Moist despairing eyes told more than words ever could of the ordeal she had been through and the woman's fear was contagious. Rebecca had to force herself to repress the shiver of apprehension that threatened to crumble her own flagging fortitude.

Willing her body to relax she asked in a voice that held only the barest trace of a tremor, "Who are you?"

"Nan . . . Nanette," came the hesitant reply. "Nanette Dubois."

Rebecca grew uncomfortable when Nanette said no more. Instead the young woman sat up and stared at her in openmouthed astonishment. Rebecca had no idea how the gentle moonlight streaming through the window haloed her golden-blond hair in much the same way an artist would highlight the head of the Madonna on canvas.

When the French woman finally spoke her words did nothing to calm Rebecca's rising panic. "It is you!" she exclaimed, her complexion turning a ghastly white.

Not understanding the other's outcry, Rebecca was doubly disturbed when Nanette jerked back beyond reach, her eyes wide with fright.

Bewildered, Rebecca frowned fearing for the woman's sanity. "I won't hurt you, Nanette. Why are you afraid of me?"

Her shrunken frame a quivering mass of fear, Nanette retreated back into the shadows, leaving Rebecca at a loss as to what she had done to frighten such a reaction out of the young woman.

"Please," she implored once again. "All I want is to help you."

"No one can help me, especially you. Your coming has sealed my fate. Be quiet now so that I may pray for forgiveness and a hasty death."

Despite the pity she felt for Nanette, Rebecca was annoyed by the nonsense the other was spouting. After all, it was not as if she had come here of her own free will. Why, for heaven's sake, should her kidnapping affect the other's status one way or another. Obviously they were both being held prisoner by the pirates. Perhaps if they put their heads together they could come up with a plan to escape. While Rebecca did not discount the power of prayer, right now the old adage "God helps those who help themselves" seemed more

355

appropriate than petitioning for a hasty death. Even though Logan was hot on the trail of her captors and would ultimately succeed in gaining her release, she was not willing to huddle in a corner awaiting that eventuality.

Rising to her feet she took the few short steps to where Nanette cringed mouthing "Hail Mary's." Rebecca placed her hands on her hips hoping there was enough light to make the gesture effective, then spoke sternly to the wall.

"Stop that this instant!"

The plaintive supplications ended abruptly. Then to Rebecca's chagrin she heard the small voice lament, "Lord, have mercy on my soul, for the goddess is a heathen."

Certain now that she was locked in with a bedlamite, Rebecca took a deep breath and said her own silent prayer for patience.

"Enough, Nanette. What is this foolish talk about my sealing your fate and who is this goddess you speak of?"

"You are the one," the French woman answered, her tone despairing. "You are Gaspar's golden goddess!"

Then the entire story came tumbling out. Nanette related the details of her capture and her savage rape by the pirate leader ending with a description of his rage over the fact that the one at his mercy was not the golden-haired woman for whom he lusted. Rebecca could hardly credit the tale; yet, as much as her mind screamed to deny what she was hearing, she knew in her heart that her companion could never fabricate such an incredible story. Yet, instead of fear, the knowledge brought with it anger such as she had never

356

known before. She longed for the strength to face the ignoble villain and exact revenge against the man who would take a virgin's innocence without conscience. And to make matters worse, Rebecca was forced to shoulder a portion of the guilt though she, too, had been an unwilling victim.

This time when she held out her arms Nanette did not shy away but stood up and came forward seeking a measure of the Englishwoman's strength. Standing eye to eye Rebecca pledged, "He will pay. This I promise you. But first we must make plans for escape."

For the first time in many weeks, a glimmer of hope shone in Nanette's face. "But how? There are guards outside and we are on an island. Even if we manage to free ourselves and reach the mainland, we will be facing a tractless wilderness. I have heard the territory is covered with swamps inhabited by snakes and alligators not to mention red-skinned savages!"

Rebecca's irritation returned full force as she watched Nanette's eyes pool once again.

"You are right, of course," she agreed with a shrug. "Attempting to escape would be useless so I will just resign myself to spending the rest of my days on the Isle of Pine with Gaspar where you have said he plans to take me." She feigned a long-suffering sigh then continued. "At least your agony will be brief once you are in the hands of his ruffians. I should not imagine you will suffer for long."

"Don't say such a thing, Rebecca! Please! We've got to do something. I'm not ready to die!"

Thank God her spirit has not been totally destroyed, Rebecca thought to herself damning Gaspar once again. Her relief was enormous for she knew that despite all Nanette had been subjected to, she would be all right once they managed to escape this den of iniquity.

"Listen to me," Rebecca demanded taking Nanette by the shoulders and shaking her gently. "Help is on the way," she assured her. There was no doubt in her mind even though she had no idea where they might be or whether the pirates had left a trail to follow. Logan would find them and she said as much aloud.

Nanette looked perplexed. "Who is this Logan you speak of?"

Rebecca's green eyes lit with pleasure and anticipation. "He is my husband, and he will make Jose Gaspar wish he had never been born," she answered unable to disguise the pride in her voice.

Rebecca was surprised to hear Nanette chuckle. "Gaspar is in for a big surprise all right! I would like to be around when he discovers his golden goddess is married. I think somewhere in his demented mind he is convinced that you were waiting just for him."

Nanette's humor buoyed Rebecca's sinking spirits. "Well, we are not waiting around so that you can watch his reaction," she said making her way to the narrow opening to peer cautiously out into the night. Two pirates stood just a few feet in front of the door sharing a cheroot and talking softly in Spanish.

"No escape there. We will have to tunnel our way out the back."

"But what about your husband?"

"Don't worry. Logan will be here," she voiced confidently, "but wouldn't it be a nice surprise if we met him on the beach?"

Rebecca winked conspiratorially at her companion.

Nanette's face split into a grin as the light at the end of the tunnel, they had yet to dig, grew brighter.

The horses ate up ground as the band of riders headed south on an inland course parallel to the western coast of Florida. But soon there were no trails to follow and in places they were forced to cut their way through the dense foliage where creeper vines tangled with the ever-present Spanish moss forming a natural barrier to slow their progress. They swam the horses across rivers swollen from the summer rain storms but had to skirt the treacherous mangrove swamps wasting precious time they could ill-afford.

Gray clouds of mosquitos disturbed by plodding hooves rose up to torment the passing horsemen leaving itching welts on any body parts left exposed. Around them they heard the music of birds chirping overhead and frogs croaking among the rushes, while occasionally the hoarse grunt of a lone alligator added a bass note to nature's choir.

In years to come Lance would be hard-pressed to recall any detail of the journey. His only objective was to recover his wife unharmed and to make certain her safety would never again be put in jeopardy. He was a man possessed. If not for the fact that he hadn't the slightest idea of where they were going and was, therefore, forced to follow behind the tall, arrogant Indian chief, he would have refused to stop when Nokomis declared it too dark to proceed.

Visions of what might be taking place within the pirate stronghold tortured Lance far more than the pesky insects that pricked the skin between his collar and his bandana or the humid heat that caused his shirt to stick uncomfortably to his muscular back.

"Why have we stopped?" he demanded as the Indian leader held up his hand issuing orders in the guttural language of the Calusa. The handful of braves that accompanied them immediately began to make camp for the night.

As if speaking to a child, Nokomis explained the obvious. "We stop because we lack the power of the owl and the jungle cat to see in the dark."

In the middle of the clearing a small fire flickered to life. Nokomis brushed past Lance heading for the circle of light. Impatiently Lance grasped his shoulder pulling him to a halt.

"Damn it, man! I want Rebecca back and I'm not stopping until I get her!" he shouted up at the aging warrior.

Nokomis flicked his hand away with no more effort than he would use to swat one of the bothersome flies drawn by the light of the camp fire. Deep hooded eyes stared down into the face of the angry frontiersman. "So be it," Nokomis declared his voice devoid of emotion. "Go your own way, white man, and we will catch up with you in the morning." He paused before adding, ". . . if you happen to go in the right direction."

Lance turned in disgust and beat his fist against the nearest tree trunk, his face racked with pain and frustration. He knew Nokomis was right, but he could not think clearly while his heart ached for his lost love. He continued to pound the rough bark of the lofty pine until his hand was bruised and aching. He reared back his mighty head and roared into the night like a ferocious beast calling for its mate. No one dared stop him. Only when two twinkling stars moved together overhead did Logan's logic return. He would wait out this long, endless night, but soon, very soon, Gaspar would pay full measure for what he had done. And if he had harmed one hair on Rebecca's beautiful head, his death would be slow and painful.

Some time later Lance stretched his long legs toward the fire, more from habit than from any need of warmth on this muggy tropical night. Resting back upon his elbows he stared into the dying embers.

"Where are they?" He spared not a glance at the solemn Indian sitting beside him.

Nokomis grunted, his gaze never straying from the fire. "We will find them on Gasparilla Island," he replied, knowing his answer would be of little help to his inquisitor.

Not a muscle moved in Logan's face to indicate he had heard the words of the chief. He pulled a splinter of wood from the fire and held it between straight white teeth. After awhile he rolled to his side, took the slender toothpick from his mouth, and began to tally figures in the loose earth.

Soon curiosity overcame his companion. "What is it that you are doing?" he asked nodding down at the cryptic ciphers.

"I'm making a list of what I know about Gaspar," Lance answered without looking up. "I know he is a cowardly son-of-a-bitch who preys on the defenseless and unsuspecting," he said pointing to the first crude figure. Moving the end of the slivered wood downward, he continued, "Secondly, I know he is a cold-blooded murderer and a despoiler of women." Lance leaned ever so slightly toward the chief. "Thirdly, I know he's an egotistical bastard who dares to give land belonging to the United States of America his detestable name."

Without warning he reached up and pulled Nokomis off balance until they lay sprawled nose to nose on the grass. "Lastly," he snarled inches from the other man's face, "I know Jose Gaspar is a dead man!"

Not for a moment did the chief doubt the fate of the notorious pirate for the murderous intent on Logan's face was clearly evident.

"Now tell me something I don't know," Lance gritted out savagely. "Where is Gasparilla Island?"

As Nokomis straightened to a sitting position once more, fastidiously brushing a bronzed hand across his hairless chest, Logan wondered if he had pushed the proud chieftain too far by demanding to know the location of the infamous pirate's hideaway. He knew that no amount of persuasion would induce the old man to talk unless he was so inclined. If Nokomis turned stubborn, refusing to lead the way to the mysterious island, there would be little he could do to rescue Rebecca from the bloodthirsty brigands. Lance waited in silence hoping that his unbridled temper would not prove fatal for the beautiful woman he loved more than life itself.

His sigh of relief was audible when the inscrutable Indian deigned to reply. "Gasparilla Island is a full day's ride south not far from the Caloosahatchee River. It's a fair sized piece of land with the small island the pirates call *Captiva* not far away. Captiva is surrounded by a wall. Prisoners are kept inside until they can be sold as slaves."

"What about the main island?"

362

"There are three warehouses and a number of huts belonging to Gaspar and his men. A long pier juts out to the west. There is no wall on Gasparilla Island but the only way to get there is by boat."

"One could swim," Lance mused picturing the place in his mind.

Nokomis shrugged noncommittally. "Do you think Kearny's plan will work?" he asked after another long silence.

"It's just a matter of timing," Lance replied with more confidence than he really felt. "Everyone must be in the right place at the right moment."

"There is one other important element to be considered, my friend; one no amount of planning can assure."

"What's that?" Lance asked impatiently unable to consider the possibility of failure.

"Gaspar must take the bait!"

Chapter 24

Judging from the brilliance of the sun streaming through the tiny window, Rebecca supposed it must be close to noon as she arched her aching back and wiped beads of perspiration from her forehead with the hem of her skirt.

"Quick, Rebecca! Someone is coming!" Nanette hissed as she scurried from her lookout post beside the narrow aperture.

Rebecca dropped the pewter mug she was using as a scoop and jumped to her feet. She brushed the dirt from her hands as best she could, then together the two women pushed the cot over the hole they had taken turns digging. The mound of earth beside the half-completed tunnel had grown so high there was a telltale hump in the mattress once the bed was back in place, but there was no time to worry about it now. They had no more than turned around when the door opened to admit an unsmiling Spanish woman bearing a tray on which were two plates of rice topped with a fishy-smelling concoction and a loaf of dark bread.

Rebecca guessed the woman to be near fifty by the tiny lines etched in her clear olive skin though not a trace of gray could be seen in the glossy blue-black hair combed straight back to fall below her waist. She had the generous breasts and well-rounded hips of a Spanish matron yet her narrow waist denied the comparison. Her sharp black eyes took in every inch of the scantily furnished room. She reminded Rebecca of a gypsy fortune teller she once saw at a country fair held in the village near her family's estate. Though Rebecca had been but ten years old at the time she still remembered the dark penetrating eyes that seemed able to read her innermost thoughts.

The stranger said not a word as she moved the water pitcher aside to make room for the heavy serving tray, but Rebecca felt her heart lurch as the woman's brows peaked. She suddenly remembered the single mug now hidden beneath the cot. When the Spaniard's gaze shifted to that very same piece of furniture Rebecca ceased to breathe as she willed the suspicious protrusion to disappear.

Only when the woman silently exited on bare feet did Rebecca dare to expel the air in her lungs, feeling like a convicted felon receiving a last minute reprieve.

"Who was that?" she murmured in an undertone as they heard the latch fall into place.

A visibly shaken Nanette whispered back. "Her name is Ramona. She is mistress to Gaspar's cousin, Leon. Do you think she suspects that we are up to something?" she asked unsteadily.

"Suspects?" Rebecca's laugh held no mirth as she took one of the warm plates and plopped down on the bed. "She doesn't suspect. She knows!" she answered without reservation. "The question is will she tell?"

Nanette wrung her hands nervously.

"You had best eat your dinner," Rebecca suggested. "We have to keep up our strength if we are to finish the tunnel."

"Do you think we still have a chance?" she queried then continued without giving Rebecca an opportunity to reply. "What makes you so certain she knows about the tunnel?"

"She noticed the missing cup, and didn't you see how she looked at the mattress?"

Nanette stared thoughtfully at the plate resting on her lap. "I do not think she will tell Gaspar. I have heard her arguing with his cousin begging Leon to take her away. She is afraid the madman will get them all killed!"

The news was reassuring yet Rebecca had no reason to trust the Spanish woman. "Even if she doesn't tell Gaspar, she may tell her lover. And, if she does, will his loyalty force him to recount the story to his cousin?"

"I wish I knew. What shall we do now?"

Stubbornly Rebecca placed her half-finished plate of food on the table. "Far be it from me to tell you what you must do, but until someone stops me I intend to keep right on digging!"

"You are insane!" Leon Gaspar accused jerking his cousin roughly around to face him.

The two men were standing on the western edge of the island where in the distance a lumbering ship floundered in the water silhouetted against the late afternoon sun. From its masts, remnants of canvas

366

billowed in the breeze as though the sails had been shredded by an ungodly force. The flailing vessel appeared to be drifting backward helplessly drawn by the current of the Gulf.

The greedy pirate leader yanked his arm free, slamming the spy glass he had been holding against the chest of his accuser.

"You stupid fool! Look there and tell me if that is not a gift from the gods. We've only to reach out and take it," he exclaimed holding one hand palm up as he curled his callused fingers into a ball. "Look!" he demanded again, his expression smug. "The deck holds no cannon. That ship will be ours and we won't have to fire a shot!"

The old sea dog squinted into the sun, his cracked lips stretching into the vague semblance of a smile, but Leon refused to be swayed even by a guaranteed victory.

"No, Jose! No more! You have more gold than you could spend in three lifetimes. And now you have the woman. You agreed to put an end to the plundering. The men have the goods packed for transport from the warehouses to the *Dona Rosalia*. We have no time to play games with a sinking ship!"

Gaspar spun around, grasped Leon by the shirtfront, and shook him. The telescope fell, forgotten, to roll across the damp, glistening sand at their feet. His eyes were like the devil's own, glazed by an unbalanced mind.

"You dare give orders to Gaspar?" he shouted, the pitch of his voice rising ever higher. "You who have been nothing more than a bloodsucking leech living off my bounty?"

"Let him go, you bastard!" Ramona could no longer stand by listening to the ravings of the lunatic as he belittled the man who was both her lover and her benefactor. "You, of all people, should recognize a parasite for you are king among them," she spat, her black eyes flashing hatred.

Jose released his cousin with a shove that caused Leon to stagger, but he quickly righted himself moving to encircle Ramona's waist and pull her close. The older man stood looking malevolently at the two of them but Ramona refused to back down.

"Go ahead then! Attack that weaponless ship. Don't stop at robbing and raping those on board! Blow your helpless victims right out of the water to prove what a big man you are! Have your final triumph!" she goaded.

Her biting sarcasm infuriated the object of her scorn. He raised his arm preparing to remind her that no one questioned his decisions. But Leon stepped in front to shield her from the promised blow, his angry visage daring Gaspar to strike his woman. With a grunt of dismissal Gaspar lowered his arm and began shouting orders to his men. As the arrogant old pirate swaggered toward the longboat making ready for launch, Leon shook his head.

"You should not have provoked him to do this foolish thing." His reprimand rekindled the ire of his mistress.

"Bah! Nothing could stop that stupid jackal from attempting to add one more prize to his conquests!"

Instead of defending his cousin's actions as was his wont, Leon stood unspeaking as he watched the boat weighed down with black-hearted knaves bump against the side of the dark-hulled pirate ship flying the dreaded flag of the brotherhood.

"I don't know, Ramona," he said at last. "I have a bad feeling here." And he placed his hand upon his heart.

"So do I. I cannot explain exactly but I foresee a final confrontation about to take place. One that could change the course of all of our lives."

"Or end them," Leon added portentously.

"We've done it, Nanette," Rebecca cried excitedly as she bent to peek at the waning light filtering through their narrow pathway to freedom. "All we have to do is wait until full dark. Then we make our move."

From her position by the window Nanette looked both hopeful and frightened. "What if someone happens around back and sees the opening?"

Rebecca refused to be deterred by the other's pessimism. "From the sound of things outside everyone is on the far beach," she replied joining Nanette by the window. "Can you tell what all the commotion is about?"

"Not really, but there was some sort of disagreement between Gaspar and his cousin. Now Gaspar is being rowed to his ship."

"He seems to have forgotten all about us."

"Then we should count our blessings," Nanette shuddered. "But as far as I can tell the two guards are still outside our door."

Both women drew back as Ramona turned to glare at the hut where they were being held. Even from a distance her anger was evident. A torrent of Spanish followed as the dark-haired woman beckoned with both arms almost as though she were motioning for them to join her.

"What is she saying?" asked Nanette.

"How would I know? I don't speak Spanish." Rebecca immediately regretted the sharpness of her tone but it was so frustrating not to understand what was happening.

After a low mumbled conference the two swarthy pirates who had been stationed outside the door strode off toward the couple standing on the opposite side of the island. The guards continued to argue among themselves. At the same time Ramona and Leon appeared to be having a heated debate with each other, their hands moving rapidly in gestures obviously meant to stress the importance of the rapid flow of words.

Rebecca smiled as the truth dawned. "Ramona is purposely drawing the men away. I don't pretend to understand why, but she is giving us a chance to escape. And I for one plan to take it!"

Without giving Nanette an opportunity to point out the possible pitfalls in their plan, she spun about and crouched down beside the tunnel just wide enough to allow the two slender women to squeeze through.

Glancing back at her nervous companion, she said, "I'll go first. Stay here until I give you a signal to leave."

She balled her skirts up around her waist freeing her knees to push forward, wriggling her body through the tunnel and out into the sultry tropical night. She paused resting on her knees listening to the distant voices still squabbling as the sun continued its descent throwing the area behind the shanty into shade.

As Rebecca prepared to signal Nanette to follow, a large hand reached out of the dim shadows to cover her mouth. In less than a moment she was dragged to her feet as the other muscled arm of her attacker came about to draw her hard against a solid masculine chest. She could feel the back of her dress growing damp from the sodden shirt worn by the man who held her within a bearlike grip. The hand clamped over the lower half of her face slowly came away.

"Sweetheart, have they hurt you?"

The soft words whispered into her ear were the most welcome sounds Rebecca could ever hope to hear. She pivoted folding herself into her husband's warm embrace. Knowing she no longer had to rely on her own courage she felt her knees buckle with relief as Lance took time to devour her lips with a long passion-filled kiss that gradually eased her trembling.

Supporting her as he continued to kiss her temples, her eyes, her nose, he repeated. "Has that monster touched you?" The underlying fury in his voice made Rebecca glad that his wrath was not directed at her.

"No, Lance. He didn't . . ."

"Rebecca! Where are you?"

Her assurances were cut short as Nanette scrambled through the hole they had dug and emerged into the faint light still visible in the clearing.

"Ssh! We're all right now, Nanette." Rebecca reached to assist the surprised French woman to her feet. "This is the husband I was telling you about," she introduced hugging Lance proudly.

Nanette looked puzzled. "Are there more that you haven't told me about?"

Then it was Rebecca's turn to look perplexed.

Logan grinned marveling that the two had managed to make good their escape, despite the obvious language barrier. "Come," he commanded motioning them toward the eastern shore where a small boat rested half in, half out of the water. "We're not out of this yet."

Rebecca, remembering Logan's wet shirt and breeches, questioned him as they ran swiftly toward the dinghy. "I thought you swam from the mainland."

"I did, but I found this little craft up the beach and figured we might put it to good use," he explained settling his charges, then shoving off. "Of course if you prefer to swim . . ."

"No, thank you! The only place I want to swim is in the hidden lake."

Thinking back to the romantic afternoon they had spent at Lona's secret place, Rebecca blushed, her stomach growing tight with the need to lie naked once more in Logan's arms. But there would be time. Thank God, there would be plenty of time. For once again she could look forward to sharing a bright, happy future with the man she loved.

Jose Gaspar chuckled as the *Dona Rosalia* drew within firing range of the still floundering ship. The ragged bits of sail flapping in the breeze beckoned like dozens of white flags signifying surrender. He hoped there would be treasure aboard to enrich his coffers but if not it mattered little. His warehouses already bulged with the gold and silver he had accumulated over several decades. But no measure of riches could equal the ultimate reward for the many years of isolation and loneliness he had endured in order to exact his revenge on those who had made him an outcast. How ironic that just when his luck had seemed to be running out, when nightmares plagued him with visions of defeat at the hands of his enemies, he had captured the greatest prize of all, his golden goddess who would reign as queen of the south seas and hail him as her king.

Gaspar watched as the *Dona Rosalia* drew ever closer to the large gray vessel whose deck was hidden behind a wall of solid planking, most likely meant to safeguard its passengers against being washed overboard during a storm. Apparently such precautions had been in vain. The ship appeared deserted except for the seagulls lining the barren masts. Perhaps the crew and passengers had abandoned the craft after its sails were torn from their rigging, choosing to take their chances among the sharks and other predatory creatures of the deep. Gaspar found the thought amusing.

From habit more than necessity, he lifted his voice to shout across the short distance separating the ghost ship from his own. "Surrender or die, you impotent bastards!"

His words seemed to echo back at him. Then suddenly he realized it was no echo at all but a new voice answering his challenge, a voice deeply timbred and filled with self-assurance.

"Not this time old man! It is your turn to surrender!"

As Gaspar watched incredulously the sheets of wood enclosing the deck of the opposing ship dropped away and he was faced with a solid line of cannons pointed directly at the *Dona Rosalia*. Midway along the line of mounted guns, Lieutenant Lawrence Kearny stood with one hand extended toward the darkening sky. He was ready to give the command to his waiting troops, an order that would let loose a cannonade the pirates could not hope to counter. Never in his worst nightmares had Gaspar foreseen the possibility of a trap in which he would be compelled to submit to the superior force of the raw young navy of the United States of America.

In an instant his past victories vanished in a puff of smoke as the first shell hit the pirate ship broadside. The deck trembled beneath his feet. His dreams for the future disappeared into thin air as a second missile flew like an arrow arcing into its target. There followed the sound of splintering wood. Slowly at first, like a soldier wounded in battle who refuses to go down, the main mast teetered high above then gave up its fight falling with a thunderous crash. The screams of the dying entangled beneath the debris testified to the hopelessness of the situation.

"No," Gaspar whimpered as he closed his eyes to the carnage around him. He refused to watch those members of the brotherhood, sworn to defend him to the death, vault the railings and hurl themselves into the sea. "No!" he shouted to the heavens, balling his fists in rebellion against an unfair God.

Struggling to keep his footing, he made his way to the stern of the vessel where the anchor chain lay coiled ready to stay the ship with the release of a lever. Purposefully he stepped within the circle of couplings then bent to lift and wrap the heavy links around his body. Arrogantly he refused to spare a glance for those so insolent as to demand his surrender. Instead he fixed his gaze upon the first star to light the evening sky. He saw again his golden goddess who would be waiting atop the mountain where they would be joined forevermore.

Above the thunder of cannon, Kearny heard the final epitaph of the infamous pirate keening through the unforgettable night, "Gaspar dies by his own hand, not the enemy's!"

As Jose Gaspar disappeared over the side of his devil ship, Kearny gave the signal to open fire. The reverberation rocked the surrounding waters creating a miniature tidalwave that could be felt for miles in all directions. No longer would the Gulf be plagued with pirates.

Florida had overcome one more obstacle and could now continue on the path toward securing her place as a cornerstone of the new Republic.

Chapter 25

Clothes lay scattered upon the floor exactly where they had fallen. Lance stretched his long, naked body, flexing his powerful muscles, then reached over to draw Rebecca close against him. The cabin was warm, their bare flesh damp with perspiration but neither cared as they languished in the aftermath of a sweet, passionate homecoming.

"What are you thinking, my lady love?"

Rebecca sighed then turned into his arms, her innocent beauty rekindling his just sated desire.

"Nothing much," she replied running her finger along his stubbled cheek. "I'm just so glad to be home again. So much has happened I can scarcely believe it."

Home again! The happiness Lance felt knowing that the bewitching, loving woman at his side was now a part of him and this land, and that they would be together forever sharing in the trials and the triumphs that were to come, made him want to leap from the bed and dance a jig.

"Do you think Nanette will be all right?"

Rebecca's concern for the young French girl cast a pall over Logan's jubilant mood as he thought how close his own beloved had come to being ravished by the villainous pirate.

Pulling her beneath his shoulder, he spoke softly, reassuringly, nesting his chin within the curve of her neck. "Don't worry, sweetheart. With Mary to look after her I'm sure by the time the next ship comes through bound for New Orleans, Nanette will have forgotten all about her misadventure."

Both knew it would not be that easy for anyone to forget what Nanette had suffered at Gaspar's hands, especially the victim herself. But wishing could not undo the evil deed. Only time could fade the horror into a bitter memory.

"Kearny's plan went off like clockwork," Lance said hoping to smooth the furrows from Rebecca's brow. "Ships can now traverse the Gulf free from the fear of attack by the murderous blackguards who have held a free rein on these waters for too long. The prisoners will be sent home and, most important, I have you back where you belong."

He held her close knowing that he would never again feel complete without her by his side.

Large luminous green eyes looked up at him adoringly. "I'm glad Ramona and Leon got away. I don't think they were evil-hearted like the rest."

Rebecca waited for Lance to say something, wondering if perhaps she was being too generous.

"Maybe you're right," he conceded skeptically. "The woman did what she could to aid your escape and for that she has earned my gratitude and undying affection."

"Whoa there!" Rebecca teased affecting a southern drawl that still held a strong hint of Mother England. "Don't be giving away what is rightfully mine, Mr. Logan."

Lance traced featherlight patterns across her smooth flat belly wondering how long it would be before she was swollen with his child. He intended to do everything within his power to hasten the day. He slowly worked his way down her silken skin until his hand rested on the golden mound of curls where her thighs joined.

Rebecca tried to ignore the heat pulsating to life within her. "Don't forget Nokomis," she reminded him, her breathing coming fast and heavy.

"On the contrary. Let's forget Nokomis," Lance teased as his fingers gently stroked the velvet soft lips that covered the center of her being.

Opening her legs to allow him entry, Rebecca ran her hand through the dark hair matting Logan's chest.

"Without him, you would never have found me."

"Without whom?" Lance murmured distractingly.

"Nokomis."

Logan rolled over to cover her body, knowing she was moist and ready.

"We'll ask him to be godfather to our first son."

"What son?"

"The one we're going to make as soon as you stop asking questions."

"Oh."

As the rising sun bathed the lovers in beams of light that promised another hot summer day, the sentry's cry of warning jolted Lance upright while Rebecca rubbed the sleep from her eyes and grumbled.

"I was having such a splendid dream. Why did you wake me?"

Lance had already donned his pants and was pulling his fringed shirt over his head. "I didn't wake you, Sleeping Beauty. An alarm has been sounded from the fort. We have to go."

Rebecca came fully alert but her bad temper at having been roused from a sound sleep did not abate.

"Damnation! Is there no peace to be had in this godforsaken wilderness?"

Lance grinned at his dishabilled little bride. She looked an adorable contradiction with her hair mussed, her cheeks rubbed rosy from his day's growth of beard, and her green eyes shooting sparks of indignation as she clutched the cover to her naked breasts.

Chucking her beneath the chin he responded lightheartedly, "You're a pioneer woman now, my lady. Rise and shine for I'm not letting you out of my sight again."

He lifted her bodily from the bed and kissed her swollen lips. "Dress quickly, sweetheart," he urged hurrying to the door where he looked toward the fort as he waited impatiently.

A short time later Lance and Rebecca stood on the glimmering white beach their arms wrapped around each other as they watched the longboat pull away from the *Victoria*, Captain Higgins seated stiffly in its prow.

As the boat neared shore Rebecca broke loose from the small crowd awaiting Jeremiah's arrival and waded into the surf to greet the man who had been so kind to her during her voyage to this strange new land. Tears misted her eyes as she hugged his ample girth.

"Captain Higgins! How glad I am to see you!" she cried with relief unaware of the impression made by the twin trails streaking her cheeks.

"Good Lord! My dear child, what is this?" the Captain spluttered clutching Rebecca to his bosom protectively. "God help them if they have hurt you! Oh my, oh my! I had no idea ... I mean ... Lady Winslow! I would never have left you here had I known they would mistreat you! I don't know what to say!"

By this time Jeremiah was standing knee deep in water that eddied around his perfectly creased trousers. He continued to hold Rebecca within the curve of his arm burying her head against his chest making speech and movement impossible as he glared daggers at those on shore.

"How dare you!" he roared at the group assembled before him. "I entrusted Lady Winslow into your keeping, fool that I am! What have you done to her?"

His face turned crimson while his immense chest swelled with indignation. "This is all my fault," he professed still holding Rebecca in his smothering grip. "I stand ready to bear the blame for whatever has happened to this innocent child."

Rebecca, her face meshed into the heavy material of the captain's coat, thought frantically that his good intentions might end up being the death of her as she gasped for breath. Lance managed to stifle his laughter though his lips quivered with the effort. He couldn't wait to see if "the innocent child" could talk herself out of her latest predicament.

"Come, Lady Winslow! We will waste no more time among these barbarians! We shall sail with the

380

morning tide and before you know it I will have you home where you belong."

Rebecca finally managed to pull back enough to stammer, "No! I mean No, sir . . . that is, I mean . . . I can't go with you!" She looked up with pleading eyes.

"You can't? What do you mean you can't? Surely you jest!" The sea captain looked at her askance. "They made you cry!" he finished as if nothing more need be said.

Rebecca realized how she must have appeared to the man as she ran forward to greet him.

"Please listen to me, Captain," she implored brushing a careless hand across her cheeks. "Sometimes a lady's tears are a mere outpouring of relief. In this case, relief over your safe return."

"I'm afraid I don't understand." Jeremiah shook his head holding Rebecca at arm's length. "Does that mean you haven't been mistreated?"

"Well . . . not exactly . . ." Rebecca hesitated.

As Jeremiah's complexion began to heighten once more, Lance took pity on the kindly man who obviously felt a keen responsibility for the lovely lady stammering like a simpleton. Stepping into the water he nudged his way between the two, throwing one arm around the Englishman while with the other he pulled his wife into his embrace.

"Actually, Jeremiah, it's a long story."

Jeremiah's black expression left no doubt that someone had best get on with the telling. Lance complied with a shrug.

"In the beginning, that is, when Lady Winslow first arrived, none of us realized what a jewel had been cast upon our shores."

Rebecca poked her husband in the ribs none too gently and at the sound of a grunt, Captain Higgins squinted his eyes at the two of them as if he had just noticed the familiar way they seemed to communicate without words. He continued to study the beautiful, dainty young woman and the strapping army scout as he allowed himself to be led ashore.

As they made their way toward the others, Lance continued. "It was not until Rebecca managed to elude the renegade Indians who had taken her captive that we began to see what an asset she might be in taming this unsettled territory."

Jeremiah stumbled in the loose sand and only Logan's firm hold on his arm prevented him from falling face down upon the beach. The man's balance was further impeded by the racking cough that seized him mid-stride.

Rebecca pounded him on the back as Lance continued unruffled by the captain's paroxysm.

"But it wasn't until we rescued her from the pirates that we knew beyond a shadow of a doubt she has what it takes to survive in this heathen land."

Jeremiah's head swiveled from Lance to Rebecca and back again, his recently high color had drained leaving his face ashen. He staggered to Rebecca's favorite boulder and sat down heavily. He studied the couple standing before him, still clasping each other possessively.

"Did you have to tell him everything at once?" Rebecca railed, looking up at Lance in exasperation.

"Now, sweetheart, you know I haven't told him *everything.*"

Secret laughter danced in the eyes of the rugged

382

army scout as he gazed down at the small woman shaking his arm as if she were used to touching him.

"Please, tell me no more," Jeremiah pleaded, placing a hand over his breast. "My heart you know . . ."

As he looked at Rebecca who was looking at Lance he saw the change occur in her flashing emerald eyes. Sparks of irritation suddenly ignited into a golden blaze of light as the two stared at one another but none could doubt they were the flames of love.

Embarrassed, Jeremiah cleared his throat. "Does this mean you are not going home?"

Leaning up to plant a modest kiss on her husband's cheek, Rebecca replied simply, "I am home, Captain."

As Lance bent to help him to his feet, Jeremiah said in a low voice only the two of them could hear, "I have a feeling this territory is never going to be quite the same again now that Lady Winslow has decided to adopt it as her own."

"Not *Lady* Winslow, Jeremiah. Her new title is Mrs. Logan. Together we plan to build a new life here in this wild unspoiled land, a life where men and women are judged solely on their own merits. I wasn't kidding when I said Rebecca has what it takes."

"I never doubted it for a moment," Jeremiah assured smilingly. "And frankly, son, I think you have it, too."

"Have what?" Lance asked casting a bewildered glance at the captain as they made their way toward the beautiful golden-haired woman waiting for them a short distance away.

Clapping the handsome frontiersman on the back, Captain Higgins laughed jovially. "You have what it takes to love a lady!"

Author's Note

Did Jose Gaspar actually exist or was he merely a figment in the imagination of a drunken sailor? In researching background material for my story, the sources I consulted were split in their opinions as to whether Gaspar was fact or fiction. Whichever may be the case, he was the ideal choice for my villainous pirate, a heartless blackguard whose death would not be mourned.

K. Willis